*D*oes it make me seem excessively young, Your Grace?" she asked softly.

He looked down at her with a peculiar expression on his face, then extended his hand again. She took it, thinking it was a gesture of acceptance and farewell he made, but then he bent and pulled her up against the horse, and up still farther until she was seated where she had not wished to be. Nature, having decreed the attraction, seemed to glow in appreciation of her handiwork. Fate, however, laced the moment with portent, imbued it with possibility, weighted it down with a sense of destiny.

The Duke of Kittridge leaned closer, touched Tessa's lips with the softest of kisses, so delicate that she might have thought it a whisper.

KAREN RANNEY

Upon A Wicked Time

AVON

An Imprint of HarperCollinsPublishers

This is a work of fiction. Names, characters, places, and incidents are products of the author's imagination or are used fictitiously and are not to be construed as real. Any resemblance to actual events, locales, organizations, or persons, living or dead, is entirely coincidental.

AVON BOOKS
An Imprint of HarperCollins*Publishers*
10 East 53rd Street
New York, New York 10022-5299

Copyright © 1998 by Karen Ranney
ISBN 978-0-380-79583-3
www.avonromance.com

First Avon Books paperback printing: December 1998

Avon Trademark Reg. U.S. Pat. Off. and in Other Countries, Marca Registrada, Hecho en U.S.A.
HarperCollins® is a registered trademark of HarperCollins Publishers.

Printed in the U.S.A.

10 9 8 7 6 5

To Mary Kay Smargiassi,
a fan who became a friend

Prologue

Dorset House
The Earl of Wellbourne's Estate
June 1788

Once upon a hill, a breeze danced merrily. Brushing through blades of grass and bright green leaf, it was a song of joy, nature's wind chime. A wizened oak stood sentinel against such foolishness—its hundred-year-old trunk broad support for spreading branches. The grass beneath the tree was emerald, the shadows welcoming. The sun had passed behind a white, fluffy cloud, and the resultant haze imbued the hill with a soft, glowing radiance.

Beneath the hill, perched halfway to the floor of the valley, was a large house. The frenetic activity of its occupants could not be seen from here. Orders rang out, summons were answered, wheels clattered upon the gravel road, guests were welcomed—all these sounds were silenced by distance and by a curious serenity present beneath the spreading oak.

Time seemed to slow. The breeze altered character, seemed evocative. Fate rubbed its hands in glee and summoned the players upon this magical stage.

The first of these, a young girl, sixteen years of age,

1

sat upon a blanket beneath the spreading branches of the tree, reading to her youngest brother.

"Harry, do you not wish to find out what happens to Sir Bethune?"

"But I'm hungry."

"You are forever hungry. Why is that, Harry? You eat as much as the other boys." She kept her book marked with one finger as she reached over and brushed his knees clean. "And how do you get dirty so quickly?"

"I don't care if I'm dirty. I'm hungry."

"We can have tea and biscuits as soon as the duke arrives."

"Why do we have to wait?"

"Because we are to be presented to the duke, that's why. And must be on our very best behavior," she said, smiling. She combed back a lock of his hair with her fingers.

"Don't want to be presented, Tessa."

"You must resign yourself to it, I'm afraid, Harry. And in the meantime, we can discover how Sir Bethune slays his dragon. How do you think he will?"

"He'll cut out his liver!" Harry drew an imaginary sword and thrust it into the air.

Tessa pretended to shiver. "Sir Bethune is about to ride down into the valley where the dragon has its lair. Can you not wonder how afraid he must be?"

"Knights aren't afraid, Tessa."

"I would be, if I were about to confront a dragon, Harry." She smiled over at him. " 'The shadows lengthened as if earth and sky darkened together,' " she read. " 'A most peculiar gloom, almost a presentiment of evil. There was the scent of it in the air, a stench of old dragon. Another odor, that of rotting meat. Sir Bethune sat straighter in the saddle.' " She put down the book, stared off into the distance. "He is about to venture into the most important battle of his life, Harry. Armed with nothing more than his sword and his honor."

"And a helmet and armor, Tessa," Harry contributed.

She smiled. "All polished to a shine, Harry." And beneath that armor, he would be tall, his chest broad, his shoulders wide. His eyes would be silver gray and his hair black and thick, worn too long for a knight. He would have even features and a decidedly aristocratic nose. His mouth was full, his lips almost always quirked in a smile. What did his laugh sound like?

"Tessa?"

She blinked. Gone was the knight with the appearance of Jered Mandeville, Duke of Kittridge.

She picked up the book again. " 'Fog, relative to the most noxious steam, lay antidote to invader. Sir Bethune raised his sword high, brought his arm down in an arc, and cut it clean through, creating a path for his destrier.' " She glanced at Harry. "Knights must be especially brave, Harry. More so than other men. Do you think it's because they are honored so?"

Instead of answering her, Harry looked up with an expression of slack-jawed astonishment on his face.

She turned her head and he was there. The knight. The duke.

He was mounted upon a large black horse, whose restive movements he easily controlled. The late afternoon sun bathed him in light, turning him into a visitor of dazzling brightness.

"Are you a knight?" Harry asked, awed.

"I'm afraid not. I am a duke, however. Will that serve?"

"Do you have any biscuits?"

"Harry!" Tessa snapped out of her reverie. "You sometimes have the manners of a toad," she whispered to the boy. The man on the horse smiled.

"I do not. You're the one who's a toad. Tessa toad face!"

"Harry! Have you no manners?"

"I have a dog." Harry said, instead of an apology.

"You do?"

The boy nodded vigorously.

"It's a mangy old dog we have to keep in a shed near the garden wall," Tessa explained. "He howls all night."

"He does tricks," Harry said defensively.

"He tries to bite everyone," she said, "and he has bad habits."

"He doesn't piss on the floors anymore."

"Harry!"

Their visitor's chuckle fueled her flush. Tessa pleated her skirt with her fingers and sent a severe look toward her undaunted brother.

Why had Fate determined this the moment for her to meet the Duke of Kittridge? It should have been at the dinner tonight had not her mother decreed her too young. But even the presentation with her brothers would have sufficed. She would have been dressed in her loveliest frock the first time he saw her, with her hair in curls. Instead, her hair was a fright and her dress one she'd nearly outgrown. And her nails were green from when she and Harry had dug in the grass to widen the path for a plump caterpillar.

Tessa had absolutely no doubt about who this

stranger was. There were not that many dukes in England, especially those blessed with such distinctive eyes, gray with a touch of silver. The Mandeville eyes.

His full-length portrait hung at her godfather's home. That he was also Jered's uncle seemed a blessing granted by Fate.

The Duke of Kittridge had no idea who she was, only that she was a beauty. A beauty who amused him, a distinctly unique trait. Too, there was something about her voice that attracted him. Some low and musical note that seemed to incite a response in parts of his body not necessarily attuned to speech. The cloud chose that moment to move away, and a shaft of sunlight struck her hair, creating a nimbus of light around her. Appreciation for the sight of her, young and innocent and beyond lovely, held him mute. Had he ever been that young? Or that innocent? Perhaps not. Beauty? An approximation he'd beheld time and again in London. Yet this rural equivalent seemed somehow more real. Her smile honest. Sincere. Touching, in some obscure way.

The breeze seemed to play with the edge of her skirt, teasing it above her ankles. It was, had she known it, a riotous announcement of intent and joy. Both players were arranged by Fate and Nature upon this stage. Both helplessly adrift in emotion. One was young and female. The other, older and male. A perfect match. A perfect tableau.

Fate, it must be admitted, was occasionally at odds with Nature. Not, however, on this occasion. Nature brushed its finger of wind across the duke's face, caused his hair to lift and then tumble upon his brow. It incited a blush to appear upon Tessa's cheek. Moments passed and neither spoke, entranced with the sight of each other. He could not remember an instance in which time seemed so perfectly slowed. How utterly beautiful she was, how exquisitely young, with all the freshness of youth and innocence and wonder in her eyes. She could not recall when she'd ever felt it so difficult to breathe.

"You are welcome to Dorset House, Your Grace," Tessa said finally.

"Is he *that* duke, Tessa?" Harry said, as if dukes were as commonplace as stones. Harry remained only long enough to receive a short nod in reply to his rudeness, then scampered down the hill to announce the visitor's arrival and thereby garner himself a biscuit.

"He is sorely lacking in manners," Tessa said, staring after him, "but he is only five."

"He will grow into them." Jered watched as Harry raced over the grass.

"And mine are as bad," she said, "for all that I've chastised Harry. I am Lady Margaret Mary Teresa Astley, Your Grace. But my family calls me Tessa."

He smiled. "That young scamp is your brother, then?"

She sighed. "And my charge for today."

"It is difficult being a older sibling," he said, a touch of humor in his voice. "I remember the duties were onerous at best."

"Yes, but you were not a girl, Your Grace," she said, turning and looking up at him. "People tend to think you wish to practice on your younger brothers. As if nappies were something one needed to do more than once."

He laughed so loud a few of the birds roosting in the tree above them took offense, flying off in a whirl of feathers and wings.

With his eyes still filled with amusement, he urged Artemis forward until the great horse was at her side.

He held his hand down to her and she put her own in it, not truly expecting him to haul her to her feet as he did. She stepped back, however, as soon as she was standing.

"Are you afraid of me?" His smile had not diminished one whit, but it seemed to have grown colder. "I but wished to give you escort to your home. Artemis can easily bear your weight as well as mine."

"I am so sorry, Your Grace. I didn't mean to be rude. You see, I really do not like horses much. No one mentions how very tall they are. Oh, they look short when you're standing on the ground, but once seated, they are very, very large. Why is that, do you suppose? Is a tree so much larger when you climb it? Or does a hill look smaller than it actually is?"

He found his smile turning genuine again. "Do you always ask so many questions?"

"Yes," she said. "Ever since I was in the nursery. All my brothers have been blessed with a similar curiosity, but theirs seem to have disappeared after a few years. Mine seems only to have grown."

Was it possible for his eyes to grow warmer, like silver melting in a long tended fire?

"Does it make me seem excessively young, Your Grace?" she asked softly.

He looked down at her with a peculiar expression on his face, then extended his hand again. She took it, thinking it was a gesture of acceptance and farewell he made, but then he bent and pulled her up against the horse, and up still farther until she was seated where she had not wished to be. Nature, having decreed the attraction, seemed to glow in appreciation of her handiwork. Fate, however, laced the moment with portent, imbued it with possibility, weighted it down with a sense of destiny.

The Duke of Kittridge leaned closer, touched Tessa's lips with the softest of kisses, so delicate that she might have thought it a whisper—except that a breath had never felt this warm. Fate crafted the kiss with the power of life itself, a force not unlike magic. It made her skin feel as if ice skittered over it. Nature encouraged the exploration, fueled the duke's thoughts with visions of soft limbs and whispers of wonder. Of welcome and joy and innocence. Made a maiden's hand grip tightly against a coated shoulder. Each participant in the kiss felt as if stars were behind their eyelids, and a drummer stood on the hillside beating a rhythm that measured the cadence of their hearts.

And then it was over. Fate retreated, satisfied. Time would prove this moment unforgettable. Time was all that was lacking to complete this pairing. Nature, never one to be appeased without satiation, echoed her displeasure in the duke's frown, in the instantly aloof expression in his eyes.

The Duke of Kittridge said nothing as he lowered Tessa to the ground, gripped the dangling reins of his horse. He turned once more to look at her. Nature carried the girl's scents to him. The shampoo of her hair, the delicate perfume allowed by her mother.

"Have no fears that you will be perceived as a child, Tessa. No man would be that much an idiot." For a moment, it looked as if he would say something else, but then he gave a silent command to Artemis and the horse cantered down the hill.

Tessa turned and watched him approach her home.

That moment of farewell seemed touched with an unearthly quality. As if time itself slowed so that each player might feel the tug of something true and lost. The Duke of Kittridge, facing away from the young girl on the hill, felt the compulsion to turn, perhaps even canter back to where she stood watching. He banished the impulse with difficulty. Tessa simply leaned against the old oak, wondering why she wished to smile and to cry at the same moment.

Fate and Nature were absurdly pleased.

Chapter 1

August 1791

It is my wedding night. *My wedding night.* Even repeating the thought did not make it seem real.

The world was changed somehow, a different place. Or was it just her? Tessa sighed, then smiled. She stood and walked around the room again. How many times had she traversed it? As many times as one could in an hour.

She was married. Truly. She twirled in a tight circle, her nightgown blooming around her. She stopped, hugged herself, then put her hands to her mouth as if to stifle the laughter.

What a glorious day it had been! The wedding ceremony might have been designed to put a new bride at ease. The only attendants had been her family and Jered's. The wedding banquet had been held in the state dining room, and although the room had been large and ornately decorated, the dinner had been intimate. Again, only the families were present. Most of the celebrations to mark the Duke of Kittridge's nuptials, she'd been told, did not require the newlyweds' presence. Instead they were to have their wedding trip, time in which to learn of the other, to form a foundation for the marriage.

10

Kittridge was close enough to her own home that her parents had chosen to return there tonight. It was either that or find rooms among the hundreds of post-wedding guests. All afternoon long a steady stream of carriages had arrived, disgorging their passengers at the steep steps that fronted the east entrance.

At one of the windows, she stopped her pacing, knelt in a pouf of silk. Her nightgown, adorned with the most delicate lace, flowed from neck to her ankles. It was quite beautiful, sewn in London, conveyed on a special coach in order to reach her on this day.

She opened the latch, raised the window, then knelt with both arms upon the sill. The view was unfamiliar, only one of the things she would have to learn. There were no rolling hills, no gurgle of water from a nearby brook, and the rose garden was so distant its presence was only hinted at by a gentle breeze. The park stretched out for acres in front of her, the sweeping vista broken only by the gazebo, its shadows seeming not as mysterious as beckoning.

Night was almost upon them, descending over the landscape and Kittridge itself like a soft blanket. It obscured sounds, encouraged whispers, softened colors.

Soon he would come to her.

She leaned her chin upon her folded hands, looked out at the home that would be hers for the rest of her life. She'd passed Kittridge often, but tonight was the first time she'd sleep beneath its sprawling roof. The iron gates had swung open this morning to admit her as if knowing she would pass from earl's daughter to duchess by noon.

And tonight she would travel from maiden to wife.

She had never dared to hope that she would be married to him. Even after her godfather had suggested it, she'd not let herself believe it might really happen. Instead she had pretended it would not, to prevent disappointment should the Duke of Kittridge object. But he hadn't. He'd sent a short note to her parents accepting the union; and to her, the betrothal ring that all the Kittridge heirs presented to their affianced brides—an emerald ring with the Mandeville crest carved into the surface of the stone.

She told herself that if she were wise, she would remember the exact nature of this marriage. This was not like her parent's union. They had married for property and then discovered love. She should not remember nights when she and her brothers had giggled over the sight of them dancing upon the terrace in the moonlight, the only music a tune her father hummed. She truly should forget the glances between them at the breakfast table, or the teasing that made her mother blush or her father laugh heartily.

This was a marriage of convenience, especially on the Duke of Kittridge's side. She would provide him heirs to the dukedom and he would provide for her future and her children's protection. Most girls did not receive as much, nor dared to dream of more.

And most girls were not married to Jered Mandeville. Their betrothal contract had been signed by proxy, as if the duke could not bear to tear himself away from the iniquities of London for something so tame and mundane. It did not matter, though, did it? She was married to him now.

She pillowed her cheek upon her hands. Kittridge was a great house, a magnificent heritage. Her son would inherit it, her daughter would marry from it. Her suite of rooms—parlor, withdrawing room, private dining room—occupied a full corner of Kittridge. Jered's rooms did the same, but on the opposite corner. And between them, bedrooms that adjoined. She wondered if his was decorated with such lavish detail and then realized that of course it would be. This was Kittridge, the home of legendary ducal majesty.

She turned and looked over her left shoulder at her bed. It gleamed whitely—a perfect maiden's bower.

She should have been afraid, not so excited. But fear was not an emotion she experienced when she thought of Jered Mandeville. Anticipation, yes. Or joy. Or the heady feeling of being granted the most wonderful wish in her whole life.

For some damn reason, his fingers trembled.

His valet paused from unbuttoning the last of his waistcoat buttons, turned, and offered Jered the salver. On it rested a generous portion of brandy in an etched crystal goblet.

"The hair of the dog, Chalmers? Bless you and all your progeny," he toasted as he lifted the vessel from the tray. The candlelight glanced off a facet of glass, creating a diamondlike prism. It shined in his eyes as if to illuminate his headache, devil-sent to welcome this day with a vengeance.

"Is Mrs. Smython still whining?" His agitated housekeeper had demanded an audience to complain that there were not enough rooms to accommodate all the guests he'd brought from London.

"I believe, sir, that she's managed to regain her usual equanimity."

Jered sat and allowed his boots to be removed and then his stockings. He flexed his toes at the comfort of being unconfined.

"As Your Grace knows, there were other guests already invited. Mrs. Smython was concerned that there would not be accommodations for all of them.''

Jered stood, frowning, spread his arms wide as his shirt was stripped from him, then his trousers. He motioned with one hand for the undervalet to cease brushing his coat where it hung and remove himself from the room. Once they were alone, he made his displeasure known. ''Mrs. Smython is paid a king's ransom to ensure that Kittridge is well-run, Chalmers. Tell her to do her job and cease prattling to me of her concerns. Especially tonight.''

''Very well, Your Grace.''

Jered was down to his small clothes, which he removed himself, uncaring that he stripped himself naked in front of Chalmers. It was a routine they'd practiced at least twice a day for most of his life.

''Was Mrs. Symthon truly angered, or was this your way of indicating your own displeasure?''

He raised his arms and allowed Chalmers to place the robe around his shoulders. It wouldn't dispel the chill, however. He held out one hand. His fingers still trembled. *Frightened, Jered?* He thrust that thought from his mind.

''I beg your pardon, sir?''

''I doubt it,'' Jered said. ''Why do I think you disapprove of my returning to Kittridge only today? Should I have been ensconced in a monastery in the fortnight prior to my nuptials, Chalmers, thinking of the state of my eternal soul? Some sort of purging regimen?'' He walked to the window, glancing over his shoulder at his valet.

''Sir?''

''Why do I keep you on?'' He turned and Chalmers was still there, outwardly servile. But the devilish twinkle in his eye had softened to become something else, an emotion that was almost difficult to witness. Fondness, of a certainty. They had racketed along together for nearly twenty years, the old man and the young one.

"Because I tie a cravat just so, sir?" There was a ghost of a smile on the man's lips.

"Adrian asked if I'd part company with you, did you know? As if you were a horse or a favorite pup. Oh, don't look at me like that, man. He's a harmless idiot." Jered turned his head and peered at himself in the pier glass. Other than a certain pinkness about the eyes, there was nothing that indicated he had spent the last week in a frenzy of debauchery. Or that he'd been unable to sleep last night, kept awake by unwelcome thoughts. "I take it by your shiver of revulsion that you would rather not leave my employ."

"I think, sir, that you outrank the vast majority of your friends in nobility and intellect."

"I would almost think that a compliment if I did not realize the character flaws of my companions," Jered said dryly.

He stared beyond his reflection to the chapel at the end of the east wing. A spike of disquiet seemed to pin him in place. Had he done the wrong thing, after all? Selected the wrong bride? He could not rid himself of that odd notion.

It was true that he'd assented to the match without any objection. He'd known ever since he'd inherited the dukedom that he would have to marry, set up his nursery for the heir to succeed him. Tessa Astley was not unsuited for the role of duchess. She came from an acceptable family, she was possessed of beauty. Years would add to her poise. And charm? He could not forget her effortless candor, the smiles she'd bestowed with no thought to their effect. That is why he allowed his uncle to believe himself a Machiavellian schemer. The old reprobate had offered up his share of the family shipyards in exchange for Jered's promise to wed. Jered had, albeit not as reluctantly as Stanford Mandeville believed, agreed to take her to wife.

I kissed her once, did you know? An unwise question to pose, even to Chalmers.

He'd seen her last year, at some ball or another he'd attended. It had been difficult slipping in and out, half the room stilled and bowed to him in that absurd bit of ducking and billing. It reminded him of the mating dance of the swans that floated upon Kittridge's lake, except that the swans had reason to arch their necks and extend their feathers. She'd been dancing with some young fop who'd looked alternately stunned and bemused at his good fortune. As well he might; she'd been gloriously lovely.

He turned to find that Chalmers had left him. Alone.

He hesitated at the door that led to his wife's suite of rooms. Since he had become the tenth Duke of Kittridge, this door had been rarely used. Oh, of a certain, to allow the maids to dust. But never on an occasion, such as now, so portentous and steeped in heritage. The rules, those unspoken bits of folklore interspersed with tradition, dictated that he swive her right enough, sow her hopefully fertile womb with the progeny who would inherit the ducal estate. Then he need not have anything further to do with her other than an annual visit to reacquaint himself with his duchess. Or perhaps she would wish to come into the city and form alliances of her own. Not until, of course, the paternity of his child was no longer in question.

He reassured himself that they would deal well together: a little complicitious sex, some tots of affection; an agreement that they would ignore each other in perfect harmony.

He opened the door between their rooms with little ceremony.

She started like a forest creature. A rabbit, perhaps, or a squirrel, what with all that luxuriant chestnut-colored hair. No, an owl, whose large brown eyes stared up at him, as if he'd taken her from her moonlit perch and shone a torch into her face. She was swallowed up in the large bed, attired in a lace-trimmed silk gown squared at the neck. She should have looked little more than a child. Instead she resembled a voluptuous and recalcitrant mistress who, having erred, waited for punishment with fevered anticipation. An idiotic thought.

There would be no visitors to this act. Once it had been custom. He was, after all, a prince of the realm. Now it seemed a bawdy sport—and one that he had forbidden, else twenty of his friends would be storming into this chamber with little decorum, hooting and howling like wolves having scented a wounded prey.

An examination of the bride in order to ascertain her innocence was another antiquated and barbaric custom he had waived. He had disliked the idea that the next duchess would be touched by someone other than himself.

He spoke to her for the first time since their vows. "Will there be any requirement for me to lie to the assembled guests?"

At her look of confusion, he smiled. Still, he needed an answer. His child's parentage rested upon it. "Will it be necessary to fabricate evidence, madam?"

She shook her head from side to side, dislodging the curls arranged artfully at her shoulders.

He suddenly realized that she had no idea of exactly what he was asking, just that the tone of his question had required a negative response. He walked closer to the bed, recognizing that each step made her more tense. And yet, owl that she was, she did not pull away, or back, or make any wise attempt to forestall his approach. Courageous forest creature.

"We shall, as tradition has it, be required to fly our bedsheet from the east wing. If you have any doubts as to your virginity, madam, I would advise that you reveal them now. Such lack, while lamentable, can be remedied given enough preparation."

"I have no doubts." How soft her voice was. How tremulous, as if a gentle breeze had been given speech. Was it fear that made it appear so, or was she as normally soft-spoken? He did not know, having only exchanged words with her once. Then she'd been a teasing sprite who had laughed up at him and then been silenced with a kiss.

He bent and kissed her now, perhaps in gratitude, certainly in apology. It was too swift a gesture to give her any warning, too sudden a move to fuel her fear of him. Her lips were soft and pillowy beneath his. Ah, there she was, then. Three years had not dampened the memory after all. How utterly odd that of all the women he'd romped with, of all the whores he'd rewarded and wives he'd taken, that this one kiss should remain so close in his memory.

"And there will be a virgin's blood upon that sheet, madam?" Words of implacable intent against lips as soft and as welcoming as crushed velvet. At her start, he pulled back, looked into eyes that had softened. "Come, you are not that innocent, surely."

Had she paled? And was he being intentionally cruel?

His fingers trailed down her arm until he captured her hand. He held it within his larger one. Which of them trembled? He sat beside her, intrigued.

"I am a virgin," she said, "but I would rather not spill any more of my blood than necessary." Her eyes sparkled with some emotion. Fear?

Her hand lay trustingly on his, like a baby bird solaced by the nest. His family ring looked at home there. Her fingers were long, slender, topped by pale well-buffed nails. He turned her hand over, tracing a path slowly from her wrist, across the palm to the tip of the longest finger. Her fingers curled inward and he smiled. Then he tenderly tucked her hand into a fist, stroked the ridge of her knuckles. Immediately the palm uncurled, a gesture of trust as unconscious as her shiver of sensation.

This lovely bride with her wide owl eyes and her sensitive skin promised an erotic feast.

"Tell me," he said, rising, "did your mother do the dutiful thing and frighten you with tales of this night?"

"She spoke with me," his bride said, not moving her gaze from him. "I am supposed to be silent and not ask too many questions, I think. And certainly should not evince any curiosity as to your actions."

Her lips were tipped up in a smile, infinitely sweet, with a taste of tartness. It charmed him down to his toes. It was not the first time she'd done something outside of his expectations. This morning, in the chapel, it had been the same.

She had, in the manner of all brides, been dressed exquisitely, but she had departed from the script in that there had been no hesitation in her movements. She had stood when he had entered the small anteroom, had stepped across the rounded flagstones of the chapel floor with an effortless grace, reaching him and placing her hand on his sleeve as if he had beckoned her by some unseen and unbidden gesture. She had turned and together they had provided her parents and brothers, his uncle and sister with a united front, two personages advancing their mutual cause, if not their family's aims, with dispatch, decorum, and not a little pride. He had found himself momentarily bemused by her tactic, by the effortless way she seemed to embrace the occasion, by the smile she accorded him and the welcome she gave him. It was absolutely perfect and too unfeigned not to be real.

And now she ridiculed her own innocence.

His fingers toyed with the belt of his robe, his attention on the branch of candles beside the bed. The kinder thing would be to snuff them. He wondered if he would. The temptation to view her in the light was almost too powerful to resist.

"And have you any curiosity?"

"I'm afraid I do." Her expression was too complex to attribute to one single emotion. Bemusement? Perhaps. Certainly a flush of embarrassment. And beneath it all the sparkle in her eyes hinted at excitement. A willing virgin, besides a curious one.

"I am not expected, certainly, to explain the entirety of it to you?" His own expression must have betrayed his reluctance to do so, if the smile on her face was any indication.

"I believe I have all the particulars in order. But I've not yet put it into practice."

"You make it sound like learning French." He sat on the edge of the bed again, torn between laughter and lust. One strap of her gown had fallen down and the rounded shoulder that was exposed seemed to catch the light of the candles' shine with a particular allure. A shadow of collarbone pointed the way to other curves, hidden by fabric, protected by darkness.

"Oh, you mean conjugating verbs before learning to speak it? Do you think conjugating and conjugal have any similarity in meaning?"

"I think it a matter of coincidence only."

She tilted her head, dislodging those glorious curls once again. "Don't you think it's amazing how many true coincidences there are in life?"

He threaded the fingers of his right hand through the ringlets that fell past her shoulders and paid no attention to her words.

She flushed, gripped the sheet and coverlet tightly in both hands, but she did not look away.

"Do I frighten you?"

"Are you not supposed to?"

"I do not believe so," he said, placing a tender kiss at her temple. It was not so much that she shivered, but as if every part of her body became alert. He could feel the sudden tension, see its effect in the way her gaze dropped to the sheet and she licked her lips. Curiosity had too quickly reverted to innocence.

"Would it allay your fears if I told you that I am as frightened?"

She drew back and stared at him. "You?" It was an accusation.

It was his turn to pull back. "You seem to believe that impossible." This, somehow, was not the conversation he'd imagined for his wedding night.

"You are considered dissolute. With a penchant for high living that makes you considered quite the rake. I have heard that had you not been a duke, it is doubtful you would have been received in fashionable circles.'' A statement as wifely as any he'd heard.

"Fashionable circles feed on rakes such as I." He smiled down at her. "The old biddies titter behind their fans, yet they are the first to open their drawing-room door. The moment they cease to be shocked is the moment they begin to be bored."

"You do not have a high opinion of the society in which you reside, do you?"

He stood and walked to the fireplace, where he snuffed out the candles upon the mantel. "I think," he said, glancing over his shoulder at her, "that since the position you occupy is one of probable duration and of a certainty some intimacy, you might begin to call me by name."

Even by the light of the single remaining branch of candles on the bedside table, he could see her flush. He divested himself of his robe. Those owl eyes became even wider; her breath seemed to halt in her chest. He watched the flush travel from her chest up her neck to her cheeks, where it blossomed into brighter color. She had never seen a naked man before, that was a certainty. And, from the looks of it, was startled by his aroused state.

She didn't demur as he threw back the same covers she had clutched just a moment ago and nonchalantly moved her aside. Nor did she say anything when he gripped the pretty silk nightgown and, with an economy of movements, slipped it over her head. When they were both naked, he rolled over and extended an arm over her. She lay as still as a corpse, hands clutched together under her chin, elbows shielding her breasts, knees crossed in an altogether futile gesture of trying to hide the soft triangle of hair. Her eyes looked everywhere but at him, even when he gently turned her chin in his direction.

"I am not about to ravish you," he said softly, conscious of the rapid beat of pulse beneath her skin. Her neck pounded with it, a frantic sign of panic. He wished there was some way, besides actions, to make the fear dissipate. But he could not talk her out of her virginity.

"I'm not afraid," she said, nearly choking on the words.

"And I am not duke," he said, before kissing her.

It was only a kiss. Nothing more. Yet it took him down a dark spiral, a deep and melting warmth where temptation and surcease waited. The soft, timorous gesture of her tongue made his blood leap, the warmth of her breath, the softness of her lips lengthened the kiss, until he felt as if the roles had been reversed and he was the innocent.

He pulled back, confused.

Her hands had fallen to her side; her lips glistened wetly; in her eyes was a soft, lambent look such as he suspected he wore.

It was layered with curiosity and expectantly eager. He wanted, in a gesture uncharacteristically benevolent, to make that look last. Wanted her to wake in the morning not with the same shyness, but with a knowing glance overlaid with that same ardent excitement. An expectancy that spoke not of fear nor of ennui, but of discovery.

He lifted himself closer, trailed his fingers from her shoulder to her chin. One finger played with the outline of her mouth, brushed back and forth against her full lower lip.

"Your lips are made for kissing," he said softly, before quickly bestowing one on them. He smiled when she reached for him, but drew back. "Some women paint theirs, or rub them fiercely. Yours require no artifice."

"Thank you."

"So eternally polite," he murmured, before kissing her again. "You are welcome." He trailed a series of kisses down her jaw. She squirmed at the sensation, which made him smile. "You are exquisitely sensitive, Tessa. Everywhere?"

His fingers trailed down her shoulder to a half-hidden breast. She had armored herself again. He tucked his fingers beneath her elbow, following the swell of flesh. "Let me touch you." Gentle entreaty. A seduction of words. Her arm fell down upon the bed again, reluctantly, or so it appeared. He raised his head and looked at the breast he'd exposed, brushed his palm over the tip, beading the nipple that rose in tight supplication.

A soft sound from her, almost a gasp, and he was nearly lost to lust. He felt himself swell even further, tighter, harder. His lips encompassed a coral nipple, his tongue flicked against it. Tessa seemed to grow warmer beneath him, as if a tide of heat built inside her sensitive skin.

His lips found hers unerringly. It was she who rose into the kiss, her hands gripping his shoulders. She held him as if he bequeathed life with his mouth, fueled her with passion. The woman beneath him, the innocent, the almost-child enchanted him. Her hands braced against him, not to push away but in a shy and uncertain exploration. And when he placed his fingers on her abdomen, above her mound, she didn't pull away but merely caught her lip with her teeth, almost trapping the moan. The sound that escaped was both faint entreaty and barely voiced excitement.

Her knee was raised; he gently cupped it, slid his fingers down to her thighs, to hips, to waist. She shivered in sensation, small bumps rising on her skin. Again the soft exquisite journey as he learned of her, small discoveries that mapped an entire body. Her ankles were as sweetly responsive to his touch as her beautiful breasts. A touch upon the back of her knees startled her; that was an exploration that needed to be continued later. The inside of her thighs were infinitely alluring; here her flesh seemed to grow hot as if leading to an inferno hidden beneath soft petal-like folds. When he touched her there, she nearly shot up from the bed, so shocked was she, an admission of naiveté given not in voice but in gesture.

The compulsion—no, need—to take her was so overwhelming that it almost conquered him at that moment.

Innocent.

He lay back against the sheets, one arm shielding his eyes. A slight movement at his side, and then a cool hand upon his chest, one not content to lay there quietly. Fingers explored and combed through the hair growing there. It was like adding wood to embers. Except of course, that his physical response was not close to burning out.

''Why have you stopped?'' She raised herself up on one elbow and stared at him.

He turned his head to look at her. Her eyes were as wide, but they were darker than before, as if the pupils had expanded to engulf all of the brown with black. There were traces of gold in those eyes. Her flush was concentrated upon her cheeks, her lips seem fuller. Her hair lay in wild disorder.

''Because you are not ready and I am exquisitely so.''

''Oh.''

"You do not understand, do you?" He closed his eyes so that he wouldn't see her. She looked too damned alluring right now. "If I took you right this moment, it would be painful for you. And I do not think myself capable of touching you without doing so."

"I am sorry." She sounded penitent, the last emotion he wished in his marital bed, from either participant.

"You are not to blame," he said, "anymore than I am. It is simply a matter of male and female. I simply need to withdraw for a moment."

"Will this happen often?" She sounded curious, damn her. As if this were an object lesson, and he supposed it was. Virgins were too much trouble. Even this one.

"I do not imagine it will happen more than this one night."

"Oh." Now she sounded disappointed. He opened his eyes and looked at her.

"Not unless you have a penchant for regrowing your virginity, madam. Virgins are delicate creatures. The first time you engage in this activity, I understand you're easily wounded."

"Is that why?"

She looked too damn pleased. Aphrodite in training. No, this one needed no education. A fact that should have made him happy but which had the oddest effect of irritating him. Why, he had no idea.

"I don't mind if it hurts. Really. As long as it's only once."

"Well, I do. I've no wish to have a woman squirming in pain beneath me."

"You make it sound dreadful."

He frowned at her. "Don't be ridiculous."

"Well, you're the one who refuses to continue." She lay back on the bed beside him.

Seconds later he rolled over and covered her. "This is truly a ludicrous situation," he said.

"You're smiling. Am I to take it that you've rested long enough?"

"You need to learn some manners," he said, surprising himself by teasing her. "Don't you know I'm a duke?"

"I am dutifully awed." Her hand cupped the side of his face, her eyes sparkled too brightly. Kissing her was like falling into air, into the night sprinkled with stars. His arousal, which had not dampened one whit in the intervening moments, grew even larger.

"There's no use for it, I'm afraid," he said, surfacing from their kiss like a swimmer nearly beached by a wave. "If I hurt you, I'm sorry. It is not well done."

Her eyes seemed to swallow him. "I'm not afraid, truly."

"Stop saying things like that."

"Well, I'm not, and it's no use frowning at me that way. I cannot help it if I've never engaged in behavior of this sort before."

"Damn it, some people call it making love."

"Then why are we yelling at each other?"

Laughter had no place in the bedroom, truly it did not.. But it was the most natural thing in the world to lower his forehead to hers and to allow the silliness of this moment to overwhelm them. Her lips tasted sweeter when curved in a smile, and her skin warmer when she was suffused by laughter.

"You must tell me what you're thinking," he said a moment later. All his breath seemed suspended. Every thought focused on the look in her eyes. Wide and alarmed. The feel of her, so soft, trembling in his arms, seemed infinitely fragile. He ached to finish this, to complete the act that would render them bound by law and flesh.

She blinked at him, her smile tremulous.

"Have you had much practice in this?" Her voice was faint, the laughter muted beneath another emotion. Fear?

"Enough," he said. He bent and kissed her again, banishing her anxiety in the only way he knew how.

"Why on earth," she mumbled against his lips, "do they call it deflowering?"

He raised his head to look at her. Her lips, full and pink, curved into a smile. "It's not as if I'm a rose, after all. But I'm quite willing to be plucked, Jered."

And he did so, with as much skill as he could muster, even half insane with lust. Later Jered realized he'd never before taken a woman who smiled at him and urged him on with a gasp and a giggle.

Chapter 2

S unlight flickered like tongues of flame across the pale ivory sheets of the bed. Tessa blinked, stirred from her dream by warmth and by the niggling feeling that something was not quite right. She stared up at the emerald velvet tester above her head, a mammoth thing supported by four towering carved mahogany posts. A bed suitable for a duchess.

The sunlight fell upon her face, brushed against her sleepy smile. A hand reached up, fingers trailed across her swollen lips.

Full wakefulness came with a jolt. She turned her head. She was alone. A full range of emotions flooded her in one moment. Awareness. All of the sensations communicated by her body clamored for attention. Soreness, first. She ached in places she'd never ached before. Then embarrassment—a full, wide, and hot flush of it—as she remembered the night before in painful clarity. He'd seen her. All of her. In the light. He'd touched her. She pulled the pillow over her head and muffled the sound of her moan. Oh God. He'd touched her. And more.

She surfaced from beneath the pillow, propped herself up on both elbows and stared toward the window and the offending glare of sunlight. No. She would not think about it. The sheet fell from her, and she glanced down at her own nakedness. A faint red mark glowed against the paleness of her breast. He'd kissed her, suckled her, placed his lips there.

She fell back against the bed, clutched the pillow to her chest. She turned her head to the spot where he had lain. The sheet felt cool against her cheek. He'd called her innocent. And if he saw her now, he'd certainly know how true a statement that was. She stared up at the tester again. Surely she should feel more experienced now. Almost wanton. But she didn't. Instead she felt more lacking than ever before, still a child.

They had laughed together and it had felt wonderful. Even talking with him was something more than real, as if the god Eros had decided to perch upon a cloud and converse with her. With his black hair and his mouth and those gray eyes that mirrored all the emotions in the world, he was absurdly beautiful, her husband. Husband. The word curled up in her stomach, warm and rich.

He had shown such consideration for her, such tenderness. Did all brides receive such treatment? She suspected not, just as she knew there was no occasion to ask such questions. People simply did not mention such things.

Husband. Tonight they would do *this* again. After the first time, it had not hurt at all. In fact, it seemed altogether promising. And today? Today they would talk, and perhaps he would tell her of their bridal journey and the places he'd planned for them to visit. Rome? Paris? She wanted to see all of them, and with him, especially.

She knelt up in the bed, staring at the spot where he

had rested the night before. *Please, let love come to him. Not a great and lasting love. That would be too much to hope for. But let him want to know me, to talk with me. Let me be his friend.* It was a prayer of few words. But, oh, dear God, if he could only see her not as an impediment to his happiness but an adjunct to it. Perhaps then there would be something more to this marriage than simply convenience. He was so utterly marvelous, and she was perfectly prepared to adore him.

When she was sixteen, she had been certain of what love was. In two London seasons, her illusions had been overcome by practicality. It was hard to retain a view of romantic love amidst the marriage mart that was London, among the swirling rumors and girls she'd known gone to brides and wives, with their laughter turned brittle and their eyes roaming the ballrooms for a mate for, not a lifetime but a night. It was an inbred society, her peers, and their disillusionment a disease too easily spread.

She'd seen the best the ton had to offer. Young men with bright smiles and hesitant voices who begged for her favor and nearly wept when she allowed them to fetch her a glass of punch. Or the suitors who sought her father's fortune more than her face and deemed it unnecessary to find out if she could even speak, let alone what she thought. Mostly she was simply bored in their company. Occasionally she was irritated. And more than once, she'd ventured to open her mouth and tell them exactly what she thought. None of the young men who courted her had appreciated the degree of her honesty.

She'd been a child when taken to London for her fittings. And barely a young woman when set adrift upon an ocean of other girls searching for a husband of wealth and nobility. It had taken two seasons, but she had realized that romantic love had no place in London, and rarely in life itself. That it was rare to have what her parents had, a union of minds and bodies and hearts.

Still, she could dream, couldn't she? And last night had been so magical, it was as if the dream actually had a chance of being true.

She was a bit disappointed that he had left her, her parents had slept together for years, shocking the servants. But perhaps his way of leaving her to awake alone was another sign of his touching regard. Perhaps he would come through that door any moment. And find what, Tessa? Her hair in a disastrous mess, her face unwashed, her nakedness not at all enticing—but simply bare!

She scrambled up from the bed, grabbing her wrapper as she did so, racing to the attached room that had been wonderfully converted to a *salle de bains*. A scant thirty minutes would be all she needed, and then she would present herself to her husband as a proper wife should.

"What do you mean, he's gone?" Tessa gripped her hands together tightly, determined that she would be every inch a duchess. How could she not be, with at least fifty people watching her every gesture?

She stood at the foot of the curving stairs, the major domo in front of her. People poured out of the dining room. She'd no idea Kittridge was so heavily populated by guests. But then, the marriage of a duke was not a commonplace thing.

"His Grace has departed for London."

Just like that.

"Did he leave any word?" How odd that it was so difficult to swallow.

"No, Your Grace."

No instructions for her to join him, no explanation of when he would return, no indication that he was apologetic or that it had been an emergency that had summoned him, or that he even inquired as to her health.

She turned, picked up her skirts, and ascended the steps, hearing the buzz of voices behind her.

She walked with great dignity down the massive hallway to her rooms, entered, closed the door quietly, leaned her forehead on a gilt wall panel. Only then did she cry.

Chapter 3

"**S**uch a sweet looking thing," the woman said. "But then, I suppose all virgins are supposed to look that way."

"If I know Jered, she's no longer in that condition." The slim, effeminate young man leaned on one hip and surveyed Tessa with the same nonchalant disdain.

It was not the first time she'd been subjected to that intense scrutiny. Tessa closed the book and raised her chin. The library had seemed a safe place. Rarely had any of Jered's guests ventured there. But she had been wrong, evidently.

The woman who surveyed her was shockingly garish. There was paint on her lips and her eyebrows were too dark to be natural. She wore a yellow gown that showed too much bosom. The young man in his ivory satin suit was as magnificently dressed as a prince. They were a striking pair, but a rude one, as the moments ticked on and neither ventured an introduction.

Of course, she was well-known. She was Kittridge's little bride. Hadn't she heard that enough times to feel bilious? Such a sweet thing. Such a dear child. Every time she heard that, Tessa wanted to fling something at the speaker. Instead she'd kept quiet. Those comments were at least better than the ones she'd heard the last few days, the buzzing of gossip that ceased at her entrance to a room. *Too innocent for him. No doubt bored.*

She tilted her chin up further, stood up from the window seat. "Did you wish something?" she asked. A lady of the manor sort of voice. Would they recognize it as such? She doubted it. All of Jered's guests had been more than a little contemptuous of her position.

They tittered. Even that was an insult. This false version of laughter was so brazenly rude it was difficult to combat.

Thank heaven she didn't have to. The door opened and Stanford Mandeville entered, his arms outstretched, a broad smile on his face.

Tessa turned and allowed herself to be enveloped in a hug. The pair of guests melted away. Vultures who had been denied a meal when the victim showed signs of life.

"Heard my nephew bolted for London. Is it true?" Stanford Mandeville asked when he released her.

Her expression must have unwittingly revealed the answer because Mandeville swore. Her godfather did not bother to apologize for his language; he never had. People tolerated his temper or they saw his back. How odd that she had been counseled all her life to restrain her opinions, to remember her breeding, her family, her position in the world, while other people behaved as they wished with impunity. Or was it simply the Mandevilles who thought themselves above manners or decorum?

"He's always been a wild one," her godfather said, motioning a footman forward. "Came from his mother."

The footman brought an enormous wrapped bundle

to the side of his chair and, at Stanford's nod, elevated it.

"His mother was Scots, you know," Stanford said as he made quick work of the muslin wrapping. "Died when he was but a boy. Racing, she was, on the heath, and him with her. I'd not say that he caused her death, but I suspect my brother blamed him for it. Called him wild ever since, up until the day he died. Wild. Like a kilted Scot."

She could barely hide her smile. A kilted Scot? Not a description she'd use to describe the Duke of Kittridge.

"I am sure Jered had his reasons for leaving for London," she said, compelled by an odd loyalty to protect her husband. Especially strange since he had evinced no such feelings for her.

"I really had thought you would have a softer influence over him."

She avoided the look in her godfather's eyes, the one that said as clear as words written upon the wall that he knew how she felt about Jered Mandeville. Still, such a thing should not be confessed aloud, should it?

Her godfather finally managed to pull away the muslin and the cotton batting, unveiling a portrait.

"You made a stunning bride, my dear. A credit to your parents. And I wanted to commemorate that moment with this gift. The painting was, after all, a great matchmaker."

She stood in front of it, stretched out her fingers and touched the hand that rested upon the pedestal, then the smile that looked out upon the world with such disdain and secret amusement. The sight of it made something turn in her chest.

During the last three interminable years, she had

waited for the announcement of his nuptials. But he had not married; instead the word filtering throughout the countryside was about his excesses, rumors flying about the madcap deeds of the Duke of Kittridge. Where there was scandal so was his name. Where there was dissipation, he was in the thick of it. And wherever people gathered, the conversation returned, sooner or later, to the duke, his misdeeds, tales told with a roguish eye and a whisper, out of consideration for the maidens in their midst. Tessa learned enough of the details to paint a picture of a licentious life. It should have colored her impression of him. How strange that it had not.

In the painting, he wore no wig but affected his own raven hair, clubbed at the back with a black silk ribbon. His knee-length coat and knee breeches were dark blue, the short double-breasted waistcoat, heavily embroidered with flowers. His stockings were similarily adorned. One hand was posed holding a walking stick that no doubt concealed a sword, the other rested upon a marble pediment. He was a tall man, the Duke of Kittridge, with a broad chest that, her godfather had said, made his tailor curse. There was nothing apologetic in that gray glance, nothing that indicated in any way that the man who stood before her regretted his appearance. It was as if the world and its opinions simply did not matter to Jered Mandeville, as if instead he created his own, rarefied existence.

Over the years, the expression had altered. Gone was the challenge in his eyes, the soft, mocking glint of suppressed humor. There was a tiredness there, a sense of desperation that seemed to emanate from the figure posed so perfectly. Or had a child turned to woman and seen what had heretofore been missed? Or even worse, had she imagined what had never been there at all? Had there ever been any gentleness in his expression, any humor half-hidden in his eyes?

Wild? Perhaps he was, after all. And she was too tame for him.

"So," Stanford said, patting her hand. "What are you going to do?"

Tessa looked up. "I haven't quite decided, sir."

"I am your uncle, child, now by marriage. I insist upon being addressed in that fashion." His smile was too fond for the imperious nature of his command.

She stood on tiptoe and kissed his cheek. "Thank you, Uncle."

"I still say you're the best thing for him, Tessa. But it might take you awhile to make him realize it."

She glanced at the portrait again.

Frankly, she doubted that the aristocratic young man standing there could be easily convinced—of anything.

She was going to London. At least she thought she was.

Tessa wondered why she was hesitating. Her trunks were packed, the only thing remaining was to instruct them to be taken to the carriage.

A knock upon the door was answered by the maid, who led her visitor through her sitting room.

The women who entered was tall, her stride not as sweetly feminine as simply determined. She stripped off her gloves with the same single-mindedness and eyed her daughter with a grim look. She had once been considered a beauty. Her hair, while no longer the color of gold, was still full and lustrous. Her features still the same, although age had softened them somewhat, as if blurring the effect of perfect lips and noble nose. Helena's eyes, however, defied the passing years. They still flashed like topaz.

"I'm very much afraid," Helena Astley said, "that your father will shoot him. Barring that, one of your brothers has forgotten his advanced age of eight and has threatened to bite him."

"Harry," Tessa moaned, correctly naming her protector. "I suppose that every neighbor within five miles also knows that I've been abandoned, Mother."

Helena eyed her daughter, as if gauging how much of the truth to divulge. "Few of your guests are known for their tact, Tessa. I'm afraid even London probably knows Kittridge deserted his bride the day after his nuptials. Not well done of him at all."

She sat down on the window seat beside Tessa. "It simply will not do, you know. I detest seeing you staring off into the air the way you were doing when I walked in, no doubt sighing romantically about your loss. Are you not the least little bit angry?"

Tessa sighed. "I am not angry," she said. She held up a hand to forestall her mother's comment. "Perhaps I will be later. Right now, I simply feel that I've misunderstood somehow. I had thought, you see, that we had begun to be friends. That he would grow to know me and to like me. Especially after . . ." Her words trailed off into an embarrassed silence. Only a flush punctuated it.

"Your wedding night?" Helena reached out, covered her daughter's hands with her own. "Then I am grateful that you were not left totally in ignorance of what it entailed."

"You did not tell me everything, Mother."

It was Helena's turn to flush. "And rightly so, Tessa. Some things should be best explained by your husband."

"It would help if one's husband was near."

Helena stood, walked to the east wall, where a tapestry was featured. Age had darkened the edge until it was nearly gray. A castle sat in the background, turrets flying a minuscule emblem. In the foreground sat a lady, her skirts adorned with picked blossoms. "A castle," Helena murmured, "fit for a princess, except that the prince has escaped."

"Perhaps that prince sent his bride a note, if nothing else."

Helena turned. "Is that what upsets you the most, Tessa?"

She glanced at her mother, then outside the window. "No," she said softly. "I would have, no doubt, made it soggy by now. I simply cannot believe he left me."

"I am at fault for your misery now, Tessa. I should never have agreed to the match. But I'd hoped Kittridge would settle down and become a good husband."

"No doubt Jered finds it difficult being a husband when he can barely remember he has a wife."

"Your father is furious. Yet he rarely admits to feeling anger. You get that deplorable trait from him. I would feel much better if both of you would confess to feelings of irritation from time to time."

Tessa smiled. How odd to experience humor when she was feeling so low. But her mother and father had argued about her bad traits and the identity of the responsible parent for as long as she could remember. And for just as long, it had been a gently waged battle, one filled with humor and fond looks. Why could she and Jered not form such a relationship?

"Would you rather I toss the cushions on the floor, Mother? Stamp up and down, pull the curtains from the windows?"

"I would rather you do anything than weep for Kittridge. He does not deserve it."

"Then you'll be pleased to know I am doing something. I'm going to London, Mother."

It was not often that Tessa surprised her mother. Even more rare that she rendered her speechless. Long moments passed during which Helena simply stared at her daughter. When she spoke, the question did not surprise Tessa. She had been expecting it.

"Why?"

"In order to be a wife. I find it rather difficult when my husband is ensconced in London."

"Do you think that wise?" There was a forbidding frown on Helena's face. One that counseled prudence. Except, of course, that Tessa was certain her mother's irritation was singled out for Jered.

"What other alternative do I have, Mother? Wait for Jered to remember he is married?"

"Perhaps he should be reminded."

"I would prefer if you did not take it upon yourself to talk to Jered, Mother," Tessa said.

"Nonsense, someone needs to tell him how ill advised he's being."

"You will not, Mother." She sent her parent a stern look.

"You are my daughter. He evidently labors under some notion that hurting you is acceptable. It is not."

"He is my husband. Promise you will not interfere." Helena returned to Tessa's side, bent down and kissed her on the cheek, oblivious to her daughter's frown.

"Very well."

That was entirely too easy. Tessa stood, eyeing her mother suspiciously. "I want your solemn promise." Helena opened the door and turned. On her lips was a perfectly charming smile. Tessa was not fooled for one moment. "Promise me."

The smile faded. "Very well. I promise."

"You will not suggest, hint, allude or otherwise insinuate any advice to Jered."

Her mother's lips seemed to thin as Tessa watched. "I said I would not."

"Nor will you send him a note, implore him by a third party, or communicate with him by any means whatsoever."

"I am not amused by your implication, Tessa." Her mother sounded regal when she was irritated. However, Tessa also knew that Helena Astley had the oddest ability to adhere to the letter of her promises while slipping quite ably behind the words.

"Promise."

"Very well," Helena said, drawing herself up. "You have my solemn word. But he deserves to have his ears singed off."

"Mother . . ."

"I detest that note in your voice. You sound just like your father at his most pontificating," she said, conceding defeat. She was not quite able to hide her smile at Tessa's laughter.

Chapter 4

❦◁◁─◯◯◯─▷▷

"**W**hat the devil is that noise?"
Jered flung open the door of his chamber, determined that whoever was making that racket was going to be sacked, and immediately. Damn it, he'd only gotten to sleep a few hours earlier. The sun was obscenely high in the sky. Blindingly so.

An armoire blocked his path. Four Hepplewhite chairs, a carved pier table, a tea table, and the framing of an elaborate bed—fluted posts, carved head, and footboard—occupied every square inch of space from hallway to landing.

At that moment, the one woman in England he did not particularly wish to see peered around a rather magnificent tapestry.

"Oh, Jered, I am sorry, I expected to have this out of the way before you awoke," Tessa said, smiling brightly. "Why is it that time seems to slip by so quickly upon occasion? And it is not simply when one is occupied with something that is entertaining, either. Haven't you found that it goes equally as fast when you are involved in a pursuit you do not particularly care for?"

He wedged himself around the armoire, found himself blocked by a carved side table, was forced therefore to simply frown at her. "What are you doing here?"

"I've decided to have my suite redone, Jered. I hope that won't inconvenience you, but I simply cannot abide the color yellow. It is almost too optimistic a shade, don't you agree? It is as if it commands you to be cheery. At least you should be able to start the day with the mood of your choice. Don't you think?"

"You know as well as I do that wasn't what I meant. Why aren't you at Kittridge?

"I have found that my presence at Kittridge is entirely superfluous, Jered," she said. "I do believe that not one of your guests has yet realized I am gone."

"Is my home infested with the plague, madam?"

"I do not believe so, Jered. Each one of its many visitors were quite healthy when I left." She smiled agreeably at him. "You truly have attracted an odd assortment of friends. They do nothing but eat and sleep and gossip from morning until night."

"If they disturb you, throw them out."

"They're your guests."

"They're no one's guests, madam. They simply congregate wherever there's a gathering. They're minor nobles and hangers-on whose chief duty in life is to deplete the purses of the wealthy. Get rid of them."

"They will not listen to me."

"You're the duchess of Kittridge. Make them."

"How? I truly doubt they would heed anything I say. It is very lowering to be called the Little Duchess in my own home, but I cannot fault their rudeness, truly. They were only mimicking your actions."

Was she chastising him? Surely she had more sense than that.

"I only wish they had become your student in all

things—and disappeared as abruptly as you did.''

She *was* chastising him.

''Then if my actions disgust you, madam, I can only wonder at your presence in London. I have given you no leave to attend me here.''

''I cannot be your companion, Jered, if you insist upon sending me back to the country.''

''You're my wife, not my companion.''

''They are one and the same. Did not Ruth say 'entreat me not to leave thee, or to return from following after thee; for whither thou goest, I will go, and where thou lodgest, I will lodge?' ''

''She said that to her mother-in-law, Naomi. Not to her husband.''

''Oh.'' She blinked at him. ''Well, the sentiment is the same, don't you think?''

''I do not. Nor do I wish to continue this conversation. Safe journey, Tessa.''

And with that, he closed the door behind him. Perhaps with more force than was necessary.

The circus was too damn loud. It had seemed a worthwhile diversion at the time it was suggested. Now Jered wished he'd vetoed the idea. People were so boisterous that it was difficult to be heard, and when they approved of an act, the bellowing, foot-stamping, and whistles were almost deafening.

''The least you could do is pretend to look amused,'' Pauline said.

Jered turned his head to look at his latest mistress. He didn't feel extraordinarily amused at the moment. Nor was he in the mood to be gracious.

She seemed to sense it, too. All week he had ignored her, had not visited her once since his marriage. Even this meeting had been accidental on his part and no doubt cleverly orchestrated on hers. His mistress had all the subtlety of a warship, with the jutting prow to match.

He blinked away the recollection of his wedding night. How strange that those memories should be filled with laughter. His own, unrestrained, unfettered. How long had it been since he'd laughed like that? And tenderness? Should he be remembering that as well?

He hoped Tessa was gone.

"He's been like that since his nuptials, Pauline. Getting wed has turned him off his feed." Adrian Hampton, the second son of the Earl of Amherst, did not seem displeased by the news.

"He has not been the same, I'll grant you that, but did you see that prize he nipped in the third race this afternoon? The King will knight him for sure. I hear the royal treasury grew by at least a thousand pounds."

"Kittridge will never notice another title."

"Or another purse." That desultory announcement from Pauline.

"Cheer up, sweet," Adrian said, chucking her under the chin. "Maybe Kittridge will buy you a bauble with his winnings."

She smiled brightly.

Jered sat back in one of the upholstered chairs of his box, ignoring his companions. Of late, their conversation was unnecessarily dull. His left hand shot up into the air, and within moments a servant was there, replacing his depleted glass with a filled one.

His glance encompassed the scene before him, the throng of people, both peer and commoner alike. It was, he noted to himself, one of those rare events in which prerogative had no influence. The most important aspect of this evening was entertainment, from the slack rope vaulting to the clown on horseback.

At the moment, an exhibition of shadow figures was being performed, all to the jangling sound of a hornpipe. The crowd seemed to surge forward with the addition of several mounted figures to the yard. One jumped up on the saddle and rode, standing, around the enclosure. Another spangled figure was swept up from a standing position by the second rider, joining him on the back of the horse.

He lifted his looking glass and trained it on the figure of one of the riders. Attraction of another sort, above and beyond horseflesh, then. Undoubtedly female. As if she'd heard the thought, Pauline leaned over the table and smiled at him. The feathers of her outrageously pendulous hat tickled his nose, and he moved slightly away, a gesture as warning as the cold smile he gave her. She settled back in her chair, faced forward stiffly. She was vacuous but had the instincts of a born survivor. Even she recognized he was not in the mood to be cozened.

He lifted his looking glass again, studied the crowd, focusing upon the figure of a woman on the opposite side of the building. He could understand why she seemed to be the center of attention. Her walking costume was scarlet, almost shockingly French, with its fitted bodice and sleeves and wide waist sash reaching to the underside of her breasts. There was no effort to disguise the fullness of her dimensions with a few rows of concealing lace. The only concession she had given to propriety was a white shawl of impossible length that trailed in the dust and which several eager admirers strove to contain for her. The scarlet feather on her hat jiggled merrily whenever she walked.

He nearly overturned Adrian as he stood abruptly.

"Darling, what is it?" A drone of a voice as someone spoke.

He trained his looking glass upon the scene at the other side of the amphitheater once more, cautioning himself that it was only because he had been recently thinking of her, that was all. He was imagining things. He had left his young bride returning to Kittridge.

She *wouldn't* be at Manson's Amphitheater.

He kept telling himself that as he walked quickly from the box and circled the building. In the mornings, the place was used as a riding school, therefore the construction closely resembled an indoor track, although of necessity much smaller.

It was not until Pauline nearly trod upon his heel that he realized the inhabitants of his box had followed him, or that the words he'd spoken had been aloud.

"Who wouldn't be here?" she demanded.

"His bride," Adrian said, with such obviously perverse delight that Pauline scowled at him.

Pauline drew herself up and frowned down at Jered, despite the fact she was a tiny thing and he towered over her. Pauline had a way of becoming as autocratic as any blue blood when she wanted, a trait that kept unwelcome admirers away and had had the ability to amuse him in the early days of their acquaintance. Now it only annoyed him.

"Does she mean to make a scene, then?" Pauline asked.

"We'll see, won't we?" Jered said, and approached his wife.

Chapter 5

She couldn't find him.

But then, she hadn't counted on all these people. It seemed half of London was packed inside the building to witness the circus. Right at this moment, the scenery was being changed to represent the ocean, complete with a huge sea monster. A large sheet of hammered metal had been transported on its side and was then hung from the suspended rope. She was captivated by the sound it made once it was lifted in the air. As it was struck with a large padded stick, it quivered and then made a loud boom like rolling thunder. The people holding boards, upon which were painted waves, ducked and stood, moved back and forth. It really did look like the ocean. How utterly wonderful.

It was quite warm inside. Perhaps she should not have brought her shawl after all. She'd deliberately worn this new dress, a bit of fabric courage. It might be, however, like waving a flag in front of a bull. It was a bit snug in the chest and nearly pinched her waist, and it certainly attracted attention. It was not, perhaps, exactly proper. At least that's what the modiste had said when she'd ordered it.

That word again. Well, what she was doing wasn't

at all proper. She should have returned posthaste to Kittridge, but she could not bear to do so. What on earth would she do in that huge house all day long? She simply wasn't the type to pine away. Marriage had done nothing but elevate her in status. It did not bring her joy or contentment, or even a child, a discovery she made two days after Jered had left.

It wasn't what her godfather said, or even the nastiness of the guests that had resolved her to come to London. It was, oddly enough, her childhood. *"Tessa, you must truly not ask so many questions. Cook has complained again. Can you not simply watch in order to learn? Tessa, will you please cease? I don't go off to school in order to teach you once I've come home. Tessa, a young lady does not ask so many questions of young men. Tessa, you really must take de la Rochefoucauld's motto to heart. 'The height of cleverness is being able to conceal it.' "*

All her life, people had poked and prodded her to be more circumspect. Being herself might truly be worthwhile now. She had nothing to lose.

She was going to remonstrate with one of those too attentive men for placing his hand on her arm when she looked up to see the glowering face of her husband. Those famous Mandeville eyes didn't look at all friendly, more like smoke from an internal fire.

"Jered, how clever of you to have found me so quickly," she said without giving him a chance to speak.

"How did you get here?" His voice was low, quite evenly pitched, but left no doubt whatsoever of his emotions at the moment. Her husband was blazingly angry.

"I walked," she confessed. After all, it was not that difficult a feat. "Your phaeton is quite distinctive, if a bit dangerous looking." London's crowded streets were sometimes so difficult to navigate that it was possible to outdistance a swift carriage while walking to one's destination. It was advisable to wear pattens, avoiding the gutters. It was even more preferable to remain on the wider thoroughfares. Otherwise it was just as likely for the innocent traveler to be splattered with contents thrown from an upper window as to be assaulted by the offal left by the thousands of horses stabled in London. Both facts, the reason why most people chose to take a carriage to their destination. But she had no choice and only enough time to grab an industrious downstairs maid and follow Jered. She seemed to have lost the maid in the last few minutes, but she had certainly found her husband. Tessa smiled at him, a gesture that did not seem to soften his anger. She glanced at the woman at his side and then back at him. One of her eyebrows arched. She would have spoken, had Jered not calmly and deliberately stepped between them.

He bent closer. "What the hell do you think you're doing here?" he whispered.

She stepped aside, smiling brightly.

"Do not think of doing it, Tessa." It was a warning in few words.

"Aren't you going to introduce us, Jered?" Tessa had the oddest thought that the other woman's voice sounded like a purr.

"You must be Jered's mistress," Tessa said. "I have heard so very much about you from all of Jered's friends. Is it true you can twirl tassels from your nipples, or is that another woman of his acquaintance?"

She would have said more, but Jered's hand clamped firmly over her arm and he pulled her away. "Have you lost your mind?" he whispered.

The roar of the crowd drowned out what she tried to say. She gazed at the spectacle behind him. No more than fifty feet away, three mangy lions were being led into the amphitheater. They would have been more frightening if they did not look so terribly emaciated and tired.

"Do you think they feed them?" she asked.

"What?"

"Well, I for one would like an introduction. I'm half-way respectable," Adrian Hampton said. He stepped to Jered's side, bowed to Tessa. His smile was particularly charming. Too much so, as if it had been rehearsed for just such an impression. A faint smile touched her lips in return.

"Go away, Adrian," Jered said "And take her with you." A nod of his head indicated the other woman.

"I really don't think it's fair, do you Jered? After all, they look half-starved." Tessa turned back to watch the big cats. The crowd was screaming, and all she could think of was that it seemed so cruel to be waving a torch at them.

"You can't just send me off like I'm a smelly parcel, Jered," the mistress said.

"Why don't you ask your bride to join us, Kittridge?" Adrian asked.

"I will not be ignored." The other woman stamped her foot.

"I think they're more frightened than frightening. Don't you, Jered?" Tessa shook off his hand. He grabbed her jacket and pulled her back.

The crowd roared again, and whatever the others said was lost in the cacophony. Jered gripped her arm, shook off his mistress's hand, and strode to the entrance to the building. Tessa had no choice but to go where he was leading, scrambling so that her feet caught up with her arm. She didn't know what he said to his companions as they left, but she doubted it was as effective as the look on his face.

It did not seem quite proper to feel excitement at this moment, but she did, and the look in his eyes did not frighten her as much as it probably should have. Of all his misdeeds, she'd never heard of him harming a woman. But then again, she was his wife and perhaps all former rules did not apply. She smiled up at him again, but it did not seem to alter his expression.

Once outside, he walked down the lamp-lit street, pulling Tessa after him, until he came to his own carriage. At least their audience had not chosen to follow them.

"I'm sure you thought this was a very good idea at the time. And I'll forgive you for it because of your youth, but I want it firmly understood that I will not tolerate any more scenes of wifely interference."

"Then the very reason for our marriage is in jeopardy, Jered. You see, I have discovered I am not with child. Since that is the singular reason for our union, I have decided that your absence, in this case, does not quite suit."

"I suggest you return to Kittridge, madam. My visits to you will be sufficient in time to satisfy your maternal cravings."

"Yes, but you are older than I, Jered. You may not have that much more time."

He only stared at her.

Her dress was new, but catching it upon an exposed spring was not what elicited a groan from Tessa. It was the sheer height of the vehicle into which she was pushed. Tessa bit her lip and concentrated on the shawl between her hands and not the distance from her perch to the ground.

She looked down at her husband who had one foot on the small brace beneath the wheel. How handsome he was, an observation she'd made at least twice today. She looked away from him, aware that his appearance sent her thoughts to wandering. And remembering. She could not look at him without recalling the night of their wedding. How had he so quickly forgotten?

She glanced away from his glare, concentrated on not feeling the ardent sway of the perch phaeton as it lurched in the air like a child's swing. She would have gripped his arm for balance and a measure of security had his look not been so vehement. It did not seem the moment for confession.

How long could he remain angry? As long as he could remain silent, evidently. A full ten minutes passed while he navigated the streets, the perch phaeton swaying in a manner that coaxed her stomach to her throat.

He glanced over at her, his concentration evidently wavering from controlling the high-spirited horses. Keeping them upright was a task she did not want him to lose sight of, especially since it was quite evident that the phaeton was delicately balanced.

"Should you not watch the road?" The panic in her voice caused him to swerve his gaze to the horses, and then back to her face.

"What is wrong with you?"

"I do not like being this high," she confessed as she sank back against the upholstered bench.

"You look green in the lantern light."

"It is a look I am cultivating." She gave a small, strangled laugh. "I have known ever since I was a child that I do not like heights, but I suspect your phaeton is even more a challenge for me.''

''Bloody hell,'' he said as they approached the square. He directed the horses to the side of the wide, paved street. The phaeton swayed even more as it came to a stop, testing her resolve to appear unaffected by the traitorous state of her stomach.

''Are you going to be ill?'' It was said with less than perfect grace, more of a growl, but at this moment, she felt too unwell to comment upon it.

She only nodded, pressing her cheek against the upholstery. Her forehead felt clammy, her mouth dry.

He withdrew his coat, threw it on her lap, turned his head.

''What is that for?'' She fingered it; it was still warm from his body.

''My favorite coat, madam. Make use of it if you will, but do not spoil the interior of my new carriage.''

She would very much have liked to counter his rudeness with a comment of her own, but she wasn't sure she was up to it. At least the phaeton had stopped. And if she could just remain still for a moment, she was certain she would be fine.

She took long breaths, closed her eyes, wished her stays were loose, or better yet nonexistent. She smiled at the thought of the Duchess of Kittridge roaming around London without a corset. Behavior not at all modest or unassuming. *Oh, Tessa.* She chided herself for the falsity of that thought. In truth, she was not at all modest or unassuming. She had hated the rules she'd been forced to follow, the endless regulations that followed a girl's entrance into society. One moment she'd been banished to the nursery, the next expected to put her hair up and become all things fashionable.

Marriage had not improved her lot. She was a wife, a duchess, and yet she was expected to do exactly what she had done as a debutante, act demure and steeped in propriety, wait until someone told her what to do, while spending the majority of her time occupied with fashion, servants, gossip.

"If this is a ruse to convince me not to send you back to Kittridge, it will not work, you know."

She opened her eyes and glanced up at him. "I had thought it was quite a remarkable gambit myself. I succumb to a sweating sickness, become ill in your carriage, and you find yourself riddled with pity for me."

She closed her eyes against his frown. It was a very good thing she was feeling better. A discussion of imminent consequence loomed on the horizon.

"I haven't the slightest intention of returning to Kittridge, Jered. If you send me back, I shall only return. I am your wife, and it is not the best thing for wives and husbands to be separated. I have often thought that the ton encourages division in a union, that marriages would be quite happy if society only accepted a few elemental notions."

"And what, pray tell, would be these elemental notions?" His temper did not seem the least bit modified in the last few minutes. Men, on the whole, do not like to be given instructions. Nor did they like being told that women will not follow theirs. A lesson she had learned from having six brothers. It was simply easier to remain silent and do what you wanted. But being a sister was not being a wife, and she didn't wish to begin her marriage with lies.

"Well for one, that married couples ought not to live separate lives. Do you not recall your Bible, Jered?"

"Not another quote about Naomi, surely?" He glanced at her, then away.

" 'Therefore shall a man leave his father and mother, and shall cleave unto his wife: and they shall be one flesh.' Hebrews." She smiled at him.

" 'One fool at least in every married couple.' Fielding." His smile was effortlessly charming. His eyes, however, remained clear and cold.

"Then there is the idea that a man should never take a mistress, at least not while he is married," she said, ignoring the fact that she had been outquoted.

"But it is perfectly acceptable should he be callow and unmarried?" His smile warned her that perhaps she had been too precipitous in bringing all these ideas to the fore at this moment. "Any more notions?" he asked, urging the horses forward. She leaned back in the carriage, closed her eyes, then decided that it only made the nausea worse. She concentrated on the lantern, but it swung from side to side in such a pitched motion that she decided that was not such a good idea, either. Finally she folded her hands in Jered's coat, warming their chill. And prayed not to disgrace herself.

"You truly are ill, aren't you?"

She nodded.

"We will soon be home. Shall I stop again?"

"No, let us not delay our arrival."

"It will only be a few more minutes."

There was silence while she concentrated on the far horizon, the sight of London burrowing down for a night's sleep. Why is it the city never seemed to rest, only trade its daytime inhabitants for those who prowled after dark?

"I wonder what people will think seeing us?" she asked finally.

"I don't care what people think."

"Truly?" she said, smiling. "Do you not ever look at someone and wonder at his errand, her life? Take that man there," she said, pointing at a man alighting from his coach. "He has a look of such intense purpose on his face. Where is he going? What is his mission? Why does he leave his companion in the carriage?"

"All that with one glance? Why should you even be concerned?"

"It is not that I am concerned, only curious. Are you not, Jered?" She glanced around her. "Why, for example, are the lamps fixed with that odd glass?"

"It is called convex, Tessa, and it is placed in such a way as to accentuate the light."

"Oh," she said, smiling over at him. "Now, you see, I shall know that forever. And should anyone ask me, I shall tell him."

"I doubt anyone at Kittridge should be concerned about London's lighting." The phaeton pulled up before the entrance to the town house. A footman sprinted down the steps but Jered waved him away.

"Very well," she said, leaning back against the cushions. "Send me back. But your chances of ever having an heir are dwindling each day, Jered."

He didn't speak for a long moment, time in which he looked at her, really looked at her. For a moment, it was as if his eyes softened, then he blinked and another expression appeared in them. Speculation, curiosity, perhaps even something harder, colder. It should not have had the effect it did on her, to make her tremble, to wish to melt in his arms.

"You want a child, Tessa?"

It was as good a reason as any to seek him out. She was not so silly as to tell him it was his love she wanted, that she had decided upon a campaign of aggression in order to gain his attention. That was as pointless as wishing she had blond hair and blue eyes. Instead she nodded, captivated at the smile he gave her, an effortless gesture of considerable charm.

His hands went around her waist and she was lifted down into his embrace as if she were no more weighty than a feather, as if she were not taller than most women of her acquaintance.

She placed her hands on his shoulders, looked at his mouth as it loomed larger and larger in her field of vision, softly gasped as his lips touched hers. Her hat was too weighty and her hair needed to be unbound. Her body readied for him, her mind remembered. When he set her back on the ground, she only sagged against him, leaning her head against his chest. It was with a great deal of effort that she managed to step back, away.

"Oh my." She blinked a few times, then looked up to find him staring at her, a look she could not decipher in his eyes.

What would he say? Would he wound her with a trite remark, something viciously mundane and exquisitely polite? After several long moments, he spoke. "Before you leave London, you will be promised of one. And my child will be born at Kittridge, is that agreed?"

She nodded.

"And you will never interfere in my life again?"

She shook her head.

"Then you will find me an assiduous husband, Tessa."

The smile he gave her was oddly triumphant.

Chapter 6

Tessa was seated at her dressing table, her maid stood behind her fastening the cap that would protect her hair for the night. Both of them turned at his approach.

Did she know that he had stood in the hallway counseling himself that this was not the way husbands sought their wives? He should have met her at breakfast and indicated that a schedule between them might be the more prudent course. She could therefore expect him on Mondays and Thursdays, and perhaps Saturday evenings if he had no prior engagements. That way, he could amply provide for the possibility of future heirs while controlling this absurd and maddening feeling that led him to improvident gestures such as the one he was making now.

He shook his head and the maid placed the cap on the dressing table, stepped back, and looked once more at her mistress.

"Thank you, Mary."

The door softly shut.

"Don't thank the servants, Tessa. There is no need."

"For common courtesy, Jered?"

"They are thanked each time they are paid, Tessa. That is all they care about, anyway."

She looked only at her hands, as if their folded condition was a new and unique trick they'd not done before. He could have reassured her that she was demure to a fault. If he had not known better, he would have thought her virginal and innocent. But the memory of her denouement, that moment of giving surrender, had stayed with him long after his pulse had slowed and his breath restored. Was that why, then, he had argued with himself over the last hour, regretting his impulse to keep her in London? She was safer at Kittridge. *He* was safer with her at Kittridge.

"Will you not miss your family if you remain in London?" With one finger, he tipped up her chin, traced the line of her throat, back up to her nose and over to her ear, a triangle of flesh mapped out with delicate precision.

"My parents are here. Their home is not far, and the three boys not off at school are with them."

That was news he could have done without.

She stared at him as if to study him, a curious assessing gaze.

"And Harry? Is he still precocious?" His fingers seemed fascinated with every aspect of her face. How odd that she should be so lovely, and yet it was not her beauty he had recalled this last week. Her way of smiling, perhaps?

"He is no longer five, Jered."

"And you are no longer a maiden."

She turned and faced the mirror again, fingers trailing the edge of the silver handled brush. She didn't expose, by word or deed, how she felt about his words. It was a trick she must have discovered, only hours old, that disconcerted him. It was as if she were a fleshed statue. He placed his hands upon her shoulders. Statues did not tremble. Lust, pure, sharp, and feral hit him then.

"Do you remember our wedding night, Tessa?" There. Such insouciance gave lie to the scampering beat of his heart. There was nothing to anticipate with this woman that he had not experienced with a hundred others. And this time, surely, bedding her could not be as strangely delirious as that previous time had been. He would acquit himself well, but would find her as human as any other woman. She would not lift her hand in tenderness and brush her fingers against his lips, causing his flesh to shudder in response. And she would not look at him in the same way again, as if he were god and hero made whole for the purpose of bringing her joy.

She stood, still clothed in silence and in a soft peach confection that pooled on the floor like a court train. She clutched the front panel of her wrapper with one fist, the other gathered the folds closer to her legs. One knee was impudent enough to escape, its roundness and pink tint almost a lure. He'd been fascinated by her long legs—scenes from his wedding night had tantalized him for days.

She was a detrimental aspect of his life, a deterrent to his enjoyment of the season and his friend's antics, certainly a goad to his conscience, a spur to his sensibilities. But she was, after all, only a wife. And wives must know their place. Hers was at Kittridge. How long would it take for her to learn that?

He threaded his fingers through her hair, felt a tendril brush against the back of his hand, wondered when he'd been so affected by a lock of hair.

Once he'd thought she was pretty. At this moment, she was more than simply attractive, she was radiant.

There was color to her face, a flush that lent her skin a soft glow. Her chestnut hair was riotous around her shoulders, a mass of tangles and tendrils. She looked like a Florentino cherub Venus, only more slender and fair of face. He knew better, however, to say such a thing. Women sensed a man's appreciation and called it capitulation.

"You are quite lovely, wife."

"My name is Tessa," she said softly, endearingly.

He knew it well. Hadn't he shouted it, near screamed it? Once more, he had the daunting feeling that he should have sent her back to Kittridge.

It was the perfect opportunity to sever the tenuous bond that bound them together. He should have damned her naiveté and strangled his reluctant yearning. He should march from her presence and seek out his mistress.

But he'd promised her a child. And she'd promised him his freedom.

"He'll kill himself for sure this time."

"Not him. He rides like the devil himself."

"Still and all, it's a bit foolhardy, isn't it?"

The front door was open, servants congregated in the doorway, their attention fixed on something happening in the square. Tessa came down the stairs just as one of the maids turned and, catching sight of her, bobbed and backed away. The major domo cleared his throat, and the rest of the servants scattered.

"What is going on, Michaels?"

"Nothing, Your Grace."

She smiled. Harry had often worn the same look of half-buried excitement. It cried out for investigation. She peered over her shoulder and then frowned.

In front of each of the town houses was a tall black iron lamp. Each of them was lit, the effect being a dotted line in the form of a square. And following the outline, two mounted riders each holding a tankard in their left hand. They were racing through the square, the object of the impromptu game evidently to douse as many lanterns as possible with the contents of the tankard while attempting to remain mounted.

Jered was one of the riders.

The other she recognized as one of the party at the circus last night. The one whose smile she distrusted. The laughter and applause accompanying each doused light was coming from the woman who had so proprietarily touched her husband's arm. His mistress.

"What are they doing, Michaels?" It was an idiotic question, especially since she could very well see what was happening. But it seemed to be called for in that moment.

Michaels glanced at her but refrained from answering.

Jered won the contest, turned his horse, and trotted back to what was evidently the starting point, draining the tankard as he rode. Her husband was quite obviously drunk, and just as obviously unconcerned about it. He stopped in front of the woman, bent down, and in a gesture oddly reminiscent of three years ago, pulled his mistress up into the saddle and kissed her. Ardently. Lovingly. With much leisure and no haste.

"Your Grace?" Michaels spoke beside her. She turned her head and forced a smile.

"You may close the door, Michaels," she said.

It was the oddest feeling, really. Like the scrape of something sharp against her skin. Not penetrating but threatening all the same. A needle perhaps. She mounted the steps feeling oddly heavy, as if she had become aged in the five minutes since she'd descended them.

And someone told me she heard he dressed up as a beggar and spent the night huddled in the corner of Whitechapel only to count the whores who seduced his friend. Imagine, for a silly wager. . . . he nearly lost 10,000 pounds, and got it back again, and more, on a turn of a die. . . . his mistress was an actress who performs those scandalous dioramas—you know the ones, Betty, where she pretends she's someone from history. Stark naked, she is on the stage with her arms held out and not moving a muscle . . . he rides that horse of his through London's streets with his friends, all of them like nothing more than bo,s, yelling and screaming and waking decent citizens.

She'd heard the rumors of course. Everyone had. She had believed them, too. He'd been not unlike her brothers, who were wicked on a whim, who pushed the measure of their parent's benevolence. But none of her brothers were cruel, and she'd not thought Jered to be. Until he had looked at her, had sat straight up in the saddle, and noticed her before he had kissed his mistress. A calculated gesture. He had accomplished his task well.

She closed the door to her chamber carefully, so that the latch barely made a sound. It seemed of infinite importance that she do so. She braced an arm against the door, leaned her forehead against it. She'd cried when he'd left Kittridge, but she would not cry now. This hurt did not demand tears. It was a bone-deep, jarring ache that made her want to turn herself inside out so that the hurt was exposed to the sun and therefore had a chance to heal in greater degree. She took a shaky breath, then another until she felt more composed, then pushed away from the door.

She felt sad and furious and wanting, and confused that above all she should feel every single one of these emotions at the same time.

"Are you coming back with me, darling?" Pauline purred. Her voice seemed to grate on his nerves like the contraption Michaels used to sprinkle nutmeg into his mulled wine. Her affection had at its roots the magnificent bracelet she wore. It was a gift he hoped would atone for his future behavior.

His blood still thrummed in his body, a combination of the race and brandy. He felt vibrantly alive. He pocketed the money Adrian grudgingly handed him, patted him absently on the back.

"You have the devil's own luck, Kittridge."

"Cheer up, I'll let you win next time."

"I'll bet on a cock fight first. I can't match your horseflesh."

Jered laughed, glanced at the entrance to his home. She was gone. The door firmly closed.

Pauline reached up and traced a hand from his knee to his thigh. He had every intention of ignoring her for the present. He had, after all, his ducal responsibilities to consider.

He dismounted, an action that was performed with ease despite the fact he was not exactly sober.

"Perhaps later," he murmured. It would have been simpler to tell her straight out that he had no intention of visiting her in the foreseeable future. Women, however, were an unpredictable breed, and she was as likely to sharpen her fingernails on his face as she was to collapse in tears. It was easier to allow her to come to the conclusion on her own.

Besides, his young wife was keeping him well occupied. If she was not with child after last night, this morning, and early this afternoon, it was not for want of trying.

She had looked devastated when he'd kissed Pauline. Absolutely crushed. Very well, it was what he had wanted. She really must learn her place. He had envisioned her established at Kittridge, out of his way, aloof and disinterested. He had not married in order to be bedeviled by an innocent, yet pertinacious, chit.

He turned away from his home. The night was early and there were parties planned.

No, she was *not* going to dictate his life.

"Don't forget your promise, Helena."

"I made it under duress, Gregory. We've been in London exactly three days and already there is talk." In fact, this entire evening had been filled with rumor and the type of gossip that ceases the moment the subject of it walks into the room. She had been, as the new mother-in-law, sufficiently close to the personage in question that voices had skittered to a halt in her presence. Yet she'd heard enough. She ached for her daughter.

At the moment, however, she was not filled with pity as much as she was righteous indignation. She had spotted Kittridge across the room, smiling at a particularly lovely young chit who looked positively entranced.

"Tessa is more than his equal, darling. She has your stubbornness and my intellect."

Her frown had absolutely no effect on her husband. Gregory shook his head at her, his dark eyes warning her off her course. Her husband was the most wonderful man she'd ever met, and one of the ugliest. He was nearly bald, with a fringe over the ears nature had crafted, as if creating a reverse nest for his shiny pate. His nose looked out of place on his face, a cute little pug nose not at all suited for the crags and weathered creases of his face. His paunch seemed to grow in girth every year; he was shorter than she by two inches. She adored him, however, an emotion that no one except she and Gregory could understand. She knew he adored her as well.

"I really believe I could dislike that man intensely, Gregory," she said now, staring through the crowd.

"He is your daughter's husband. I suggest you attempt to find his good qualities."

"What if he has none?" It was a very real worry.

"No one is ever truly without redemption, Helena."

"Keep telling me that, Gregory, and I will endeavor to believe it. I still maintain we should never have agreed to the marriage," Helena said.

"It's a bit late to be thinking that, my love," Gregory replied. "The time for objections was when Stanford suggested the match. Reformed rakes make the best husbands. Isn't that what women claim?" His fingers trailed over her shoulder. Even in public they touched often.

"In your case, it was the love of a good woman." She smiled at him.

"Not to mention the lowering effect of seven children."

"You are a wonderful father, Gregory. I knew you would be from the first. But then, you were not as much a rake as the Duke of Kittridge."

"And how am I as a husband, my love?"

"An outrageously good one, Gregory."

"Or just outrageous?"

"That, too," she laughed.

He wiggled his eyebrows at her, and once again she wondered how she'd been so lucky to have attracted this man. Granted, there were still some people who could not see past appearances to the man beneath. But they were to be pitied for being denied the essence of Gregory, which was all well and good. She preferred to keep the essence on home ground so to speak.

Now, if only Kittridge would do the same.

She smiled brightly at Gregory before proceeding on her errand. He only shook his head at her.

"Where is my daughter, Kittridge?"

Jered looked up and the smile he'd used for the young miss flattened as he stared at his mother-in-law. He straightened, towered above her, but Helena was well used to the strutting behavior of males, especially those caught in acts of an illicit nature. And charming another woman while her daughter was absent from the scene was definitely unacceptable behavior.

"My wife was not invited, madam."

Helena had an almost overwhelming desire to strike him on the forehead with her fan. She did not like the look in Kittridge's eyes. It was not quite challenge, but it was most certainly not regret. Or any other concilia-tory emotion.

"I will not have her hurt, Kittridge. She is not your equal in depravity."

He smiled at her, and for a moment, Helena thought it might actually be humor in his expression. It was gone too soon for her to be certain. "Your daughter is my wife, madam. I need not account to you for any of my actions. Or hers."

"Perhaps with any other woman, Kittridge, but not with Tessa. I do not relinquish what is mine that easily."

"A trait your daughter has acquired from you it seems, madam." He bowed, then resumed his stance. He was too handsome, Helena thought. There was something about him that even she recognized, an effortless sensuality.

"Shall I give Tessa your greeting? Or shall I refrain from telling her that her mother chastised me in public?"

Helena was silenced by his taunt. Did he know that if he spoke of their meeting, Tessa would be furious with her?

"Tell her, Kittridge. I shall, perhaps, have tales of my own."

They locked gazes in that moment, the mother and the rake. Neither doubted that a battle had been joined.

Chapter 7

"It looks idiotic, Charles."

"It's what's done, all right? How do you think to muffle the sound otherwise?"

"Well, I don't think highwaymen wrap their horses' hooves in black batting, Douglas. It looks like the damn horse is in mourning." All three horses were tied to a tree, awaiting the arrival of the last of their group.

"Will you both shut up? Your yammering will waken everyone, and then all Kittridge's efforts will be for naught."

"Don't see why he just wouldn't lend me the money." Adrian's voice was less melancholy than irritated.

"You know Kittridge doesn't lend money."

"But why the hell does he want to rob a coach? He could get us all shot."

"Why does Kittridge do anything, Adrian? Because he's never done it before. Because he likes the danger."

"I'd much rather he gave me the two thousand pounds. I could spend the time at the tables, getting my capital back instead of standing out here in the middle of the night. It's deuced wet."

"It's called rain, you fool."

71

"Shut up, Charles. You're half the reason we're here."

"Me? Why? I wasn't the one dead set on winning a fortune so much so that I couldn't stop until I'd lost everything."

"Why don't you just stand in the middle of the road and shout your intentions, gentlemen?" For a moment, Jered wondered at the wisdom of the actions he would take in the next few minutes, but too soon the thrill of excitement and the thought of the escapade to come banished every restraining thought.

He rode ahead of the others to a place he'd picked that afternoon. The coach would approach from the north and curve around this bend in the road. Just south of there was where they would take their stand, at a place not seen to be an ambush point, after the armed outriders would have already passed. Then he and the others would approach the fast-moving carriage. Adrian would slow the lead horses, while Charles would keep watch. This was, after all, a well-traveled route to London. Jered would be the one to approach the driver while Douglas followed close behind, watching his back. The robbery would be executed flawlessly, a perfect exercise of precision, planning, and intellect, an adventure that even now made his heart beat faster and his breath quicken.

Except for one thing. Sounds were coming from that bush, just east of their current location. It sounded like some sort of wild animal. From the crashing and the moans, a crazed and brutal beast.

Tessa had heard her parents arguing ever since she was a child. They took great pride in the fact that they vehemently disagreed upon occasion. She had heard her mother call her father a stubborn fool, and her father announce that her mother was the most falsely opinionated woman he'd ever met. Yet it was obvious even to strangers that they loved each other dearly. And they spoke of each other as if each was their greatest friend, prized above all other people.

How did one become friends with a rake?

Despite the fact that he had so obviously wished to hurt her, to parade his mistress before her and therefore send her scuttling back to Kittridge, she was determined to discern her husband's good qualities. Understand him, in other words. Only then could friendship come, and it would act as a solid foundation for their marriage. They were already quite compatible in other areas.

She could feel her face flushing.

The decision to embark upon a friendship with Jered, however brilliant, was easier decided upon than implemented. Take this evening, for example. She hated horses. Detested them. They were huge smelly beasts, covered in spiky sharp hair. They had nasty dispositions and they knew she was afraid of them. She'd only ridden once before tonight, and that was as a child of six. Ever since, she'd avoided the great smelly beasts as though her life depended on it. The rain only made the smell worse.

She sawed on the reins, and the blasted animal veered from the path, nearly knocking her unconscious when a low-slung branch swung into her view. She ducked, held on to both reins, wished she'd had the courage to ride astride, then she could have bent her back and extended her arms around the horse's neck and held on for dear life. As it was, she was perched upon the side of the horse, quite ladylike but without much control at all except to hang on to her own hat, pray that the mare choose to once again ride down the muddy road instead of stumbling through the damp underbrush.

Another branch nearly pulled her hat from her head, and she snatched it back. It was so dark that the trees looked like skeletons; their branches multilimbed arms that seemed to scratch the night sky. Her eyes had finally adjusted to the scant light, but not enough that she had any idea of where she was going. In fact, her destination was as much in doubt as her current location. She'd been following Jered, when he'd suddenly veered into the trees and disappeared.

It was not the time to recall all those really horrifying nursery stories she'd read, Bluebeard, Babes in the Wood, Little Red Riding Hood. Why is it that children's stories are so filled with monsters like wolves and witches who eat children, and men who kill their wives? And to think, that people actually sat and told their children such things. She remembered one her nurse had read. *I had a little doggy, who used to set and beg, but Doggy tumbled down the stairs and broke his little leg.*

She shivered. But then another poem came to mind. She smiled and recited it from memory. " 'I had a little pony, his name was Dapple-Gray. I lent him to a lady, to ride a mile away. She whipped, she lashed him. She rode him through the mire. I would not lend my pony now, for all the lady's hire.'

"You see," she said, addressing the beast beneath her, "for all that I do not care for horses, I would never whip you."

"I do not bloody well believe it," Adrian said, turning his horse so that he was beside Jered. "Isn't that your wife?"

Jered felt the flash of recognition, closed his eyes,

opened them again, but she was still there. "Yes," he whispered. A moment later Jered wondered why he'd bothered. She was making no attempt to be quiet, but then she'd no knowledge of their intentions.

The Duke of Kittridge said nothing as his Mother Goose quoting wife emerged from the copse of trees. She was ambling down the road like a drunken sailor, her hat askew, her left leg not even in its stirrup.

Her riding habit consisted of a redincoat with double collar and bodice, so deep a shade that it appeared almost black in the darkness. It was buttoned from waist to collar with tiny pearl buttons that acted like little lanterns, catching the wink of any available light. Her hat had a wide brim, tall crown, and absurd feathers that bobbed wetly each time the horse stepped heavily into the mud.

All in all, she was hard to miss.

"She's going to ruin everything," Adrian said loudly, evidently feeling the same lack of caution. Why bother, when Tessa was doing everything she could to attract attention?

What the hell was she doing here? Was she following him? Why? He urged his horse forward, grasped the bridle of Tessa's mare. She didn't look the least startled.

"Oh, hello, Jered. I am so glad I found you," she said, quite ignoring the fact that it was he who had discovered her. He frowned at her, but the look had absolutely no effect.

He pulled out a dark scarf from his pocket, threw her hat into the bushes, and handed her the scarf. She took it in silence, a feat for Tessa.

"What are we doing here?"

The peace was too good to be true.

"Did you know, I was thinking the oddest thought

about nursery tales. Why do you think they have so many monsters in them?''

"To frighten children into obeying," he said, giving her another frown.

She thought about it for a moment. "Like a morality tale, you mean?" Another pause. "Perhaps. But don't you think it could be accomplished with a bit less fear?''

"*Some* people would pay no attention, then," he growled, but she was as inattentive to his meaning as to his mood.

He extracted the knife stowed in his boot, sliced off each one of her buttons.

"Jered, I quite like that button. And that one," she said as another flew. He concentrated on his task, paying no attention to her gasps of alarm. So the bodice was not as tight, and the material sagged a bit. She was still decent, and the absence of the light-seeking buttons meant additional safety.

"First time I've ever heard of you being unable to control your women, Kittridge," Adrian said. "Congratulations, little one. I count myself amazed."

"Shut up, Adrian."

"Yes, please," said his surprising wife. "I truly do not like being called names. While it may be commonplace in your group, I dislike it."

Adrian sketched a mock bow from the back of his horse. "God forbid that you do not approve, Your Grace."

"Are you truly a friend of Jered's?" She peered at him in the darkness, as if to view him more clearly.

"Perhaps your husband has no friends, little one," he said in a mocking tone. "Only sycophants."

"I am his friend, sir."

That surprising remark made Jered turn his head and stare at her.

His fingers slid along the bridle of the mare. He drew her closer, a whinny of protest as if she felt too constrained, too near his stallion. Eyes rolled nervously, the whites like tiny moons, the only spot of light in this dark and shrouded night. Were Tessa's eyes as wide and as frightened? He couldn't tell.

He could hear the carriage coming down the road, a heavy coach lurching in the mud.

The surge of excitement he felt was neither commonplace nor unexpected. He relished it just as he savored this moment, when it was as if he stepped off a cliff into the nothingness of adventure. There, in front of him, was darkness and nothing else. The future was not ordained or planned, practiced or rehearsed. It was fluid like water over stones, simply there to be shaped by events as they unfolded.

A hand upon his arm captured his attention.

"Jered?" A whisper in the darkness, a goad. Now was not the time for her to speak. And to mention his name no less. He frowned, thinking he had been unwise to believe her docile even for a moment.

"Why are we here?" The scarf he'd given her dangled from her fingers. The hand that clutched his arm did so with talonlike strength. Was that what she was, then, a small falcon? At this moment, he wished he had a hood for her eyes and perhaps something to place across her mouth.

"We are robbing the coach, my dear," he said, and laughed as she thrust the scarf at him. It draped over his chest, fell to his leg, hung upon one shiny black Hessian boot, then fell to the ground beneath his horse's hooves. There it would stay, mired in the mud.

He shook off her hand, urged his horse forward, and dashed into the night, intent upon his prey.

He can't be thinking of behaving like a highwayman. He cannot! But it was all too clear that he was, and that his friends were intent upon doing the same. She remained where she was, still mounted, heard the sound of the brake against iron-bound wheels.

"Stand and deliver!" A shout then, a demand from one of the wealthiest men in England.

There had been a note in his voice, something oddly exultant, as if he'd been excited beyond measure to be lawless. The Duke of Kittridge robbing a coach!

She jerked, startled by the sound of a shot. A gun? Dear God, were they shooting at him?

She lurched forward in the saddle, dug her heel into the mare's sides, but gently so as not to hurt the huge beast. The mare did not seem inclined to move, even when another shot was fired and a female scream ripped apart the night. Tessa grabbed both reins and rocked back and forth in the saddle, murmuring those words she'd learned surreptitiously from her brothers, who were expected to excel in swearing in the same way she was expected not to know what any of the words meant.

The mare, bless her, seemed to pick up on the sense of urgency, or perhaps it was the third shot that made her turn her head and sprint in the other direction. It was, perhaps, the very best thing that could have happened, because Tessa heard shouting behind her, then a shadow raced by, tearing the reins from her hand. All she could do was stifle a scream and hold on for dear life to the mound of leather that supported her knee, hoping that the lurching feeling inside her stomach was due to all the excitement and not from incipient illness. It simply would not do to shame herself at this moment, especially since her husband was determined to cast enough dishonor upon the family name.

The pace was much faster than she was used to, the sum of her experience being when she was six and had fallen from her pony, and the placid walk of a few minutes earlier. The scenery flew by. She was so immersed in trying not to fall to her death, and alternately being certain she would be horribly sick, that Tessa wasn't even aware they had stopped until Jered dragged her from the horse and set her behind a tree. The horse was urged on by a slap on its rump. Tessa had the oddest thought that it would have worked as well on her.

She nearly fell against the tree, forehead pressed to the bark.

"Are you going to be ill?" His voice sounded absurdly cheery.

She supposed she said something, because he pushed her even farther back behind the tree and held her close. Strangely, his warmth did seem to make it better. Or perhaps it was simply the fact that her stomach had stopped its riotous disregard for propriety.

"You really don't like being jostled, do you, Tessa?" Was it her imagination, or did his voice sound almost tender? She buried her head into his chest, allowed a sigh to escape her lips.

"How on earth did you manage to travel to London?"

"Closed carriages don't seem to bother me. Just swaying phaetons—and now horses, I suppose. Why do you think that is?"

She knew he was about to say something else, but a

whisper in the darkness cut short that remark. Another whisper, one quite audible, and then an answer. So no one had been shot to the death, then.

She drew back, fixed her husband with a fulminating stare, then realized her anger could not be seen. She grabbed his coat and shook it, strongly enough that he bent his head.

"What is it, Tessa?"

"How could you do something so foolish, Jered? For what reason? Why on earth would you chance your life for money when you're as rich as Croesus?" She hoped that the tremble in her voice could be construed as a simple chill. She was, in fact, terrified, both because of his actions and the resultant gunfire.

"Are you rehearsing for the part of harridan?" he asked, patting her arm absently. It was done the way one might pat a dog upon the head, or pet a cat. Without much thought or intent, a gesture designed to appease, placate, calm. She wasn't sure what she felt at this moment, but she was certain it was not calm. Fear? Anger? Or simply confusion that he would have done such a thing.

She pulled on his coat again.

"What is it, Tessa?" Barely veiled irritation. Well, she was irritated, too.

"I really must insist upon your attention, Jered," she said. "I wish to return home now."

"As soon as possible, Tessa." And with that he put his hands on her arms and pushed her back until she was pressed against the tree. The shadows coalesced and became his three accomplices.

"Did you get the money, Adrian?"

"The entire chest, Kittridge. However did you know they would be carrying gold?"

"Luck, Adrian."

"It doesn't seem quite fair, though, Kittridge. Being a duke and all. Don't seem to need much luck in your position. Should be meted out to the rest of us. Could use a little damn luck at the gaming tables."

"Here, here," said Charles.

"Well, it's his own luck that we didn't get shot tonight, that's for sure. A damn bullet near creased my scalp. What about your vaunted luck, Kittridge? Me lying on the ground with the rain washing my face. Wouldn't have felt bloody lucky then."

" 'Time and chance happeneth to them all.' "

"Now is not the appropriate time for a quote, Tessa."

"Well, I do not believe in luck, and I think it's a bad thing for your friends to. Look what luck has done to you. Forced you into robbing carriages."

"Your little bride's got a mouth on her, Kittridge. Hope to God you train her to use it to good purposes."

"You are an exceedingly rude sort of person," Tessa said to the still-mounted Adrian. Nothing she had seen of his character had impressed her.

"I am devastated, Your Grace."

"Quiet!" Jered's left hand was braced against the trunk of the tree, the other was splayed across Tessa's bodice. His attention was not on the fact that his fingers dislodged the scarf at her neck. Instead he was focused on the sound of iron-banded wheels again clattering down the road to London.

"Jered," she whispered, but he only moved his hand upward until the tips of his fingers touched her lips. Just that, a fleeting caress that warned.

He turned back, pulled her up against him so that their bodies could not be seen behind the tree. The other three had already scattered for refuge in the overgrowth lining the road the moment they'd heard the sounds of the carriage.

The coach swayed ponderously from side to side, its crowded condition evident from its movement and the number of trunks piled on its top and rear bars. Two outriders followed it, and as they passed, Tessa could only thank Providence that Jered's choice of victim had not been so armed and protected.

Jered himself might have been a shadow except that a shadow never possessed such warm hands, hands that were spanning her waist.

She angled her head away from him, pretending that the urge had not been to lean into his caress. "Is it that your fortune is only rumor, Jered? Is that why you felt you must steal? Truly, I do not mind. I've my grandmother's inheritance, you know, and we can live so much more cheaply than we do now."

"My wealth is intact, Tessa."

"Then why, Jered? I do not understand." She shook her head. The danger had passed evidently, the moment gone, and all that was left was this odd night filled with actions that startled and shamed her.

He dipped his head, murmured in her ear. "Do you not like excitement, Tessa?" His tone was chiding, the tip of his tongue against the rim of her ear a taunt.

"Is that why? Only for excitement? What if one of those bullets had struck you, or if the coach was accompanied by mounted patrols? You could have been killed, Jered."

He said nothing, just pulled her in the direction his mount had strayed.

"Come here," he said, mounting his horse. Her own mare had been found and now followed docilely behind, as if she knew that the time for recalcitrance had ended.

Here was a person who could control her. Jered extended a hand and Tessa took it, then found herself swept up before him on the saddle. It was not an entirely comfortable position, being set sideways. She simply did not know where to put her left shoulder. In the end, she slouched down and allowed Jered to extend his arms around her. It was only after long minutes of fidgeting that she realized two things—they were in motion and Jered was laughing.

"Are you settled in yet?"

"Yes." If her voice was terse, then it was the way she felt. She disliked being the source of amusement.

"Are you feeling ill?" There was still a note of humor in his voice, one that stiffened her spine even more. A difficult position to maintain since her head was against his shoulder and her left arm was, by necessity, stretched around his back.

"No."

"You've been quiet for too long, I'm beginning to worry."

"If you must know, I'm trying to understand you."

He tilted his head. She knew he tried to see her face, but the shadows made that impossible. Just to be on the safe side, she burrowed her head against his chest.

"Ah, I see. Instead of being my nemesis, you have decided the role of nanny is more attuned to your character."

"If I were your nanny, I should box your ears," she said.

"But you are not, and I do not ask for your comments, wife. Critics one has in plenty. A wife should not be one."

"You are a duke, Jered. Surely your time could be spent for better purposes than this. And your companions are nothing short of titled hooligans. Your leadership could be better served in greater causes."

"And your tongue to better purposes than castigation, wife. Or do you prefer to return to Kittridge and await my arrival? You would have no reason to criticize me then, Tessa. I would be at my best behavior when I visited you."

"Was this your ultimate mission, then, Jered? To have me return to Kittridge in a huff, certain that you are a rake in true form? And this charade as highwayman, has it been enacted for my benefit alone?"

"Do you never stop, Tessa? Do not question everything I say or do, wife. Simply accept it."

"You would have me be as silent as during my season."

"I doubt you were ever truly mute," he said sardonically.

"I would have you know that I was quite acceptable. I said nothing unless I was spoken to, did nothing untoward, was utterly proper."

"And you did not question anyone? About anything?"

There was silence while she weighed the benefits of the truth against a falsehood. His laughter was warm, but she smarted nonetheless.

"Very well. If you must know, since the list of acceptable topics was rather limited, I spoke mainly of the weather."

"And what did you ask? How clouds are made? What causes the rain? How can you guess if it will be a fair day?"

She smiled at him. "Very acceptable questions, Jered. Did you ever see a snowflake up close? Have you never wondered why it seems warmer when it snows than if there is no snow at all?'' She tilted her head up, stared at the impenetrable sky. ''Can you drown in the rain?''

He pulled her close, flattened her cheek against his chest. ''I concede, Tessa. I do not know the answer to any of your questions.''

A warm spot edged out the cold. She said nothing further, only gripped him tightly, wishing she could ask him the one question she'd dared never utter, the one that was always present in her heart. *Who are you, really?*

Chapter 8

Halfway home, their companions disappeared, slipping onto one of the crowded streets that led to the square. Jered led both horses to the rear of the town house where he dismounted and held up his hands for his wife. She slipped down from the saddle with precarious grace, leaning against him for a moment before standing on her own.

"How do you feel?"

"Quite well, really. Isn't that the oddest thing? Do you think horses know when they're being ridden by someone who honestly likes them? I'm quite afraid that I did not hide my aversion from the mare. Do you think that's why she ignored every one of my commands?"

"It is my belief that animals can sense fear. Horses, dogs, even perhaps those wild animals such as wolves."

"Do you really think so?" She seemed excessively interested in the subject.

Dawn was beginning to extend its fingers of light over the horizon, enough that he could see her face. Her cheeks were tinted with the palest peach, her lips were delectably full, but she would not meet his eyes, and her hands were twisted together in front of her. *Anxious? Undoubtedly. Perhaps even fearful. But of what?*

Me? He discounted that thought immediately. He was not the type to frighten women. Any nervousness he induced in women was normally that of arousal. He turned from handing the reins of both horses to a sleepy stableboy and studied his wife.

He always felt alive, refreshed after one of his forays, always too filled with vitality to sleep. His energy dictated some other type of activity, and who better to satisfy that urge than his wife? But from the look of her, it would require a bit of persuasion. Her lips were pursed, her demeanor stern and unforgiving. He smiled. It was a challenge he would easily accept.

He was looking at her with a smile on his face. A flush warmed her cheeks. She felt young and countrified and inadequate in a way she'd not felt since she was a child. No, she had never felt quite this way as a child because she'd been comforted and cosseted and protected by her parents, surrounded by the knowledge that she was beloved. Now she felt as though that protection was lost, put aside in her growing, and there was nothing but herself to sustain her. Not Jered's affection, because he had made it perfectly clear she was not held in any high emotion at all—else he would never have kissed his mistress in front of her, staging such a magnificent ruse in order to shock her, and then send her back to Kittridge.

She clasped her fingers into fists, then surrounded her waist with her hands. It was chilly and the dawn air provided fog where there had been none before, an encroaching cloud of it, light and furry and gray.

When Jered held out his hand, she placed hers on it, allowed him to lead her to the back of the townhouse, past the shocked kitchen staff, through the hallway, and to the staircase that arched and curved up to the third floor. Their suites encompassed most of the third floor, a majestic series of rooms that mirrored those at Kittridge in that they were commodious, with the bed chambers separated by more than a few rooms. Luxury and separation. It seemed to mark the tenor of the Kittridge nobility.

Jered did not lead her to the guest room she'd occupied for two days. Nor did he venture near the duchesses' rooms that she'd been promised would be completed in only a matter of weeks. Instead he led her silent and unprotesting to his own suite of rooms that overlooked the east gardens.

Even now the sun, muted by fog, lit the way. In another place, the effect would be dreary. Instead the drapes were drawn open to reveal a layer of fog not far beneath the window. It felt as if they were ensconced upon a cloud, and everything else was unreal and only imaginary. At certain times of the year, London's fog was tinted yellow, but now it was almost the color of Jered's eyes.

He allowed her to pull free of his clasp, walk to the window. A door closed, a key turned, soft footfalls, the feel of the brocaded curtain under her fingers, the tightness of her breath—all these things were indicative of a greater danger, that of anticipation.

She really, truly, should continue to be stern with him. What he had done was terrible. She held to that thought even as she sensed him coming closer.

She no longer saw the fog, instead her eyes closed. When he came and stood behind her, it was as if her body sighed in relief, the heat of his body warming the air between them. She didn't move, not an inch, not even when he brushed her hair aside and placed a warm and soft kiss upon the nape of her neck.

"What is fog, Jered? Is it truly clouds, come too low to the earth?"

"I'm sure I don't know," he murmured against her neck, and it was as if she could feel with her skin each separate word he spoke.

"When I was little, I believed it to be heaven, descending from the sky, coming to capture angels. And all the people who were chosen would simply step up on a cloud and it would take them away."

"What a hideous thought," he said against the skin of her shoulder. How on earth had her bodice been opened? Oh, there were no buttons, were there? "I'm surprised you weren't terrified at the sight of fog."

"Oh, I wasn't worried. My parents and my nurse told me only the good go young."

He stood so close that she could feel the rumble of laughter in his chest. A disconcerting experience especially since he brushed his fingers over the tendrils of hair at her nape. Had she ever before realized how especially sensitive she was there? Or that the shivers he evoked with such an effortless touch slid down her body and back up again?

"If it makes you feel better, Tessa, Voltaire said, 'It is not known precisely where angels dwell—whether in the air, the void, or the planets. It has not been God's pleasure that we should be informed of their abode.'"

His hands were suddenly at her waist, his thumbs at the small of her back. How odd that she could feel his hands even through her clothes. And even stranger that the chill seemed to seep through the window, making her front cold while her back was blessedly warm.

"Your clothes are damp, Tessa." Another nuzzle, another shiver as the sensation traveled to her toes. She arched her head back, found a comfortable spot against his chest. His hands fanned her waist, traveled around to her stomach, where they splayed against her, bringing her back against him, closer, always closer. She could feel him breathe, feel his chest expand, constrict. Somewhere, outside this room, people were beginning to stir. Morning ablutions were being performed, clothing was donned, a glance out the window, a frown, a stretch, perhaps a yawn. The world readied itself for the day.

And inside this room? Everything compressed to a touch upon her skin, at her temple, a soft thread of fingers through her hair, slowly, achingly slow, removing the pins that bound her hair up in its serviceable bun. She'd lost her hat somewhere.

A kiss upon her cheek, a slight coaxing turn, and she faced him. His hands, those hands that were tender and resolute and tenacious, were at her back now, forcing her gently forward, her boots aligned with his, until not an inch separated their bodies, only the full skirt of her riding habit and his trousers. Clothing, however, was no barrier to sensation, to the heady warmth of him, to the insistence of those hands that were at her sides now, creeping up until they were breast level, squeezing her ribs gently.

"Did you know, Jered, that there are nine orders of angels? Angels, archangels, virtues, powers, principalities, dominations, thrones, cherubim, and seraphim. Isn't that fascinating?"

A hesitation of lips upon her skin, a smile then, as he placed a kiss behind her ear.

"Tessa?" A summons, gently spoken.

She raised her head, tilted it back until her eyes met his. A soft smile wreathed his lips, but it was not of

amusement. It was too feral for that. A frisson of . . .
fear?—traveled down her spine. No, not fear but awareness. More than even her wedding night, or the night
before, this was the moment of reckoning. Male. Female. A bond as old as the world, as new as this next
moment.

"Are you frightened?"

"Yes. No. No, I'm not. I think fear is truly an awful
emotion, don't you? And I have spent the entire night
filled with it."

"You have?"

"Yes, and your horse knows it, too."

He leaned forward, placed a kiss upon her forehead,
a tender benediction that charmed at the same time it
confused. One hand slipped open her jacket, a gesture
made easier by the loss of her buttons. She glanced
down at the sight of his hand against the blue fabric.
An aristocrat's hands, long-fingered, surprisingly strong.
His palms were callused from years of riding; his fingers, however, were smooth, capable of creating the
most delicious sensations.

"I'm very glad you're not frightened of me." His
voice was soft, a near whisper in the morning light.

She glanced up at him again, a little disconcerted to
find that his gaze had not veered from her. His fingers
did not seem to need sight to complete their unveiling.

"I have never been afraid of you, Jered. You confuse
me, and concern me, though." He bent forward, placed
a kiss upon her neck. She shivered.

"Hmm?" He didn't seem to be paying the least attention to her words.

"I'm very much afraid I disapprove, Jered."

He reared back and stared at her.

"You disapprove?"

"You really shouldn't go around robbing coaches, Jered. It's not well done of you. Surely you can find something more suited to your position. Something that is not morally unjust?"

"Such as?"

"Any other occupation, Jered. Something that might speak well to your rank."

"Good works?"

"Well, yes."

"Are you volunteering to lead me into virtue, Tessa?"

"If you wish, Jered." She smiled softly at him. "Although I've little experience, I'm sure we can find something that will suit us together."

"The birth of an heir seems like a good enough goal for this moment, Tessa." He traced a finger across her lower lip. His eyes seemed terribly intent upon her reaction. She smiled but could not hold the expression very long. If the truth be told, she very much wanted to kiss him.

"Yes. Well."

Chapter 9

S he knew better than to ask for darkness, remembering too well the candles he'd kept lit to better see her. What would he see now, in the morning's light that he had not already seen? She had neither grown taller or shorter, fatter or thinner. She was as she had been, neither beauty nor troll, but somewhere unremarkably in between.

But a woman could wish to be beautiful, could she not? Especially when her clothes were gently taken from her one garment at a time. First the half-redingote had been undone so quickly that she'd been divested of it before she quite realized it. Then the blouse and skirt that made up the rest of her riding habit were gone with a whisk, as if Jered's fingers were magical and this moment made even more so by his slight smile. She was left finally with her light stays, but even they were no match for his nimble touch, because a moment later both front and back openings had been breached, and they dropped to the floor in a tangle of boiled leather and canvas. Only her chemise separated her from nudity, and even that was no more a barrier than a breath or a flutter of eyelashes, as she kept her eyes determinedly closed.

A fingertip whispered against her lids, an amused voice whispered in her ear. "Where are you, Tessa?"

"Wondering why I feel so much more naked now than I've ever felt before. And while I'm sure I am supposed to feel gloriously adrift in sensation, I simply must admit to the truth."

"Which is?" His fingers had stilled upon her skin. She glanced up. There was the oddest expression on his face. It convinced her to close her eyes again.

"You see, Jered, I am quite aware of my faults. Too plenteous a bosom for one, legs that are too long, a waist that will never be tiny regardless of how tight my maid laces my corset. I would very much like a darkened room and a warm blanket right now."

It was with great relief that she felt his arm beneath her knees, and another at her back. She was being carried to the bed—she was certain of it, a quick flash of vision behind half-closed lids confirmed it. The room was canted and then the tester appeared, massive carved mahogany posts draped with velvet.

Instead he deposited her on the hearth before the fire. While she stood there shivering, he pulled down the embroidered coverlet, the sheets, then retrieved her as if she was a parcel he'd left behind, installing her between the cold, damp-feeling sheets. She began to shake, as if the chill was seeping into her bones. He murmured something that sounded too reminiscent of the curses she'd muttered earlier and took off his own clothes, uncaring where they landed.

Enough light filtered in from the windows that she could see him quite clearly. Recall had not furnished her with enough details. Had she seen the ropes of muscles in his arms, the power of his thighs before? Or had his chest been quite so broad, with that dusting of black hair? The same shade that cradled a manhood of impressive proportions, even quasi-dormant as it seemed. But then, she'd had only two night's experience in such things.

Her fists went underneath both pillows as he shocked her further by not moving next to her as she'd supposed, but lowering himself inch by inch over her body, until nothing remained untouched. From neck to toes, she was draped by a living blanket, if such could be said for Jered's body.

"I quite like your plenteous bosom, Tessa. And your long legs. As for a tiny waist, a man would be a fool to trade the two for the one." He raised himself up on his forearms, looked down at her, an expression that could only be construed as amusement on his face. "Are you still cold?"

"I am becoming warmer," she said, licking lips that were suddenly very dry. "Are you my blanket?"

"Do you wish another?"

"You are performing the task quite well. I am not quite undressed, you know. I still have my chemise."

He traced a line around the borders of her lips, a curious tingling touch. "Yes," he softly said. "I know."

Her expression must have been quizzical, because he only smiled, then bent his head to place a kiss beneath her jaw, almost at her neck. Another spot acutely sensitive.

"You wiggle when you're ticklish. Did you know? I would have thought you'd laugh." He raised his head, smiled into her eyes. "But I prefer the wiggle."

She was feeling quite warm now. Abundantly so. But she did not tell him that for fear he might move. And the feeling of him being so heavily atop her was not altogether unpleasant. In fact, it was very enticing.

But he moved anyway, all of a sudden being at her side, turning her so that she lay facing him. Toes and knees touched but nothing more, and Tessa felt an absurd loneliness. So much so that she reached out one hand and touched his chest with her fingers, then laid her palm full on his skin as if to test its warmth. His skin felt so smooth, the hair upon it almost silky to the touch. Her other arm was braced beneath her head, she reached out and threaded her fingers through his hair. As soft as this. *And the other, Tessa?* She felt the flush tingle through her skin at the thought of putting her hand there.

Could he read her thoughts? His smile seemed to indicate it.

"And what are you thinking, wife, that you would have such a look of unholy glee upon your face?"

She could not look at him as she spoke. Instead she focused her attention on her hand brushing against his chest. "That it would be daring to touch you," she admitted, her voice soft as a whisper, as delicate as a mote of sunlight.

His hand reached out to touch her face, brush back a tendril of hair from her temple, hesitate at her lips. "Please do so." Words so softly voiced it might have been no more than a thought.

Her fingers were drawn to one bronze disk, it seemed to incite a circular motion of one finger. Was it her imagination, or did his breath still and then hiss through his lips? And did his eyes narrow as he watched her, both their gazes trapped by the sight of one hesitant finger tip?

And then one finger reached out and did the same to her, circling a nipple through the fine gauze of the linen.

A rush of sensation followed his touch and then seemed to anticipate it. A tightening in her chest, a feeling of tension, of heat. Was this, then, what he felt when she touched him? A quick upward glance to eyes that smoldered in the dawn light. The Mandeville eyes. Once she'd thought they were like cold ash. How could she have missed the fire?

It was as if he mirrored her actions. Each stroke upon his skin was duplicated on hers. Nothing was initiated by him, it was as if he allowed her to set the pace. On their wedding night, it had been he who led her into discovery. Last night he had simply overwhelmed her. This time she was to be the explorer. And explore she did, a hand sliding down to rest upon his hip, then to his wrist, and sliding up to a muscled shoulder. Then into his hair, combing it back from his forehead with her fingers, avid eyes watching as an errant lock fell down again. He did not reach for her, said nothing as she skimmed his jaw with fingers that trembled with daring. His lips were quirked in a half-smile, but they lost even that when she traced his mouth, one finger hesitating at the center of his bottom lip. She pulled herself up on one elbow, leaned over, breathed softly against his mouth. A daring thing to do, especially since she'd felt the tension in him these last few moments, as if he restrained himself by will alone.

Her kiss was softly done, warm, pillowy, innocently carnal. She felt him shudder as she licked his lips, but when his head moved a fraction, she pulled back, away. Her glance was almost chiding, he closed his eyes in the face of it, lashes drooping against his cheeks. Another shadow in a room being tinted by a stubborn sun.

Her hand rested on his shoulder, her thumb brushed against his cheek. He moved, a restless gesture of legs and torso, and it was then that she felt him, huge and hard against her thigh.

Her eyes blinked open to meet his gaze, one not of restraint but of power. In a flash of seconds, it was gone. In its place was a slow, dawning smile, and a hand that reached out to push her gently back against the pillow.

He loomed over her, a shadow limned by light, a presence as overpowering as a storm cloud. And if there was lightning, it was in his eyes as he smiled at her. Both fists grabbed her chemise, lovingly sewn by a contingent of apprentice seamstresses for her trousseau and costing far in excess of any of her previous garments of the same type. This was edged in lace and embroidered with roses. It made no difference to Jered. Nor did she protest as he fisted the material and slowly pulled his hands apart, the tearing sound a soft whisper of blatant intent. The tear was even and lengthwise, and his eyes followed it all the way to her knees, as if she'd been previously buttoned up in armor and was just now being revealed. The neckline remained intact but was not equal to his determination. She lay open like a seed pod.

He reached for her, brushing aside the torn remnants of her chemise. His palm, warm and slightly callused raised her breast, pushed it up as if in offering. If this was sacrifice, it was to his lips, not as tender as voracious. Not teasing, but demanding. His mouth ringed her nipple, he used his teeth to gently graze, leaned back and watched as it drew up tighter and then tighter still, as if approving in reaction to his touch.

His kiss was intrusive, enveloping, hungry. Gone was the tender lover who encouraged exploration; this man was talented, experienced, gave no quarter and demanded nothing less. She was neither maiden nor wife nor whore. She was woman and female and mate, and the only survival was in acknowledging her weakness and burying her power.

When his hand reached down and pulled her legs apart, she allowed him this. And when his fingers trailed from her thighs to the heat at their juncture, she had only one thought of protest, but that was buried beneath another kiss. He touched her, and she gasped. His head lifted and he looked down at her, his lips wet and unsmiling. His face lupine and predatory. Another intrusion of fingers and she bit her lip. He smiled, as if her response to him had been a sign and her moan an accolade.

When he entered her, hard and fast with no sign of delicacy, and the teasing long forgotten, she lifted her hips to cradle him, sure that she would die of it, more than certain it did not matter if she did.

Chapter 10

❦❦❦

"How did it go last night, sir?"

He shrugged into his coat. "All things went quite well, Chalmers, considering."

Jered pulled the front of his waistcoat down, moved away to study his reflection in the mirror. Except for a certain look about the eyes, he appeared the same. There was something about his expression, however. That was it. He looked too damn pleased with himself. And he had no reason to be. None.

He suffered through a brushing by Chalmers, then listened to him tell the footman where to put his newly polished boots. Everyday tasks, everyday words. Nothing was out of place. His eyes strayed to the closed door that led to his bedchamber. She was still sleeping. The sleep of the just? No, more like the exhaustion of the well loved. He'd taken her three times last night—no, this morning. Or had she taken him? Was that what the problem was, Jered? Each time, it had felt as if he were being led somewhere he'd never been before, by a chit whose eyes decried her innocence as readily as her lips lured him. He was a man unused to any degree of celibacy, that was all. And prior to her arrival in London, he had managed to be celibate for almost a week. That was the reason. That, and only that.

Are you certain, Jered? He'd been hard pressed to restrain his laugher last night. Why did he always feel like smiling when he made love to his wife?

He frowned into the mirror. It was no use. There was simply nothing to be done for that look in his eyes. Complacent, relaxed, thoroughly at peace with the world. He should be running for the continent; he suspected he might be safer there despite the French problem.

She was his wife. There was no need to feel that frisson of sensation when thinking of her. It was simply that she'd surprised him, that was all. Her delicate touch had skittered over his skin like a thousand little bombs. He'd wanted her to touch him so badly he'd almost begged for it. Had nearly caught her hand and pressed it to him, urging her to satisfy that almost inhuman need. *Only a moment, Tessa. Just for a moment.* He closed his eyes, damned the memory that would furnish the sensation without conscious thought, looked down at his trousers and damned his loins.

What was she doing to him?

"And the duchess? Shall I ring for her maid?"

He glanced over at his valet. Chalmers was a study in expressionless toadyism. He narrowed his eyes and studied him in silence. Was that just an innocent question or did it have its roots in the fact that his valet had had to wait until evening to fetch his breakfast? Granted, he had been awakened this late before, but he'd not been wrapped around his wife when it had occurred. His skin felt absurdly warm. Good thing Chalmers averted his eyes at that moment. If he didn't know better, he would have thought himself blushing.

"I believe my wife is still asleep, Chalmers."

"Very well, sir."

Jered wasn't altogether sure what a proper response to that might be, so he sought refuge in silence.

"How much gold did you put in that chest? It felt too damn heavy for what I asked," he said, as he was assisted on with his boots.

"I but delivered the amount you sought, sir. I did take the opportunity, however, to place a few muslin wrapped bricks in the bottom."

"Good thinking. I'm sure Adrian thought it was a king's fortune."

"Begging your pardon, sir, but would it not have been wiser to have simply given him the money?"

Jered pulled up the boots, stood and stamped his feet down to ensure a good fit.

"And miss the adventure? Come, Chalmers, don't tell me you're growing maidenly in your old age."

"I did not inform the guards, sir, just as you advised me not to. You could have been quite easily shot."

Jered took one last look in the mirror, turned and patted the shoulder of his servant. "But I wasn't, was I? And as for telling them, it would have taken all the fun out of it, don't you agree?"

He turned at the door, looked beyond Chalmers to the darkened window. "Don't wait up, Chalmers. I fully expect to be gone until dawn."

Chalmers heard the click of the door handle and turned. There, framed in the opening, was the Duchess of Kittridge, her appearance very much different from that of a few days ago. When he'd seen her last, she'd been perfectly coifed, her dress a confection of silk and lace from Madame Fouchard, currently one of the more popular modistes. She'd worn a look of expectation about her face, an innocence that had charmed him. The woman who looked at him and then at the door where the duke had exited had aged in some inexplicable way. Her hair was tousled, there was a mark upon her cheek where the mattress had pressed into her skin. But it was her eyes he avoided after one quick look. Confusion was there and an almost painful vulnerability. The girl had vanished, but the woman was no less captivating. In fact, perhaps more so. He glanced away from the sight of her wrapped in a sheet, but he could easily imagine her nakedness beneath the material. He was not *that* old.

"Why did he do that?"

Chalmers stooped to remove the bootjack, thinking that it would be more prudent to mistake her meaning. There were, after all, confidences at stake. But he made the error of glancing at her again, and a shaft of compassion seemed to spear his heart at her look. She was staring at the door as if all the secrets in the world would be granted her if only she kept her vision fixed there.

He would only divulge what he knew: "I do not know, Your Grace."

"But to steal his own gold. Why?"

"I believe that His Grace enjoys the lure of the forbidden." There, that was both truth and exposure enough. She would gain nothing further from him.

She glanced at him then, relinquishing her vision's grip upon the door.

"Where has he gone tonight?"

"I'm sure I don't know, Your Grace."

"Some place forbidden, Chalmers?"

She said nothing else as she slowly retreated, closing

the door behind her with a smart click of the lock.

Why did he feel as if he had said too much? Or she had revealed too little?

Some place forbidden.

It really should not hurt so. After all, she was becoming to know her husband all too well. He was not the portrait, the same noble young man with pain in his eyes who looked out at the world as if seeking understanding, perhaps compassion. There was nothing of that young man in her husband. He was thoroughly decadent, a rake, a man beyond her understanding—who would leave her within hours of their wedding, who would deliberately flaunt his mistress, who stole his own gold and ducked bullets with a laughing disregard for his own safety.

Or perhaps he was more like the portrait than she'd ever imagined. Paint and canvas was, after all, without depth. Only a hint of it existed, an illusion created by the artist to trick the eye. Perhaps Jered was like that, entertaining and charming but without depth, devoid of character. Perhaps he was truly bereft of those qualities she so admired in her father, his uncle, the being she'd created who'd stepped out of a wooden frame and listened to her and advised her and kept a lonely heart brimming with love.

She sat at the end of the bed, his bed, and surveyed the room around her. Its size was intimidating even now. With night barely upon them, it was dark as a dungeon, swooping shadows barely lit by the lone candle that sputtered at the bedside table. How odd to be awakened at a time when others were ready to sleep. Did Jered revel in nights turned to day and days of sunlight and fresh breezes only a backdrop for a stuporous sleep?

The lure of the forbidden.

She'd taken her own reputation and nearly shattered it in her actions of last night. Granted, she had been accompanied by her husband, but even so, the winds of rumor were less favorable for those of the female of the species. Society would have castigated her for her role in the affair while speaking of Jered in hushed and admiring tones. Not to mention what her parents might say.

The lure of the forbidden.

His mistress, of course, that was his destination. Even after last night, he would go to her. Even after most of the morning had been spent holding her and teaching her, whispering the most deliciously decadent things in her ear, he would go to his mistress.

Wives do not demand fealty from their husbands. They accept it or they pretend they have it. There is no other behavior to be tolerated in polite society. And to follow him would be the most forbidden thing of all.

It was an absolutely scandalous thing to do, of course, but she was very much afraid that the rest of her life was going to be filled with adventures and episodes that would cause tongues to wag. That was the price, she was certain, for a true marriage to Jered Mandeville. She had wanted to be his friend. Friends share adventures, have similar interests. She shook her head. There was nothing about last night's robbery that she would choose to relive.

Still, it did not seem quite fair that she should do all the accommodating and he have nothing of it.

She stood and wrapped the sheet around her, opened the door, brushing by Chalmers with nothing more than a nod, utterly uncaring. She would return to her own chamber and dress and have the coachman take her to Jered's mistress. Certainly a forbidden action, a thoroughly scandalous behavior.

Perhaps she was more like her husband than it appeared.

Chalmers leaned back, flattened his hands palm down against the wall. Perhaps he was only hallucinating and had not heard correctly. Perhaps it was simply a case of too much wine with dinner. Or perhaps he was coming down with a nasty cold, something he grew accustomed to suffering whenever they were in London. It could not possibly be true. Not at all. The Duchess of Kittridge could not be thinking of doing what she was doing.

She had quite brazenly asked the major domo if he knew the address of Jered's mistress. Just like that. Out into the open with no more tact or diplomacy.

He contemplated the advisability of racing down the stairs and blocking the doorway, either that or convincing Michaels not to tell her a damn thing. But the man looked like he felt, as if someone had given him a very sharp blow to his gut, one totally unexpected. And he heard the man stammer out the address with something like sick horror, and knew that he had nothing left to do now but inform the duke. Jered Mandeville was not going to be happy. Not happy at all.

It was a pity, too. He was beginning to like the young duchess. But after tonight, he was certain she would be sent back to Kittridge in disgrace. Very certain indeed.

Chapter 11

❝**I**t's quite strong, isn't it?'' Tessa took another sip of the brandy. It had seemed, initially, like a good thing. Rather like this evening. Tea was not at all appropriate when visiting a mistress. But after much reflection, perhaps the brandy was a little too adventurous. The roof of her mouth was numb.

The woman simply stared at her. A state of continued amazement, perhaps even fascination. At first she'd looked absolutely terrified. Of her? How idiotic. Still, it was quite an enlivening thought. To induce terror into one of the demimonde. How utterly improper.

One did not visit a mistress. If it was not a cardinal rule, it was certainly not something discussed. In fact, Tessa was certain she was not supposed to even know about the woman's place in Jered's life.

She was expected to sit in the background and allow him all sorts of liberties while never questioning his actions. Of course, women of her rank were rumored to have lovers. But what if the one man you craved as a lover was also your husband? Not often done and perhaps even a little provincial. Except, of course, that her parents were a perfect example of a marriage that could be wonderful. Was she a fool to wish the same?

The woman was quite lovely, if one could ignore the state of her hair. It was piled up in the front, like a precarious nest. Was such a style demanded of a mistress? Her state of undress left few of her attributes in doubt. But Tessa could boast of the same. In fact, too much of some things, she thought, glancing down at her own bodice.

The town house was decorated in a bit too much of the French fashion, with too much lace and acres too much velvet. Scattered everywhere were plump little cushions in shades of pink and purple. And above everything, a cloying perfume that was so strong it was a presence in the room. How could Jered stand it? Did all dukes pay for such love nests, or did Jered have the misfortune to support a mistress with outlandishly poor taste? Tessa felt the spike of tears, blinked them away. Tears were silly things, and she simply did not have time for them right now.

She took another sip of the brandy. It grew more acceptable with every swallow. How odd that she'd never tasted it before. But then, she really didn't care for spirits.

"I do not, you know."

"Don't what?" Tessa turned her attention from the level of brandy in her glass to her hostess.

"Twirl tassels." How odd that her voice no longer sounded like a low, throaty purr. Or was that reserved for Jered? The woman's voice was very high pitched, almost grating to the ear. Tessa frowned, ran her tongue over her teeth. No, she could still feel her gums. She pressed her lips together. They tingled.

"What a pity," she said, once the inventory of her parts had been completed. "I might have asked for lessons."

The woman looked quite surprised. How odd.

"Is it your first time in London, Your Grace?"

"No. I've had two seasons. And you?"

"I was born here."

"Oh." There was not much to say to that, other than to offer her sympathies. It didn't seem quite polite to do so, however. "Do you like the theater?" she asked instead.

"To attend or perform?"

"Do you? How utterly fascinating. An actress. I'd never hoped to meet one."

"I'm sure you did not," the woman said dryly.

She really must learn her name. But the occasion of an introduction had never come up, nor had Jered's mistress been disposed to give out her name once the terrified young maid had summoned her to the parlor. She'd taken one look at her, poured herself a glass of brandy, and downed it in one gulp. It had seemed to Tessa only convivial to request a glass for herself. Were the woman's lips numb, too?

"Do you sing?"

"Do you want me to perform for you?" There was absolute amazement on her face.

Tessa shook her head. She would never be so crude. One performed only when one wanted. She, herself, had managed to escape many impromptu concerts on the claim that she was suffering from a sore throat. If she had known about the powerful properties of brandy, she would have imbibed and then never worried about the fact that she couldn't hold a tune.

She leaned against the back of the settee, then forward again. It seemed quite a comforting thing, almost like being rocked. Once more. Ah. Her nose felt odd.

She touched it with the tip of her finger. Missed. Found it finally.

"Your Grace?"

"Hmmm?"

"Are you all right?"

Tessa waved a hand in the air. "Perfectly well, thank you." She held her glass up in the air, stared at it. "But I seem to have finished my brandy."

"I really do not think it would be a good idea to have any more."

"Do you not think so?"

The woman shook her head.

"You mustn't be kind, you know."

"I must not?"

"Absolutely not. Then I might possibly like you, and it would be a disaster. You see, I am engaged in a duel with you."

"You are?"

"Oh yes, and this is in way of being a reconnoiter. I mean to learn your secrets."

The woman had no response to that.

"I don't suppose you would like to divulge any? Are you certain you don't twirl?"

"Your Grace, I think it would be a very good idea for you to go home."

"You're being kind again."

"I am not. Only prudent. If your husband discovers you've been here, he will not be happy."

Tessa sighed.

"Must everyone keep Jered happy? For all our efforts, he does not seem to be happy. Have you noticed that when he laughs it's almost like it's a surprise to him?"

"I don't believe I've ever heard him laugh, so I cannot comment."

"There, you see?"

"Is your carriage waiting, Your Grace?" There was a decidedly frosty tone to the woman's voice. How odd. It was as if she'd mimicked Jered's very tone.

"Yes. Although I told him to go around the block. I expected, you see, for Jered to be here."

"Well, he isn't."

Tessa stood, felt the room spin, sat abruptly. Her eyes widened.

"Are you going to be ill?"

"I most fervently hope not," Tessa said, and sank back against the cushions.

Jered strode up the steps two at a time, as furious as he could imagine being in his entire life. Nothing in his recollection could match the rage that filled him now, no memory came close to equaling what he felt at this moment.

The little maid who answered the door was new, but for all that, she didn't ask him his name or his business.

At his inquiry, she simply pointed. He noted without much surprise that her index finger trembled as she indicated the parlor door. And she might be wise to show some fear. He was in the devil's own mood.

Excellent instincts, he thought as she bobbed a few times and hid behind the door he pulled open.

"I believe you know your wife," his mistress said with quite remarkable aplomb, considering that she was only attired in a wrapper. He unfortunately had fond memories of that garment, a thought that made him feel oddly ill at ease.

"Tessa?" he asked his wife, as if needing her solemn

little nod to ascertain that it was truly her. She was seated in a chair facing his mistress, her hands buried in the black fur muff resting on her lap. She was dressed in a red-and-white dotted gown topped with a red spencer. Upon her head was a red hat with perfectly symmetrical black feathers, among which was perched a stuffed yellow finch. Jered found himself staring at the bird in fascination, wondering if it would fall off the next time she nodded her head.

She looked, however, as pale as snow, and as he watched, she wobbled on her perch at the edge of the settee.

He was engulfed in confusion so catastrophic that he was incapable for a moment of uttering a word.

"I do not bloody well believe it. I told myself it wouldn't be true. That you wouldn't be so idiotic as to do something like this." In fact, he'd thought the note Chalmers had sent him was a jest, some absurd bit of nonsense dreamt up by one of his acquaintances.

But no, there she was, his wife, and his mistress. A farce. An unbelievable bit of female nonsense.

Only silence answered him. But it was not a calm silence for all that. Nor was it one filled with womanly reserve, which he'd half-expected. No, he had anticipated that Tessa would be dutifully chastised by his appearance.

His wife stood, brushed down her skirts, straightened her ridiculous little hat with its idiotic perched finch, and made a half-bow to his scantily attired mistress.

"Thank you for your time," she said. Her voice was slurred. Nor did her eyes seem quite as focused as they should be.

"What the hell did you give her?"

"I didn't give it to her, she took it." Pauline glared at him.

"Brandy, Jered," Tessa said, smiling brightly at him. She turned to face his mistress. "Thank you."

"On the contrary, Your Grace," Pauline said, making no attempt to hide her smile, "it was quite an illuminating meeting." She turned to Jered. "Your wife is a charming child."

He was reduced to gestures a dying fish might make, a simple opening and closing of his mouth. Tessa brushed by him, sent him an insipid little smile, and then opened the door to the town house. She was halfway down the steps before he rallied himself.

"What in bloody hell do you think you're doing?" The volume of his request had taken it from the range of a simple question. But he was to be excused, he told himself, by the sheer lunacy of her actions.

Tessa turned and looked up at him. How like an innocent she appeared at this moment, with her mouth arranged in that simple little smile, no more than a movement of muscles, barely any emotion. Her hands were still buried in that ridiculous looking muff—it was nearly as large as she was. No, that was not quite true, she was tall for a woman, and not delicate at all, witness the curves pushing against the fabric of her bodice.

He could feel his cheeks flaming, felt the irritation bubble forth again.

"Are you foxed?"

She blinked at him. "It's quite possible." She pursed her lips together, sucked in her cheeks.

He took a deep breath, forced himself to calm, took another breath because the first had done nothing for his state of irritation.

"I find it's not an altogether bad feeling. No wonder

my brothers do it,'' she said, and proceeded to walk down the steps none too gracefully. The carriage, his carriage, was still parked on the side of the street. The driver, his driver, was perched upon the seat, stiff necked and seemingly oblivious to all that occurred around him. Why the hell hadn't he seen him before?

"What did you think you would accomplish by coming here? Damn it, Tessa, I expect you to answer me!'' The footman had jumped down from his position at the back of the carriage, walked forward as if to open the door for the duchess, caught Jered's look, then turned quickly and resumed his place.

Tessa reached out and gripped the door handle. He placed his palm on the door and slammed it shut.

"You're not going anywhere until I get some answers, Tessa.''

"Shall we discuss it on the street, Jered?'' She smiled, this time a brighter smile but no more pleasant.

"We'll discuss it where I see fit, Tessa.''

She turned, straightened, her muff a barrier of fur and velvet. "Very well, Jered, I thought you were with her tonight. Is that truth enough for you?''

"And you were what? Going to fight for me? And I am the prize, is that how you see it?'' She turned and opened the door, unfurled the steps herself. Her slender figure was there one moment, seated near the window the next.

"Do you think you're worth it?'' She smiled. "I would offer you a ride home, Jered, but I'm not feeling at all well at the moment. It's very possible I will be extraordinarily ill.''

With that, she slammed the door in his face.

* * *

"You did well, Chalmers," Jered said, intent upon the view from his window.

"Very well, sir. Were you in time to avoid any unpleasantries, sir?"

"If you define unpleasantries as a meeting between mistress and wife," he said, tightening the belt to his dressing gown, "I'm afraid not. Still, it could have been worse, I suppose. Though I don't know how."

"You might not have been where we could reach you, sir."

A quick glance satisfied Jered that Chalmers had not been in jest. "How many places did the footman go before he found me?"

"Only two, sir. I had given him a list, you see, of all your favorite establishments."

"I've become set in my ways, then, Chalmers?"

"Not at all, sir." He retrieved the coat Jered had tossed on the chair, began brushing it studiously.

"And is that how my wife learned of Pauline's address, Chalmers?"

A horrified glance was answer enough. "Not from me, sir."

"But you know from whom, don't you?"

"I have taken steps to have the person responsible censured, sir."

"I should keep my nose out of it, is that right?"

"I believe, sir," Chalmers said in offended dignity, "that your efforts might be better served in those areas in which only you can effect a change."

"In other words, my state of matrimony, Chalmers? Funny, you sound almost like my uncle when you chastise me like that. Should I up your wages, sit you on a chair, and prop your gouty stump up on a footstool?"

"I beg your pardon, sir." Chalmers was all stiff pomposity. "Shall I lay out your blacks, sir?"

He glanced out the window again. It was nearly midnight, too damn early to claim fatigue. Besides, he had only awakened six hours ago. No self-respecting hedonist went to bed this early.

"No, Chalmers. I don't believe so. If I went out again this evening, I'd probably shoot someone, or no doubt insult his wife and be set for a duel in the morning."

"As you wish, sir."

He glanced over at his valet again.

"I've been an idiot all day, Chalmers. A regular feat, since I've slept through most of it." Apology sent. Now would it be accepted?

A small smile filtered over his valet's face.

"Shall I fetch you a tray, sir?" Accepted, then.

"No, Chalmers. I find I'm not very hungry either."

At least not for anything Cook could send him.

Chapter 12

❝**A**re you sure you won't come? Or has the little duchess domesticated you?❞ Adrian's smile did not quite match his eyes.

"I'm sure you don't require my presence to lose all your gold, Adrian."

"There's a club I've heard about, Jered, that might interest you as well. A little departure from your standard fare. I've heard that whips are used on the more recalcitrant females. Shall we try it out?"

Jered only smiled. A moment later, Adrian left him. It was just as well; Adrian's company was growing excessively irritating lately.

He leaned up against a pillar and surveyed the crowd. He'd seen the Astleys earlier, had avoided them by simply turning his back. Helena had not yet spied him, but he did not doubt she would. Nor did he doubt he would be taken to task for some reason or another. What was it with those Astleys? They were all overwhelmingly possessive.

The last masked ball Jered had attended he had escorted his current mistress, paraded her about the room in a grand jest. He'd introduced her to several women, most of whom would have been chagrined to have been

117

in the same room with a member of the demimonde, let alone in close proximity. He suspected that several of the men had divined her identity soon enough, but then, just before the unmasking, he'd slipped her away.

It was not that he hated the world into which he was born, it was that he simply could not summon up enough concern to truly care about it. There were few things that interested him, even fewer people.

The fact that he was present at this ball surprised him. Perhaps he was here because no one expected him to be. Then again, it was something to do, and he detested being bored.

He didn't dress for these damn things, he preferred to wear a domino, an eye mask fashioned to cover half his face. The pretense allowed him the freedom of not being your graced to death for the evening, relinquished him from the endless tedium of being honored because an ancestor had been made a prince of the realm. Not that he did not enjoy his rank. He did not see how he could possibly have existed without it. The carefully structured anonymity of such occasions as this ball tonight, however, offered him a singular respite.

He milled about, leaving the card rooms for the dancing area, skirting the edge of dancers with the precision of years of practice. Not until nearly midnight did he realize what he was doing, a discovery that quirked his lips.

He was waiting for his wife.

He did not doubt that she would somehow find her way here, even though he'd given his servants strict instructions that no further information as to his whereabouts were to be given to his duchess.

She was fortunate that he had not banished her to Kittridge after that last episode. He allowed her the ben-

efit of innocence. She evidently did not realize that he
did not tolerate insolence from anyone. The fact that he
had not sent her to the country surprised him. Or perhaps it had at its roots the fact that although he had
purposely not been to her room for a few days, thinking
to demonstrate his irritation, memories of her were
never far from his mind. Humor and voluptuousness,
now there was a combination.

He should never have married. Especially her. She
had that way of looking at him, her chocolate eyes filled
with warmth and laughter. On their wedding night, in
the light of candles, her eyes had appeared infinitely
alluring, promising all the secrets women retained from
birth. She'd held her arms out to him and invited him
closer, lured him to her body as if it were a freshwater
spring and he, adrift upon an ocean unfit to drink.

He had, like some besotted idiot, once studied how
she breathed when she slept, had even matched his
breaths to hers. He had covered her with the sheet and
then experienced a sick horror at the feeling that had
come over him. He'd mated for heirs. Instead she'd offered him laughter. He'd had the right instinct to flee
her after he'd taken her virginity. He could still remember that one incredible moment when he'd plunged into
her and felt her pain, only to be forgiven for it by the
kiss she'd awarded him, heady and loving and deep.
He'd exploded within her, unable to calm his own rush-
ing release, unable to restrain the shout that echoed in
the duchess's room with such fervor and joy that the
statue in the corner almost turned its head in surprise.

Everything passes, everything perishes, everything
palls. The French had it right. All he had to do was wait
until the novelty wore off, and his life would revert to
what it had been. An ordered existence of his own mak-

ing, punctuated only by the excitement he educed when he could take the tedium no longer.

"Your mother is in the retiring room, my dear," her father said. "You might take advantage of the moment to cover yourself."

She turned and in a gesture that no doubt shocked the people around them, threw her arms around her father and hugged him tightly. She pulled back finally, smiling into his face.

"Isn't it awful? I gave the modiste exact instructions. But it looks like a bedsheet, doesn't it?" The costume was nothing more than a swath of silk, trailing from one shoulder to the floor. Something—resembling laurel leaves to the modiste—had been embroidered along the hem. Tessa wore a girdle of gold fastened around her waist and on her head a crown of gilded leaves. The remaining part of her costume was a mask of white feathers. She was quite certain no one in Greece had worn feathers.

"Half of one," Gregory said, clearing his throat and averting his eyes from that portion of his daughter's anatomy that was so obviously barely covered.

"I shall simply pretend to be possessed of the Mandeville insouciance and brazen my way through the night in this horrid costume."

"Yes, but what will you say to your mother?"

She gave him a brave smile, tried not to think of the confrontation, and vowed to be out of sight before her mother reappeared.

"How is she?"

"Irritated. She called on you, you know, and has received no answering visit."

"I planned on seeing her tomorrow."

"I would make certain you do. You know your mother." Tessa nodded.

She surveyed him from head to toe. He was dressed in a brilliant red tunic and a skirt that came only to the middle of his thighs. A series of leather straps covered his chest. "You know, of course, that you've no call to insult my costume. That's a perfectly horrid thing you're wearing. What are you supposed to be?"

"A Roman centurion."

"Aren't your knees cold?"

"Yes," he said, "but this was the lesser of a multitude of evils."

Tessa shook her head, and the look father and daughter shared was one of mutual consternation.

"Have you seen Jered?"

Her father nodded and pointed to the opposite corner. "I believe he's hiding over there, the better to avoid your mother, I believe."

Since both husband and wife had a similar notion, Tessa smiled, reached up, and placed a quick kiss on her father's cheek.

"Running, are you?" His hand cupped her cheek, his warm brown eyes met hers.

"Yes," Tessa confessed.

"Looking for someone?"

She turned and he was there. Braced against a pillar, dressed in his blacks, attired in a mask that did nothing to hide his eyes. He surveyed her from the tip of her feathers to her sandals, a rather rakish grin indicating what he thought of her attire.

"Very well, who are you supposed to be? Diana? Artemis?"

"Clytemnestra, daughter of Leda and Tyndareus. The wife of Agamemnon."

Another smile. "Rather bloodthirsty, aren't you? If I remember, didn't she and her lover kill her husband?"

"Only after he sacrificed her child in order to sail to Troy."

"How did you find me?" he asked.

"I wasn't especially looking, Jered. There are not that many entertainments in London this month. Most people have already retired to the country."

"Feel free to emulate them."

"I am trying very hard to be your friend, Jered, but you are not making it an enjoyable task."

He looked surprised for a moment, then he smiled. "I don't need any friends, Tessa."

"On the contrary, Jered, from the caliber of people you associate with, I'd say you needed friends more desperately than anyone I know."

"And you volunteer for the duty, I suppose? Leading me to virtue and approving my friends. Quite a task you've taken on."

"I am quite willing to, Jered. I would even venture to be your mistress. After all, I'm sure only experience and willingness are required."

"It's not done quite that way, little one. You should negotiate first. Hold out for a decent house and carriage. Find out how much he's willing to pay you. Never give away what you can sell."

She turned, and Adrian was there. His blond hair glowed in the light of a thousand candles. His ice blue eyes sparkled, but not with warmth. Not with wit that enjoyed a jest for the sake of it, but the type of amusement that lives on the shame of others.

"Are you sure you wouldn't care to investigate the

whips, Jered? It seems to me your little duchess could use some taming,'' Adrian said softly.

''I really do not like you,'' Tessa said, directing her attention to Adrian. ''I know that's unpardonably rude, but I find myself compelled to be honest.''

At that moment, the musicians ended their selection, and the sounds of violins dwindled into pure, distilled silence.

Perhaps her voice was too loud for such a moment, her temper urging her to words she'd have been better served to restrain. ''Perhaps you speak from experience, sir, but my husband's skill is such that a woman should pay him!''

All conversation in the room ceased. Several people stared at her, then looked away as if fascinated by the flooring, or the curtains, or the chandeliers above their heads. Glasses no longer clinked. The candles no longer sputtered. Even the breeze coming in from the open doors stopped.

Or so it seemed.

Tessa could feel her heart beating so quickly that it felt jarred loose in her chest. Her cheeks felt burned, as though they were aflame.

Jered had never before, for all his depravity, heard a collective gasp. But then, he'd rarely been as outspoken as his wife. His deeds, for the most part, were performed outside of society.

He stepped away from the pillar, summoning his irritation from beneath his shock. Did she never give a thought to her words? How dare she criticize any facet of his life? How dare she offer herself up as his friend? His mistress?

He felt himself warm in Adrian's smiling stare.

"I believe the little duchess is under some illusions, Jered. Shall I tell her how many mistresses you've had over the years? Or how many we've shared?" he added in a whisper.

"Seven," Tessa said. Jered's gaze whipped around to his wife. She stood smiling, supremely unaware that she was the object of attention, that her every word was being repeated to those who could not hear her well. "Of course," she said, her face pinkening, "I really think it's a huge number, myself. I can only hope that such an amount was not because you grew tired of them, Jered. If so, it shows a decided lack of character that you are so easily bored."

Someone laughed, and was just as quickly hushed.

He had to get her out of here.

He gripped Tessa's arm and none too gently escorted her to the door. It seemed to him that a dozen husbands sighed a bit too loudly in shared relief.

"Jered."

He really was beyond speech at this moment, or he would have told her to be quiet. He doubted, however, that it would have done any good.

"Where are we going?"

"Anywhere. Away."

"Do you realize, Jered, that you are forever escorting me *from* places, and rarely *to*?"

He sent her a frown; it did not silence her. "Why is that, do you suppose? I feel like a light being hidden beneath a bushel." He stopped on the steps, turned, and looked at her.

He was swamped by feeling, nearly drowning in it. There were too many complex emotions present to simply call it anger. But that was enough to latch on to, to grip with both hands. "Perhaps it's because you're al-

ways where you shouldn't be, Tessa. I needn't enumer-
ate those occasions, surely? Places *most* wives would
never have ventured."

There was a flush on her face, a look too virginal to
be worn by the woman who'd moaned in his arms,
who'd cried when he'd taken her and sobbed his name
into his ear.

"I really don't think it is fair for you to comment
upon my actions as a wife, Jered, when you have not
exactly been proficient as a husband."

"Were I in your position, madam, I would have been
a great deal more circumspect."

"Then shall we trade places? Perhaps I would make
a better husband," she said brightly. "Wife," she commanded, thrusting a finger at his face, "help me off with
my boots."

He caught his startled laughter midbreath.

"Your parents should have sewn your lips together
at birth."

The look she sent him was teasing, too much so for
the crowd that had gathered behind them.

He swung up into the carriage, shouted instructions
to his coachman, realizing that every person crowded
into the doorway could easily hear the address. He had
just damned both their reputations by his action. He had
a few moments in which to change his mind, turn the
carriage around, and deposit his wife where all wives
should be. At home. Perhaps reading a lurid novel. Better yet, embroidering something. A crest upon a pillow-
case. His initials upon a tailored shirt. Wifely things.

"Are you ill?" He wouldn't have been at all surprised if she was. Even though she'd told him that she
felt fine in closed carriages, he was prepared for the

opposite. If anything, his wife relished a contrariness of spirit.

"I'm fine, thank you."

How utterly polite. How restrained. How wifely of her. How irritating.

Was that why he knew he wasn't going to turn the carriage?

A daring bit of whimsy, Jered. No, more than that. Almost certainly the wrong thing to do. If he were a better man, he would tap upon the carriage roof and Simons would instantly obey. To do what he was thinking was simply unheard of, of course. One did not take a wife to their destination. It was not done.

He leaned back against the tufted bench, studied her in the carriage light, wondering if this visit would have her finally returning to the country. She must learn that his actions were not for her ridicule or approval. He was the Duke of Kittridge, after all, and she was his wife by virtue of his apathy and possible inclination. It had not been a love match, he had not handed his heart to her along with the keys to Kittridge. There was nothing affixed to her betrothal ring that made her superior to any other woman he knew. Her purpose was to furnish him his heirs, not expound upon his honor. Not question his friends. Or his occupations.

The sooner she learned that lesson, the better. The quicker she learned her place in his life, the better they would deal well together.

And that was the reason he would not turn the carriage.

Chapter 13

The building was an unprepossessing one, a three-story redbrick structure. Its door was painted black, a fanlight allowed light to stream out at night, daylight to filter in during the time most of its occupants were asleep. Most nights, there was music, a quartet played in the gallery above the second floor, scenting the air with soft sounds. There was an aura of refinement about the place, one justifiably attained. It was owned, it was rumored, by a contingent of nobles who wished a steady supply of healthy and compliant flesh and a place to play when boredom set in at home.

He was not one of the owners, but Jered could name them all. He'd played cards with most, had lost a substantial amount of money to one. In fact, the joke was that his was the second floor, the lost sum having been enough to outfit twelve rooms of the opulent structure.

It was true that the house had a name not quite in keeping with its restrained image. At first it had only been known by its address, 3606 Tattersall Lane. But time and reputation had granted it another label, one that most men who knew of its existence used with great fondness—the Pleasure Palace.

There were twenty-eight rooms in the Pleasure Palace, every single one of them given over to one vice or another, as long as there was one constant, the achievement of pleasure. The only requirements for admission to its exalted membership ranks were annual dues of a princely sum, and a title. Guests were discouraged. Therefore, it was with no little connivance and a great deal of money that the Duke of Kittridge was able to escort his wife through the hall, up the stairs, and to the third floor.

There had been no one in the tastefully furnished parlor. There would be no one walking through the hall. Discretion was not merely inclination at the Pleasure Palace, it was an imperative. Appointments were encouraged, although the staff maintained an attitude of compliancy in order to fulfill extemporaneous requests. Such as the one the Duke of Kittridge expressed. There were no eyebrows raised, no judgments made. Each servant had been employed at an elevated sum for just such a reason, to encourage loyalty and silence, both to the Pleasure Palace and its members.

Jered slid his fingers across the raised edge of gilt on the fourth panel, as directed. He had never done what he was about to do; the novelty of it was intriguing. Not to mention Tessa's reaction. His wife had the largest eyes, they took in everything. She'd remained silent from the moment they'd entered the door. Nor had she spoken as they mounted the grand staircase. Even now, as the secret panel opened, she remained mute.

Her ridiculous feathered mask bobbed, and he almost smiled at the sight of it. Instead he reached over and searched for the pins that fixed it to her upswept hair.

"What are you doing?" How odd that she should be whispering. Did she know what they were about to do? Or that silence was the best atmosphere, even though he'd been assured that the corridors transferred no sound. In fact, he'd been told that his companion could scream and it would not be heard. *Would she scream?* It was such an arresting thought that his finger stilled, then resumed their search.

"Taking this damnable thing off, Tessa. It will get in the way." He found the last hairpin, extracted it, then pulled the mask off and tossed it on a hall table. It lay perched half on, half off a blue and white china vase, its feathers trembling.

Wise of her not to ask questions. It was almost as if she knew.

Well, he would find out in a matter of moments, wouldn't he?

He pulled open the panel to its full width and preceded her, half-turning to extend a hand to her. "Forgive my rudeness," he softly said, "but it is really better if I go first. It's dark and you might lose the way."

She stared at his hand for a long moment, so still that he had an errant thought that she was not unlike a fawn, young and infinitely fragile at the moment of fatal knowledge. The closing of a trap, the sound of an arrow's arc, the instant before a bullet burrowed through fur and skin and flesh.

Without a word, she placed her hand in his.

His fingers curled over hers. Then, a slight tug as he pulled her inside. It was like walking into a puzzle box, an impression only strengthened when the door closed soundlessly behind them.

"Don't be afraid." Had he heard her swift exhalation of breath? Or did he hear the pounding of her heart instead?

The lure of the forbidden. And this place was most definitely forbidden.

She was newly wed and most certainly still too innocent, but she'd had two London seasons and she was not stupid. Places like this were whispered about in horrified tones, with just the right degree of piety to indicate that the teller of the tale was not as fascinated as it might appear. But Tessa *was* fascinated and terrified and, more than anything, curious about the next few moments and that odd smile that played about Jered's mouth.

It was dark as night. No, even night was not this dark, because there was always a light from a dwelling or a sliver of moonlight, or even a coach lantern or street lamp to mark the way, Something to give dimension to the darkness, layers through which the eyes might strain to create sense from a shadow or an object. This darkness was full, absolute, so complete that she hesitated even when she felt the gentle tug on her hand.

"Don't be afraid," Jered said again. What an odd thing for him to say in that tone. As if he expected it of her and somehow encouraged it from her, a fear that he might point to as a sign that she was not adventurous enough or companion enough to partner him. What would he do if she told him she was not afraid? That the feeling that coursed through her now was not fear or trepidation or even caution, but a willingness—no, eagerness—to be on this odd and dark journey.

When he tugged on her hand this time, she walked in the direction he indicated, her feet falling upon a carpet so thick that they seemed swallowed in it. Two paces, three, then he pulled her forward again, the soft slither of something being opened—and the corridor was no longer dark, only lit by the candlelight from a room to their left and a window that allowed them to spy upon its occupants.

Jered glanced inside, then slid the window shut again, but not before Tessa saw a grimace of revulsion flash over his face. Her fingers trembled on the wall, her curiosity was almost such that she wanted to pull back the panel and discover what it was that Jered found so distasteful.

It was as if he knew her intent, could divine it in the dark. "Do not, Tessa," he said, and this time his tone was neither complicitous nor goading. She dropped her hand, felt the tug on her other, followed where he led in silence.

Finally just when it felt as if they had traversed the entire inside of the house, Jered stopped. He slid back the small window, glanced inside. The light was sufficient to see both the small smile that crossed his lips and the speculative look he gave her.

She allowed him to pull her closer so that she was standing in front of him. The corridor was not wide, so their position was made even more intimate by their location. He placed his hands at her waist, bent his head close to her ear. "Look, Tessa, and you'll learn what most wives will never know."

She had known it was to be something like this, the gleam in his eyes had given him away long before this window had been opened. She had prepared herself for the sight, for being horrified and embarrassed by what she might see. But she had also determined that he would not know it. She would see what he wished her to see, but instead of dissolving into tears or begging him to remove her from this place, she would be stoic and unemotional and untouched.

Until she saw them.

The room was illuminated by candlelight, just as the chamber on her wedding night had been. And the furnishings were not unlike, the bolsters on the bed were thickly embroidered, the four-poster had a heavily carved head and footboard, the tester was velvet. Upon the floor was a patterned carpet in the eastern fashion, a table was set with silver and crystal, the remnants of a meal sat upon the sparkling china. On the opposite wall, a bright fire burned. It alone would have lit the room had the candles not been present. But it was by their glow that the two stood bathed, a man and a woman, both nude. Each entranced by the other, as if forbidden to touch by a strange and mischievous power. Separated only by a foot or so, they stared at each other, so still it was possible to think them statues.

At that moment, Jered slid his hands upon her waist. She flinched, startled at his touch. It had felt as if she was a part of the scene in the other room.

She wanted to tell him to take her from here, that such a sight was a horrid thing, more than a breech of propriety. It was vile and disgusting and horribly wrong. But of course it wasn't. It had a purity, a beauty that was oddly compelling. As if she viewed something not profane, but rather something natural and uninhibited.

Her eyes were drawn back to the window. The woman smiled, tossed her hair over her shoulders. The gesture bared her breasts, but she did not try to cover herself from the young man's gaze, remained tall and straight and unashamed, a picture of woman at her most glorious. It was quite evident she was older than the male, his face was too young to be anything but student to her more mature tutelage. But age did not seem to matter at this moment, not even to the young man who

reached out both cupped hands to her body as if he were
a starving supplicant and she a feast.

Jered's hands moved upward, thumbs brushing the
underside of her breasts. Tessa bit her bottom lip at the
sensation. Something curled within her when he spoke,
the words so soft, so gently spoken they felt like the
faintest of breezes, a notion of sound within her ear.

"She'll teach him, Tessa." Just that, no more.

Indeed that was exactly what she was doing. The man
in the room trapped a nipple between his fingers, she
removed his hand and brushed his fingers back and forth
against her breast until the tip blushed and hardened.

Jered's thumbs brushed against her cloth-bound
breasts, enticed the nipples to display in just the same
way. He pulled Tessa back against him, leaned against
the wall, so that she was cradled by his body. She stiffened against him for a long moment, a silent tug of war
in the darkness, before succumbing to his greater
strength. But all he did was lock his arms around her
waist, rock her slightly back and forth, it would have
been a comforting cadence if she had not heard his
breathing and knew that he was as affected as she by
the scene before them.

It would have been easier, later, to admit that she
closed her eyes, remaining in the darkness untouched
by Jered's odd seduction. It would have been more acceptable to ignore his teasing caresses and softly voiced
taunts, demand that he allow her to leave. If she had
spoken above a whisper, they would have been heard
by the couple in the other room. She remained silent.
Curiosity won out over shame. The lure of the forbidden. It beckoned her, too.

A soft groan from the man in the room. A sound of
nuance, entreaty, pleasure, it encompassed all of these

and more. Tessa looked beneath half-shuttered lids, the tableau oddly even more evocative filtered by her lashes. The woman extended her hands to the man, touching him lightly on the shoulders, cupping the mound of muscle and bone. A skimming touch of hands down his arms then over to his chest. There they halted in their exploration, a gentle touch of teasing wonder. A glance to his eyes, a pinch to bronze nipples. Another masculine sound of entreaty. Hands upon his hips, a soft smile. So would have a mature Eve have looked. Enticement in a glance.

Jered reached up with both hands and swept her hair from her nape. His grip seemed oddly tight as he held her still and kissed the back of her neck in a place that made her shiver. His breath was hot, but so was her skin.

"Let me teach you, Tessa." Whispered words.

His fingers felt too warm through all the layers of her clothing. Tessa looked down. He had insinuated his fingers inside the sheath of silk that had been her costume. His fingers matched her skin for heat. Her face felt flushed, a peppery feeling not unpleasant. But it was difficult to breathe while feeling so, and even more difficult to appear unaffected.

The back of his hand pressed against the fabric of her bodice, creating a pocket of air between her breast and his palm. Just that. Not a touch, nor intrusion. A warming, as if he gentled her for his touch, acquainted her with his nearness. When his palm slid over a nipple, brushing back and forth, it was almost a release. A breath escaped her at the sensation, an approving murmur from Jered. She felt strange, parts of her body seemed swollen. It felt as if there was an itch that needed to be satisfied, but that was impossible because it came from deep inside her, as if her body needed something she had not provided. Hunger? Relief from pain? Passion? She didn't know, only that it grew in intensity each moment, each soft touch of Jered's fingers and breath of words.

For a moment she closed her eyes, felt herself ease backward into him. For a moment, just a moment, she forgot that he was not the man she wished him to be and that she had been too innocent and too sheltered for this. Instead she turned her head until her cheek rested against his chest, felt the solidness of him, the warmth. She heard his quick breaths, felt the heat of his skin, the brush of fabric against fabric.

But Jered was not satisfied with that. A hand reached out and gently turned her head until she faced the window again. His fingers stroked her cheek while his thumb slid back and forth against her bottom lip, learning texture and shape.

It was curiosity that forced her eyes open and shock that kept them fixed on the pair in the other room.

The woman knelt in front of the young man, her head upturned to smile into his flushed face. One hand gripped his organ, swollen hard and large and long, the other traced a path from the back of his knee to his buttock, curved around and measured it in appreciation. It was not simply the young man's nakedness that shocked Tessa, she had studiously avoided looking lower than his waist. It was the woman's next actions. Her lips parted, her tongue emerged to lick slowly and lovingly around the bulbous head. The young man clenched his hands into fists, his head arching back in obvious and ardent pleasure.

"You look like a little owl," a warm and masculine voice whispered. Jered. Of course it was Jered. For a moment she felt paralyzed, struck dumb with absolute amazement. "What, no questions?"

She shook her head.

Jered said nothing further, simply spread his legs and pulled her back into the vee caused by his stance. She was surrounded by him, enveloped, something she might have noted if her gaze had not been intent upon the sight before her.

Jered's hands rested at her stomach, one above the other. His breath was warm against her cheek. She tilted her head so that she was closer to him, not noticing that she did so, not seeing his small smile at her actions. Nor did she notice when both his hands slipped lower, pressed against her clothing until he could feel the shape of woman beneath the costume. His soothing touch eased the ache that thrummed through her.

The young man moaned.

Tessa blinked.

"She'll take him full into her mouth now," Jered whispered. He bent and nuzzled behind her ear. She arched her head to allow him access, bit her lip against her own moan. Seduction, of course it was that. Artful and practiced and planned. That, too. It should have mattered. It did not.

She looked away from the tableau in the window, her breathing constricted. There was something oddly beautiful about such carnality. It made no pretense of being love, not in this place so obviously set aside for pleasures of the flesh. And yet it was not constraint. There were no bonds on either party, no reluctance. Only sensuality for the sake of it, hedonism without hypocrisy. Enjoyment for its own purpose.

"Tessa." A soft command. Not entreaty, Jered did not entice. He was ruler, not supplicant. She turned her head, her cheek once more pillowed against his chest. A finger tilted her chin, a soft, inquiring gaze in the faint light from the window.

"Tessa?"

She only looked up at him. The next moment she was being kissed, whirling away into a spiral of sensation.

A sound interrupted them. Slight as it was, it was enough to call them back into themselves, away from that slippery place that shared one mind, one thought, one desire.

The woman was practiced in her art, so much so that Jered had felt himself harden even more as he watched. *Not perfectly true, was it Jered?* He'd envisioned Tessa on her knees before him, her untutored hands learning him, her mouth, that luscious mouth on his flesh in the tenderest and then the most brazen of kisses.

And then she'd looked up at him, her brown eyes widened in confusion, her face tinted by a flush he could see even in the faint light. Desire, in its purest form, unadorned by artifice. Need so powerful that it called out to him, found its answer in his own halting breath and swelling loins. He'd had no choice but to kiss her, to explore the truth of her look, to touch tongue to inner lip and feel her shiver. Hold her, feel her, hear her moan.

He'd brought her here to shock her, and she had managed to startle him. No, more than that. He wanted to mount her now and be damned to the place. Had he ever felt that for a mistress? Lust, surely, but not this fierce need.

He turned her again so that her back was to him.

"Put your arms around my neck, Tessa," he said,

and reached down to cup her elbows. She arched back against him, her hands clasped behind his neck, a position that lifted her breasts. He reached inside her bodice, hooked a finger into the delicate lace of the chemise, shredding it without a qualm. Only then did he free each breast from its cloth prison. Tessa sighed, then caught the sound as it escaped, a wordless admission of sensation.

He pulled her back against him, his hands pressed once more to her abdomen. He closed his eyes, rocked her in a motion as ancient as the seas, as heady and as voluptuous as the scene he ignored in the other room. One glance had showed him a young man with his hands fisted in his partner's hair, a look of exultation and joy as he thrust into her talented mouth. Jered placed the palms of his hands at the juncture of Tessa's thighs, pressing through fabric and lace until he could feel her contours, her softness, her heat.

He did not doubt that her gaze was still fixed on the scene through the window. Voyeurism was a heady sport, one perhaps too much for an innocent like his wife. But she did not move like an innocent, and she did not feel naive, and the heat from the core of her could singe him. She may be innocent of what she was feeling, but it did not negate the fact that she experienced it. As did he.

One hand pulled up her skirt, while the other pressed still harder against that soft triangle. Her breathing was erratic, almost mirroring that of the young man in the other room. Jered reached beneath her chemise, pressed his palm against soft skin and softer hair, dipped his fingers into the swollen and heated flesh.

He rocked her again and again against his hand, uncaring that his technique was supplanted by the desperate need of this moment. He wanted her, had to be within her, but all he could do was taunt her until she had no choice but to bite her lip to keep from screaming. The young man moaned loud and long in a song of exquisite pleasure. Tessa began to shiver, her body rigid. He pressed harder against her and urged her on with erotic words remembered from long-ago purloined texts, and wished and prayed and damned this moment for not being different, and the circumstances for preventing him release.

Chapter 14

"Is there anything else I can get you, Your Grace?"

"No, thank you, Mary. I'm planning on retiring. Please tell cook that the meal was delicious and I appreciate the extra effort of the tray."

"I'll tell her, Your Grace, and I can just hear her now. You tell Her Grace that we've all the time in the world to do her bidding, we do. And if she wants a cuppa or a biscuit, all she needs do is ring the bell."

"All that?" Tessa asked with a smile. The young maid was so earnest and so eager that it was difficult to be in her presence. It would be easy enough to squelch such pronouncements in the future. Simply give her a cool glance and a sharp reprimand. Effortless disdain. Except of course, she could not treat someone else that way, let alone someone employed on a whim and just as easily dismissed. She smiled again as the young maid nodded, bobbed from the room, decorum barely restrained beneath an answering grin.

The door shut behind her and Tessa was once again alone. She stood, surveyed the room. It was quite lovely, more sumptuous than she'd planned. She had no training in such things, but she knew enough to allow others who were more knowledgeable a free hand. The sofa was new, covered in a forest green velvet. The chairs had been recovered in a floral pattern. The carpet beneath her feet was one that had been in a guest bedroom at Kittridge. It had captured her attention with its panorama of a basket of fruits as the central theme. Its brilliant colors had been restored after a thorough brushing and airing and now it framed the room as if it were a painting. Along with the mahogany pieces that made up the parlor furniture, the furnishings were warm and inviting, coaxing a visitor for an intimate chat, urging its inhabitant to light the fire and prop feet upon the ottoman and open a good book.

She walked through the connecting door to her bedchamber. Here, too, the changes had been made in far shorter time than she would have believed possible. Being a duchess was useful in some ways. The bed hangings were of the same green as the sofa, a shade that made her think of a forest at dusk, shadows enhancing the color. In that corner was a massive armoire, its curved panels done in the French style, its contents bulging with a trousseau crafted for a princess. Or a duchess. And in the back of it lay a balled up scrap of silk that had been her chemise.

Everywhere she looked there were touches of wealth, a miniature of her mother and father given to her at her wedding, the gilt frame resting on a solid gold stand. A vase of priceless value resting upon a four-foot-tall marble pediment. A Copley painting hung from one wall, a Reynolds from another, a Jacques-Louis David on a third. Upon the table footing her bed rested an exquisite porcelain bowl of fruit, sculptured in Italy. Each individual grape, orange, persimmon, and fig, seemed edible, glistening with droplets of eternal rain, succulent and appealing.

She had lied to the young maid. She had no intention of retiring. She doubted she would even be able to sleep. Her body seemed as tight as the velvet weave of the bed hangings, as knotted as the gold braid that affixed it to the posters.

Jered had said nothing to her as he had helped her restore her clothing. Had spoken not one word as he reached in front of her and slid closed the viewing window. Nor had he said anything as he had escorted her from the corridor and down the exit stairs, leading her by the hand through the darkened and hushed stairwell. There was not one word exchanged by either of them during the coach ride home, and if he looked at her and studied her in the darkness, she was not aware of it. She'd held the curtain open with one finger and pretended a nonchalant interest in the nocturnal view of London.

She wrapped her hands around one poster, leaned her forehead against the carved wood, clenched her eyes shut. Oh, what was this feeling? This heat that coursed through her like a fever? She felt as if she could not take a free breath. The sound of her sigh was too loud for this room of comfort and elegance. She willed herself not to remember, but the scene had been too often recalled for that not to happen. This time, as in all the previous occasions, it was not the young man being pleasured she saw but herself. A curious and arousing scene, one in which he'd barely touched her and yet had brought her to completion with just his proximity, words, and a few strokes of talented fingers.

How had he done that?

She could feel her face flush, just as she'd felt before,

every time she recalled the scene, the seductive rocking movement of his hips, the touch of his palms upon her breasts. She'd undressed and hidden her chemise in the back of the armoire, but she could not hide herself as easily.

Oh, but if she only could.

The door opened almost silently. There were people who saw to things like that, drawers that opened with a creak or a groan, hinges that were oiled often and well, shoes that were polished, food that was prepared, sheets that were laundered. The necessities of life raised to an art form. A world of effortless service. Well paid for, of course.

If he made a sound it was not his bare feet brushing against the carpet, nor the hiss of an indrawn breath. It might have been in the click as the door swung shut and the lock engaged. Or she could have been alert and aware and waiting for him.

Absurdities, Jered? Again?

She was standing in the darkness, her hands clasped around a bedpost, her nightgown as sheer as imagination could make of it. A sense of déjà vu caught him as ably as if she were a cannon and he a four master, broadsided and sinking fast. Except of course the look she gave him was not one of censure or even innocence, but one of complicity. And awareness.

It almost drove him to his knees.

"When I agreed to take you to wife," he said, honesty the only antidote to her look. "I did not quite expect someone like you. I most certainly did not anticipate all those questions you ask me, the way your mind flies from one tangent to another like a drunken bee. I never envisioned you shocking me with those things you say. I thought you'd stay in Kittridge, perhaps growing roses and reading arcane poetry and anticipating my visits to you with barely veiled . . ."

"Fear?" she interrupted. "Or anticipation? Or was I to bless the day you left me and pray that you did not return often? And perhaps I would become with child and rear him alone in the country?"

"That was the plan," he admitted.

"Then shall I pretend to be terrified of you? Is that what you want?"

"It is too late a pretense, I'm afraid, after tonight. I barely touched you and you exploded in my arms."

"How did that happen?" Her question hinted at more. Did she need reassurance. Even now?

"It happened the way it normally does, Tessa, when there is desire between two people."

"And that is why you are so angry now, isn't it?"

He took one step closer. "Not exactly. I am angry because I have no mistress to assuage my needs. It would take more than a pretty bauble to convince Pauline that you will pay no more visits to her. I've realized I don't have the patience to woo another woman."

"Is that something you should admit to a wife?"

"Oh, not to any wife, but I'll have to concede that it does not seem as if you are just any wife."

He took one step closer. "In fact, since you have become such an adept companion and since you have offered me your portrayal of mistress, I believe that it is only fair you play that part."

She said nothing. Not even when he reached her and extended one finger down her exposed arm in slow exploration.

"Would you have taken your mistress there, Jered?"

"No, Tessa, I would not have." Pauline was more

than a little adept at that little trick, but that was a comment he would not make.

"Then why did you take me?"

"Is it not enough that I've given you another subject to ponder?" Her hair had been brushed for the night, but left untouched. As if she expected a lover. "Isn't it enough that it happened, Tessa? Can you remember? It was not that long ago. A matter of hours only." He stepped closer, extended his arms around her, pulled her back against his chest. "See how easily it's recalled?"

"Don't."

"Don't what, Tessa? Don't touch you, don't hold you?"

"Please don't talk about it."

He stepped back, turned her gently in his arms. He could barely see her, but something stopped him from lighting a candle. Not a sensibility for her feelings. Not a surge of unwanted compassion. Certainly not in apology for what he'd done to her. Perhaps honesty was too much a weapon. And perhaps speech was simply beyond him at this moment.

He did something he'd wanted to do for hours now, he bent and kissed her again, silencing his thoughts and her pleas in the simplest way possible. Except that kissing Tessa was not a simple thing, it was rife with sensation. The rasp of his tongue against her lips coaxed them open, the warmth of her mouth solicited a neophyte's moan from him. Her tongue was first shy, then wanton as it dueled with his. A simple kiss? It was as if his depth of field compressed until the world was only a black dot, as if he were swooning like a maiden aunt.

He backed her up to the bed, lifted her by the waist until she fell back against the covers. He spread her legs, opened his dressing gown, thought fleetingly about speed and finesse and all those things that had made him such a reputedly good lover. But nothing mattered but easing this ache, this gnawing dissatisfaction, this damnable hunger. Nothing, not her wishes or needs or his experience or knowledge. Nothing.

He came into her too suddenly, but she was hot and slick and ready for him. He groaned and nearly cried aloud at the sensation. He was too experienced a lover to think her that quickly aroused.

"You've been like this for hours, haven't you, Tessa?" He thrust once, impaling himself in softness and heat. "Ready for me. Waiting for me."

"I don't know." A soft admission, a gasp of awareness. He thrust again. Her fingernails gripped his arms, her head writhed back and forth upon the coverlet.

He felt like an animal cursed with the instinctual need to mate, fevered with it, desperate, wanting to claw and bite and scourge anything in its path, anything between it and the expulsion of his seed. He gripped her hips tightly, pulled himself closer, burying himself to the hilt. He glanced down and the shadows made even more erotic the dance of flesh against flesh. Like an animal he thrust again. All sophisticated play banished the moment he howled like the creature he felt himself to be. A surge of ecstasy with words was forced from mind and heart at the same moment his body quaked and shivered and rejoiced: "Damn. Damn. Damn. Damn."

A song of anger sung to a melody made for love.

Chapter 15

"I rescind my promise," Helena Astley said to her daughter. "I most definitely intend to interfere in your life." She poured a cup of tea, passed it over to Tessa, watching her with a stern eye as she took the cup. Tessa remembered tea parties with her dolls. They had been more friendly than this event.

"Your father said you were half-naked. And three people have told me that you and Jered were arguing in front of everyone."

"What was your costume, Mother?"

Helena averted her eyes. "That does not matter, Teresa."

She was in trouble. Her mother rarely called her Teresa. When she did, it was as powerful as a witch's spell, invoking all kinds of childhood terrors. Helena was a proud parent, but she was also a strict one. Tessa used to think her mother had eyes in the back of her head. None of her seven children ever got away with anything their mother didn't secretly condone.

"You went as a Valkyrie again, didn't you, Mother? With the breastplate and those cones?"

"That is not the point."

"I bet you carried a spear, too."

"A staff. I was encouraged not to continue with the spear."

"I should say not, after nearly stabbing the Countess of Vestmere with it last year."

"That, too, is off the topic, Teresa."

"I don't particularly care for this topic, Mother." She took a sip of her tea, added more sugar. "I'm no longer a child."

A raised eyebrow. Her mother had the most talented of facial expressions. Tessa could almost hear the words. *"Then do not behave as one."*

"I do not, for all my minor idiosyncrasies, choose to argue with your father in public."

Tessa smiled into her cup. The walls of Dorset House had occasionally trembled from their shouting. She had no doubt her parents loved each other, just as she was never in any doubt that both her father and her mother were possessed of deeply held beliefs and strong opinions. And while they may not have argued in public, there had certainly been times when Gregory and Helena let anyone within arm's reach know how irritated each was with the other.

"Jered and I weren't exactly arguing," Tessa said. "I was merely commenting upon his choice of friends."

"Unfortunately that is not the tale that is circulating."

"I have no control over what other people say, Mother."

"No, only upon your own actions. Has Kittridge not been treating you well?"

Tessa could feel the flush rising from her toes. If Jered treated her any better she would be dead of ecstasy within the week.

Helena raised another eyebrow. Tessa replaced her

cup upon the tray, stood, circled her mother's sitting room. The Astley's London home was a gracious retreat, nearly quiet since the three younger boys were at their lessons and the older ones off at school. This room was her favorite, with its soft green silk walls and the thick carpet upon the floor. The chairs were thickly upholstered and comfortable, the sofa the same. The tables were mahogany, polished to a sheen. It always smelled of her mother's perfume, something hinting at sandalwood. An oriental spice, as unique as Helena.

Today a fire was lit, bringing warmth and cheer to a gray day.

A clock ticked upon the mantel, and Tessa could hear the individual clicks of each passing second.

Her mother would not speak. It was a trick of hers. She would wait in patient silence for however long it took the recalcitrant to confess a sin, beg for forgiveness, promise it would never happen again. Her brothers were all reduced to quivering apologies within minutes. Tessa wondered how long she could hold out before talking.

"Are you happy, Tessa?" Reprieve both in a name and in the fact that her mother had spoken first.

"I am not unhappy, Mother." There, that was the truth. But there was something missing, wasn't there?

"There are degrees of misery, darling. All found within that broad framework. Not being unhappy is not quite the same as being content with your life."

"I love my husband." Another truth. A blinding one. It dazzled her sight, rendered every other trouble invisible.

"And what if Kittridge does not love you, Tessa? Have you considered that?"

Tessa traced her fingers upon the mantel. How did

she tell her mother that she had resigned herself to the fact that he probably did not? She amused him. She knew that quite well. She had been able, for a while, to interest him. How long before he would turn from her? A week? A month? It was a very real fear. She turned and looked at her mother. Not something she could impart to another soul.

"Yes," she said softly. "And it doesn't matter. How do you stop loving someone?"

"I wish you could, Tessa. I would counsel you to guard your heart. I do not believe unrequited love has any redeeming qualities." Helena stood, came around the table, and faced her daughter. "I will not have you hurt." On her face was the same look she wore the day Robert had come home with a broken arm. He'd been in a fight with a boy four years his senior and had not fared well. Helena had treated her son, tucked him into bed, and then marched off to dispense justice in her own way. Rumor told of the young bully being punished on his father's knee while Helena watched. The lesson being not only to pick on someone of his own size but that it was best not to choose one of the Wellbourne children to torment.

"I always hate it when someone tells me I cannot do something, Tessa. I see no reason why my child should not have the benefit of my expertise." There was a faint smile on Helena's face.

"You may have rescinded your promise, but I have not released you from it. It is my marriage, and my husband."

"Yes, but you are my child." And that, according to Helena Astley, was that.

Tessa sighed, and wondered if she ought to warn Jered. Her mother was extremely possessive. A pity the Duke of Kittridge did not feel the same way.

Chapter 16

❝ **I** cannot tell you how much we appreciate you inviting us to use your box, Your Grace. Indeed, my sister and I have thrilled at the very notion of being able to view *The Beggar's Opera* once again. And how delightful that such a droll comedy is being performed even after the season.❞

"On the contrary, Miss Crawford," Tessa said, stepping aside so that the elderly ladies could seat themselves. "You and your sister are the ones who have done me the favor. Tragedies should be partaken in silence, with a great many handkerchiefs, while laughter should be shared. Don't you think?" She waved her fan in front of her, the slight current of air enough to stir the damp tendrils of hair at her temples. The ton thought nothing of being packed together like salted fish in a barrel. Not to mention the heat generated by the thousands of candles. Pity the poor spectators below the massive candelabras. They could not help but be periodically splattered by candle wax as one by one the candles sputtered and died.

The box in which she and the sisters Crawford sat was commodious in comparison. It was specifically reserved by Jered, an inscribed brass plaque attesting to that fact was mounted upon the wall beside the door. There were six comfortable chairs crafted of mahogany and fitted with thick, soft cushions. There were twelve such boxes along the gallery, the majority of which were filled on most occasions, but not by patrons who possessed a great love of opera or comedies. The inhabitants of the gallery came for only two reasons, to see and be seen.

A few of the boxes were still empty, but then, it was considered fashionable to be late, even arriving in the midst of the first act if necessary. Depending upon the rank of the late arrivals, the play might stutter to a stop while the ladies were divested of their cloaks and the gentlemen found a comfortable chair. Then all would resume, the entire theater having come to a halt over the rudeness of a chosen few. But that's what most of the people under this roof had come for, to gossip and castigate and, above all, whisper to their hearts' content and make no apologies for what they were doing.

It was theater night, after all.

In the box next to her, an old gentleman sat happily fondling the leg of a particularly lovely young woman. Her blond ringlets were artfully arranged with ribbons and feathers, her gown was more apropos to a ball than to a night at the theater. The white-bearded gentleman seemed particularly besotted, especially since every time she bent closer to ask him a question, she revealed more of her attributes.

A mistress and a husband. Not at all an uncommon sight. Perhaps even a farcical one. Tessa had heard of at least one occasion when a husband had come face-to-face with his very own wife one night. Both of them had nodded politely and pretended not to know each other. A most advantageous attitude, especially since each had been accompanied by a lover.

It was theater night, after all.

Would she be that way in five year's time? Brittle and disillusioned and quite happy to build her own life apart from Jered, content in adultery as an opiate to her husband's infidelities? She didn't think so, but then, a month ago she could not have imagined all her adventures in London.

Her dress had been fashioned in the Russian manner, a silk and satin gown with a waist just below her bosom, small puffed sleeves and a scooped neck. The shoulder train was affixed with tiny silk ribbons in a shade almost pink, but pale enough to mimic her own flesh. The train itself was embroidered with ribbons, a hundred deeply hued rosebuds that enhanced the severity of the pale pink silk sheath. It was a contradiction, a bold dress, yet one of stark simplicity. She wore no jewelry, not even the long drop earrings recommended by the modiste. Her hair was pinned up in a style that hinted it could just as easily be undone. Her laces were quite as tight as they would have been in a less freely styled gown—the better to push her bosoms up, the modiste had said. Indeed, they looked to overflow her bodice at every indrawn breath.

What would her life be like if she could move with ease? She might possibly even slouch a bit in a chair instead of the posture required by such constraint. Every bit of clothing worn by man or woman was designed to pinch or itch or otherwise mold the flesh into some other form. Would Jered act different if he were not hobbled by his clothing? Odd thoughts for a duchess to have. But the flush that mounted from neck to cheeks was not so strange after all. It had at its root the quick and annoying vignette of her husband attired in nothing more than the skin God had given him. He moved quite well without his clothes.

She clicked closed her fan, opened it again, resolved to think no more of Jered for the moment. It would undermine her determination for this evening. She smiled at the sisters Crawford, who were scanning the crowd like eager little birds. Friends of her mother's, they were delightfully charming, literate, and filled with opinions on everything from the proper way to measure tea to the manner in which life should be lived. The sisters Crawford were two of the twelve members of a literary salon her mother attended while in London. It was no accident that every single member of this literary gathering had called upon Tessa in the last few days. She suspected her mother had called upon every one of her friends with, no doubt, a hint that her daughter might welcome a visit.

If that was her way of not interfering, Tessa would eat her fan.

As much as she might chafe under the interference, she could never remain angry at her mother. It was like cursing the wind, or being angry at the rain. Helena Astley was a force of nature in her own right. It was simply easier to let her have her way, wait until it was over, and then resume her own plans. She had invited the elderly sisters to the theater not only because she needed companions in order to attend, but also because she was very conscious of their limited resources. She doubted they would have the funds to purchase a ticket to the theater, let alone the means with which to arrive here. Therefore, her mission for this evening had a dual purpose, that of garnering her husband's attention while being kind to two ladies she very much liked.

The noise in the theater was like the drone of a hundred bees trapped in a jar. Laughter, shouts, calling from one aisle to another, they all added to the cacophony. The play should have commenced nearly fifteen minutes ago, but there was no sign that the curtain would soon be raised.

As if she had spoken a demand, one by one the candles were snuffed in the higher candelabra, leaving only the branches outside the boxes, centered so as to avoid the voluminous drapes. It was as if the light from the candles outlined each box, called out to the other spectators: Here is the real play. Witness these dioramas presented for your pleasure.

And it was just then that Jered arrived.

He had given up attempting to ascertain how his wife obtained her information. Be it maid or chambermaid or Chalmers in his most verbose form, she somehow was able to divine his intentions for an evening and follow him there. Or, like now, lie in wait for him like some sort of virtuous and patient spider. He had been alerted to her presence by one of the ushers, just in time to procure another box for the evening.

She was dressed in palest pink, an exquisite color for her. No damn spider had ever looked as fetching.

He frowned across the crowded theater at his wife, certain that everyone below him was more fixed on the sight of her smile and delicate nod than on the play. Pity. They would not see what they evidently expected.

His guests gathered around him as the music began. He seated himself in the corner, a spot from which he could not be readily seen. He did not wish to spend the entire evening bandying looks with his wife, or adding to the speculation no doubt rampant in the gallery. What difficulties he experienced with Tessa would be better served to remain private. For her sake. He did not, after all, wish her hurt. Only tamed.

He'd avoided her again. For nearly five days this time. It had not been especially easy to do, a fact that added greatly to his irritation.

His companions for this night were a diverse group. Three women and two men. A perfect pairing, if he was inclined for it. The invitation had certainly been made more than once this evening by the woman with the coal eyes and the riotous mane of red-gold hair. She was quite lovely, really. And she was quite available. Looking for a protector.

His right hand fingered the drape half-shielding him, his left remained upon his knee, tapping an idle rhythm against the fabric of his trousers.

Why is Tessa here? To incite my irritation? She has performed that feat quite ably. And who the hell designed that dress? She is half falling out of it.

She was *not* going to get under his skin.

"I adore a good farce. Do you not, Your Grace?" The woman with whom he'd been paired smiled, her lashes fell over brilliant black eyes. It was a coquette's gesture, one of supreme practice, he had no doubt. He bent forward, smiled, extended one finger and traced the line of her cheek. Such soft skin. Pity she'd used so much rouge upon it.

He glanced over at his wife. Her gaze was fixed upon the stage, but a flush tinged her cheek as pink as her dress. A part of him wanted to warn her that she did not enter this battle well-matched. He had superior weaponry and a knowledge of the field. She would not find herself the victor, and the outcome might well signal defeat for her entire strategy. He was not such a fool

that he could not discern it easily enough. She wanted
to fix herself in his mind, his every thought, make it so
that his entire world was colored with Tessa. A fabric
backdrop against which he'd decorate his life. A frame
for it. She wanted no mere partnership, she wanted in-
corporation. She wanted him to offer up his freedom,
nay, his very existence, in an oblation to marriage.

"I am so grateful I was invited to attend the theater,
your grace. I really didn't wish to come, but my friends
assured me I would be welcome." Her lips pouted se-
ductively.

What the hell was her name? "Of course," he said,
smiling fixedly at her exposed bodice. His wife's was
lower.

He sat back, stared at the stage. He barely paid attention to the first act. The second was made memorable
by his companion's repetition of MacHeath's song:

> *"If the Heart of a Man is deprest with Cares,*
> *The Mist is dispell'd when a Woman appears;*
> *Like the Notes of a Fiddle, she sweetly, sweetly*
> *Raises the Spirits, and charms our Ears,*
> *Roses and Lilies her Cheeks disclose,*
> *But her ripe Lips are more sweet than those.*
> *Press her,*
> *Caress her,*
> *With Blisses,*
> *Her Kisses*
> *Dissolve us in Pleasure, and soft Repose."*

"Isn't that lovely, Your Grace?" Again he was
treated to a tremulous portrayal of a virgin quivering in
excitement. A tawdry example, he wanted to tell her.
Most virgins were not so skilled that they captured their

lower lip beneath their teeth and shivered as if in rapture. Some virgins even laughed at inopportune moments and opened their eyes wide in alarm and amazement, and captured the essence of bliss in one softly whispered, "Oh my."

But she didn't need to know that, and he shouldn't have remembered it. He sent a fulminating look across the theater to his wife. She was watching him.

Why should he care? And why should he feel the warmth gather on his face as if he were no more than five and had been discovered doing something wrong? He was the Duke of Kittridge. She was just a wife. He knew his place in the world. Pity she couldn't learn hers. And just who the hell was she smiling at with such a look of humor on her face?

She bent to the side to answer a question from one of the old biddies, and nearly fell out of her dress. He grit his teeth, lifted his left hand, and wiggled his fingers in the air. Almost instantly, a footman appeared, bearing a silver tray upon which were arranged several glasses. He took two, gave one to his companion, nearly downed the second in one swallow. Another lift of fingers and he was provided with a second glass. This one he sipped more slowly, studying his wife over the rim.

Why is she really here? What could she possibly hope to gain? Did she think to make me jealous? Not likely, when her companions are two elderly ladies. Is she waiting for someone else? Some male companion?

It may well be the custom for other wives to take lovers, but he was damned if he was going to allow Tessa to do that. Why, he'd kill the idiot who thought he would touch his wife. And Tessa? Tessa would be beaten to an inch of her life, that's what. Despite her piteous screams and pleading for his mercy, he would

lower her chemise and touch that delectable rear of hers
and . . .

What the hell is happening to me? He shook his head
as if to dislodge such troubling thoughts. He realized
two things in that moment. He was as little pleased at
the idea of Tessa being at the theater as he was by the
abrupt recognition that he had acquired her habit of endless questioning.

Chapter 17

"Hello, Jered."

He inclined his head. *Most certainly a noble gesture,* thought Tessa. *But in Jered, one only almost regal.* No one could question his demeanor. As arrogant as a prince. Was that why he'd studiously ignored her presence for the last few days? Five days, to be exact. To prove yet another point? She was quite certain it was not going to work.

She turned and introduced her guests to her husband. He was more cordial to the sisters, infinitely charming. The elderly ladies were nearly atwitter with excitement when he finished kissing their hands.

"Are you enjoying the play, ladies?" he asked.

"Indeed, yes, Your Grace." Cecily Crawford chirped. Denise bobbed her head like a sister sparrow. Both women's eyes had widened when Jered had entered the box, and their gaze had not swerved from him since. Tessa could understand their fascination. He was too wonderfully handsome. And very aware of it.

"It's a lovely farce, isn't it, Your Grace?" Denise asked, then looked down at her lap. A yellowing lace-trimmed handkerchief was being strangled between her clenched hands in an excess of excitement.

"It is indeed a farce," he softly said, and Tessa was quite certain he was not discussing the play.

"It is quite one of our favorites," Denise said. "And Teresa was such a dear to invite us."

"Oh, Teresa is a dear. There's no doubt about that," he said agreeably.

Tessa just smiled at him. Amiably. Did he know she could have as easily bitten him? He must, else he wouldn't have sent her that look that goaded at the same time it warned.

He sat on the chair closest to her.

"We rarely visit the theater anymore, Your Grace," Cecily contributed. "And when Teresa extended the invitation, it was a godsend. Truly a godsend."

"Then you must consider my box at your disposal, ladies. There are quite a number of plays I'm sure you would enjoy."

The Crawford sisters were silenced with that sentence. Indeed it was an effortless act of charity on Jered's part. Because it was so casually gifted, it did not appear as such. It was truly a magnanimous gesture. She smiled at him in approval.

"Why do I not think you are here for the play, Tessa?"

"I am here for the same reason as you, Jered. To enjoy myself, of course. Are you not having fun with your friends?"

"Quite assuredly."

"There are some lovely ladies with you. Have you taken a new mistress, then?" Her smile was bright.

"Rest assured, Tessa, that when I do so, it will be none of your concern." It felt as if he had slapped her.

"Then you have not, as yet. Are you auditioning for the part?"

His look freed her laughter and she blessed it. It was either laugh or cry at that moment, and she'd much rather have him incensed at her mirth than pleased by her tears.

"However, the lady who accompanies me is rumored to have some remarkable talents, Tessa." His eyes were cold, so cold that she could easily have been rendered chilled from them. Except such a statement had the opposite effect on her that he evidently intended. She did not feel the least subjugated or cowed by his chastisement. In fact, she was blazingly angry. So much so that perhaps she raised her voice a little too loud, forgetting that sound carried very well in the old theater.

"Does she stand on her head when you swive her, Jered? Please, do tell me it's something I can aspire to. Perhaps I can quote Ovid while nibbling on your cock. Although I imagine it would be even more of a feat if it was in the original Latin. Not your cock. Ovid."

The two elderly sisters had grown silent after one gasp. The theater was absurdly quiet, as if all movement, all sound, all whispers and sotto voce speech had simply stopped. On the stage, MacHeath, Ben, and Matt ceased their acting and stared open-mouthed at the Kittridge box.

She had done it again.

His eyes weren't cold. They were very hot. Like steam, perhaps, or fog obscuring the gates of Hell.

She found herself pulled up from her chair by a grip fueled by fury. Well, she had certainly gleaned his attention—and that of at least three thousand other souls. If someone could have been rendered invisible, it would be Tessa. In only moments, he swept her from the box, pulled her down the grand staircase, and pushed her into the coach.

She managed to say something about the Crawford sisters, a sentence that garnered her a few minutes respite when Jered left the coach to make arrangements for their return home. Too soon, however, he was back in the coach, seating himself facing the rear of the carriage. At least he had not lit the lantern.

The only sounds were those from the outside. The clop of horses hooves on the cobbled pavement. Someone laughed. Someone cried. A faint scream. London night, never quiet. Even so, it was infinitely preferable to the atmosphere inside the carriage. For a long time he did not speak, but it was not a restful silence. She could feel his rage, could almost anticipate it, as if it was a beast breaking free of its chains.

"Have you no sense whatsoever?"

She frowned at him in the darkness. "Why do you mind if I've caused a few people to talk, Jered? Your own actions are not beyond reproach. I would think you would be lauding me for my behavior since it so impugns the family name. Isn't that what you're after?"

"Do not turn this around, madam wife. My behavior is not at trial here."

"The gossips will simply attribute it to your character. They will say you have had too much influence over your poor countrified wife."

"Were you never reigned in as a child?"

"You were evidently not, Jered." She straightened, stared at him. "You could do so much more with your life. Instead you comport with idiots and bring a harlot to the theater."

"She spent most of the time quoting the entire second act."

Was there humor in his voice? She pressed her lips together over words that were too improvident to say aloud. *Oh, Tessa, if you had only thought that earlier. Will you ever be able to return to the theater?* Not in her lifetime. Perhaps disguised, with a mask.

"Oh? 'A wife's like a guinea in gold, stampt with the name of her spouse.' That sort of thing? I prefer 'Gamesters and highwaymen are generally very good to their whores, but they are very devils to their wives.' It seems quite apropos, don't you agree?"

"You evidently have not matured enough to be seen in polite society, Tessa." No, she'd been mistaken. There was no humor in that voice. It was like shale, flinty and hard, brittle to the touch.

"Therefore, I'm to be sent back to Kittridge," she shot back. "How utterly convenient an excuse for you."

They were home. Too soon. Now he would leave her again; this time he would not return until dawn. She knew that as well as she knew that he would do it in a calculated gesture to make her into the kind of wife he wanted. Silent, submissive. Absent.

It was finally too much.

She waited until he helped her from the carriage, strode by him saying nothing. The stairs were too high, too long. She stopped in the middle of them, reached into the alcove for the Chinese vase that rested there. It was nearly three feet high, a lovely piece of porcelain.

She picked it up and threw it.

Shards of something wickedly sharp flew in his face as the vase exploded onto the foyer floor. She was throwing things at him! No, only one thing, the Chinese urn that had been in the family for too many years to count.

He felt the edge of his temper flare again, as if someone had ringed the lip of it with gunpowder. He really

should turn her over his knee. Again, unbidden, came
the memory of her almost perfect back, the violin flare
to it, the smooth, pink skin of her. And then another
memory. Her voice in the theater, the mocking tone of
it as she set the ton on its ear. And his uncle called *him*
wild.

"I don't want you ever treating me like that again,
Jered." Her voice was quite low, but in that tone a cat
might use before pouncing on its owner with teeth bared
and claws extended. *I have had enough,* it seemed to
say, *of pawing and petting and your insistent interference. Leave me alone.*

He was certain that he had misinterpreted, but after
another look at her face, decided that he had not. His
wife was more than upset. From the flags of color upon
her cheeks, he could only deduce that she was embarrassed. Or even, as difficult as it might be to believe,
enraged.

"You are my husband, and husbands do not humiliate their wives."

He only stared at her.

"You have shown more concern for this bloody vase
than you have ever shown for me." She actually planted
her fists on her hips and glared at him. "I've seen you
pat the blasted thing, you even smile at it!" Was she
actually yelling at him?

He walked up the stairs, judging her mood. There
wasn't anything else to throw. He wrapped his arms
around her, trapping her arms. He hauled her up until
she was eye level to him, no mean feat because his wife
was not exactly dainty. Willowy, true. Well-endowed,
certainly. Tiny? No. He braced her against the wall,
thinking that such close confinement might make her
cease her murderous behavior. No, his wife looked over

his shoulder as if searching for more ammunition.

"Stop it!" he shouted, except that the shout sounded suspiciously breathless to his ears. It did, however, have the unique ability to startle Tessa. She stilled. He grit his teeth, closed his eyes, and then reopened them seconds later to find that her expression had not softened one jot. She was still frowning at him, and her lips were clamped together in a stern and reproving gesture that reminded him oddly of his old nanny, who had given him that very same look when she was blisteringly annoyed. The buried emotions of shame and embarrassment surfaced long enough for him to realize that he was feeling all of those emotions because of his wife. Another sin to lay at her door.

"What on earth is wrong with you?" Now *that* was a shout. She blinked at him as if confused by the question. He repeated it, although he was certain the second rendition would give him no further clue. She looked at him as if he were one of those lunatics at St. Mary of Bethlehem hospital, a look that combined pity, irritation, and abhorrence all in one measure.

"I will not have you touching another woman, Jered. It's not something I'm willing to accept."

One of his eyebrows winged upward. He could feel the tug of it as if it was a gesture completely out of his control and perhaps it was, just as he was oddly speechless in the fact of her anger.

"My father has always been devoted to my mother. It is something I had grown to expect. Your behavior is simply not to be borne."

She was all pink fury, trapped there glaring at him. Her eyes flashed fire, and her mouth was pursed out and her chest heaving with each breath. She was a summer storm come to command him to behave, a female Zeus all power and passion.

She smiled and again he caught an edge to it, not to mention the fire that had once again sprung to life in her eyes. "And as to returning to Kittridge, I do not think it would be fair to concede the game before it's been played—fairly."

Had she just accused him of cheating? Surely not.

"I will not be a target in my own home, wife."

"Then do not give me reason, husband."

What made her think she could speak to him in this manner? What insolence of spirit caused her to believe herself immune to his anger? Was she simply foolish? An errant thought, and a worthless one. She had irritated him, amused him, bedeviled him. She was willful and spoiled and charming and stubborn and irritating. But she was not stupid.

"Do I have your word never to throw anything at me ever again?" He waited until she nodded before he would set her down. A little conciliatory humiliation might be a good sign also. A little rueful shame. His wife, however, merely slitted her eyes and smiled a particularly thin smile.

"Only if you agree to treat me with the respect you treated that bloody vase."

"That vase was three thousand years old."

Her eyes widened, she looked past him to where the shards were being swept up by a silent footman.

"Truly?"

He nodded.

"Oh dear."

"Is it enough to promise to venerate you when you're an ancient crone?"

"No."

He stared at her for a long moment. Then nodded. Once. In truth, the capitulation eased a tightness in his chest. One that had been present ever since this damnable evening had begun.

His arms were still wrapped around her, and he still had her braced against the wall. Not exactly an inopportune time to recognize that the dress she wore rearranged her curves in some very tantalizing places.

"Did you know that lust and slut are the same words, Jered, only turned around? Do you think it true that men feel more passion than women? Or is it that women have so many more things with which to occupy themselves?"

He closed his eyes. It did not effect the state of his hearing.

"I suspect, Jered, that it would take no more than a few soft looks to turn you into a ravening beast. Why do you think that is so? And why is it that I would very much prefer being left alone tonight? I believe it is because you truly have not apologized all that graciously. In fact, I do not believe you have done so at all. And while it may be extraordinarily ducal of you, it is not quite husbandly."

He dropped her as if she were an armful of hot coals. She straightened, frowned at him, and jerked her dress into place. She mounted a few steps. He wanted to warn her that the distance was not quite far enough away.

"Are you now about to lecture me on how to comport myself, madam? I will leave you, then, with a question of my own. Why is it that I find myself wishing a great distance from you?" He speared a hand through his hair and glared up at her.

"You needn't shout at me, Jered," she softly said. "And I am very much aware of the answer, if you would wish to know it." She was looking at him with that small smile playing around her lips. The same one that was capable of infuriating him.

He mounted the steps behind her, opened the door to his suite, glanced over his shoulder at her. "Very well. What is the answer?"

"You feel badly about the way you have acted, and your conscience is bothering you. That's why it would be just as easy to avoid me tonight. Do you know what my very favorite quote from *The Beggar's Opera* is, Jered? 'The comfortable estate of widowhood is the only hope that keeps up a wife's spirits.' "

He shook his head and closed the door behind him. Perhaps with greater force than was necessary.

"Damn it to hell!"

"I beg your pardon, sir?"

"Nothing, Chalmers. Simply an expression of my life."

"Is there anything I can do, sir?" Chalmers hesitated, his fingers poised at the knot of Jered's stock.

"Unfortunately, no," Jered said, whisking off the constricting garment and handing it to his valet.

"As you say, sir."

"You may go, Chalmers," he said abruptly, striding to the door of his bedchamber. He opened it without looking back to see if his valet had obeyed his order. Why should he? The man had been given a direct command, to disobey it meant dismissal. His servants understood the nature of his autocracy, what a pity his wife had yet to learn it.

His conscience bothered him? He felt badly? He slammed the door again, but while it gave him a great deal of satisfaction, it did not mitigate the gnawing suspicion that Margaret Mary Teresa Astley Mandeville may have been correct.

Chapter 18

~~~~~⌒⌒⌒⌒~~~~~

"**Y**ou rarely come to London, Uncle," Jered said. "Am I to assume there is pressing business that calls you here?" He entered his library, irritated that his uncle had appropriated the chair behind his desk. It was a calculated move, one of power, and both men recognized it as being such.

"You may well say that," Stanford Mandeville said, studying him. It was not the first time he had been looked upon so, as if he were a particularly interesting bug his uncle had just now discovered. He would study it before he squashed it beneath his boot.

Other than his sister, Stanford was his only relative in the world. And yet there had always been this constraint between them. Jered had been fifteen when his father died, young enough to need affection, old enough to pretend he did not require it. It was a good thing, for he had not received any. Only an endless recitation of the complaints his father had uttered. Truth to tell, there were times he'd thought his father had not died at all.

He had thought once that his uncle might have felt bitter about being outranked by a boy barely shaving. He could even understand if his uncle had ever expressed any envy. But Stanford Mandeville simply didn't care that he had been prevented the title because of Jered's birth. As long as there were a set of ship plans before him, as long as his connections at the Board of Commissioners for the Affairs of India still relied upon his advice, as long as there were men to summon him to His Majesty's dockyards, Stanford Mandeville was sublimely content.

Then, what the hell was he doing in London?

"Have you ever spoken at length with Helena Astley, Jered?" His uncle surveyed him from above steepled fingers.

"Why do you ask?"

He went to the sideboard, turned and held up the decanter. His uncle nodded. He poured two glasses, walked to the desk, and handed him one. He walked to the mullioned window and stared at his garden, unwilling to sit opposite his own desk like some sort of recalcitrant schoolboy.

"You must admit, she's an attractive woman. I fancied myself in love with her once."

Jered turned at that admission. "Is that why you were so dead set in my marrying the daughter?"

His uncle smiled, looked down into the glass. "No, Jered. And I have long since decided that I would have been miserable with Helena as wife. She is a rather headstrong sort of woman."

Jered remembered his confrontation with her. "She has passed those traits on to her daughter."

His uncle ignored that comment. "Helena wrote me the other day, Jered. She's not at all pleased by your actions. Says you are making her daughter miserable."

Jered took a sip from his glass, stared out at the path that led from the rear entrance to the stables.

"Why complain to you, Uncle? Surely she did not think you had any influence over me?"

"For all my manipulations, I thought I was doing the right thing by both of you. I was giving my goddaughter what I thought she wanted and perhaps by doing so, curbing some of your wildness."

Jered's laughter choked in his throat, the burning of the whiskey seared a path from his chest to his nose. "*My* wildness?" He turned, slammed the glass down on the sideboard, glanced at the door that stood as a barrier to the outside world. One hand pointed in that direction. "My wildness?" he repeated, the words hesitating on his tongue, restrained there by surprise, irritation, incredulity. The same emotions he felt in his wife's presence.

"Seek out my wife if you would wish to chastise someone, Uncle. She follows me everywhere! She rides through the woods quoting fairy tales, she does not cease asking questions from dawn until dusk. She has even had the temerity to visit my mistress! That is only the shallow end of her transgressions, Uncle, and you have the gall to label me wild? Hah!"

He speared both hands through his hair, clamped both hands on the back of his head, spun to face the window again.

"I am sick to the death of being labeled wild simply because my mother was Scots."

There was a strange look on Stanford Mandeville's face, an odd melding of humor and compassion. "It is not for your mother's birth that I've called you wild, Jered, but for what happened to you after her death."

"I do not wish to talk about it."

"And so you have spent the majority of your life crowding it with excess so that you needn't do so."

Jered turned, amusement wreathing his lips in a genuine smile. ''Is that what you've always thought? My
life is not defined by one event. If the way I live my
life does not meet with your approval, then do not study
it so avidly. Limit your dissections to those involved
with timbers and masts and ship plans. Leave my life
alone.''

''While you flounder in the shoals?''

''I am not some damn ship!''

''Then what are you, Jered? And what are you going
to do about your wife?''

Tessa moved away from the door. She did not wish
to hear Jered's answer. Not because she was eavesdrop-
ping and such a thing was not considered polite or even
decorous for a duchess. She didn't want to hear his
plans for her. They no doubt included sending her back
to Kittridge. Nor did she truly want to hear what he
might declare as his true nature. *What would he have
said? I'm a wastrel, uncle. I'm a lost soul. I'm a man
who was adrift and have found myself back to shore by
the love of a good woman.*

Oh, Tessa, do not be such an idiot.

She placed a palm on the oak door, wishing that the
contact might convey something of her tangled
thoughts. He was angry with her, infuriated at his uncle.
Why, then, should she wish to open this door and comfort him? He did not wish her comfort, that was plain
from his words.

He did not want anything from her.

No, perhaps that was not correct. Sometimes, he slept
in her bed or she in his. In the soft light of dawn, they
turned to each other, each offering wordless comfort.

Yet there was still a gulf between them, one not of

culture but of inclination. She wished him to know those tiny details about her life, her needs, her wants. He guarded his thoughts too well, with excruciating reserve. She was exuberant, he was reticent. Family, it meant so much to her. Did it mean anything to him?

She was afraid to question him too closely about his life, his wishes. Each time she wanted to, she was stopped by the fact she exposed her own vulnerability with each request. She hadn't the slightest doubt that his answer would be a cutting one designed to put her into her place and send her scurrying back to Kittridge.

But she was not going.

Chapter 19

Why the hell was he here?

To prove something to his uncle? Why? His uncle would have his opinion regardless of his actions. And why did he even care? He did not. He simply wished to be away from London for a while. The shipyards was as good a destination as any.

He'd not been able to answer his uncle's question. *Then what are you, Jered? And what are you going to do about your wife?* Had not been prepared to do so for one overwhelming reason. He didn't know the answer to either question.

Jered stood in the Admiral's day cabin, looking out through the steeply canted windows of the stern gallery. Closed wooden cabinets were built against the lower third of the windows, and upon these rested the voluminous set of plans for the *Conquest*. He didn't need to read them; every foot of rigging, every square yard of sail, every iron bracket, every timber, every plank, every instrument was engraved upon his mind. He knew the *Conquest* well enough to rebuild her himself.

The dockyard was the scene of frenetic activity. A new ship was due to be launched in a matter of weeks. Nothing as grand as the *Conquest*, in fact this sloop was small enough to be run by twenty seaman. It required over a hundred men just to raise the *Conquest*'s anchor. There were two more ships of the line being readied for battle, sent here because the navy dockyards were filled to capacity with ships waiting for refitting. Rumors kept the Mandeville heritage well-greased with funds. Each time the French did something absurdly stupid, the fleet geared itself for action.

Would it come to war, then?

Louis XVI had fled Paris with his family. A king deposed while a nation rioted. Jered's attention was fixed on the scene below him. He employed hundreds of workers, artisans, ex-sailors, boatwrights, all Englishmen, added to all the sailors who would occupy this ship once she was sent back out to sea. Hundreds of men multiplied by hundreds of ships. His entire life had been punctuated by one war or another, and each one filled the Mandeville coffers.

For years, the dukes of Kittridge had played with their industries like toys they kept in a musty schoolroom. It had taken Stanford Mandeville only a few years to turn the shipyards into not only a highly profitable venture but a prestigious one. The Mandevilles could rightfully boast that they did not rest upon their laurels but contributed to the crown even to the present day.

The sun glinted off the ocean, a reflection of light to warn of night approaching. Another day, then. He had been here nearly a week. His initial interest in the *Conquest* had turned into something more. *Only curiosity, Kittridge,* he told himself. *Nothing more than that.* She was the greatest of the Mandeville ships. Who would not be intrigued?

She was the largest Mandeville ship ever commissioned by the Admiralty, with one hundred guns fitted among her three decks. The figurehead was of a voluptuous woman, her head thrown back as if in defiance of the waves, her titian hair carved with such attention to detail that it seemed to coil over the timbers. Across her bosom a scarf was draped and on it the words *annus mirabilis* carved. A fateful year indeed. And a fateful ship. She had taken seven years to build, using more than two thousand oak trees for her hull alone. She had three masts, twenty-seven miles of rigging, more than five acres of canvas sails, and could house more than eight hundred officers and men.

Three years ago, she had come home to the Mandeville dockyards that birthed her for a complete refit. Her bottom was being coppered, her hammocks painted; she was destined to fly the flag of Admiral Lord Hood when work was completed. She was, this grand old girl, Jered's birthright. He had been more than intrigued, he had been caught up in it, lost in her spell just as he'd been as a child and watched wide-eyed as she slipped into the sea for the first time.

He shook his head as if to dislodge the memory of that day, with the sun beating down on his head so fiercely it seemed to be afire. The seabirds had flocked and swooped and swirled, and he had been alight in wonder at their antics, pulling his mother this way and that to show her the bravest one, the most acrobatic, the one that seemed to wear a smile. And his mother had bent low and laughed with him, her eyes gleaming with an echo of his own childish wonder. Then she had told him to be still, with her warm hand on his cheek and her smile for him alone, and together they had watched as the great ship had slid into the sea, rocking and swaying and then settling down like a broody hen into its nest.

Why the hell *was* he here? Certainly not to engage in melancholia. He could do that regardless of the locale. And certainly not to usurp his uncle's position as head of the Mandeville Ship Works.

Introspection and memory were a deadly combination. And he didn't want to dwell anymore on what had been. He would much rather concentrate on what was. In the present. Now. Here. Tangible and touchable and as solid as the timbers aging in the sun, the pile as high as the *Conquest*.

It was her fault, of course. Nothing had ever been the same since he'd taken a wife. His very life was shifting, as if he were sinking into sand. While everyone had always been nauseatingly curious about him, no one had ever truly cared what he thought, or felt. At least not before Margaret Mary Theresa Astley had become the Duchess of Kittridge. His dreams had remained inviolate in the sanctity of his mind; memories had been relegated to the dungeon of his past, to rot with all the other half-fleshed ghosts.

But she wanted to understand him, to pull him apart, devour him bit by bit, until there was nothing of him left. Or, like a clock, take him apart to see how he ticked, while having no earthly idea how to put him back together again.

And if he recalled her a bit too much, then it was simply a function of this unease he felt, this notion that he was correct all along—wives should be sent away, to live a life of peace and contentment.

Her lower lip was too full, her face average. Pretty. Perhaps even beautiful at times. Her body, although wonderfully curved, was not extraordinary. Then why can you remember the last time you touched her with such precision, Kittridge?

Her hair had been spread over the sheet in riotous disarray. He had thrust his fingers through it, combing it, then clutching it in fistfuls near her skull. He bent over her, delicately stroking the edge of her ear with the tip of his tongue, feeling her shiver beneath him. His hands went to her throat, bracketed it, thumbs resting in the hollow there, measuring her collarbone, cupping her shoulders. She was like a delicious chocolate that the boyhood Jered wanted to plop into his mouth and crunch in one greedy mouthful. The adult in him urged patience, the tasting of each morsel, savoring the flavor, the continuation of sensation. He licked where her throat curved into her neck, gently brushing away her hands.

Damn her! Damn her. Damn all the saints in heaven. And him, for marrying her. She was an irritant, a complication, a ripple on the smooth surface of his life. She was a wife, and determined to be all that wives were, contradictory, intrusive, maddening. Nothing had been the same since he'd married her. Everything was a bit off, as if he was looking at his own world through leaded glass. There was nothing wrong with his life. He had friends, he had occasional excitement, he had London. What else did a man need?

Not a woman who shouted at him in crowded theaters or threw Chinese vases at him. Not a woman who followed him and got drunk with his mistress.

There was going to be a reckoning, he vowed. Tessa may have run her parents a ragged course, but he would be damned if she was going to dictate the terms of this marriage. Wives were to be silent and submissive. They were to be genteel, docile, and unassuming. Perhaps beautiful so that they did not embarrass a husband, but not endowed with a nature or a disposition that gave other men an idea they were loose or willing to bend the matrimonial bonds.

Perhaps that was the secret to Tessa. Keep her luscious body filled, keep his mouth clamped firmly on hers. Keep her moaning so that she could not question him. Keep her gasping and sobbing so that she could not talk.

She would kill him in a month. Worse, she would make him a besotted fool; and while he was quite content to ardently admire a mistress, he was not prepared to worship a wife.

He felt the chill seeping in through the sill. He stood in the sun and watched the birds swooping down, heard their raucous call and the rhythmic splash of water against the timbers of the docks. He was oblivious to those who glanced up at the stern gallery and noticed his presence.

Chapter 20

It *is blessedly more elevating being in company as a duchess than as a young woman on the matrimonial mart,* Tessa thought as she glanced around at the strangers who surrounded her. *Or even an innocent bride.* She'd acquired a reputation as being scandalously outspoken. People simply did not know whether to be afraid of her or to pity her for her lack of sophistication. Now if she said something considered a little outré, half the people laughed as if she'd told the most charming tale. The other half smiled, uncertain what to do.

On the whole, people forgave her for her idiosyncrasies simply because she had married well. It was not like a scant year ago, when she'd wanted to know all about Mr. Devoncourt's trip to India. Females, that gentleman had informed her, should evince curiosity only about a certain set of topics.

She had sent her mother a look, and Helena had rescued her from commenting upon Mr. Devoncourt's stupidity. As if the world fit into the weather and the opening of Parliament. As if a man really cared about fashion. She certainly didn't. Except for those rare occurrences when she was at the same event as Jered, she could have been dressed in leaves and wouldn't have cared.

Someone laughed, and the sound grated on her nerves. What did she want, then, for the world to be in mourning? It would have more closely matched her mood. But she smiled and accepted the greetings of those who were presented to her, murmuring something pleasant while their eyes seemed to tunnel into her soul. Ah, Tessa, you are very much mistaken if you think those eyes can see past the Mandeville diamonds. The glitter alone rivaled a hundred candles. Why did people place such value on something that was little more than a stone? A pretty stone, to be sure, but a rock nonetheless. Where exactly do diamonds come from? She placed a gloved hand upon her neck, felt the solid weight of them, smiled, stepped back and away from the group that surrounded her.

Why had she come? Because she was so miserable in the town house, adrift in a type of loneliness she'd never felt before, cushioned by a silence that was more apropos to that of a sepulcher. She missed her brothers, the noise they made when home from school, their teasing, their protectiveness. She missed her father, the way he would always take time from his reading or his correspondence to talk with her. And she even missed her mother, but she would never confess that aloud. A family who loved her, people who cared. How simple it seemed now, and how horribly elusive.

It was certainly permissible for a married woman to seek a bit of fresh air, perhaps even safe to do so upon Whitsund's terrace. The house was not far removed from London, a carriage ride of no more than fifteen minutes. It had seemed a good idea to come, to spend an evening being entertained by the sound of voices other than her own, to talk to someone about the world and all within it. Except that oligarchies do not change in a manner of weeks. Most people chose to discuss other people rather than ideas. And while it might be titillating to discuss the Earl of Whitsund's newfound wealth, or the fact that Lady Hargrove smelled of spirits of late, Tessa could not quite forget how she felt when people whispered about her and heads nodded in her direction.

She exited by one of the floor-to-ceiling doors thrown open to freshen the crowded ballrooms. A few couples strolled along the flagstone terrace, a more courageous pair walked along the crushed-shell path to a stone bench.

The entrance to the garden was guarded by two massive granite griffins, beaks pointed outward, wings taut and windswept, haunches carved as if ready to spring. She traced the line of wing with her gloved fingers.

Had Jered gone back to his mistress? Was that why he had not been home for over a week? Only a few of the questions that kept her awake. She closed her eyes, forced away the sight of him naked and muscled and arching with delight over another woman.

Kittridge was looking more like a haven each day.

The raised voices was her first clue to the commotion within. She turned, and the assembly seemed to stop, separate, bowing and nodding. No less a personage than a duke, then, would stir the merry from their revels. And such a duke. A man garbed in night, with eyes the color of mist.

As if he read her mind, or she summoned him, he turned. In that instant, it was as if there was no door between them, as if no one stood in their path, as if the terrace had blurred and become something else.

She turned her back to him, each single motion of her body seemingly difficult, almost agony. She felt him approach, heard his soft footfalls on the terrace stone.

"Whitsund chose well for his heraldry, don't you think?" A voice she'd heard too often in her dreams of late. Rich and warm with a touch of sardonic humor always lurking beneath the words. She turned, and he was there, dressed in his blacks, as was customary for his night prowls. She could not help but note with an eye not entirely dispassionate that he looked splendid. But, then, he always did.

She concentrated upon her fingers' movement against the stone wing. "Did you know, when he was made Earl, he begged the king to bestow the favor upon his late father, so that he would not appear to be newly made noble?"

He joined her at the steps. "A legendary figure, the griffin, with an eagle's head and wings atop a lion's body. It is said, you know, to have originated in Persia." How utterly polite they were being.

"And symbolizes strength and vigilance. Why do you think those attributes are the ones most prized?" she asked.

"Because Persia's history is one of mass murder and deceit, no doubt. A shah makes a practice of killing his brothers or blinding them after he becomes ruler."

"How horrible to kill a brother simply in order to rule. I would think one's brothers would be an asset for a leader."

"Were your brothers always such?"

She smiled. "No, especially not Harry. But I would not murder him, all the same. Do you know, I think it would be quite terrible to take a life. To know that you were responsible for ending someone's existence. The guilt of it must weigh heavy on a person's mind forever, don't you think so?''

''Do your thoughts always meander in this fashion, Tessa? I find that I am not required to make a comment for your mind to go flitting from topic to topic.'' He smiled, but it did not take the sting from his words.

''I am just interested in a great many things, Jered. You would have curiosity be a bad thing.''

''No, Tessa,'' he softly said. ''I believe that I have myself encouraged it.'' A scene of candlelight ecstasy. A flush rose on her face.

She turned away from him. There were few places she could go. To the shrouded darkness and interrupt horrified lovers who had sought the shadows for a forbidden touch, to the ballroom where laughter and conversation was almost overwhelming. Or to home, that was almost the worse choice of all. To the solitary companionship of her room, to wonder and wait and remember.

''Am I to infer that you are about to give me a direct cut, wife?'' There was that hint of humor, but beneath it a cool warning. She was not fool enough to ignore it.

She glanced over her shoulder at him. There was a slight smile on his lips, but the Mandeville eyes were as cold as frost—or crystal, so finely crafted that it was nearly ice thin. And yet she'd seen that look warm until his eyes reminded her of steam so heated by thoughts and wishes and hopes, it was as if his soul was made of fire.

''I was about to return to the ballroom.'' *Because I do not wish to make a fool of myself, and the question burns at me. Have you been with another woman all this time, Jered?*

''Were you? Several people directed me out here.

Sounded inordinately pleased that I had arrived, in fact.''

''The better to whisper about you, no doubt. Why is it they bow and scrape at your face and cannot wait until you turn your back?'' They were evidently the focus for a great deal of speculation, if the number of eyes trained upon them was any indication.

''Because there are not many in that group I would call friend.'' He looked toward the crowded ballroom.

''They seem to spend an inordinate amount of time intrigued with other people and their lives.''

He shrugged. ''It enlivens their own lives, I imagine.''

''But there are books to read and plays to see, and so many other things to do other than to spend it gossiping.''

''Careful, Tessa, you are being as critical as they.''

''And what is the best way to treat such blatant disregard of good manners, then, Jered?''

''Ignore them.''

''And they will go away? Most things are not that easily solved.''

''It has been my experience that they are, Tessa. You really must try it sometime. Apathy works far better than attempting to change everything in your path. And, now,'' he said, bowing, ''I've planned on a night with friends and cards.''

The light from the ballroom was sufficient to cast a shadow upon his face. Tessa found it oddly arresting. Half-shrouded, half-illuminated, he looked the twin faces of man himself. It was an odd thought, but then, it was the moment for it, with him looking at her as if she were a threat to his peace, a source of his irritation.

Those eyes were not cold now but simmered. The fire still glowed.

"Is that what you've done with me, Jered? Ignored me and hoped I would go away?"

A question released was not one answered. Her husband turned on his heel and left her.

"Would you summon my carriage, please." The footman was dressed in stiff brocade, his wig powdered so heavily he created a cloud around him when he moved. He bowed slightly and Tessa stepped back, thinking it a blessing that powder had lost its fashion except on state occasions and on nights like this, when the Earl of Whitsund was desperate to impress his guests.

"Has Kittridge's carriage left?"

"A few minutes ago, Your Grace. Shall I send a runner to intercept him?"

She shook her head, waited for her own carriage. Another benefit of being a duchess. The matter of wealth was often whispered about, in fact her own seasons had been filled with conversations of less than romantic intent. Her girlish companions had been equally astute and knowledgeable about the history of a suitor's family as the sum of his inheritance. In those instances when the matter of wealth was in no doubt, but the degree of it was a mystery, other tangible assets were assayed, such as property. A man was considered acceptable if he had a carriage and four, well-off if he had a landau and a phaeton, and a Midas if he had more than one town carriage, a landau, a phaeton, and a stable filled with matched pairs. The Duke of Kittridge satisfied that requirement and more. But all it meant was that she need not wait until Jered was finished with the carriage but could use her own to return home.

She seated herself, waved the coachman off, and signaled through the open door for the footman.

"Where would you go for a bit of depravity in London?" she asked when he stepped forward. She kept her voice lowered, conscious of the listening ears of the coachman.

"Your Grace?" He was bent nearly in two being, like most footmen, extremely tall. The carriage lanterns mounted on the postern of the carriage illuminated his face and the flush that spread from ear to ear.

"If you were a man, where would you go?" His flush seemed to recede a bit.

He cleared his throat and looked up and down the crowded street.

"There are a great many places in London, Your Grace."

"Then where would you go gaming?"

"Am I a noble?" He had quite the loveliest smile.

"You are a duke."

He blinked at her.

"Then there are only three places, Your Grace, that I could recommend." He named them off, and she asked him to give direction to each of them to the driver.

"Where the bloody hell have you been?"

The ebony door had been opened by the major domo who stood aside, bowed, and then quietly shut the door before melting away into the shadows.

Tessa peeled off her gloves, not an easy task since she'd had them on for hours. They seemed to have become affixed to her like a second skin. To her left was the drawing room, to the right the hallway to the kitchen, the servant's staircase, and the less public rooms. Before her, the steps to the upper floors swept up grandly, and beside them, an anteroom that led to Jered's study, the library, and a small, intimate dining room. The more pretentious quarters were located on the second floor, their suites on the third. It was a perfectly lovely home, decorated in restrained good taste and filled with priceless possessions.

And its owner stood not ten feet from her scowling at her as if she was an intruder. He did not repeat the question, simply stood, barely suppressing his anger. That was quite obvious by the fact he kept clenching and unclenching his fists at his side, and that his gaze had not moved from her for one moment since the door had been opened. She could *feel* it.

"I have quite gotten used to my days being nights and my nights being days, Jered. Isn't that unusual? I feel quite awake, even considering that it's nearly three o'clock in the morning. Why do you think that is?"

He took one step closer. The look on his face was not at all friendly, but she didn't suppose he was to blame. He was fully dressed; the only concession to the hour was that he'd removed his coat. Otherwise he was as he had always been, sartorially correct. A man in his prime, graced with good looks and health, features that were nearly perfect alone but together created a face a sculptor might adore.

That curious feeling came over her again, as if she could not quite control her breathing, as if her heart were racing in her chest, or taking extra beats.

She sighed. "Answer my question first, Jered, then I answer yours. Where were you for a week?"

His eyes were like flashes of lightning, warning of a

storm to come. "I was at the ship works. To inspect my sinecure, if you will."

An answer that surprised her. The relief she felt would be rewarded with the truth then. "I went looking for you," she confessed.

"You went looking for me." A statement. Not a question. As if he could not quite believe it.

"Yes. Well."

"And where might you have gone?"

"I am quite sure I enhanced your reputation, I'm afraid." Another tidbit of truth.

"Explain." How curt his voice sounded.

She brushed by him and raised her skirt with her right hand preparatory to mounting the stairs. The other, gripping her gloves, rested upon the banister.

"You will no doubt be regaled with stories of a mysterious woman coming to inquire for you at your gaming clubs." She named the establishments, and with each he grew more rigid. She really couldn't bear looking at his face, or the expression in those Mandeville eyes, so she looked at the floor instead.

But he asked no further questions, and he did not move, even turning his head so that she could no longer see his face.

"I am not Naomi, Tessa."

She studied him. He hid so easily in plain sight.

"But I'm very much afraid I'm still Ruth."

She mounted the steps and did not look back once.

Chapter 21

~~~ o~o ~~~

S *he's a sweet girl, she'll do you proud. Intelligent,*
healthy. Couldn't do better for a wife. His uncle's
words marched through his brain. So, too, did other
comments. Pauline, who was capable of discerning the
most hidden vulnerabilities in those who came within
her sphere could find nothing more scathing to say
about Tessa other than that she was a charming child.
She was no child. *Tessa toad-face.* The words of a five-
year-old brother. An unwilling smile trembled on his
lips before he forced it away.

I ask too many questions, and I have a lamentable
habit of saying what I'm thinking before I know it. It is
quite disconcerting. She had not outgrown those habits.

The ton did not abide by the rule that if you cannot
say anything good about a person, remain silent. Gossip
was suspended until such time as the individual had
proven themselves worthy of being spoken about, or
decried. Tessa had done all she could to ensure herself
a spot in the compendium of harpy's tales. Shouting at
him in the theater, making a spectacle of herself traipsing around London after him like a lost puppy. He
would not have been surprised if she were the topic of
fevered conversation all about town, the fact that he'd

not heard the gossip owing more to the state of his precarious temper of late, and not to any gentility or restraint among his acquaintances. No one, quite simply, had had the courage to tell him.

Yet she dared to look at him, as if she found him sorely lacking. As if he was beneath her contempt.

He walked up the stairs slowly. She was like a damn flame, and he the proverbial moth. He hesitated at her door, turned and walked to his own suite of rooms. He entered the connecting door without so much as a knock. He didn't need to seek permission from her.

She turned at his entrance. No maid attended her.

The gown she wore was silk; it concealed nothing. Her breasts jutted upward, pressing against the cloth, testing its strength. Her nipples were large, deep coral circles with round, pointed, pouting tips, their protuberance a taunt beneath the thin layer of cloth. He wanted to suckle her through the material, brand her with a wet mouth. Instead he walked closer, reached out and stroked a palm over her left breast, in tender appreciation and delicate seduction. She shivered but did not draw away.

"Tessa?" His voice was a question, a ribbon through the darkness, a curve of crimson satin. She raised her hands, placed them on his shoulders. Her fingers on his skin, thumb welled in the indentation where neck met chest was assent enough. Still, he did not kiss her, simply stood where he was and scented the air. Lavender and warmth. She stood before him with her hair in riotous tendrils, breathing so heavily that he knew she was aroused by the sheer fact of his presence. Still, he did not move, content to savor the moment.

"Yes," she said finally. A word that had been crafted in granite with a blunt stylus, Jered thought, for all the endless time it had taken to be uttered. The fact that it had been only seconds was something he noted with a twist of his lips. His fingers trembled, his insides quaked.

Wives were not desired in such a fashion. That knowledge alone made him wish, with an infinitesimal portion of his mind that was not tied to any other organ of his body, that she wanted it stopped. It would have been safer if she had pushed the door shut, answered him in the negative, even demanded that he leave. She did not deport herself as a wife should. Instead she tempted and coaxed and all with only one word spoken. Yes. It was not a word of defense or enticement, only assent.

She was a candle in the near darkness, luminous and smiling softly, her lips pink, open, slightly moist. She was to be respected not lusted after; revered, not wanted. She was the mother of his future children, but to be so, he would need to thrust inside her with all the force and need of which he was capable, giving her pleasure and ease and sending himself into delirium.

Blessed duty. He had never shied from it.

Her feet were bare and primly together, her toes curled as if in delight. It was ludicrous to feel tenderness for a pair of feet. It was the first time in his experienced life he'd ever felt desire and sweetness melded together. It was a heady mix, one he regretted feeling at the same time he bent to kiss her, hungry in a way he'd never been before, wanting to touch her, to make her feel the same improvident feeling he experienced. He breathed in the scent of her, the breath she exhaled, knew that what he wanted was not simply to possess her, but that this need had transformed the boundaries of simple lust into something imminently more terrifying. He wanted, he realized in a spark of clarity that terrorized him, to be succored by this woman.

When his lips touched hers, hers pillowed them in a comforting, gentle way of long standing. There was no hesitation when she opened her lips, no reservation of sharing breath, tongue, gentle moisture. It was a kiss of lovers, companionable in their passion, well acquainted with each nook and crevasse, curve and angle of body. It was a gesture of welcoming, of satisfaction, of bodies remembering rapture.

Her hand brushed against his chest. His two hands pressed against her back, brought her gently forward until not a breath could separate their bodies. She could not help but feel him, hard and angled and granite where she was smooth and curved. It was almost a perfect joining of bodies, even clothed, that it sent a spike of fear through him. A fire seemed to leap between them, roaring and strange and so filled with passion it was as if a conflagration was promised in that spark incited by tenderness.

He pulled back, looked down into her face, believed in that moment in witches and Wicca and things not of this earth, of the power of sorcery and the power of a woman.

He bent and blew out the lone candle.

The world outside the window was touched with moonlight, a faint sliver of color that dusted the emerald trees and made even more mysterious the blackness of the shadows. Here, in this room, there was the same darkness, but it was tipped by fire and a scent of flowers, and a feeling that grew in the silence.

His lips feathered hers, a gesture not of passion but of testing—or perhaps of taming. His hands ran from the rounding of her shoulders to the violin curve of her back, a delectable and seductive undulation of feminine flesh, awash in a cloud of warm scent.

She cupped the back of his head with one hand, her palm curving along the line of his skull. An invitation given so artlessly to deepen the kiss.

A rhythm began to softly erupt between them, something fed from trembles fading to a soft hum, a gentle crooning not heard and only barely felt. They swayed together as if brushed by a gentle wind, both holding on to the other in wordless passion. It was lust empowered by need, tempered with a melting tenderness.

Her arms surrounded his neck, pushing into him with an urgency that startled him. The touch of her body against his was not so much spark to tinder as it was water to parched soil, a gentle rain of feeling that nourished him at the deepest level. He pulled her even closer, swept his hand down as if he could do nothing without another touch of her, the sensation of his palm against her flesh.

She made a little sound at the back of her throat, something that sounded like a whimper, a sound so provocative and feminine that it aroused him even further.

This sudden quickening, the violent need, was because his body was simply used to being appeased at regular intervals—it had nothing to do with this particular woman.

He reached out and with a hand that shook a little, buried it in the mane that was her chestnut hair, stroking through the heavy tresses and pulling her head back so that her throat was bared for his kisses.

The damnable gown, softly insistent upon veiling her, maintained an ironic chasteness he had every intention of breaching. Impatiently he pulled it from her, twisted it above her torso, freed her arms. Then, just as he was inclined to rip it from her, it magically loosened enough that he tossed it to the floor.

He pulled her onto the bed, pushed away the sheets and comforters. If she trembled, it would not be from the cold. He must, however, maintain some control. Not like he'd felt over the last few minutes when it seemed he was drowning in the hot cavern of her mouth. He'd felt as if he'd been trapped by a whirlpool, mind and body being sucked down into a vortex he could not control.

Where was it written that men were the seducers? He felt less like the instigator of this sweet scene than the lamb led bleating and dumbly happy to the slaughter. Tessa smiled at him, a tremulous, innocent smile with an edge of daring to it. Or perhaps he only imagined it.

His palm slid up her ribcage to the fullness of a breast, cupped it, felt the smooth globe of its perfection, its tip so tightly drawn and needy. Her nipple puckered in invitation; he soothed it with a small kiss, a gesture accompanied by a hiss of Tessa's breath, a short, abortive sound of awareness.

Exploring fingers created threads of sensation as they brushed against her closed eyes, counted the eyelashes, sank into the hair at her temple. And all the time he touched her, he said nothing. Silence, except for their breathing.

She was silk and satin. Nothing was rough about her, not the skin of her elbows or the bulb of her heels. His palms replaced his fingers, and he began an exploration of her that was fiercer than before, more domineering.

Her lips softened beneath his, her mouth was a hot cavern willing to be explored, her tongue touched his with tentative, gentle wandering.

His fingers skimmed over her skin, testing sensation. When they lingered at the inner juncture of her arm, he bent to touch his lips there, marking his possession with a soft kiss. His lips played in the hollow of her underarm, exploring the paradox of tensile muscle abutting tender femininity. Her breasts lured him, their creamy softness a pillow for his tongue, their jutting nipples tender and defenseless, an easy conquest given his determination. He held her captive by that touch, her nipple hot in his mouth, ringed by lips not willing to surrender their prize. Wherever he touched her, her female heat curved and bowed in response to his mouth's greedy demand. Jered wanted to consume her with the carnivorous fervor of a predator, and wanted her to need to be possessed with the obeisance of a sacrifice.

He moved to her side, his fingers skimming along her legs, clasping thin-boned ankles, the curve of knee, dotted along the flesh of her hip where his hand splayed out to measure the angle of pelvic bones, softly stroked through the soft fleece at the juncture of her legs. She moved, a gesture of self-protection, modesty, withdrawal.

It seemed as though the air stilled, waited, expectantly for the continuation of his movement. Instead, she only sighed softly when he continued his tender exploration, having learned more in that silence than she should willingly have taught him.

Yet being prey was not a role she was equipped for; even in her newness to love, she had not been passive. She reached up with a demanding hand, pulled his head down to steal a kiss, absorbed the soft chuckle he made at her gentle tyranny.

He bent his head, his lips touched hers upon the side of her neck. Just that and no more. A brush of tongue to the curve of her shoulder. No heavy passion, no slavering need, yet her trembling accentuated.

Her hands slid around his back, her lips opened wide for the intrusion of tongue, her pelvis rocked up to cradle him, invited his assault. He did nothing but kiss her, spiraling into the sensation of Tessa with a profound sense of gratitude that relished the sensuality of this moment as much as it ignored the niggling voice of warning.

His chest brushed her breasts, tantalized them with the gentle abrasion of hair, teased them with a soft side-to-side movement. Her hands brushed impatiently against the skin of his back, her nails groping for purchase against his sweat sheened skin. Again her hips rocked forward, her legs spread wider, her core of heat invited, entranced, beckoned. He slid forward, a gentle movement, an infinitesimal distance that caused her to shiver again.

When he entered her, slid slowly inside, her nails gripped him so tightly that he wondered if he would bleed from her assault. A question he dismissed when he was rooted deep inside her, his welcome eased by incredible heat and a wet friction unbearably wonderful.

He pulled out of her and she gasped, an open mouth expression of loss and wonder and surprise. He bent and trapped her breasts between his hands, scraping his teeth along the edge of both nipples, creating fire with his sucking mouth, branding her. When he slid inside her again, she sighed, a long awaited sound of welcome.

It was not enough. It was an empty promise of sunlight in a darkened cave. It was not enough, even when he kissed her, mouth to mouth, tongue to tongue. She ravaged his mouth, his amusement over her boldness long since dissipated to become equal ardor.

His lips moved to nuzzle in the soft, damp tendrils of hair at her temple. "Tessa." Her name seemed to be uttered in praise or benediction, or entreaty. "Tessa."

He moved then, and she made a soft, delicate sound, nature and instinct writhing her hips forward to cradle him on his withdrawal, entice him on his return.

She was sobbing now, insistent sounds that ground at his composure, ate away at the remnants of restraint. She could not know how much he wanted to impale her upon him, make her swim in this feeling, the moment, insistent desire, heavenly passion.

He bent his head, mouthed one nipple as she rocked, sucked hard as she made little gasping sounds that were both entreaty and demand.

He slammed hard against her, touching her womb, driving into her with a dominant ferocity. He felt her explode around him, her gasps transformed into a low moan, her convulsions shattering to become tight little shudders in the channel that surrounded him, grabbed him with greedy tremors, inviting him to surrender, nature's plea.

As he filled her with himself, imploding gratefully into the creature they'd become, the niggling voice of warning surfaced, half-buried beneath the ecstasy of the moment. He pushed it away, sensation, fulfillment, satiety more important in these seconds. It was not quick enough however to dismiss the caution.

He'd never felt like this before. Not experienced the wonder of it, the sheer joy of lust and affection. Never before had he wanted to dominate and protect so fiercely together.

It was a warning he could not ignore.

Chapter 22

When her visitor was announced, Tessa sighed. She stood, greeted her mother with a quick hug and a kiss.

Her mother peeled off her gloves while continuing to watch her. Not unlike the stare a lioness might give its prey. A very hungry lioness.

"Well?"

"I take it you've heard," Tessa said. "Frankly, I expected you days ago. What kept you?" She signaled for the tea to be served.

It was rather remarkable, really, to be surrounded by people who knew that a nod of the head or a wave of the hand signified certain things. Almost as if they read her mind. No doubt another privilege of being a duchess. At home she was lucky to get anything firsthand. A biscuit, a scone, a rasher of bacon, all prizes to be won by the quickest or the most sly and held aloft away from her brothers' sticky fingers.

"You're father's been ill." At Tessa's look of concern, she continued. "A cold. He is better. Though, I have no doubt word of this misadventure delayed his recovery. Tessa, how could you!" Here it was, the lecture she'd dreaded. "And not only that, but your father learned of your behavior before me."

"And didn't tell you." She sat. This was worse than she'd expected. Her mother loathed it when her father attempted to shield her. How many times had she heard her mother tell him that she'd born seven children without his help, she could manage her affairs quite ably. Her father never had a response to this, was left to sputter and snort and look helplessly at Tessa.

"You look terrible. Has marriage to Kittridge done this to you? In addition to turning you into a foul-mouthed harridan?"

"In my own defense, Mother, King Henry VIII used one of those words quite often. It was one of his favorite things to say."

"Where on earth did you turn up that drivel? It doesn't matter if the Archbishop of Canterbury is fond of repeating it daily to his roses. You were not raised to comport yourself in such a fashion. And in a theater!"

"It wasn't a bawdy house, Mother." She was careful not to admit she'd been to one of those. There were a great many things about her life that she never wanted Helena Astley to know.

"Cecily Crawford cannot look me in the eye. And Denise is still abed."

Tessa privately thought it had more to do with the cold weather and the fact that the elder Crawford sister was in her sixties, but wisely refrained from saying so.

"And you haven't been sleeping. I can tell, Tessa. You always get those dark circles."

Tessa rolled her eyes and tried not to sigh too loudly. When she heard the tea cart, she sent a blinding smile to Michaels. He looked a bit taken aback by it, but made no comment, simply slipped back out the door with that unearthly silent glide that characterized all of those who served her husband.

"How is Harry?"

"Fine."

"Stephen? Robert? Alan?"

"All fine. And so is Michael and James. None of your brothers, whether they're in school or at home, have done anything to bring shame to the family. Not one. I must tell you, Tessa, that I am extremely disappointed in you. The tales I am hearing are not at all pleasant."

Tessa poured the tea, handed her mother a cup. Smiled and passed a plate of pastries. Smiled again. She wished she had some brandy. But that would be like putting a torch to tinder. Pity. It would have been nice to have been drunk during this encounter. The day after her first episode, she hadn't suffered a headache, merely a dull ache in the middle of her forehead. It had, however, remained there for nearly the whole day, a warning that more than one glass of brandy would have sent her to her bed for a week. Looking at her mother's set face, it was still a thought that had merit.

"What did Father say?"

"Something idiotic about growing up with six brothers."

Tessa smiled weakly.

Her mother continued to frown.

"What do you want me to say, Mother?"

"That you will comport yourself decently, remember your upbringing, your father's position in Lords, the gossipy nature of the ton. That you will endeavor to spend the rest of your time in London remembering that although you are a Mandeville now, you will always be an Astley first, last, and forever.''

That impassioned speech said, her mother sat back in her chair and smiled.

''I know better than to leave you alone,'' Jered said that night, surveying himself in the mirror.

Tessa had always found it difficult to be attended by someone. Her marriage had only worsened the state of her modesty. So many people traipsed in and out of her room with no concern as to her state of undress. Before someone saw her naked, she at least wanted to know their name.

Jered, however, was wholly unconcerned about his intimate needs being attended to that he accepted such servitude without seeming to notice it. It was as if he were simply not there. Nor did he note that this London house was curiously without sound. Not a whistle, a whisper, or a gasp intruded where it should not be. It was as if there were only ghosts attending them.

They had all been quite proper; none of the servants had ever ventured even a shy smile in her direction. The young maid, Mary, had once confessed to a tender feeling for one of the footmen. But even Mary had been less voluble in the past week, as if regretting her burst of initial friendliness. And Chalmers had taken to lowering his lids very quickly when he saw her, a servile gesture of humility that did not fool her one bit.

Jered nodded to Chalmers then motioned for him to withdraw. When the door clicked shut behind Chalmers, she looked up only once, then concentrated upon the pattern of the carpet beneath her feet.

''You might as well come with me, Tessa. If I don't invite you, you'll simply follow.'' She looked up at his words, meeting his eyes in the mirror. She looked away first.

Shyness should have been burnt out between them. Especially after last night. But it seemed as if there were more constraints there than before, as if all the actions taken and all the words expressed in the darkness were being silently refuted in the light of day. If she did not know better, she would have thought Jered angry.

Why? Because she had wept in his arms? Because he had whispered words that were soft, tender? Almost loving? Because last night, she'd begun to think that it might be possible for him to turn into the man she'd always known he could be, someone warm and giving. A man with honor, who used his rank and privilege for good, not simply frittering it away.

"Are you coming with me or not?" He glanced at her and reached for his walking stick. An affectation of his rank? He hardly needed it, not like his gouty uncle, but who was she to tell him that he looked slightly ridiculous with it. It was part of the persona, the dissolute noble. She did not quarrel with the appellation. It fit him too well. But she'd glimpsed parts of him that hinted at something else beneath the slightly mocking smile. Something fine and worth admiring. But it was rare enough that she might have been mistaken, and no doubt an accident that he'd shown her at all.

"Where?"

Those Mandeville eyes seemed to burn into her. Not coldly, not even disdainfully, but with an intensity she could not understand. She looked away again, felt as helpless as if she were a child about to be chastised for some infraction. But she was not a child, she was a woman and a wife. She was no longer the innocent he'd claimed and would not be treated like one.

"Where?" This time, the word was not curiosity but demand. He smiled at her and she wondered if such a peremptory attitude had been the best possible action on her part.

The answer was to a tavern, too close to the docks and catering to a variety of clientele, most of whom would not be admitted in polite society.

She stepped out of the carriage, took Jered's arm. He brushed by the men slumped against the side of the building. War veterans, no doubt. There were too many of them, men without an arm, or missing a leg, blind, diseased, or simply sick. A man cried out to her, not an oath, but a simple entreaty. She pulled away from Jered, reached into her reticule and dropped a few coins into his palm.

Jered pulled her away, his hand on her elbow none too gentle.

"Don't ever give money to them, Tessa, or they'll never leave you alone."

"The man does not have an arm, Jered. Surely you can spare some sympathy, if nothing else?"

"No doubt he was drunk and his loss was as a result of misadventure. Don't see him as a romantic, Tessa."

"How can you not see him at all?"

He stopped, looked down at her. The light from the open door cast them both in barely hidden shadow. "Now are you criticizing my social conscience, Tessa? Next week will it be my attire, madam wife? Or perhaps my table manners? Shall I consider myself fortunate that you do not inspect me each evening to ensure I've changed my linen?"

"If I criticize you, it is only because I wish the best for you, Jered."

His hand sliced through the air. "What is your right, madam? Are you without fault, that you can see mine so well? Who appointed you the vestal virgin of my conscience? You do not wish the best for me; you wish to alter my life into something of your making." He was so close now that she could feel his breath upon her forehead.

His hands reached out and gripped her shoulders. His hands flexed, his fingers gripped tighter. It was as if he restrained himself from further movement by holding on to her in such a way.

"I do not wish to change you, Jered," she softly said. She looked down at the shadows that enveloped her feet. "I just wish to understand you."

"Why should you? Was that a part of the marital vows you took? I was there, madam, I cannot recall one such word."

"It seems you have a problem with most of them, Jered. 'That marriage is ordained for the mutual society, help, and comfort, that the one ought to have of the other, both in prosperity and adversity.' Or have you forgotten those as ably as you have the other dictates of our vows?" At his silence, she added, " 'Forsaking all others, keep thee only unto her, so long as ye both shall live?' "

He said nothing, simply released her, and strode into the tavern. She had no choice but to follow him.

Inside there was no crystal chandelier, no maroon carpet or softly playing musicians. If this was a gaming hell, it was unlike the others she had seen. In fact, it was as disreputable a place as she'd ever seen in her life.

The room reeked of smoke and fish and a faintly rotting odor reminiscent of mildew. As she stepped into the room Tessa realized that while she was not the only women in the room—there were a great many females seated upon men's laps—she was certainly the only one dressed so fine. The gown Jered had told her to wear was of sapphire silk, shot through with gold threads. The bodice was snug, the décolletage dipped low in the center, a dress that would have been considered the height of fashion had she been anywhere but here. In this large room with hundreds of pairs of eyes trained on her, Tessa realized she was horribly overdressed. Worse, she was one of the few women whose breasts were not exposed to the fascinated gaze of the men present.

She followed Jered into little more than a curtained alcove set off from the main room. There three other men sat, waiting impatiently, if she judged their looks correctly. One man with a thin, aesthetic face and wearing a mustache, took his time surveying her from the tip of her shoes to her hair piled upon her head. The look managed to be contemptuous at the same time it seemed to render her naked. She moved closer to her husband, but Jered removed her hand from his arm, a gesture as implicit as his casual glance. There was little comfort there, and it was doubtful if he'd care that she was suddenly wishing she'd remained home tonight.

She had been childishly pleased he had requested her presence. Almost grateful, in fact. A penny tossed from a carriage with a careless hand could not have been more eagerly received. *Do not be an idiot, Tessa.* He did not truly wish her here, that was quite obvious from the way he'd ignored her in the carriage, to the disagreement they'd just had.

Did he think she was an absolute idiot? He had not shocked her before, but he had evidently not given up the attempt. He wanted to have her revile him and hold his occupations in such disdain that she chose to remain at Kittridge rather than be with him. His wife must not slip from the carefully proscribed boundaries he had set for her. And those limitations included saying nothing when he spent time with his mistress, never questioning his choice of entertainments, never making comments about his friends, his future, his way of spending his money. Never, in other words, caring anything whatsoever for Jered Alexander Mandeville.

A barmaid appeared, tray filled with brimming tankards. She slapped the last one down in front of Jered, and then stood with her tray against one hip, smiling at him. She was quite pretty, a young woman with black hair worn curly and short, lips that had obviously been reddened. Her blue dress was simply constructed, with a ribbon threaded through the edge of the bodice. It fell to her ankles, managing to conceal while at the same time advertising her body's curves. There was a clear invitation in her eyes as she stared at Jered. She bent low and said something to him that made him smile. Even from here, Tessa could see her breasts, unconstrained and barely concealed by the blue fabric.

As she watched, Jered untied the bow that fastened the ribbon, slid his hand inside her bodice and pulled free a full and brown nipped breast. To the accompaniment of his companion's laughter, Jered's thumb brushed over her nipple with casual masculine appreciation. The barmaid only smiled back at him, a saucy invitation before she brushed away his hand and hiked her bodice back into place.

He did not turn to see if Tessa had even noticed.

*   *   *

Even the cards stank.

There was something cloying about the air, as if someone had thought to spray perfume to mask the stench. And everywhere Jered placed his hands, they came away with a feeling of stickiness, as if the accumulated filth of a hundred years had never been cleaned from table or chairs.

It was not one of his favorite gambling sites, but one of the most fascinating. Men rarely cheated at cards in this waterfront tavern. To do so meant death at the end of a wickedly sharp knife or simply being coshed over the head and rolled off the end of a pier to drown. And most did not like losing, either, which brought an added spice of adventure to the game. He didn't mind losing, but he often won. Either way, it was more exciting when surrounded by a hundred men who didn't care if he lived or died.

He glanced at his wife, not betraying any interest in his casual scrutiny. She looked shattered, much as he had expected she would.

He nodded as one of his companions suggested a game. Vingt-et-un was uncomplicated enough that it didn't require his concentration.

She looked tired. As well she might. He was damned lucky he could stand up. Another sin to lie at her door. Was she trying to kill him? A ghost of a smile made its way unbidden to his lips. *You really are desperate, Kittridge, if you are blaming her for that. And an idiot if you will discount the fact that she was at the center of the single most erotic event in a life devoted to them.* He could still feel her, arching back against him, holding his neck and quivering as if she were a bow and he an archer, plucking her with skill and strength and . . . damn it, she should be back at Kittridge.

He forced his mind away from recall to the game. He nodded and realized he'd lost this hand. A hundred pounds, then. Price enough to pay for a memory.

He glanced over at her. Her eyes were wide, her gaze focused on a particularly amorous sailor, the view of his lovemaking not at all obscured by the half-closed curtain. Jered followed her glance, winced as the sailor sucked avidly on the exposed breast of the whore on his lap. She was laughing, pressing his face to the white flesh, all the while reaching for a tankard of ale.

Tessa turned, her eyes met his, and as he watched, a flush rose from her neck to her cheeks. He turned back to the table only to realize that he'd just lost another round.

He was disconcertingly aware of her. A warning, if nothing else. She might even become a necessity to his life. She was better off at Kittridge, tending to flowers and children.

He lost another round. This evening was going to be ruinous. Five hundred pounds so far and the evening not half over. Well, he had not come here to win at cards, anyway. It would have been a bonus, but it was not his driving determination for this night.

He glanced at Tessa. "Are you breeding yet?" She glanced at his companions and then back at him. Twin scarlet cheeks bloomed like poppies on her face.

"No." And then, just when he'd thought she had nothing more to say, she straightened and leveled him with a look reminiscent of his grandmother's rather frosty hauteur. She'd been dead twenty years, but it was as if Tessa had acquired her poise and her regal demeanor in the last five minutes. "It is rather difficult for the hen to lay an egg without a potent rooster."

His companions thought that statement hilarious.

It cost him another hundred pounds.

The night grew later, the atmosphere became even more dangerous. Two fights erupted in the other room, one ended in a knife to the belly. The victim was carried off and no one in the alcove knew if he lived or died. Jered found himself losing more and more money, an almost unheard of venture for him. He normally had the wits to stop when it was evident he was out of sorts and losing so badly. But this night and this place and that woman had a deleterious effect on his mind, if not his common sense.

When the entertainment began, he realized he didn't care how much money this evening cost him. It was quite evident that it was going to achieve what he wanted.

The Three Bells was renown for two things, neither one being the quality of its ale or its atmosphere. But a man could win a fortune at cards here, and watch the contest between the whores every Wednesday night. They could even, if they chose, become a participant.

Where the idea had originated, no one knew. Jered suspected it had occurred to someone with a literary mind who had read of a similar test between a Roman empress and a whore. But the Wednesday-night affair was between two well-paid prostitutes, both willing to test their stamina in return for a hefty fee to be paid by the owner of the Three Bells. It had been said that on a good night the pot amounted to enough money to allow the winner to retire from her trade. It was, however, not a spectacle he would willingly choose to watch.

The two women were hiked up onto the tables. They

remained fully clothed, the only concession to the event was that they pulled their skirts to their waist and spread their legs. Whichever woman won was determined by how many men she serviced. No gentleness required, certainly no affection. It was only sex, sometimes quick, sometimes longer. The men lined up in front of the tables didn't care about finesse.

Jered toyed with his cards, lost some more money, intent more on Tessa's reaction to the events in the other room than in his playing. He glanced up, looked away from the sight of two masculine pairs of pale white pumping buttocks. Not a sight to induce passion. Voyeurism was an acquired taste, one he'd not often indulged in despite what Tessa might believe. Yet a young man's initiation into love by an accomplished older woman was much more palatable than this disgusting display. How many cases of syphilis would emerge from this night's fun? Frenchmen labeled it the Neapolitan disease, Italians the French pox. Most Englishmen simply called it the pox, when they referred to it at all.

He had been right to assign her his grandmother's poise. She had not moved, nor had her eyes veered from the spectacle. If anything, she appeared more regal than before. A princess in disguise. He had given her that poise. He was responsible for that look upon her face, the almost frozen countenance. Not an accomplishment, Jered. A shame, instead.

Her hands were folded one over the other upon her skirt, her chin erect, her lips firm but not unsmiling. Simply fashioned, her profile, as for a painter's view or a sculptor's touch. How odd to hear grunts and groans while witnessing such purity. She appeared to be above it, this personage. Was she the same woman who artlessly captivated him with passion? Yes. And trapped him in the web of it.

Why did he feel as if he were punishing her for it?

By the time the evening was over, he had lost almost five thousand pounds, more money than he'd ever gambled away in his entire life. It did not please him to sign the chit, but he did so, along with directions to his solicitors.

He escorted his wife to their carriage with no more thought to their danger than he'd evinced on their arrival. He could acquit himself well with a pistol, and the walking stick he carried, like most, had a concealed rapier. Besides, he was a duke, and it would be death to touch him.

He waited until Tessa was seated in the carriage before he mounted the steps and pulled himself inside. There was a trace of light in the eastern sky. Dawn was approaching. He loved this time of morning, the slow awakening of the night. London was never quiet, but it seemed particularly hushed in these few hours just before dawn as if watchful and still, waiting for the approaching sun. He liked to be abroad on mornings such as these. It made him feel as though he had conquered nature itself, as if he were alive and waiting for the day while all London slept unaware.

Tessa sat in the corner, staring out at the lightening sky with little interest. For a fleeting moment he wished he could tell her how he felt, to share what he was thinking. But to do so would be to diminish all that he had accomplished tonight, wouldn't it?

A great feat, indeed, Jered.

*　　*　　*

It was enough money to support twenty families for a lifetime. Thrown away in one evening. And the other. No, she could not think about it.

She closed her eyes and leaned her head against the cold glass. What kind of man had she married? What kind of man had she believed herself to love? One who could humiliate her so totally when he wished it, who cared so little for his wealth that he tossed it away? Who could evince so little concern about the world in which he lived that he simply did not see the poor, the maimed, the needy?

She wanted to be away from him before the pain she was experiencing could be read on her face. An inch beyond her and the world was a strange domain, peopled by a stranger she thought she'd known. Inside her mind the memory of a lover lived, one who had stroked her skin and held her and soothed her while she sobbed.

She wanted the world back the way it was a month ago. She wanted it back so that she could turn away from him, announce her departure for Kittridge in words as soft and deadly as his had been in the tavern. She wanted it back a day ago, so that she could close the door upon him and never experience a hint of tenderness, a world in which touch conveyed words he was too proud to say. She wanted the world back the way it had been an hour ago, because even shattered as it had been then, it was still better than it had become.

And all the times in the past weeks, when she'd held him close to her heart and thought about how much she was coming to truly love him, despite what he did and what he said, and how he acted, she wanted those times back, too, so that she could tell her heart he did not deserve her affection, certainly not her love. She felt as if something bright and beautiful, something fragile and delicate had curled up inside her. As if all the possibilities she'd dreamed and hoped had given an inward shuddering sigh and then quietly died.

He sat opposite her and remained obdurately silent. Words of apology would never come from his lips. He would never venture an explanation, never wish to help her understand. He was not simply an autocrat, he was an island unto himself, separate, alone. Perhaps even adrift.

Was this his life, then? All her horrible imaginings, all the whispered rumors, all the stories she'd heard had not prepared her for this. Had Jered no interests, other than those of amusing himself? Did he not have causes that interested him or ideas that festered in his mind impatient to be born or spoken or written? Was anything of value to him other than his own entertainment?

Her life had been spent surrounded by nobility, and yet the men who'd been born to their titles had not been simply satisfied to be their rank. They wanted more. Her father was impatient to end the slave trade, banding with William Wilberforce in working to prevent the further importation of slaves into the British West Indies. He had sat with her many nights explaining why he felt so passionately about trading in human flesh, how he hoped one day to see the House of Lords adopt a similar motion.

Stanford Mandeville spent his days designing and building warships, most sold to the crown. He was as passionate about the brigs that bore the Kittridge stamp as Jered was in a pursuit of pleasure.

And there were other men of similar purpose who wished to strengthen their nation, who prepared for the future with the strength of their will and the talent of their hands and the power of their purses and names.

Yet Jered Mandeville was not one of them. Was there nothing Jered wished for in life? Was being a duke all he wanted to attain? Questions she wished she had the courage to ask him. No, it was not the questions she feared. She was very much afraid of the answers.

When he touched her, it was as if he carried fire in his fingertips. Her body was enslaved, her mind was unfortunately free. And spirit? It dwelled apart and alone, horrified and disillusioned, and more than a little sick at the thought of living an existence such as Jered's for the rest of her life.

A portrait was easier to love.

"You seem a bit morose, my dear."

"I believe the word you are searching for is tainted, Jered."

He didn't respond to her taunt, ignored the frisson of emotion that coursed through him at her words. Who was she to judge him? He took a deep breath and exhaled softly, attempting to hide the depth of his irritation. It was what he wished for, was it not? Her retreat. The battle they waged was as important as any for territory. His life, her interference.

"Tainted? A bit melodramatic, aren't you?" He smiled at her but she avoided his eyes.

"Whatever you say, Jered." Her voice was weary. So too the look she gave him. As if she had aged in a day. No, a month. That's how long it had taken for that innocence to leave her eyes. He knew because he'd counted it off in that damnable little clock inside his chest, the one that boomed like a cannon whenever she was around, the one that slowed and then thumped and then nearly stopped when he remembered how it was with her.

A dangerous woman. A woman equipped with a powerful smile, a daunting laugh, and the effortless and unrestrained passion of a nymph. Once she was back at Kittridge, this feeling would leave him. Once she was away, tucked into that little niche he had grudgingly carved for her in his life, he could go about as he had planned. Living his life without the constant judgment in those dark eyes.

"Do you hate me so much, Jered?" The question startled him.

"I don't hate you at all, Tessa. On the contrary, you have many traits I admire." Courage. Persistence. Humor. Intelligence. It irritated him that his wife's virtues seemingly outweighed her faults. She was no paragon. She argued with him, asked endless questions. She was also possessed of an almost maniacal optimism. An emotion that decreed she awaken each day with her smile dusted with hope and anticipation. Had he ever felt that way?

"And yet," she was saying, "whenever we are happy one moment, the next you do something terrible to push me away again."

"I am really not in the mood for the dissection of my character, Tessa."

"No, but then, you do not countenance criticism do you? Is it being a duke? Do you know what I think, Jered? I believe all those entertainments that crowd your days are planned because you cannot tolerate your own company. I believe that you are no more substantial than meringue. Solid looking, but inside you're hollow."

How had this moment been turned on its ear?

"I quite liked the buxom blond," he said. "She may be in the market for a protector, don't you agree?"

"You are doing it again. Trying to hurt me. I wonder why it has taken so long for me to understand that about you. You wound whenever you feel threatened in order to protect yourself."

"Shut up, Tessa."

"Why, Jered? So you can think of something else horrid and depraved and vile to do to me? So that you can plan something that pierces the ennui of your days, provides something to interest you? You grasp depravity and hold it close like a lover, Jered. But even that pales, doesn't it? You become like that poor beggar in the street. Each day it takes more brandy to render him drunk."

"I doubt he drinks brandy, my dear," he said, amused.

She rapped sharply on the roof, and when the carriage slowed, she pushed open the carriage door, shocking him. Even more was the look she gave him, illuminated by the passing street lamp. It was filled with anger, blazingly perfect in its execution. He had done his job well, then.

"I'm not sure exactly what the emotion is I'm feeling right now, Jered, but I suspect it's hatred. I've never felt it before, isn't that provincial of me? How utterly naive. You win, Jered. You can have your races and your circuses and your mistresses. You can rob coaches and parade women naked through your home for all I care. Wager your entire heritage or give it away. Disappear into the ether. It is not my concern any longer. I'll return to Kittridge, and I will never again willingly wish myself in your company again," she said tightly.

She had managed to startle him more times than he could count during their abbreviated union. Now her rage discomfited him as if a perfectly charming lap dog had suddenly become rabid. She managed to shock him even further by jumping from the opened door of the coach.

"Damn it, Tessa!"

She wrenched her ankle in her less than graceful descent from the carriage. But she would not return to it. She could not bear to be in his company one more instant. It was as if all the awful things that had happened in the last month coalesced in that moment to render her sickened. She glanced over her shoulder to see him alighting from the stopped vehicle. She continued walking.

"Don't be a child, Tessa. This is not safe."

He was lecturing her? She nearly choked on brittle laughter.

"Don't be an idiot."

She glanced over her shoulder again. Jered would be on her in two steps.

"I will take a hack home, Jered. Leave me alone."

"The Duchess of Kittridge does not utilize the services of a hired coach."

She turned to look at him. Except for the brightness of his shirt, he might have been a pool of shadows. How apt. He dwelt in darkness, in the worst of human emotions.

"It will be of no consequence, Jered. Footpads and thieves hold no threat to me. I would rather be in their company than yours."

She began to run, her soft kid slippers almost no protection against the wet cobbles. It had rained earlier, and while it had dampened the dust and cleansed the air, the moisture had turned the streets into muck.

"Damn it, get in the carriage!"

She had always been able to outrun her brothers. She dropped her shawl, wished she could have easily divested herself of her stays. But what she lacked in speed, she made up for in determination. She heard the pounding of his boots behind her, for a moment felt a spiking of fear and just as suddenly it changed to become something else. It was not a pleasant feeling, an emotion comprised of anxiety and grief and anger. Still, it kept her racing through the streets with him close at her heels.

St. Agnes was just ahead, and two streets away, the Wellbourne town house. Strange, how the instincts of youth pulled at her. Home. It became not the stately edifice created for the Mandevilles, nor was it their ancestral seat. It was her mother's embrace, her father's protection.

St. Agnes was an old lady of a church, grown to maturity amidst sprawling London. Tessa had attended services there herself. The north of the church fronted the street, so she cut across the south of the church. The dead were always buried to the south of a church for two reasons. The Devil could only enter a churchyard from the north, and the shadow of the church should never fall upon a grave. Superstitions that governed the placement of the dead. But the most touching of all was the fact that a grave was always oriented with the head at the west so that the eyes could view the rising sun. Scraps of knowledge she'd gleaned from some place and which now flew into her mind. Warning against hiding here? The dead could do her less harm than her husband.

She ducked behind one of the tallest tombstones. Some of them dated from the twelfth century when St. Agnes had first been built. Their history had only been fascinating in the past. She had never been squeamish, having brothers would have been a misery if she had been. But still, now was not the time to recall every single story one of them had told her—of ghosts and goblins and women who had been walled up in castle masonry, punishing their offenders and descendants by roaming the earth as vengeful wraiths. She could almost hear the call of their spirits. She touched the stone to retain her balance, and drew back her glove. The full moon illuminated something on her fingers, something shiny, almost phosphorescent. She wiped her glove clean upon the wet grass.

"Tessa? Damn it, answer me!"

She had no intention of answering him. No intention of returning to the town house. She'd no choice but return to Kittridge, even though she'd much rather go back to Dorset House. Life there would be simple again, among people who valued those things she cherished. There would be no more nights turned into days, no more certainty that people cared more for her title than they did for her mind. She would spend her time reading instead of worrying; she might walk in the park and enjoy the fresh air instead of clamping her handkerchief over her nose and wishing that there were not quite so many horses in London.

And the other, Tessa?

She would forget that, too. Memory would fade eventually. Perhaps one day she would not be able to recall how effortlessly he'd introduced her to lust, how joyfully she'd experienced passion.

The moonlight was bright, illuminating the ironwork on top of the older graves, ironically making the shadows appear even darker. The full moon might have made it possible for him to have easily seen her, but then, she doubted Jered would think to look for her here, among the graves of the ancient dead. He would not understand that she would have done anything at this moment to escape him.

Short, thick upright slabs marked the newer graves. She used them as places to hide in order to traverse the width of the churchyard. Ledgers, designed to protect against body snatchers, those men who profited at stealing the newly dead and selling them to medical students, were a more modern innovation. They covered the entire portion of the grave, sometimes even enclosing the body in a solid stone tomb. She skirted the edge of one, ducked behind a tombstone.

"Tessa?"

His voice seemed to come from farther away. He was headed in the opposite direction then.

She stood, tired of her cramped position. There was little chance he would find her now. Still, she took precautions following the line of graves that bordered the small path to the west of the church. She was nearly to the street when she edged by a new grave, stepped on something hard embedded in the ground. It made the oddest sound as it exploded beneath her foot.

The shock of something hitting her chest threw her back against the ground. A sensation of breathlessness kept her there looking up at the sky and the moon. It was directly overhead, looming large like a child's white ball. The ground was wet; the dampness seeped into the back of her dress.

Get up, Tessa. You'll ruin your dress. A lady does not recline in a public place. What would your mother say?

"*Comport yourself decently, remember your upbringing, your father's position in Lords, the gossipy nature of the ton. Remember that although you are a Mandeville now, you will always be an Astley first, last, and forever."*

I am trying, Mother. Truly.

She rose on one elbow. Her right arm was numb. She tried to raise it. It would not move. A sensation of wet warmth trickled over her chest. She glanced at her bodice. The sapphire material had turned black in the moonlight.

She was going to be violently ill. Oh, dear God, not *now*. She forced herself up to her knees, swayed. Her heart wasn't beating. Yes, it was. So faintly that she could barely feel it. But then, she could not breathe either, a giant fist squeezed her chest, reached in and pushed her lungs up into her throat.

She tried to breathe again. All that emerged was a shallow pant. She couldn't even cry out, only emit a tiny little cry weaker than an infant born too soon. She clutched at herself, felt the wetness seep through her gloves, coating her fingers.

What was happening to her?

"Jered?" It was a whisper. No one heard, not one step echoed near. She looked up at the sky, tried to breathe, to call out again. The scene wavered, shimmered in front of her eyes. She extended her left hand. Her gloved fingers scraped against the ground, touched a corner of a ledger stone. She stared down at it sightlessly.

"Mother?" A child's cry, one of confusion and supplication.

She fell back against the ground, mute and defenseless.

This place of gray stone and looming shadow was a monument to death. The pain she felt was oddly out of place, a testament to the agony the living could endure.

Chapter 23

"It was a spring gun," the Earl of Wellbourne said. "Perhaps the intention was good. One that I could, perhaps, understand under different circumstances. I would not want my loved one's grave tampered with either. It just seems to me that other provisions could have been made to prevent grave robbers." *Pray God, Kittridge would not have a grave to tend.*

"I've summoned my own physician," Jered said.

"That won't be necessary. My wife has decided opinions on the medical sciences. She has already sent for someone she trusts."

That news did not seem to set well, either. But then, Gregory Astley didn't give a flying farthing what Kittridge wanted or didn't want at this particular moment. The whole thing had been a horror. From the moment the footman had arrived at their home to inform them that Tessa was ill and had been calling for her mother, to now with both of them standing outside Tessa's room and pretending some sort of conjoined concern.

His wife was attending to Tessa now, alternating between shuddering sobs and a raging anger. It was better for the state of his health that Kittridge not be anywhere around Helena at this particular moment. Not that she would let him into the room, anyway. Tessa's eyes had filtered open only once to spy Kittridge at the foot of her bed. She had simply turned her head away, murmuring, "No." That whispery voice had the effect of a papal decree, a royal edict. Kittridge was not to be allowed near his daughter.

"I want to see her."

He looked over at Kittridge once more. He was providentially glad of the fact that he had a face that did not betray emotion. Otherwise he was certain his son-in-law would be able to measure the degree of his contempt.

"I'm afraid she doesn't want to see you."

"I'm her husband."

"It's a bit late to be claiming marital privilege, isn't it, Kittridge? Why the hell was she in a churchyard? She should have been at home. Or barring that, at a ball or the theater. She should not have been stepping on a spring gun installed beside a new grave. Why was she there, Kittridge? Tell me. If I like your answer, I'll judge whether or not to plead your cause with my wife."

He was not, evidently, the only one schooled in controlling his features. He was treated to a glare from those odd eyes, and then no other emotion flickered on Kittridge's face. Not concern, not compassion, not guilt. Nothing. And not one word of explanation passed his lips.

It was just as well. He doubted if he could have cloaked the distaste he felt long enough to urge Helena to allow Kittridge a glimpse of Tessa. No reason could have been enough to explain what happened; nothing Kittridge could say would be been valid enough or sane enough to balance out the insanity of this moment.

A spring gun! My daughter! She'd been too pale as if all her blood had drained out upon her dress. Her lips had been nearly bloodless, and for the first time in his adult life, Gregory wanted to raise his balled fist to the heavens and scream and rage at God himself. His darling daughter. His Tessa with her laughter and her intelligence and her smile, her brown eyes with their flecks of gold. When she was a child she'd had a habit of coming into his library when he was working, crawling beneath the well of his desk to stand at his side. She'd remain quiet for a time waiting for him to notice her. He'd been unable not to ever since she'd slid open the door. He would hide his grin, though, until she became so impatient she'd tug on his trousers. Then he would put down his quill, pull her up onto his lap and tell her a story until she fell asleep in his arms.

When she was grown, she'd smiled at him and told him, *Yes, please,* that she wanted Jered Mandeville very much as husband. What father could refuse such a daughter?

But that assent might well have killed her.

They stood in silence cloaked in a civility that wore thin as the minutes ticked by. Gregory finally sat in one of the chairs provided. Kittridge stood, his attention occasionally directed to the domed roof that topped the staircase.

Or did he call to heaven itself for guidance?

Gregory doubted it.

It had only been fortuitous that his driver had found her. They had separated to look for Tessa, and just when he was certain she could not be found, he'd heard the shout. He'd raced down the street that led to the church-yard by calls as panicked as they had been loud. Once he'd reached her, he'd realized why there had been fear in his driver's voice.

She had been covered in blood. Her blood.

At first he'd thought her dead. And then she'd moaned, a soft little entreaty that had the effect of stopping his heart. The only word she'd uttered had been a plaintive call for her mother. Not for him.

What the hell did you expect, Jered? It was exactly what you wanted, what you'd planned for was it not? To chill that look of love in her eyes, to harden that soft smile. He wanted nothing to do with emotion, wanted to send her back to Kittridge. To keep his wife docile and submissive, absent and silent.

She was too silent now. Only that one word directed at him. *No.* Simple, to the point. Absurd that he should feel betrayed by it. Unwelcome in his own home.

An hour ago, he'd tried to humiliate her. She'd only sat and took his planned punishment with a regal demeanor that had impressed and then shamed him in equal measure. He'd done what he'd attempted. She repudiated him as ably as he'd wished.

No. A simple word.

His father-in-law looked like he would rather hit him than speak to him. That was all to the good; he didn't know what he could say. What would Gregory Astley have done if Jered had told him the truth? Could the truth be spoken? Could words frame all the confusion he felt, the regret?

He looked up at the cupola, at the stained glass depicting the Greek goddess Gaea, daughter of Chaos, mother and wife of the sky and the sea. It had been fashioned by skilled artisans to attract the eye. The brilliant blues and greens of it were visible even in the foyer on sunny days. Today it appeared oddly muted, dulled by a sun barely risen.

A clatter of footsteps and a short, mustached man scurried up the steps. Behind him came his major domo, no match for the stranger's eager ascent. Jered waved him off when his father-in-law stood, welcomed the man and escorted him into Tessa's chamber.

Then he calmly shut the door in his face.

Peter Lanterly leaned over Tessa and with the apparatus he called his cylinder, listened to her chest again. The cylinder was a foot-long piece of wood, two inches in diameter and hollow. "It is possible," he explained, "to perceive the sounds of the heart in this manner much more distinctly than with the sole application of the ear."

He moved to the other side of the bed, knelt on the side of it, and bent over his patient again. "While the bleeding from the wound has been reduced, it is a bad sign that she has traces of blood upon her lips. Respiration is not audible on the anterior and lateral portions of the right side of the chest. Indeed, percussion is much more distinct. And there is the characteristic noise of fluctuation."

"What the bloody blazes is he talking about?" Gregory asked Helena.

Peter Lanterly glanced over at his patroness's husband. "I am very much afraid, sir, that it means your daughter's lung has collapsed."

At both parents' questioning look, he continued. "There are two lungs in the body. I do not know if it is possible to live without one lung. There is an operation we might try, to inflate the organ once again. But it requires the adoption of a certain risk."

"What risk?" Helena held tight to Gregory's hand. Her gaze had not left Tessa's face since she'd entered the room an hour earlier.

"Pus in the cavity of the pleura, followed by emaciation, frequent cough, yellow, opaque sputa, dyspnoea, diarrhea. Peripneumonia, almost certainly fatal."

"I don't understand a damn thing he's saying," Gregory said.

Peter Lanterly spoke up. "I am sorry, sir, I forget sometimes. What I meant was that infection could set in. Although your daughter, sir, was fortunate in that the bullet did not strike her heart or nick a vein, infection is a very real concern."

"What are the alternatives?" Gregory asked.

"There is no alternative, I'm afraid. As I said, I do not know if it is possible to survive with only one lung. Without the procedure, your daughter will probably die. With it, she may die. There are only degrees of risk I'm afraid."

"What can we do?" Helena straightened. Her back was rigid, her intensity so palpable that it could be felt.

The operation began a few minutes later. The bed was ringed with candles, most shielded by glass, some sputtering in their holders. Clean sheets had been piled beneath Tessa's right side, both to elevate her body and to soak up the blood that would inevitably be shed by the incision Dr. Lanterly would make.

If he erred in preparations, it was in discussing everything he was going to do in such detail that twice Helena wanted to ask him to cease. They were instructed that no one was to speak or ask questions once he began. Nothing was to veer his concentration from the delicate surgery. Their daughter's life was at stake.

A quill, not unlike the ones each of them used to pen their daily correspondence, would be inserted into Tessa's chest. Dr. Lanterly would blow into it to inflate the lung. Tessa had not regained consciousness, a blessing because otherwise she would have felt both the incision and the insertion of the quill.

Helena wished she believed in magic. Or if not magic then, please, let there be miracles. She clutched the footboard of Tessa's bed, looked at her daughter lying so still and pale.

Mother, please? Dorothy gets to wear her hair up and everyone knows what a flirt she is.

Why do I have to have six brothers? Why six? They make rude noises, Mother. I would much rather have had sisters.

Mother, aren't the roses lovely this spring? I think we should name one for you. It has the most wonderful delicate green leaf, just the shade of your eyes.

Oh God. Her throat closed up and she caught her lower lip with her teeth. She looked up at the ceiling and didn't even feel Gregory's arms around her, intent as she was in not sobbing aloud.

"Darling, it will be all right."

She leaned her head against his shoulder, turned her face into his shirt. "Please keep saying that. Over and over. Please."

"How is she?"

Peter closed the door behind him, rolled his sleeves down and fixed his cuffs.

"You are Kittridge?" There was not an ounce of servility in his tone.

"Yes." There was not an inch of warmth in Jered's.

"I have been asked by the young lady's parents, sir, to refrain from communicating with you. If you would know of her condition, then I would suggest you ask them."

"Will she survive?" Obdurate silence. Jered sorely wished to boot the man out of his house, but he couldn't with Tessa's life still in danger.

"That is my wife in there, you idiot," he said finally.

There was a small smile beneath the mustache, one that indicated quite plainly, more than any words, that the physician didn't give a damn what the Duke of Kittridge wanted, whether or not he was Tessa's husband or a stranger off the street.

"Lady Wellbourne told me to convey her sentiments to you should you prove difficult. I am pleased to echo my patroness's words, sir. All her parents can do at this time is to consider what is best for their daughter. That does not seem to be you, Your Grace."

And with a small smile he descended the stairs.

Chapter 24

In the end, it was decided to remove Tessa from London. The dirt, the smell, the noise, in addition to the crowded conditions of the city, could prove a detriment to healing, Peter advised. The decision to take her to Kittridge was made only after hours of arguing. Helena would much rather have preferred to bring her daughter back to Dorset House. But perhaps their home was a bit too noisy, even with three of the boys away at school. In the end, Helena deferred to Gregory, only because she recognized that they were powerless in the face of the law.

Tessa was Jered's wife; he could command her presence if he so chose. As for Jered's assent or denial, his advice had not been solicited. Nor was he informed that his wife was to be taken to the country. It was simply done, the blanket-covered litter moved to the specially fitted coach. He had said nothing. Not one word. That, if nothing else, instilled in Helena a certainty that their decision had been a just one.

She vowed to remain with her daughter. If needed, she would even move the three boys to Kittridge until her daughter improved. And improve Tessa would, or the might of Heaven itself would hear Helena's screams.

When she said as much to Gregory, he only chuckled. Laughter had been a sparse commodity in their lives in the last two weeks.

Every day, however, proved to be a milestone. Tessa still breathed. Each day her wounds healed, both the one from the spring gun and the incision made to save her life. Helena rigorously followed the rules of care Peter had dictated, changing the bandages twice each day, washing the wounds with a mixture that emitted a foul odor whenever the bottle was uncorked. She dusted the powder upon the bandages as instructed. She prepared steam infusions as directed, poultices containing odd ingredients that she did not question. She had sponsored the young doctor since she'd heard of his successful work among the poor, she was not going to second-guess his techniques now.

Each day Tessa survived it was as if one of the bricks pressing down on Helena's chest was removed.

Tessa remained in a sleeping state until the beginning of the third week. It was obvious she was in pain when she roused, but there was no sign of disease, for which both parents expressed a heartfelt thanks to the young doctor. Only then did they learn of his own misgivings, and the fact that Tessa had been one of the fortunate ones. More patients died of infection than their underlying disease.

That night Helena sat beside her daughter's bed, held her flaccid hand and wept.

It was near dark, but the evening did not bring repose to the square. One by one, the candles were being lit in the homes that faced him, light against the encroaching darkness. Soon the street lamps would be ablaze, and the calls would begin as the watchman sounded out the hours, less dramatically on this imposing street due to the rank and the wealth of its occupants. A carriage or two would emerge from behind the structures. A few young titled members of society would become foxed and wander home thinking themselves excessively daring by singing lustily from the tops of their voices. It was London and never truly quiet.

His home, on the other hand, was a tomb. Silent with that well-paid-for muffling of noise. There was no sound of leather slippers upon the floorboards, no lively tune hummed in a hallway, no trill of laughter that incited him to investigate its cause. Nor was there a soft murmur of a voice uttered in thanks. Not one question broached to a servant. They were gone. Only furnished by a memory. Excellent recall was one of his newly discovered talents.

In his hand he held a letter. It had been brought to him this afternoon, and he had barely set it down since. He had avidly broken the seal, then pressed his fingers against the folds of paper to prevent its being opened. Did he want to know? Something seemed to tear within his chest. Something foul and dark with fluttering black wings. His soul?

He had walked through his home for nearly two hours now in a restless summoning of courage. His fingers had dusted along the keys of the pianoforte; his memory had furnished him with a laugh. She'd hated to sing, claimed her voice was somewhere between a croak and a scream. A wisp of a smile made him clutch the letter closer in one fist. Even now she could make him smile. He walked through the kitchens, ignoring the servants who stared wordlessly at him. He brushed aside a question or two, barely heard what they said, emerged alone between his house and the stable—remembered another night when he'd played highwayman.

Where had happiness gone?

But was it ever truly happiness, or only counterfeit, something he'd created to keep himself excited about the prospect of life?

He walked back inside, took the stairs quickly, opened his sitting-room door, went through another connecting room to his chamber, another room, then hers. It was a damask and roses room, warmly alive with her scent. Even now. She'd lain here for weeks, too pale not to be dying. She'd not awakened, had not even stirred. This information he'd gleaned from Mary, who'd cared for his mother-in-law with the same assiduousness Helena had cared for her daughter.

Something fluttered in his chest again. Some demon bat that squirmed in pain.

He had watched them take her from his house on a litter, her face unnaturally white, her sleep so deep it could not be mere slumber. What had he felt? Nothing. He had simply shut off that part of himself that engaged in emotion and felt nothing. Yet now it was as if a tourniquet had been removed abruptly, with no thought to the consequence. The pain of it surged forward, nearly blinding him in a red haze of agony.

Did God hear his prayers? Or were entreaties from such as he intercepted by the angels? Did they act as bulwark against an impassioned plea to God lest he sully the very air his message traveled upon?

Open it. Coward. Open it. He'd told himself that three times before summoning the courage. It was as if he had an anchor embedded in his chest.

"She will live." Three words. The image of Tessa

flowed before him, a ghost of his mind and memory. The sight of her holding on to one of the posts of her bed, her hair unbound and falling down her naked back, her head turned, her lip caressed in a smile. The look she sometimes wore, her eyes as soft and as honest as those of a child's. But no child had clung to him in her sleep, or shocked him with her demand for an heir. Sometimes when she smiled at him it had given him a queer little tug to see such delight on her face, only one more expression in the plenitude of emotions she expressed. He'd seen rapture and amusement, apprehension and shyness, anger and a look so pure in its joy that it almost had the power to shame him.

He forced open the folds of paper again. It quivered in the air held by his trembling hands.

"She will live." He clenched the letter from his mother-in-law tight in his fist. Of course she must. An angel had shown pity after all.

Chapter 25

❦❦❦

"**W**hat are you doing out of bed?"

"Standing. Not very well, I admit, but nonetheless, I have promised it to myself for a long time now. You may even consider it my birthday present to myself."

With a start, Helena realized they had missed Tessa's birthday. She did not ask herself where the time had gone. She knew the answer only too well.

"I no longer celebrate birthdays," she said. "Certainly not yours. To do so gives people the impression that I'm much older than I am."

"Of course," Tessa said. Her smile made Helena bite her lip and look away. Too many nights she'd wanted only for her daughter to live. Now Tessa was smiling at her.

"Are you crying? I am sorry," Tessa said, teasing. "I will tell everyone I'm twelve or that Papa stole you from your cradle. Whichever version you prefer."

"I am not crying, you silly goose," Helena said, wiping the tears from her face quite overtly. "But if that's what it takes to get you back into bed, then so be it."

"I can feel every single feather in that mattress, Mother. Please do not ask that of me."

"Then sit in that chair. Here, I will help you."

The process took a great deal longer than Helena would have liked. But the five-foot journey across the room to the chair beside the window was accomplished with much humor. It masked, perhaps, the degree of Tessa's weakness.

"Do not look so disgusted, Tessa. You will soon get your strength back."

"Well, it's either that or prop me against the door. I can keep it open if nothing else," she said with a laugh.

"Nonsense. You will be standing and running before long. In the meantime, shall I ask Harry to come in and practice his chess game with you?"

"Please do not. Your son does not lose at all well, Mother. He has a lamentable habit of whining. Worse, he accuses me of cheating."

"Then, I could read to you or your father could discuss his new motion with you."

"I have no desire nor necessity to be entertained. Truly." She smiled at her mother. "I'll just sit here and look at the world outside my window." She glanced outside as if to match gesture to words.

"Are you certain?"

"More than anything," she said. "But I know you, Mother. You will check on me at least four times in the next hour. If I change my mind, you will be close at hand."

"Very well," Helena said, straightening the covers upon the bed and vowing to send for the maid. It was the perfect time to change the linen again.

"Mother?"

Helena glanced over at her daughter. Ever since her injury, Tessa appeared older, as if during the weeks' long sleep she had aged somehow—though, not overtly so. There were no lines showing. Perhaps it had been the pain. Perhaps it had been other things.

"Yes, my darling?"

"Thank you." Tessa blinked several times, turned and gazed out at the landscape once more.

"You're welcome, Tessa."

Helena closed the door softly behind her, wondering exactly for what her daughter had thanked her.

Sometimes when she looked at the air it looked as if there was a haze about it. As if there were so many tiny pieces of dust that she could see them falling to the ground. Or as if she witnessed the mist that would shortly change to dew. It was a phenomenon she experienced only in the early morning hours or in the late afternoon as now.

The parkland was covered with frost. It glittered in the sun as if tiny bits of light had been trapped within each blade of grass. The hills that surrounded Kittridge undulated into the distance, dense and shaded with at least three shades of green.

There was the gazebo. She'd escaped there too many times in that first horrible week of her marriage. Someone had told her it had been designed by a famous architect. It was a separate building, its interior carefully screened from the main structure by a clever series of lattices. It was redolent of the scent of roses, and always delightfully shady, with the sun filtering through the intriguing little roof. It had been her favorite spot at Kittridge. An intimate bower within which to sit and think, away from a home built on a large and splendid scale. It had been the only place in which Jered's guests had not come to interrupt her. She'd taken a book of poetry, a volume of Voltaire, a purloined Fielding novel, but instead, her thoughts had drifted to her new and absent husband—much in the same way they did at this moment.

She'd cried there, her face buried in her hands, the tears so wonderfully tragic and piercingly sweet. A lost love. A longed-for love.

There was much about Kittridge to like. Much to dislike as well. She wondered, but had never asked, if her mother had felt the same about her father's home. When she had traveled as a young bride to Dorset House, had it been with misgivings? Had she loathed her new home or loved it? Or like her, had she felt an odd mixture of both emotions?

The house was not to blame. Houses do not create memories, they only hold them inside. People create them with words and actions. Some wise. Some not so wise.

She had not said his name. Had not asked about him or spoken of him. Everyone was so careful not to mention him, as if in doing so they might render her wounded in greater degree.

Jered.

There. She'd spoken it in her mind.

It was the strangest thing, but she could not remember how she'd come to be shot. She could recall everything but that moment, each second leading up to the time in which she must have stepped upon the trigger that activated the spring gun. Except for that instant, nothing about that night had been blessedly numbed or dulled or whisked from her memory.

Nothing.

If he had written her, she did not know of it. If he had tried to call upon her it had not been to visit her inside her chamber. If he was at Kittridge right this moment, she would never be aware of it because she was so insulated by her family. But she doubted he was here, just as she doubted that Jered had more than a passing thought for her after she'd left London.

She glanced at the portrait hanging in her sitting room. From here it was visible through the doorway, a fact her mother had not discerned. Tessa did not doubt her mother would have closed the door, or worse, removed the painting if she'd known her daughter could see it. How strange that she could feel her mother's enmity toward Jered even though a word had never been uttered. Not one word of questioning, condemnation, or accusation. Yet it was still there, hovering in the air like the stench of something foul.

She stared at the portrait. It was almost life-size, certainly prepossessing. But not as much as the man.

His Scots heritage shone in the blackness of his hair, in the grin his uncle had claimed was inherited from his mother. But he'd never spoken of his mother or his father—or the sister who had attended their wedding and been whisked away by a husband oddly nervous and out of place.

As a child she'd felt as if she'd known him forever. Was it because she had spent so many years talking to his image? Even so, such familiarity had not prepared her for the presence of the man. She could render a sculpture of him. Her fingers echoed with recall the shape of his jaw, the tender fullness of his bottom lip, the way his eyes tilted down at their corners, lending him an air of vulnerability.

She folded back into herself. It was a useful trick against emotion. Without much difficulty, she could pull a gray mental blanket over her thoughts, guarding them from such unwise feelings such as regret, pain, longing—emotions that would only get in the way of her living her life from this point on.

It felt as if her innocence had not truly been shed until now. The final barrier between being a girl and a woman had not been severed that first night when Jered held her in his arms and been her tutor and her lover. Nor had it been in all the nights in between, when he'd shown her lust and passion and all its facets.

It was this moment as she stared at the face of the man she loved—and realized with a clarity made painful with the fullness of time that he would never love her.

Chapter 26

The boy halted in the middle of the hallway, stared at him as if he'd grown two heads. For a moment it was a contest of wills, the adult against the child. And for just that amount of time, Jered thought he might lose the exchange. But at last the boy looked down, bent to retrieve his ball and held it tight in his hands. Protection against theft?

"You shouldn't be playing in here. There are too many things you might break," Jered said. When had the ghost of his father inhabited his body? "Priceless things," he heard himself mutter in an agony of maturity. Had he not once looked just as this boy had, narrow-eyed, willful? Jered wanted to jerk the ball from the child's grasp and hurl it through the nearest window just to prove his father's voice had not been uttered through the son's lips. But he did not.

"I'm guarding my sister," the boy said, instead of the curse Jered might have uttered at his age. No, not that young. He had been happy then. The anger had come later when he was nearly grown. Or thinking himself almost a man. Taller than this boy but no less stubborn. The lips were drawn together, a tight purse. The blue eyes were unfriendly. The hair shorter than his, blond where his had been dark.

"You must be Harry," Jered said as the boy only stared at him. "Do you still have your dog?" he asked in an amiable attempt at conversation.

"He died."

So much for that.

"Why must your sister be guarded?"

"To protect her." A look of some emotion—contempt?—crossed his features, nested there. Well, he had not expected anything else, had he? Perhaps not this invasion of Astleys, but certainly no welcome home. And yet, already at the first bout, he was tired of it.

"Where is Tessa?" He had already visited her suite. She had not been there. No one had, lending the rooms an unearthly air of silence. A feeling not unlike the one he'd experienced after his mother had died had drifted over him then, as if a tiny cloud had lowered itself from the sky for the sole purpose of obscuring his view, surrounding him with melancholy. He had left, determined that it had been an errant emotion, one of too many sleepless nights.

"Where is my wife?"

A mulish look but no response.

"Well, she is certainly not in the hallway, is she? If you're guarding her, you're doing a poor job of it."

"What are you, Kittridge—thirty-one? And Harry only eight. A bit unmatched, aren't you?" Gregory Astley stood on the landing, no doubt summoned by that instinct that governed all good fathers. *A child in danger? Yes, dammit.* Jered had wanted to, in a suddenly ungovernable fit of irritation, paddle the youngest Astley. He would have, too, if he hadn't thought the boy capable of biting him.

It had been an unjust pairing. But Wellbourne had been wrong if he assumed that the child would not have fared well. Was it something due to their birth? Or the water at Dorset House? How did the Earl of Wellbourne produce such stubborn offspring? If the rest of his children were like these two, Jered wished a long and active life for Gregory in the bosom of his progeny. That seemed a just enough punishment for interference in his own life. Perhaps more than he deserved.

"Where is Tessa?" he asked again, prepared once more for intractable silence.

"In the conservatory," Gregory said, surprising him. "And quite willing to talk with you." Another surprise. "Eager, in fact," were the words that drifted down the stairs after him.

"Hello, Tessa."

She was dressed quite simply in a green embroidered wrapper that looked as if it were designed after the French fashion. Little more than a saque, it nonetheless clung to her curves, its scoop neck leaving no doubt that its wearer was female and bountifully endowed by nature.

The chaise upon which she sat was new. Or taken from some other part of the house. He could not remember seeing it before this moment. Her posture could have been taken from a Roman etching, a woman reclined, resting upon one elbow. The only concession to an English winter had been the soft throw over her legs.

A slight nod was the only greeting she gave him. No wonder, then, that her father was so willing to divulge his daughter's whereabouts. This was no sickly patient, no whimpering woman.

What should I say? The truth was too onerous a burden to bear, especially for him. *I wondered how you were*. It sounded too conciliatory. Too effeminate a response to weeks of silence. Still, it popped free.

"Are you well?"

A small smile curved her lips, one of secret amusement. Once again, he felt himself outmatched by Astleys, but this time he did not experience the same irritation. Shame, quite possibly. A patently ridiculous notion.

"Quite well," she said, her voice low, effortlessly modulated. Had she practiced it? Rehearsed the tone, the facial gesture of polite disinterest?

"Well."

"Yes." That smile again. Or had it ever left her lips?

"You are still pale," he said.

"I believe that being shot does that to you."

"It was a stupid thing to have happened."

"Indeed."

"You are certain you are well?"

"Quite well," she repeated. And smiled again.

"Other than the paleness, you look quite well."

She was utterly still. Not a finger moved, the only sign of life was her soft breathing, regulated, lifting the material of her bodice. That and the smile that was identical in nature to the first one. Even her eyes, blank and flat in her face, promised no warmer a response.

"I am well," he offered.

She inclined her head. A corpse might have looked the same, head lolling to one side. An eternal smile affixed to a face that showed no more emotion than hers.

"Then having satisfied myself you are fit, madam wife, I see nothing to keep me here." He slapped his riding gloves against his leg, grateful for some movement. Someone in this room was alive. "I shall return to London."

She said nothing to his announcement.

"It is no less than we expected." A female voice, one he knew before he turned his head. Helena Astley regarded him with the same narrow-eyed gaze as her son. It was quite evident Gregory was the politician in the family; his antipathy had not been as evident.

"Go back to London, Kittridge."

"As a send-off, that's quite amiable of you," he said, his irritation blossoming again. Perhaps it was the contempt in the Astley eyes that made it bloom.

"There's nothing amiable about it and you know it. The sooner you're gone, the quicker my daughter can recover from your visit."

He glanced over his shoulder at his wife. Her head turned and she smiled at him. Another innocuous gesture, but was there something in those eyes? A flicker of some emotion not easily buried?

"My wife," he said, looking at Tessa, "seems perfectly recovered, madam. I might go so far as to say that she looks untouched. Almost virginal. Is it your aim that she remain so?"

A slight movement. Tessa's expression betrayed itself still further. *Did I make her angry? Good.* Even that was better than this frozen apathy.

"Untouched, Kittridge? Tessa almost died."

Did she think he'd forgotten Tessa's appearance? The blood staining her dress? The weeks of remaining still and cold, unmoving?

He glanced back at his mother-in-law. "Truly, madam?" It seemed the most innocuous thing to say, especially since he wanted to shout at her.

But she matched him well in temper.

There was not simply contempt in Helena's expression. It was fury. She was unsmiling, a golden virago just at the instant of flaming retribution. Jered wondered what would water her wings and keep her from shooting fire at him.

She walked to her daughter's side, jerked Tessa's wrapper off her right shoulder, the opposite of the one upon which she reclined. Some sound of protest came from his wife, and she tried to pull the material free from her mother's grip. Did Helena mean to shock him? She did so.

"Do you doubt it?"

Once Tessa's skin had been perfect, the hue so pale he had likened it to ivory. This was the breast he had fondled and teased, the flesh he'd kissed and nuzzled and praised. The wound was halfway to the nipple, an ugly mass of red, a knot of scar tissue from which a tracery of scarlet lines flowed. A tentacled horror.

"And she boasts another beneath her breast, Kittridge, where a physician cut her open. He blew his own breath into her lung so that she might live. Do you think her untouched now?"

He must get his nails trimmed. Those of his left hand were much too long. Quite capable of causing four tiny holes in his flesh. Was he bleeding? His right was spared that indignity simply because he was holding his gloves. Strangling them. As he might have done his mother-in-law.

He bowed slightly, a gesture as perfectly chilled as Tessa's eyes, and removed himself from the room.

It was of infinite importance that he escape.

"There. Do you see?" Helena asked.

Tessa pulled up her dress, swung her legs off the

chaise carefully. It had been six weeks since she had been wounded, but she still found it difficult to move without pain. Not as much as there had been during the first few weeks, of course, and every day was better than the one before, but she was never totally free of the knowledge of her injury.

And now neither would Jered.

"Yes," she said, "I see. Exactly what you wanted me to. What did you expect him to do, Mother? Fall to his knees weeping?"

"A little contrition on his part would have aided his cause."

"Jered didn't do this to me, Mother. It was an accident."

"What were you doing in the churchyard, Tessa?" The first time the question had been asked of her. What would her mother say if she spoke the truth? *Running from Jered. Escaping my marriage.* Instead she told another version of the truth. One that had been made painfully clear by Jered's visit.

"It doesn't matter, Mother." Not now.

Helena sighed. "You still love him, don't you?"

Tessa smiled, the gesture no warmer than earlier. It was extraordinarily difficult to smile lately. "I am not sure I even know what love is anymore. Do we love someone because they are like us or because they are not? Did I love Jered because I found things in him to admire, or had I only pretended that there must be something there? Or was I just so certain that my love could change him?"

"If you married thinking to change him, Tessa, I could have told you that was futile. Women have been doing it since time began, and it has never worked."

"But we still believe it might happen. Is it our own arrogance, then?"

Her mother's laughter surprised her. This afternoon had been devoid of all humor. "Good heavens, you sound like Diderot. He wasn't at all fond of women." Helena hesitated, looked up at the ceiling as if to find the words engraved there. " 'Impenetrable in their dissimulation, cruel in their vengeance, tenacious in their purposes, unscrupulous as to their methods, animated by profound and hidden hatred for the tyranny of man.' " She waved her hand in the air as if to summon the rest of the words. "And something about an eternal conspiracy to dominate."

"We sound terribly dangerous," Tessa said, smiling with more amusement now.

"Oh, and indeed we can be. But we women must begin with a bedrock of the truth about life itself. Then, and only then, can we build on it. We must believe not in what might *be* but in what *is*. Then learn to live with it as best we can."

She smoothed the back of her hand over her daughter's flushed cheek. "Oh, I don't know if that makes any sense, my child. Simply accept. Don't struggle against it."

"And happiness? How are you ever happy?" Tessa stared off into the profusion of plants that lined the wall of glass.

"Acceptance, again, Tessa. By taking pleasure in each day. By seeking to find the best of yourself and in yourself. By being grateful for love when it comes."

"What do you do if the person you love isn't capable of loving back?"

"I'm not the person to ask about Jered Mandeville.

My view of your husband is somewhat biased, I'm afraid.''

"You do not like him, do you?"

Helena smiled, brushed her hand over Tessa's hair. "Arrogant men give me hives. And I will confess to being absurdly pleased by the sangfroid you displayed. But if I dislike him, Tessa, it is due in large part to the pain he has caused you. But in the end it really doesn't matter what I think of Kittridge. It is your opinion that matters the most, isn't it?"

"Jered used to hate my questions, Mother," she said, a small, wobbly smile accompanying her words. "Until this moment, I never knew how he felt."

He loved his home, loved the history of it, the sheer theater of its magnificence. Loved, too, the fact that he was the tenth generation of Mandevilles, that his lineage could be traced back to the first duke, ennobled because of prowess in battle.

There were more than three hundred windows to his home, a hundred of them visible from the entrance road that skirted the Nye River. He loved riding down the stretch of old oaks until he came to the curve of the road. Separation made him even more conscious of the beauty of the sandstone-colored edifice that had been in his family for so long.

The Nye flowed under the arch of the south battlements, ensuring a steady water supply even when under siege. Two turrets remained, flanking the outer courtyard, their curtain-wall construction still boasting broken brick and chipped mortar where cannonballs were leveled against Kittridge during the Civil War. There was a piece of history everywhere he looked, as if his home were a living lesson, a monument to the tenacity and stubbornness of the English people. Kittridge reminded him of all the best and brightest that was Britain, a certain indomitable resilience, a belief in the continuance of what had gone before, a smug acceptance that what was here yesterday would be here tomorrow. But right now he could not wait to be quit of it.

His skin felt as though it belonged to someone else. Too tight for this body. He felt shriveled, as if he'd been too long at a bath. Even his heart appeared to belong to another; the tinny little booming sound belonged more properly in a child's body. Not his.

How odd to feel so disconnected. To be himself and yet not.

His horse was fresh, one of the beauties kept in his stables for guests or for his own enjoyment. He was eager to run and Jered let him, over the grass made brittle with frost.

A memory. A damn memory. She laughed at his side, proud of him, every single glance suffused with that pride. She was like a girl with her hair flowing out behind her, her thick burr of a voice caught like the wind and thrown back at him.

He loved to race with her, even though she beat him most times. She would never let him win, either, saying that a cheated victory was much worse than an honest loss.

"Hurry up, Jered," she called, his name rolling on her tongue. It sounded long the way she said it, not simply two syllables. She glanced back at him and he spurred his horse harder, but she was going to win. He just knew it.

The rolling ground was deceptive. There might be a rabbit's warren, a fox's lair, a hole made by a fence post once dug and then never filled in again. Or ice upon the grass.

He slowed on the crest of a hill, forced into prudence by memory. She was gone, his mother's ghost only a mist of recall vanished in a moment. A queer tug upon his heart. But he was not fourteen anymore. And it was wiser not to remember.

He stared back at his home, golden and red in the winter afternoon. Sprawling, magnificent.

Tessa's eyes. How bright they'd once been, even as she'd chided him. How filled with laughter. He should not remember that, either. Or that moment framed in pain. Tessa, helpless and exposed, her wound a target for his eyes. A sign of vulnerability, of mortality. Of how close she'd come to death.

His eyes stung. It was the breeze. A breath of something in the air. A hint of snow, a winter chill. Perhaps even sleet. He brushed his gloved fingers over his cheek. Pulled them away, stared in wonder at them.

His horse was given its head and he bent low over the saddle, banishing caution and prudence and, above all, memory.

And raced the wind.

Chapter 27

❦❧

"You spent too much money on the final details, Jered."

He only smiled at his uncle. Despite the state of the Mandeville coffers, Stanford Mandeville was a notorious skinflint.

"The *Conquest* is a beauty of a ship, Uncle. She deserved the best."

"And what the hell happens if she sinks? Not going to mean a tinker's damn if she has carpet on the Admiral's cabin floor."

"That wasn't where the majority of the money went and you know it."

His uncle grumbled, looked at the ledgers again, squinting. Jered doubted that the overt study of the journal was necessary. He was quite certain Stanford Mandeville could quote each of the *Conquest*'s expenditures verbatim. In fact, he'd stake his inheritance upon it.

"Yellow paint?"

"I was tired of red waterproofing. You realize of course that everyone thinks we paint the decks red to mask the color of blood."

His uncle glanced over at him, removed his spectacles. "Well, it's not a bad idea. But yellow?"

"The paint was a better quality, the timbers will not rot as quickly."

"Yellow." His uncle jiggled his spectacles in his hand, as if considering. "What about the Admiralty? They've quite grown used to red decks."

"Tell them we know that any ship of the line will sustain relatively few casualties. Tell them that the French paint their decks red. Tell them that it offends my artistic sensibilities. I frankly don't give a flying farthing what you tell them, Uncle. The Admiralty is your concern."

"Until I die, and then they're yours."

"Remain healthy for a long time, for my sake."

"I'm surprised, you know."

"That I even knew where the shipworks were? Or that I expressed an interest?"

"Both I suppose."

"Don't bother to look at me with that speculation on your face, Uncle. It was a momentary aberration. A flight of fancy."

"There wasn't a horse race or a party to attend, is that it?"

"Correct."

"And I am not to ask for more from you, Jered? No familial obligations, no interest?"

"Correct again."

"Your sister gave birth to a child last week. Did you know?"

"*Jered! Watch me! Watch me!*" An excited laugh, a pony bouncing beneath her. A giggle and a smile, broad enough to encompass the world. Susie. His little sister. Too damn young to give birth. How old was she? His mental calculations provided something astonishing. And terrifying. She was seven years older than his wife.

"No," he said, surprise melting the words to the roof of his mouth.

"A boy. They've named him Michael Jered."

"It's a common practice, Uncle, to name a child for a titled relative. Done, no doubt, to soften my purse."

"Not because of the fondness in which your sister holds you?"

"I doubt, frankly, that Susan has given more than a passing thought to me these years."

"How long has it been since you've seen her? Your marriage does not count. I do not think you exchanged one word with her on that occasion."

"Too many years. Is that the confession you want?" Jered stood, walked to the window. "I doubt the story is unusual, Uncle. She was five years younger than me. A child still when I was grown."

"Orphaned, however, as quickly as you. Did you spare no thought for her?"

He glanced over his shoulder. "Have there been no rumors about me lately, Uncle? Is that why you have pulled something from the past, some memory with which to pummel me? I confess, then, to being all that you think about me. A poor brother. I rarely thought of her."

"She was ten when she lost her mother and eleven when my brother died. A child."

"And I was not much more, Uncle. If it's permissible to claim some preference for oneself. Susan was taken to a cousin's bosom. I was expected to be a man. Sent off to school again with barely a word."

"Was that the reason, Jered, you've cut yourself off from those who would love you? Why you've never once asked about your mother's family? Because one old man did not know how to look into a young man's angry eyes and explain life and death?''

Jered turned. ''I do not fault you, Uncle.''

''And yet, you do. You said a few weeks ago, Jered, that you were not defined by one event. Sometimes people are. Your father was. I would even venture to say that your mother was the single most important person in his life, and her death the one defining event. He died because he could not bear to live without her. How could I explain that to a boy?''

There was silence while Jered turned and stared out at the snow, thinking of all the things that the blanket of white covered—rocks, hills, crevasses carved when the earth was mantled with glacier and lake. Not unlike what his uncle would have him be, cloaked in ritual, raiment, duty, honor, all the catchwords and icons of his position, if not his time.

''He drank himself to death, Uncle.''

''Slower than a gun, Jered, but just as effective.''

''Do you know, my father never mentioned her. From the moment I carried her, lifeless, into the house until the hour he was dying, her name was never spoken.''

He looked out at the ice-shrouded landscape, focusing on it. Words were so much easier when he could pretend no one heard them. Especially these. A confession of the soul. ''He blamed me, you know. Told me the accident would never have happened but for me. He was crying. And then he died.''

''The question is, do you blame yourself?''

''I don't know. Perhaps. I loved to ride, to race along the hills. It wasn't always safe, especially in spring. And she loved to race with me. Her mare stumbled and she was thrown. Would it have happened if she had not gone with me? No. Could it have happened at a later time? Some other day? Yes.''

"Fate, Jered? Or simply bad luck?"

"I don't believe in fate, Uncle. Or even luck."

"Is there anything you do believe in?"

Jered smiled. An icicle dropped from a branch, shattered. "Precious little," he said.

"You're headed down a ruinous path, you know."

"You've said it before. And, no doubt, you will continue to say it until the day one of us dies."

"You're very close to evil. Or do you even recognize that fact?"

A vision of Tessa's stricken face. A hideous scar upon white skin. He huffed out a breath of air, focused his gaze upon the crown molding at the ceiling and beyond, to where cherubs were painted among a pale blue sky.

"And one day my name will be used to frighten young children, I suppose, Uncle?"

"The difference between wickedness and evil is only a matter of intent, Jered. One must try to be wicked, balancing that which he knows to be right against what seems to be enjoyable. True evil is effortless because that line has already been crossed. Too many times. I perceive you as standing on the edge of a precipice. So delicately poised upon the brink that even the wish to aid you might be enough to send you plummeting to the ground."

"And you wish to spare me that descent, is that it?"

"Evil does not allow for happiness, Jered."

He had no answer for his uncle's predictions, only a question that had sent him here. "What did you mean," he asked in the silence, "when you said that you thought you were giving Tessa what she wanted?"

He thought his uncle was not going to answer. And then, just when he would have retracted the question or turned the conversation to some other course, his uncle stood, came around the desk. He joined him at the window, affixed to the view the way Jered was, as if it were easier somehow to talk to snow.

"She's in love with you. I would have thought you'd know by now. But the very fact of asking the question indicates your ignorance of its answer."

Stanford turned and looked at him. A piercing gaze, Jered thought, understanding the effect of the Mandeville eyes. He had used the look himself on more occasions than he chose to remember. To study, to intimidate, to indicate displeasure, it was infinitely effective.

"She has loved you for a very long time, Jered. I cannot help but wonder if she feels the same as she once did or if your actions have caused her to feel differently."

"Evil, again, Uncle?"

"Yes," Stanford Mandeville said, surprising him. "Exactly that."

"Helena, please be still, darling or I'll never get the silly thing fastened."

"It's only fair, love. You were in such a hurry to get it undone, a taste of putting it back together won't hurt you."

He frowned, staring at the laces threaded through his fingers. "Silly damn thing. Glad it didn't take this long to get the blasted thing off."

Helena wiggled into place, trying to restrain the chuckle that welled up from her toes. Too late. It escaped, bubbling forth into an eruption of laughter as she took pity on her husband and pulled the corset from his hand.

The statue that graced the corners of the library weren't discomposed by the sound of her merriment. No doubt they'd been privy to human grunts and groans for the past century. She and Gregory could not have been the only lovers to have taken advantage of the commodious window seat. When she mentioned as much to Gregory, he just grunted.

"Not in the midst of the worst ice storm to hit the country in years, love. Damned cold next to that window. Not to mention my southern exposure."

"It was a wonderful afternoon, darling." She couldn't help herself, the grin that laced her words betrayed her enjoyment of their play.

"We took a chance, Helena. Even if the boys were at their lessons, Tessa could have walked in on us, not to mention Kittridge himself."

It was a totally improvident thing to do, of course, Gregory thought, eyeing the wrinkles on the knees of his new trousers and then his wife languidly covering her nakedness despite the icy chill of the room. But then, at least they'd been spared the dark and gloomy interior of their guest room upstairs for a few hours.

"I doubt Kittridge will find his way back here for a decade, Gregory. You did not see that look he directed at Tessa. Either shocked or repulsed. It does not bode well for her marriage." She held up a hand. "Please, do not do me the disservice of telling me that I am reading too much out of this. In return, I will not mention that I had premonitions of failure from the very beginning."

He sighed, extended a hand to his wife, now fully dressed.

"All I am going to say, my love, is that I am eternally grateful that God Himself saw fit to grant me only one daughter. He knew that it was all I could handle."

She leaned forward and kissed him, a hot and fiery kiss that recalled the hour spent upon the window seat. He was getting older, didn't she realize that? He decided, as the kiss deepened, that although he was getting older, he wasn't dead, and having a determined wife was not altogether a bad thing.

Chapter 28

"I've a morsel waiting for you upstairs," Adrian said. "A rather exotic variety I smuggled into your bed. She's rumored to be quite talented with her mouth."

Jered only smiled.

"No doubt your initial response will be to find some way of sending her home without taking advantage of her talents. Why do I know this? Because you have been decidedly dull this past week."

Adrian stood, walked to the other side of the room where a crystal decanter resided. "You have not bedded one female in that time and have spent most of the evening staring into the air as if witnessing some specter. I think you would be better served by taking advantage of my largesse. She didn't come cheap, you know."

"Nothing worthwhile ever does, Adrian."

"Good God, but that sounds like the uncle talking again."

"No," Jered said, "only the voice of experience this time."

"How utterly noble you sound. Is this part of a trend? Something to emulate?"

"Do you believe in evil, Adrian?"

"Evil? I have no aspirations to heaven, Jered. I frankly do not believe that I will be punished for my sins if that's what you mean, despite what my Methodist parents tried to instill in me."

"Do you believe in the concept of evil? That it is easier to be unconsciously wrong than it is to be consciously right?"

"Good God, you have been reading too much. What ever brought that on?"

"Something my uncle said. He believes, like Thomas Hood, that evil is attained without conscious thought."

"Your uncle thinks too damn much, and you have taken up that nasty habit."

Jered smiled into his brandy.

"It's the bride, isn't it? Your conscience bothering you? You should have let me have a taste of her, you know. Then we could have compared notes. That would have rendered you less romantic."

One moment he was sitting in the chair before the fire, the next he was pressing Adrian against the wall, his throat beneath his hand. And a thick throat it was. No hindrance, however, for the rage that was flashing through him. Dry tinder to a spark. And that flame had been lit by impossible words from a mouth flattened by his other hand.

"Don't ever," Jered said, his face only an inch from Adrian's, "speak about the Duchess of Kittridge in that fashion." A moment, a breath, a conscious control of his rage. "If you do, I shall have to kill you. Do you understand?" A quick nod of assent, a flaring look of panic.

"Now, get out of my house!" He flung Adrian away from him and strode from the room, not looking back.

In the mood he was in, Adrian would be seeking his own death to remain.

He sent the prostitute home. It amused him that he managed it with such ease. She had claimed herself enchanted by his magnificent eyes, his beautiful smile, his so lovely body. The clink of coins tumbling into her hand evidently rendered him as quickly beneath her notice.

It was an irony that he had not been unfaithful to his wife since the moment the minister decreed them wed. It had not been inclination as much as logistics. Tessa had insisted upon following him everywhere. Then, another factor had added to his fidelity; his wife kept him more than satisfied. Eros could not have been more pleased. Or exhausted.

She had once thrown a vase at him in a fit of pique at the thought of adultery. How amused she would be to know he wanted no woman but her.

A frightening thought, that. One almost as fear-inducing as the knowledge that his life had been altered without his cooperation and certainly without his agreement. The entertainments he'd found so necessary to stave off the ennui now only bored him. *Had she been right? Had the occupations of his life been only to fill a gaping emptiness?* From the moment of their marriage, she had taunted him, irritated him, challenged him. Because of her, he had begun to remember. And he had not even realized how much he had forgotten.

He might have been able to understand it more if Tessa had been the focal point of his recollections. But it was not just his wife who occupied those mindless moments. His mother with her auburn hair and green eyes and laughing smile appeared prominently in his memories. And Susan, little Susie, with doll dragging behind her, thumb stuffed in her mouth, came crawling into his mind the way she'd often sought comfort in his bed during a storm. Even though there had been five years between them, sometimes they'd gotten the giggles so bad the entire bed had shook.

And his father. How odd that he could barely recall the man who had wept as he lay dying, his wife's name an icon he carried into death. Instead he remembered his father teaching him to ride when he was a boy, adjusting his stirrups himself instead of instructing one of the grooms. His father's concern, and then laughter the first time he fell from a horse. Walking with him through the west wing of Kittridge as his father explained each portrait. The feeling of being overwhelmed by the huge paintings that stretched to the ceiling and occupied each square inch of the walls, but being reassured by the feel of his father's large and warm hand encompassing his.

Damn memories. And yet the curse was not shouted even in his mind. It seeped in between the remembrances and recollections like mortar between brick, holding them together but not changing their shape or identity.

The most painful reminisces were the youngest, the least aged by time or distance. Tessa. A woman who might always hold within her the precious qualities of childhood.

"I was but thinking that it would be nice to be a man. Just for a day. Even an hour. To give up my corsets. To swear and spit and scratch. To tell ribald stories and laugh at risqué humor."

"Is that your opinion of men?"

"I have a great many opinions of men, and they vary with each of them. Do you think it's because I have six

brothers? Should I have six points of view, then? Or seven, counting you?"

"Do you think Thomas Paine was correct, Jered? That the monarchy and aristocracy will not continue more than seven years in any of the enlightened countries in Europe?"

"Why do you think birds only have two feet, Jered, and not four? Or are their wings really feet with feathers?"

"My modiste said the oddest thing, Jered. Did you know that black is not really a color according to fashion? It is a combination of all colors. And white is the absence of color. Don't you think that odd?"

"Why do you think silk feels so wonderful? It shouldn't, once you know that all those little worms have had to die for it."

Curiosity, thy name is Tessa.

Too innocent. Had I ever been as inexperienced, as guileless? Yes. Once. A very long time ago.

Had she been correct that night?

A question he'd asked himself too many times.

"Whenever we are happy one moment, the next you do something terrible to push me away again."

He walked into his sitting room, restless. *No wonder, Jered. You poke and prod at yourself with words that are as sharp as daggers.* An unwilling bout of honesty, this. And yet he could not drink enough to drown the questions. He should know, he had tried. When Tessa lay in her chamber, her parents guarding her door, he had remained in his, drinking.

It had been a worthless exercise. He now knew his capacity for indulgence had been lengthened and broadened and extended again. *Another slip, Uncle?* Another line he'd crossed?

He had dismissed Chalmers earlier this evening. It was a cold night, one that did not encourage travel. Ice upon the roads sent a chill into even the warmest coach. Nor were there any places he wished to go. Adrian was right, most of the entertainments he'd seen lately had paled in comparison to his own memories.

What was happening to him?

"She has loved you for a very long time, Jered. I cannot help but wonder if she feels the same as she once did, or if your actions have caused her to feel differently."

No doubt, Uncle. She looked at me as if I were the devil himself.

How's that for evil?

The candle sputtered and was finally extinguished. There were a supply of them in the drawer below, but Tessa did not bother to light another. It did not matter whether she sat in the dark or not.

She had not slept well since Jered had left. A palm rested against her nightgown, over the scar on her breast. Was that why he had left without saying another word? Without asking to speak with her alone?

She really should not care, should she? After all, he'd made it pointedly clear that he did not wish her in his life.

London was anathema to her. She didn't want anything to do with the entertainments that so delighted her peers. She hated the sulfurous smell to the air, the incessant noise, the filth of London, the hint and promise that anything that could be wished in life could be obtained for enough money or power. The Duke of Kittridge had both and used neither to good purpose.

She placed her hand over the scar, rubbed it carefully

back and forth. It itched abominably. A sign, she'd been told, that she was healing. In all outward respects. She could stand and move and walk without pain. But inwardly? Inside where all the thoughts and feelings hid, were cowering?

Memory furnished too much detail. Sleep brought dreams. She was never free of it, this sense of shame so deep it was a part of her. Not only for what she had done but for the knowledge that there were still depths to which she would descend. If he smiled at her. If he crooked his finger. If he whispered. She would smile and venture near and shiver in response. *Oh, Jered. Please love me.*

Her mother was wrong. Maybe not willingly so. But her mother had married a man who had adored her from the moment they'd met. A man who was noble and proud and who was a blessing not only to his family but to the world in which he lived. It was easy to accept life when it was offered to you on such terms. Glowing and radiant and dressed up with greens on a platter crafted of ornate silver.

It was more difficult when everything you wanted was destined never to happen.

Chapter 29

❦

"Your Grace, you cannot mean to climb up there?"** *Chalmers's eyes are so round, they look like tiny moons mounted in his face. A rather apt analogy,* Jered thought, since the moon was full tonight. The better to go plundering in the night. Isn't that what his mother's ancestors would do? Maybe there was a virtue to being half Scots after all.

"Of course I do. I've done it hundreds of times."

"Pardon me, Your Grace, but that was years ago."

"I'm not exactly in my dotage, Chalmers. And you are a poor companion if you've nothing to speak but cautions."

"I beg your pardon, Your Grace. But is there no other way?"

"Not unless you wish me to meet a gorgon or be challenged to a duel. Or possibly brained with a ball."

"Are you certain, sir, that I could not simply slip in the back door and open the staircase? It's for the servants, and they're most likely all in bed by now."

"Why the devil didn't you mention that before?"

"I would not have liked to diffuse His Grace's pleasure in the planning of this adventure."

"I take it I'm being chastised, Chalmers?"

"Sir, could you refrain from laughing?" his valet whispered. "It may well signal our presence."

"I shall remain mute while we proceed to the rear. Although I must admit taking the stairs depletes the romance from a kidnapping."

"I am afraid, Your Grace, that I see nothing the least romantic about this moment."

"As soon as I am upstairs, you can pretend to be a hedgehog, Chalmers, and roll yourself back to the carriage."

"Are you certain, sir, that you require my presence?"

"Come, Chalmers, a bracing sea voyage is just what you need to chase away the cobwebs."

"I truly believe I'm coming down with a contagious rash, sir."

"Or some other type of malady? The sea air is just what you need."

"If I could possibly speak freely?"

"When have you not?"

"There have been numerous occasions, Your Grace, in which I've held my tongue."

When Jered said nothing, he continued. "Are you quite sure you're feeling well, Your Grace? I have not, in all the long years of service to you, sir, seen you in such a mood."

"What you are experiencing at this moment, Chalmers, is an excess of excitement."

"Are you certain, sir?" They were at the back of the house now, not a simple exercise since Kittridge was so large. "It could not be sickness of some sort?"

"Like your nonexistent rash? As no other adventure I have been on, Chalmers, this one is the most stimulating. It is the dead of night, during a full moon. What could be more wonderfully planned?"

"Sir, your capacity for exploits far outweighs my own, I'm afraid. I am a full twenty-five years older than you."

"I shall treat you with the greatest of care. You're to share a cabin with the first mate, and I've been assured he does not snore. Look at it this way, Chalmers," Jered said as he opened the kitchen door and stepped inside. "It could be worse. I could be stealing someone else's wife. This one is mine."

He had waited until her candle had been extinguished, then a half hour after that to be certain she was asleep. She might well scream at his appearance or do some other thing to attract her parents' attention. The very last thing he wanted to explain was why he was attempting to steal his wife out from under their noses. Indeed, why he was attempting to steal her at all. It had come to him, in one of these brandy-laced moments that accompanied brilliance, that he was going about this all wrong.

His heir was now his nephew, a thought he did not particularly espouse. Not that he had anything against the infant. He was no doubt a model baby, and just as certain attractive, given the hereditary qualities of the Mandevilles. But Jered was a young man still with quite a lovely wife, and there was no reason why the two of them could not provide the heir to the ducal inheritance without much effort on their part.

The fact that his wife was not, to all intents and purposes, speaking to him at the moment was a situation he planned on alleviating. After a few weeks alone, she would come to understand him better. He would begin to know how to handle her. They would live happily ever after, and all this nonsense about good and evil could simply be dismissed as philosophical claptrap.

Life, as he had planned it, could recommence.

Her found her sitting-room door without much trouble. He could navigate Kittridge blindfolded if he needed to. In fact, he had on many occasions when he and Susie and some of the servants' children had played on rainy days. Strange, he could recall a number of childish faces that had subsequently grown older still at Kittridge. Grown men and women, taking their parent's places. Some were missing, boys gone off to war, girls lost to marriage or childbirth or both. His mother had been a generous employer, taking in women with children, sometimes adopting whole families. *Was it still the same?* How odd that he didn't know.

The bedroom was dark, but his wife was not asleep. She sat unmoving in the center of the large bed, her face turned toward the door.

"Hello, Jered."

"Do you have the eyes of a cat, Tessa?"

"In the full moonlight, yes."

He smiled at the note in her voice, half amusement, half amazement.

"Are you well?"

"Do you realize how many times you've asked me that since we've been married?"

"It has been a substantial number, has it not? Have you recovered from your wounds?"

"I am considered a model patient. Kittridge has had a salubrious effect on me."

"No fainting, chills?"

"I'm quite healthy, Jered, but you did not sneak into my room in the middle of the night to ask me that, surely? A note would have sufficed."

"Perhaps," he said, his mood quite vibrantly happy,

"but I could not have stolen you away with a note. I am very sorry, my dear, but this is quite necessary." He pulled the comforter from the bed, tucked it around her.

"Am I being abducted?"

"You are, and I must congratulate you on your composure. I was quite prepared for you to be adverse to the notion."

"How? Do you have a kerchief to gag me?"

"Silly woman," he said with a smile, "I was going to kiss you senseless."

"Oh."

He folded the comforter over her and calmly carried her from the room.

The passage out of the house was accomplished with the same ease. He made a mental note to admonish the major domo for not, at least, hiding the silver. If a thief could have entered his home with as much adroitness, he would have been stripped of all his inherited possessions long before now.

The brazier in the coach had long since died a cold death. The blankets he'd accumulated for the journey were nearly as frosty, except for the fur one he wrapped around Tessa.

"I should have thought to bring your cloak, but I did not plan that diligently, I'm afraid."

"No doubt it was not included in the manual on kidnapping," she said dryly.

"Believe me, if there had been one, Chalmers would have read it from cover to cover."

"Is he in on this, too?"

"He is hiding like a coward with the driver. Afraid to face you, I do believe."

"What are you doing, Jered?"

She did not mean his effort of warming her hands, nor of stuffing the blanket into the corner where the draft from the window whistled like the north wind.

"I want time with you, Tessa. Not in London. Not with your parents watching me every second. Time. The wedding trip we never took. Will you grant me that?"

"Why?"

"Why now? Or why ever?"

"Is it because you feel sorry for me? Or because your conscience is bothering you?"

"I do not feel sorry for you, Tessa. Do I pity you? Is that not merely sympathy and sorrow? As to my conscience, have I one?" He tucked the blankets around her, wishing the night was not so cold, that the inn was not so far away. He didn't want her ill. "Give me a few weeks, that's all I ask."

"Jered, I truly do not want to hurt you. I truly don't." She held her hand against his cold cheek. "But I don't want a wedding trip. And I don't want a few weeks. I want to go home."

He sighed. "Well, brace yourself, Tessa, you're going to Scotland instead."

The sight of the inn was blessed relief. Jered had lit the lantern, and they had each pressed their hands against it in order to absorb what heat they could. But the chill increased, and soon they could see their breaths inside the carriage.

Scotland? She didn't want to go to Scotland. But her words had made not one dent in his resolve. Instead he had simply bundled her up and whisked her upstairs, eliminating the possibility that anyone might see her in her dishabille and construe something illicit in their assignation.

The lure of the forbidden.

He was kidnapping his own wife. When she pointed out as much, he'd only smiled, amused at his own outlandishness. She should have shouted the house down, not meekly acquiesced to his plan.

It was dangerous being this close to Jered.

He had stood in the doorway of her room and her arms had almost stretched out of their own accord, as if something outside of herself had commanded—*Arms, here is Jered. Envelope him, please. Hold him close and keep him safe.* How silly. And yet, other parts of her were in accord. Legs wished to run to him, heart pounded stronger, lungs could barely breathe. Breast and loin trembled in secret anticipation.

Oh, Jered, what have you done to me?

Days of looking at his portrait had not prepared her for the sight of him, candlelit. A lock of his hair tumbled down on his forehead. She restrained herself by a thread from pushing it back into place. His mouth quirked into a smile as he placed her gently upon the chair beside the fireplace, moved to close and lock the door. He returned, bent to stoke the fire into full flame.

"I've never seen you do such a thing," she said, unwillingly charmed by his easy gestures, a tanned hand grasping tinder, a fist gripping poker. He'd always called for servants to attend him.

"I am not incapable, Tessa. Simply a duke." His voice was crisp, imbued with that inflection she'd learned to expect. Ducal authority. Nobility. Had he learned such things from the cradle?

He smiled at her look, turned to tend the fire.

"Do you know how many people are employed at Kittridge?"

"Why am I certain you are going to tell me?"

"One hundred twenty-three."

One eyebrow rose. "That many?"

"All those people dedicated solely to your comfort, well-being, your very existence."

"It seems a waste of good manpower, doesn't it?"

He stood, brushed his hands on his trousers, smiled a particularly lovely smile. "Once I asked my father why we employed so many servants. I was, frankly, complaining. There was little possibility of me escaping punishment for any infraction since there were so many eyes looking in my direction. He explained that if we practiced more economy one of the young maids might have to be turned out. She, in turn, would not be able to help support her family, which might mean that they would be forced into the poorhouse. You know your Mother Goose, Tessa. Have you ever heard 'For Want of a Nail'?"

She shook her head.

" 'For want of a nail, the shoe was lost. For want of the shoe, the horse was lost. For want of the horse, the rider was lost. For want of the rider, the battle was lost. For want of the battle, the kingdom was lost. And all for the want of a horseshoe nail.' "

"And, so, to support a family, you allow people to serve you?"

He laughed; the sound of it tied to her heart somehow.

"I see I cannot claim anything where you are concerned."

He poured himself a measure of wine. She accepted its presence in the room the same way she did the tray of bread and cheese. Something he'd no doubt arranged beforehand. As a scene of seduction, it was more rustic than most, but then, he would have been careful not to seem too overt.

"Your questions have the ability to spark my memories for some odd reason," he said. "I just remembered something my father used to say. 'Without a fortune, nobility is merely an illness.' "

He walked to the window, tested the shutters. The wind whistled around the building. The fire sputtered in the hearth, the sheets warmed by a series of bricks, if the humps at the foot of the bed were correct. It was a large room, no doubt the finest the inn contained. Nothing less for the Duke of Kittridge.

Was she supposed to feel like a bride? A feeling of anticipation raced through her—and something that felt like wickedness, something she'd never experienced before.

Let this be our wedding trip.

Tessa folded her hands carefully in her lap, bowing her head so that he could not see, but one tear fell onto her clenched fists, one tiny, betraying tear. A sudden sadness. One brought about because of who they were as much as why they were here.

"Tessa?"

His touch on the back of her hand was like the delicate filament of a spider's web skittering along her flesh with infinite delicacy, prickling nerve endings in an anticipatory shiver. She was unprepared for the softness of it, the tenderness of restraint.

"What is it?"

She shook her head, heard him sigh. He pulled her from the chair, she walked into his embrace, turned her head as if to invite the touch of lips tracing the line of her jaw, memorizing the placement of bone, muscle.

His hands were warm heating to hot, touching her

chin with a gentle grace. He pulled her closer, murmured soft words, nonsense words, words to coax her from her sudden sadness.

He stood holding her, doing nothing more than that, rocking her like a parent might a child. No more than fifteen minutes had passed since they'd entered the room. Yet it might have been years. If this pain was never eased, if this grief she felt was never assuaged, it didn't matter anymore.

If he never held her in his arms, never touched her again, she would never forget the taste of him, the feel of him, or this odd, vulnerable moment when he stood so close and waited, unspeaking, for her to explain.

How could she?

Complicity, agreement, willingness. If she did not welcome him tonight, it didn't matter, did it? Because he'd already insinuated himself past the portals of her mind, opened the heavy door that guarded her spirit, ignored the squeak of hinges rusted by tears. All that was left was consummation; the giving had been done long ago.

She sighed, her heart too full to speak.

"Are you warm?"

Her laughter seemed paradoxically wrong and yet somehow appropriate to this moment.

"Yes." She eased out of his embrace. "But I am very afraid."

He pulled back and looked into her face. What did he see there? Her eyes slid away from his.

"Why, Tessa?"

"The answer is a weapon, Jered. Truth often is."

"And you do not trust me with a weapon?"

"Perhaps you'll become too adept at it."

"What words can I say that will allow you to forgive me, Tessa? What actions?"

"Shall I write down the words for you, Jered? And then pretend to be surprised and pleased and gratified when you mouth them? Was that why you've brought me here? To coax me into forgiving you? I'd almost believe you cared, but we both know that is not true."

A look crossed his face. Anger?

"Shall you command me to forgive you, then, Jered? Wives are supposed to do that, aren't they? Very well. I forgive you. For depravity, and apathy, and wasting your promise. For being a child when the world needs men."

"Damn it, Tessa, you are not making this reconciliation easy."

She blessed the amusement she felt at his look. It banished the feeling of sadness as nothing else could have.

"Is that what this is?" She placed a palm on his chest. "Do you want reconciliation because you've never been thwarted before, never refused anything in your life? Or to seduce me into forgiving you? A bout of lovemaking and I would be a willing and compliant wife?"

"The idea has its merits," he said. "If it didn't, why did you allow me to take you from Kittridge?"

She looked down at the floor, but he would not allow her that. He tilted her chin up until her eyes met his. "Why, Tessa?"

"The truth? Perhaps I missed you. And another truth for you, Jered. We can make love, Jered. Tonight, tomorrow, a hundred days, a hundred weeks from now. And it will be wonderful and delicious and wicked. But it will never make a marriage. There will always be something wrong between us. Something lacking.''

''You've never thought so before.''

''Almost dying has that effect on you, Jered.''

It took all of her resolve not to cry as he walked out the door.

Chapter 30

The *Isolde* sat high in the water, her design making her appear like a swan gliding upon a black sea. And she was not unlike a swan with her graceful lines, the swept-back hull that was neither copper-clad nor reinforced with iron braces. Her four tall masts stretched into the sky, her white sails fluttered in the wind like feathers. Designed as a prototype for the tea trade or for sale to the East India Company, she was crafted for speed not war. Yet in these uncertain times, it was not wise for any ship to be without defense, and so she was to be refitted with cannon after her maiden voyage.

Her launch was a culmination of three long years of work and a revolutionary design that Stanford Mandeville hoped would lead to a whole fleet of similar cutters. He had been the one who'd named her, according to Mandeville tradition, and he'd done so with plans for the *Tristan* in mind. But in one regard he had not followed custom. He was not going to be present on her maiden voyage, having given this privilege and honor to his ducal nephew.

Jered stood at the poop deck. Directly below him was the captain's quarters, given up for this maiden voyage to the owner. Captain Williams would occupy the sail-

281

ing master's cabin to the port side of the weather deck, where the massive wheel and two compasses were located.

Tessa occupied their cabin now, and unless she surprised him greatly, still sat in the same position he'd left her, the edge of the one large bed.

She had been silent ever since awakening this morning to find him sleeping bundled on the floor before the fire. It was the first time he'd ever done so, but he did not tell her that. Nor did he explain that a curious sense of honor had kept him from the bed because she so obviously feared his presence there.

"Why are we going to Scotland?

"To visit my mother's relatives."

"Now?" She had been unable to say anything after that. Had only looked around the cabin, seen the clothing he'd brought from London for her, her things arranged upon the bolted-down bureau. He'd assigned one of the cabin boys to see to her comfort and had left her staring after him, an unreadable expression on her face.

"Hands aloft!" Only experienced seamen manned the *Isolde* on her maiden voyage, and several of them ran along the tops of the yards, utilizing only the foot ropes once they'd reached their station. The main mast was two hundred feet above sea level. Once they were in position, another call sounded. Holding on to the yard with one hand, each man began to haul the sail free with another. This dangerous procedure was known as one hand for the ship, one for yourself, and many an inexperienced sailor had lost his balance and fallen to his death. As Jered watched, the rigging of the sails was set to provide maximum forward thrust. The anchor was hauled aboard, and the sailing master stood behind the wheel, watching for the sign.

This one time, the signal would come from her owner. Jered lifted his hand in the air and the *Isolde* began to move.

It was not his first voyage, but it was the first time he'd been aboard a ship that had never been ocean tested. The timbers of the hull groaned and creaked beneath his feet, rope twanged as it caught tight, pulled against winch and windlass. *Whack,* another sound as the wind grabbed the stiff canvas sails and blew a kiss into them.

She smelled of fresh-cut timber and resin, leather and tar, hemp and paint. Her deck was lined with fluted balusters as finely carved as any found in stately country homes. She was crafted of mahogany and teak, brass and pewter, and as he watched, she came magnificently to life.

The sailing master turned the wheel and she responded to the touch with a delicate shudder through her frame. The wind was her lover, coaxing and pushing, easing her along, until the ocean itself took note, the waves parting to the urging of her bow.

Away from the harbor they flew, out into the ocean. Nothing but open water lay before them. The feeling of being both minuscule and omnipotent surged through him. They would veer north soon, into the North Sea.

He had a smile on his face; Jered could feel it stretch his lips. But even more surprising was the feeling of exultation, as if he himself commanded the sea. He felt himself god of the waters, Poseidon by virtue of his supreme good fortune. He held on to the bow rigging, felt the surge of ocean beneath his feet, realized he was laughing as the *Isolde* skipped over the waves.

"Sir?" A tug on his arm. He looked down.

The cabin boy was no more than ten years old, but

pink-cheeked and solid. He did not have the frail appearance of most of the young of London. How odd that he just now realized he did not have the acquaintance of any children. There was Harry, of course. But none of his friends possessed any, and as his uncle had been quick to point out, he had never wished any information about his Scots relatives. He had certainly cut off his sister's good will.

"Sir?" Jered shook his head, glanced down at the boy again. "Your Grace, begging your pardon, sir, but herself is sick."

"My wife?"

"Aye, sir. She don't want me to call you, sir, but she's been puking ever since we left the harbor."

He descended the steps, pushed open the door to the cabin. A shaft of sunlight slanted over the bed. Tessa lay with her arm over her eyes, the other hand clutching the bedcovers.

She didn't speak, just waved a hand in front of her. To ward him off, or to communicate, he didn't know. There was a look of such utter rigidity on her face that it frightened him. She didn't move, but he could hear the slight hitch of her breath, as if the movement brought her pain, as he sat on the edge of the bed.

"We don't have no surgeon on board, sir."

A look passed between the two males, a look not entirely that of employer and employee, adult and child. It was comprised of entreaty, complicity, and helplessness, equally shared and equally felt.

Tessa turned her head.

A wiggle of her fingers drew him forward. He leaned close to her lips as she whispered. "I am sorry, Jered, but I believe in addition to disliking perch phaetons and horses that I also heartily loathe the ocean."

"Are you feeling ill? Do you need a basin?"

"Yes." It was a sibilant whisper; a murmur, no more—but one of heartfelt agreement. He grabbed the one thrust at him by the cabin boy just in time. She retched horribly, over and over. It was as if her body wished to rid itself not only of her breakfast but of every meal since she'd been born.

He waved the boy outside, bid him return with warm tea and some toast if a fire had been lit. If not, he would give her some brandy in the hopes that it would settle her stomach. He wished he knew of something more worthwhile to do, something that would soothe her pain.

He brought her a wet cloth, helped her rinse her mouth, then sat on the edge of the bed and performed a ritual he'd discharged often but never with nurturing in mind. She lay silent, eyes closed, while he extracted every pin from her hair, placing them on the wooden chest beside the bed. Then he took her brush from the case he'd brought from London, carefully brushed her hair. It seemed to relax her, because she murmured something, eyes still closed.

She curled into a ball, her clasped hands beneath her chin. A shiver skittered across her skin. He reached for the blanket neatly folded over the foot of the bed, shook it out, and softly covered her.

He should have allowed her the silence in which she encapsulated herself, left her alone. Instead he sat beside her and stroked his hand down her blanketed arm. Comfort. How odd that he should wish to bestow it. Even stranger that her discomfort plucked forth his own.

"I'll be fine," she answered in response to his question a few minutes later, wishing only two things on this earth—that Jered would cease being solicitous, that he would just go away and let her get through this in peace. She was more embarrassed than she'd ever been in her entire life, a condition only increased by being in her husband's embrace. Somehow his arm had extended around her, her face was pressed against his shirted chest. He was silent and still and so warm and comforting that she felt the beginning of tears pepper her eyes.

She pulled away from him, rolling into a tight ball. The odor of sickness hung like a miasma between them; she was not about to deepen her disgrace by adding to it with her tears.

Tessa heard two loud clumps on the wooden floor, and then Jered climbed in beside her on the bed, gently moving until he was behind her and she was cradled against him spoon fashion. His arm reached out and curved over her, not touching, but making a statement as possessive as if words had been spoken. It was so determinedly male that she would have smiled if she had not felt so awful.

Hours later, he still held her, unmoving. She stretched, realizing she must have drifted off to sleep. Jered's kiss on her forehead signaled he knew she was awake, and she smiled gently to acknowledge she was willing to face him again. She moved, lay flat on her back, eyes closed. Surveying the state of her health, she was surprised by the scent of lemon and the fact that her stomach rumbled. In preparation for another bout of sickness, or hunger?

She blinked open her eyes and Jered was there, leaning over her. He smiled, brushed back her hair from her forehead.

"You snore, did you know?"

"I do not. Old bald men snore, not delicate, well-bred ladies."

His smile broadened.

"I don't really, do I?"

"Just softly. A snuffle or two."

She closed her eyes again.

"Do I?"

She opened her eyes, surveyed him. "I don't know. There haven't been many occasions when we've slept together."

An inventory of memory was taken in a flash of time. They'd rarely been together in a bedchamber and unoccupied with other, more carnal, concerns. The only time they'd allowed each other the vulnerability of sleep had been on their wedding night, and that had ended with his leaving her. Until this afternoon, adrift in a wordless world of unvoiced comfort, he'd never held her for the peace of it, for the wish to assuage her pain.

Even when she lay close to death, he had not been near.

"Were you frightened?"

She didn't ask what he meant. The source of his question was there in his eyes. "I don't remember much of it. Only that there was no pain at all and then there was. I have shadow images now, odd little vignettes of memory, but even that fades more each day. My mother and father holding me down, my father cursing and Mother crying. I remember Stephen and Alan praying over me. Stephen wishes to be a bishop and he was practicing, I think."

"And Alan?"

"He is closest in age to Harry and believes himself to be a great warrior. I am sure he lost a bet to Stephen, which is why he was holding the incense burner."

"You had your brothers with you but no husband."

"Oh, but I did have you," she said, a small smile teasing him. "I had your portrait."

He frowned. "Which portrait?"

"The one where you're standing next to a pediment."

"Is there a dog in it? One that looks like a rat?"

"No. No dog. But you look perfectly wicked in it, as if you know a secret jest."

"No doubt."

"You have the oddest look on your face right now, Jered. Are you embarrassed?"

"Hardly." He played with a fold of sheet, creasing it into a pattern.

"You are." She raised herself up on an elbow, smiled at the notion of Jered Mandeville embarrassed.

"If you must know, when I was posing, I was thinking of all the ways I could seduce the artist's daughter. As I remember, she flitted in and out of the studio on all sorts of errands for her father."

"I'd heard the artist was a woman."

"You've no doubt heard a great many things about me," he said, leaning back against the headboard. "Most of them regrettably true. In this case, however, the artist was a wizened old man."

"It's beautiful whoever painted it. You became my dearest friend, you know. I used to sit and talk with you as if you listened." *Should I be telling him things like this?* Perhaps not, but the day had been filled with surprises, from boarding this beautiful ship to the time he'd spent with her.

"And found the reality did not quite match the painted image?"

That was too close to the truth. She said nothing.

"What did you tell me?

"What I thought mostly. I had a difficult time during my seasons. Father has often told me that I must not tell people what I think, and I must, on all accounts, remember his position in the world. What I do reflected upon him, you see."

"A wise parent would say so. I needn't bring up the incident at the theater, I trust."

"Thank you," she said, looking away from his smile. "It was very difficult being a society miss. The only appropriate conversation was the weather. And the only expression allowed is one of bemused detachment. I cannot think why I thought my second season to be better than my first. I was doomed to be a failure, I think. A blossom beyond its first bloom."

"Are you certain you are not seeking compliments by that statement? I cannot think of a sillier thing you've ever said."

"Which is a great compliment, Jered. Thank you."

"Was there no suitor to interest you, then?"

"In truth, I cannot remember a single one."

"No one?"

"Well, there was Mr. Randolph, but if you ever speak with him, he will regale you with stories of how I spilled punch on his new embroidered waistcoat."

"Everyone knows those balls are too blessed crowded to breathe."

"Or Mr. Hawthorne. He declared his undying love in the rose arbor."

"Why were you in the rose arbor with a suitor in the first place?" Her husband had the most forbidding frown upon his face.

"Because my hostess declared that the new Sophie bloom was the most exquisite delight and I must simply show it to Mr. Hawthorne, whose father dabbles in such things. It was not that I was embarrassed by his fulsome declaration, it was simply that I was taken aback by it. I believed him to be amusing me at first with a theatrical rendition of undying love. I managed to restrain my shock until he got to the part that his soul would perish like a fort yielding at night, having been besieged in the morning.''

"The damn fool stole that from Cervantes.''

"Unfortunately I mentioned that it sounded like a passage I knew, at which he replied that a proper woman knows only two things, the sound of her husband's voice and when to smile.''

"Having been on the cutting end of your temper, I trust you did not enable that fool to live past a few minutes.'' His grin was anticipatory.

"I confess I don't remember exactly what I told him.''

"There you were, then, graduated from the Hawthornes of the world, yet you chanced upon a duke with the same arrogance.''

"You are quite good at letting people know exactly what you think of them, Jered, without a word being spoken. It's the Mandeville eyes. Or your effortless arrogance.''

In the past, such a moment might have been filled with irritation, anger masking hurt feelings on either side. Perhaps because of the past several hours, because there was nowhere to go other than this spacious cabin, they smiled at each other. Perfectly content for the moment.

Tessa wondered how long it would last.

*   *   *

"My wife will not be requiring the carriage after all," Gregory told the footman. With a bow, the young man backed out of the room.

Helena halted in the middle of her packing and turned to him.

"You didn't like my mother," he said.

Helena had not expected that statement. An impassioned plea not to follow Tessa, yes. A comment upon the impossibility of it. That too. But not this odd remark.

"No, I did not." She sat down on the bench in front of her vanity. "Although I tried, Gregory. You know I did."

"She was very attached to me."

"She was too attached, Gregory." She frowned at her husband. "Oh, I see. I'm supposed to have some type of revelation, is that it? Your mother made my life miserable, as you know quite well. She meddled. I am but concerned."

"A word my mother used often in conjunction with you, I remember."

"Did she?"

"She did not believe you were worthy of me, you know."

"Really."

"With that look on your face, Helena, should I be grateful that the poor dear expired of influenza only a year after we were wed?"

"The poor dear," Helena said, "was an absolute terror."

"I wonder if Kittridge would say the same."

"That truly was a horrid thing to say, Gregory."

"What you are contemplating is not wise, Helena. You could possibly mar their only chance for happiness.

Is that what you want? To have Tessa wander through Dorset House in the same wan manner she's been prowling through Kittridge? She's been miserable.''

"That's exactly why I'm going to find that bounder.''

"She's been miserable because that bounder has not been around. Like it or not, he is your son-in-law.''

"I do not like it.''

"As long as Tessa does, that's all that matters, isn't it?''

"Your mother was a harridan," she said, looking up at the ceiling. "She interfered then and she's interfering now.''

"I know your sense of fairness, Helena. Already it's surfacing from beneath your mother's indignation.'' Gregory bent down and nibbled on his wife's shoulder. He didn't seem to be able to stop himself where she was concerned, that still managed to surprise him. After filling the nursery with seven children, it would have been more normal for the bloom to be off the rose, so to speak. The opposite seemed to be true. Her reactions were always gratifying, her response to his merest touch something a man always dreamed about, a beautiful woman's satisfaction.

She stood, slitted a look at him that would have frightened most men. She had the most daunting way of being verbally lethal to anyone who threatened those she held dear, being fiercely protective of him, their children, and friends who met her lofty criteria for friendship. For all others, she had little patience, could immolate with a glance. Her humor was part of her, certainly. So, too, her absolute openness about life, her generosity of spirit, these were all qualities he admired. She seemed to suck life up like a giant sponge, willing and wanting to absorb all of it. She mothered that way, too. Children and animals loved her, men lusted after her, and most women kept away.

When he'd fallen in love with her, he'd known that he would love her for the rest of his life.

"She is my child, Gregory, and yours, if you recall."

"I remember that quite well."

"He'd better do right by her."

It was a concession and one he saluted with a kiss to her cheek.

"I can still shoot him, darling. It wasn't a bad threat you once issued on my behalf, you know."

Helena turned and looked at her husband. She extended one hand and he grabbed it. He simply sat down again with her in his arms. They sat looking at the fire for a long while before she spoke.

"I never thought about this, you know," she said softly. "I held her in my arms when she was born and marveled at how beautiful she was, how tiny and perfectly formed. I lived each new moment with her, as if I was learning at the same time she was. I've never felt anything like it since. Do you think that was because she was my first?"

He murmured an assent, pressed her head next to his chest. "I never believed I would worry about her so. I truly believed that once she had put her hair up, once she was married, she would be out of my thoughts, except for family occasions. I dreamed of having grandchildren, of giving her advice, of being her friend. But never did I realize that I would forever be so concerned about her."

"Or that you would wish to reorder the world to make her happy."

She raised her head, gave her husband a sad little smile. "Yes, there is that, too. How dare he steal her away? There must be something we can do.''

''He is her husband and he took her from his own house. Short of shooting him, there is not much.''

''The bullet would probably bounce off his iron heart.''

''If he's gone to all this effort, I doubt there's much metal there, love.''

''It's too late.''

''I agree that you may feel that way, Helena. But it is our daughter who must decide if it is too late or not.''

''Why do you think I feel so protective of her, Gregory? I do not feel that way about the boys. Yet I love them as much.''

''There was always a bond between you and Tessa. Sometimes all you and she needed to do was to look at each other before bursting into laughter, as if you'd told each other a delicious jest without saying a word. There were even times,'' he confessed, ''when I felt left out, cut off from such communion. But then I realized it was not I who was excluded but all men. How can we possibly compete with such sisterhood?''

''We were, no doubt, wondering why men were such idiots.''

''I am not the one who was prepared to chase after our daughter and her husband, my love.''

The gentle laughter felt good, like rain on parched soil.

A moment passed and the smile faded to a thoughtful look, the laughter into a sigh.

''I wish you would not worry about her. She is sensible and intelligent.''

''She is still ill.''

''Nonsense. She has healed perfectly fine. She was racing in the halls with Harry last week.''

"She will be hurt again."

"I suspect that to love is to hurt, Helena, even though I've felt nothing but joy in loving you." She lowered her head, heard the booming drum of his heart beneath her ear. How wonderfully dear this man was to her. The love of her life. Her greatest and dearest friend.

"Still, Gregory . . ." Her words trailed off. "That truly was not fair, bringing up your mother like that."

"I'm only an idiotic man, dearest. I have to use what weapons I can muster."

"At the risk of having you tell me I say this too much, how are you feeling?"

She sent him a bright smile. "Remarkably better, considering that we seem to be traveling as fast as the wind."

"And the state of your stomach?"

"Surprisingly well. Why do you think that is?"

"Perhaps you only had to become ill once, and after that, you never will again."

"Still, I don't want to chance riding again, or traveling in your perch phaeton."

"But at least you look to be a fair sailor. Come here and I'll show you something."

He extended a hand to her, helped her over the coiled rigging ropes. He braced himself on the bowsprit, pulled her forward until she was in front of him, then folded his arms around her. His hands clasped at her waist before he pulled her back to rest against him.

She did not mention that the pose was erotically evocative, calling up another time. Another place.

He bent and spoke into her ear, over the sounds of the spray of saltwater and eternal slap of the sails.

"Doesn't it feel as if we are birds? We could be flying instead of bound to the earth."

Indeed it felt that way. There were no birds above to challenge their whimsy. The *Isolde* headed west, racing toward the setting sun. The sky was indigo and gray, streaked with crimson. The only sounds were that of the white waves being sliced by the clipper, and the wind bellowing, fierce and raw.

How long did they stand there entranced by the sight of the sea? Too long.

Tessa would have attempted to smile, but her teeth had long ago frozen to the inside of her lips. She shivered as another gust of frozen wind traveled down her back and shook her head.

"Could we go below?" At least that's what she wanted to say. It emerged as something less than English. She put one gloved hand up to her lips, breathing into her palm in an effort to warm her face. Was it possible to turn to ice from the inside out?

Jered turned her and looked at her, the first time in minutes he'd done so. She'd been anchored to him by silence and by a resolve not to complain.

"Good God, Tessa, you're freezing!"

A sound emerged from her throat that might have been a laugh or simply a sound of agreement. He edged by her, pulling her below, away from the bitter wind. Once in the companionway, he pulled her close.

"Damn it. Why didn't you tell me you were turning blue?"

"Just get me somewhere warm," she said, nuzzling his neck with her nearly frozen nose. She breathed on the inch of exposed skin, felt the warmth of him with gratitude. It wasn't an erotic gesture, as far removed from sexual need as a newborn lamb's nuzzle to his mother.

"Why didn't you say something?" He wrapped his own scarf around her neck, shielded her face with it. She wanted to tell him that it was unfair to ask a question and then take away the means with which to answer it. She didn't bother, too grateful for the residual warmth of the wool against her skin.

She followed him down the companionway through a warren of cabins. Finally they reached the galley, where he addressed the wizened man who stood over the stove.

"Can you prepare something for my wife, cook? Something warm and hardy?"

"We've potato soup, sir, and a lamb leg I've been roasting for the meal tonight."

"Anything warm will do."

A few minutes later, Jered was calling for the cabin boy, giving instructions for a hot bath, the soup and a pot of tea to be brought to their cabin.

"Why do you let me do these things to you?" he asked.

She halted in the process of removing her cloak. Did that question require an answer? Evidently not, as he simply continued to mumble and peel away layers of clothing.

Tessa didn't know who he was chastising the more, her or himself. She didn't ask, too grateful to be able to scuttle behind the screen, finish disrobing. There were some things she did not wish to share with Jered, and the sight of her naked skin, almost bluish and bumped from the cold, was one of them.

In moments the tub had arrived, and just as quickly, she was submersed in it.

"Do you need any assistance?" Was there amusement in his tone?

"No."

"Are you certain? And what was that sound?"

"A sigh of bliss, Jered. I am warm for the first time in an hour, and wondrously happy at this particular moment."

She'd heard that fresh water was in short supply aboard ship, but that didn't seem to be true, because the tub was luxuriantly large and filled with hot water. The steam from the bath touching her chilled face felt like tiny blistering beads. She didn't think she could feel her feet, but it was delicious just the same.

"It does not take much to please you, does it, Tessa?"

"I am remarkably hard to please," she said, leaning her head back against the tub, "but I am trying to pretend otherwise. I am molding myself, you see, into the perfect specimen of wife. Someone once told me that he considered wives to be a great deal of trouble."

A hesitation while he measured her mood.

"They are. Or one particular wife is."

"I have tried to turn myself into a statue, you know. One that can be safely carried from place to place."

"Statues break."

"There is that," she agreed. "Then shall I seek to emulate something forged from iron?"

"Iron rusts."

She wiggled her toes, sank deeper into the tub. "You are never pleased, Jered. What about steel? Something fashioned of Toledo steel will never rust."

"Something wickedly sharp, no doubt, aimed at my heart?"

"You will find something at fault with all my suggestions. I may as well remain as I am."

"May as well," he said, and amusement was back in his tone.

"Jered," she said, some long, wonderfully warm moments later.

"Yes?" He peered around the screen, and she frowned at him. It did not cause him to retreat, however. His smile was particularly wolfish, or at least it appeared so in the shadows. Full night was almost upon them, and yet he'd made no move to light the candles.

"Why do you feel the need to visit your relatives in Scotland?"

"I wondered how long it would take you to ask. My uncle informs me that I've family there, an aunt and numerous cousins. I've never met them."

"And all of a sudden, you have a yen to? And a wife is kidnapped and a ship sails?"

"I am the Duke of Kittridge. What good is a fortune if you cannot utilize it? You look disapproving and wifely again."

"Do all things come so easily to you, then? You wave your hand in the air and most people bow and scrape because you're the Duke of Kittridge?"

"Most people do."

"I never have. Is that why you wished me sent to Kittridge?"

He smiled. "There is all likelihood that you are correct, Tessa. You are the first person who has ever questioned me, both in the sense of impugning my directives and eternally asking why."

His good humor irritated her, especially in view of her fears. "Will you be leaving Scotland alone?" she asked.

His laughter surprised her. So, too, the look he gave her, amused and chagrin vying for dominance. ''Is that what you've thought? That I'll tuck you away somewhere? Hide you in the depths of Scotland? That would play hell on having an heir, wouldn't it?''

''Is that what this is all about?''

''You thought it worthwhile once, Tessa.''

She no longer made an effort to conceal her body, most especially the scar that embarrassed her. Now she let slip the cloth she'd used to shield herself. Watched as his gaze slipped to her chest and then effortlessly returned.

His amusement had vanished. The affable companion of the last hour had disappeared. She half-expected to see the arrogant duke in his place. Instead he said nothing, simply removed himself.

She heard the sound of the door closing shut a moment later.

Jered did not return for the rest of the night.

Chapter 31

The dawn sky was glowing richly pink and orange, bathing the world with celebratory colors. A tint of it touched the window, drifted shyly onto the sill, brushed coyly against Jered's hand. He turned, an act of renunciation of nature's majesty for another pleasure infinitely more dangerous. Tessa at dawn.

He had waited until he was certain she was asleep before returning to the cabin. Honesty, that elusive commodity in his life, forced him to admit he had not wished to see her. He had not wished to view that smile, see that radiant sparkle in her eyes. How quickly it had returned. How easily she forgave him. Even as she feared his plans for her. She should have protected herself in greater degree, held herself aloof. At least been less open, less trusting.

Because that is what you have done, Jered? He veered from that thought.

He leaned back in the chair and viewed the dawn. His favorite time of day. This was normally his sunset. His and a thousand other carousers who viewed dawn as a clarion call to scurry into their daytime holes. They were night dwellers, rarely in contact with those who lived average lives. Normal lives. They fed on greed and excitement, and debauchery. *They, Jered? Who in the illustrious group has forced you into living such a life?* There was no *they.* Only himself. A reluctant leader for a group who clung to the shadows and snickered in the darkness.

He leaned his head back against the chair, closed his eyes. A vision appeared behind his lids. His mother sat upon the floor in front of the fire, his toddler sister next to her. In he walked with his new puppy clasped in his arms, proud about the trick he'd coaxed Heroditus into learning, albeit with many pieces of cook's bacon. Laughter greeted his arrival, punctuated that afternoon, that hour of his life now gilded with memory, made precious by the rarity of its recollection. Where had his father been? There, of course. Sitting in the chair, hand occasionally reaching down to touch his mother's hair, as if needing that bond between them. His adult eyes saw what his childhood had not made clear. The way his mother had looked up and smiled at his father. Often. With a special look seen only between lovers.

Another scene, instantly available for his perusal, since it had been too often recalled. His father, weakened by illness, clutching his hand, the last bits of strength used to raise himself from the bed. Then, no words had come from him, no last minute castigation. All remonstrance and curses had ceased, replaced by blessed silence. Jered had turned, following his father's line of sight, but there was nothing there but the line of windows looking out onto the private gardens. Nothing to cause that look to come over his father's face, as if heaven and the angels had stepped forth to welcome him. Or as if his mother's shade had blessed the room with her radiance, coaxing forth a shaft of sunlight from behind a cloud. His father turned his head to look at him, the joy in those sunken eyes somehow more than simply difficult to behold. It had been agony to watch as his father had looked toward the window once more. He held out his hand and softly, with the edge of his voice raspy and sounding unused, except for shouted curses to his son, spoke his wife's name. The first time he'd done so since she'd died. And with the sound of it a benediction on his lips, he lay back down on the pillows and died. His heritage had been a fortune, a dukedom, and two children, among them a fifteen-year-old son who grieved not only for his mother but for a father who'd blamed him for her death.

For the first time, Jered wondered what it had been like for his sister. Who had seen to it that she'd been sent to live with a cousin? What had her life been like? She had been barely eleven, certainly still a child. And he still too much of one to be of much help or support. The fact was, he had not tried. And in all the years since, he had never wished to see her or find out about her life. Her presence at his wedding had been a surprise, but he'd spent no more than five minutes in a stilted conversation with her, so impersonal she might have been a stranger he'd met in London.

Another memory, of his mother's face and her smiling laughter as she told the older child how possessive he'd been when his sister had been born. She'd been brought to the nursery, a tiny princess with her own kingdom, asleep in her white lace-banded cradle. He could not remember doing such a thing, but his mother had assured him that he had gone around the nursery, touching the door and the wall, the curtain and the toys, the trundle bed and the sheets, the fire grate and the floor. "Mine!" He'd named everything. Mine. Mine. Mine. He had wanted it known even then that he would not tolerate interference, the usurping of any portion of what he decreed as his. He could be excused for such actions. He had been five years old.

And now? What was his excuse now?

He opened his eyes, looked toward the east. The sunrise was almost complete, the chorus of color more subdued. He stood, walked to the mullioned window, and looked out at the black water and its white flecked waves. His hands clasped behind his back. He should have, at that moment, have felt one of the most powerful men on earth. His ship, the one his money, his heritage, his name had built surged beneath him, the only solid barrier between sea and sky. A heady freedom. A feeling of power?

Yet it was quite possible he was more miserable at this moment than he'd ever been, more dissatisfied with the life he'd created for himself.

What did he want? A month ago he would have known. To be left alone. But that time when he'd been given his wish had been oddly silent, steeped in a solitude he decided he disliked intensely. Each occupation he'd engaged in had been rendered oddly flat. And the world a spotted gray.

Did he really want to be alone? Most of his life, a good half of it, had been spent in that fashion, superficially entertained by the chaos around him.

When had he become so jaded? When had the mask begun to adhere to his skin, so that even the careful peeling back of it threatened to strip away his flesh, render him bared to the bone?

Tessa made a sound in her sleep, and his attention was caught by her again. When had he grown to need her? He wanted to know her, the way he'd not known any other woman. He wanted to understand her, in the way that friends truly knew and accepted each other. He wanted to sense her presence in a crowded room, speak to her of his wishes and his wants, share himself with her in a way that she could finish his sentences, anticipate his thoughts, empathize in a wordless communication between two people.

He wanted what her parents had, what he only now suspected his own parents had enjoyed.

You're an idiot, Jered. Because of you she nearly died.

Lacking? She'd said there was something lacking between them, when every memory of her in his arms was precious and priceless. What did she want from him? Answers to questions. His company. Neither jewels nor gold nor riches. She'd wanted a better man. One she'd seen somehow or divined existed beneath the garb of dissolute rake. Once he might have agreed with her, and been able to step out of the mask he wore. Now he did not know if it was possible to separate what he was from what he wished to be.

And the prize if he could?

Acceptance. She offered him acceptance. It seemed to him a greater gift than love, invoking caring and friendship and laughter so free it reminded him of his own childhood. Acceptance was the gift bestowed from parent to child, friend to friend, and only rarely from lover to mate.

Could he give her what she wanted? A man reborn? Would she be content with pieces of him? Shards he'd cut free with confessions from the soul?

"I am trying very hard to be your friend, Jered, but you are not making it an enjoyable task.

Once, she'd tried to be his friend. And what had he

said? Odd, he could not remember. Perhaps he could try to be hers.

He doubted she would rebuff him as ably as he'd probably repudiated her.

Chapter 32

$\sim\!\!\cos\!\!\sim$

Chalmers halted at the doorway, fingers on the handle as the sound of laughter swept under the door. He angled the tray so that he could tap once more on the heavy oak. Beyond the door, another crash came, another piece of the cabin was no doubt being sacrificed as the Duchess of Kittridge perfected her pitching arm. Chalmer's face bore its customary rigidity, lightened only by a faint glimmer of amusement in his dark eyes.

"Well done, Tessa! Now you've got it!"

Chalmers closed his eyes as the exuberant voice boomed past the portal of oak and banded iron. "We'll make a bowler of you yet. Pity we don't have enough for a team."

Chalmers sighed.

"You just have to have a feel for the ball. Here, overhand, like this."

A crash a few seconds later had indicated that her aim still wasn't what it should have been. It was when Jered had been batman that the main damage had occurred, however, a resounding rumble of sound that had resulted in the cabin boy summoning Chalmers to the door, frightened of what might have transpired within the chamber.

Chalmers had opened the door to find that an extemporaneous cricket game was being staged, utilizing, of all things, a lemon for a ball and the duke's walking stick for a bat. His entrance, instead of chastising the two, had been greeted with a request for breakfast that he was now in the process of delivering.

Evidently the cricket game carried on.

"And a beamer is a delivery that leaves the bowler's hand and goes through head-high to the batman without pitching," Jered said.

"Of course, how could I forget?"

"If you've got a duck, you've not scored. If you've got a pair, that means you've failed to score in both innings of a match."

"Jered, this simply makes no sense. Chinese cut, drag, finger spinner, how is one to understand anything about this idiotic game?"

"It isn't idiotic, Tessa," Jered said. "This game has been played for at least two hundred years. Maybe more."

Chalmers knocked once again. This time, his supplication received a response. A hearty invitation issued in a voice laced with laughter prompted a quick smile and a turn of the handle.

Inside the cabin was as it had been this morning, a charming room if one had to be adrift upon the ocean. Except, of course, that it had suffered the ravages of the game. Pillows had been knocked from the chair, one of the walls bore a faint smudge of yellow, the scent of lemon lingered in the air. He sighed again. The duchess had disappeared.

This voyage was simply one of the more unpleasant occurrences in his life with the Duke of Kittridge. The entire ship seemed nothing more than a wooden echo chamber or a musical box from which the sound of laughter emanated at all hours of the day and night.

Chalmers placed the tray on the table alongside Jered, bowed.

Jered ignored his presence as if he were invisible, a function of his life and his servitude he had long since understood and accepted. In fact, he really didn't choose to be noticed by anyone. He preferred his shadowy role. But on this voyage, he was almost completely useless other than his perfunctory duties of bringing and fetching trays. He'd no reason to lay out His Grace's clothes; nothing to brush, nothing to shine. The duke was carrying on quite well without him.

Not only was his uselessness and his position as fifth wheel, so to speak, disconcerting, but he had noticed over the last few days that the strangest thing seemed to be occurring. Both the duke and his duchess were retreating not into themselves but into an entity Chalmers could only call "them." It was as if the more time elapsed, the more they simply grew together, into a creature that discovered itself and gloried in its creation. It was an odd phenomenon and one in which Chalmers was voyeur, uncomfortably so. It began with shared silences, it grew in shared laughter, it drew on its own strength as if the two of them seemed bound by something that hummed between them. Awareness? He did not know, nor did he care to investigate. He was just as happy spending the remainder of this interminable voyage in his cabin, ignoring the hammock above his head with as much determination as he pretended not to hear the first mate's snores.

He closed the door to the cabin with a feeling very much like relief.

* * * *

"Is he gone?"

"Scampered from the place like a rabbit in hunting season."

Tessa emerged from behind the screen. In her hand was the squashed lemon she'd retrieved from beneath the bed. "I do not think Chalmers likes me," she said, staring at the door.

"The question is," Jered said as he poured some tea into a cup, "not whether or not Chalmers likes you, but do you like him?"

She considered the idea very carefully. "It would be terrible to say that I don't particularly care for the man, wouldn't it?"

"Absolutely," he said, hiding his smile behind the rim of his cup.

"Even though he's been with you—" she hesitated, "how long?"

"Nearly twenty years."

"Oh, twenty years, then."

"Does it make it more difficult if I told you that there are times in which I positively warm to the man?"

"Much," she said, with such a disconsolate air that he laughed.

"He will simply have to get used to your presence in my life, Tessa."

"A singular feat, Jered."

"But not an onerous one," he said, extending his hand. She grasped it and then surprised him by pulling it to his lips and kissing his fingers. Her smile lured him closer, and he kissed the edge of it, then stepped back.

"Or, if he disturbs you, I can simply dismiss him."

"Good heavens, no."

"Are you sure?" Her eyes were wide, and if he didn't miss his guess, censorious.

"People need their jobs, Jered. You simply cannot dismiss them like that."

"I did not. Only offered it. Do you concede the cricket game?"

She nodded, then smiled again.

"Well, what do you suggest? The weather's grown too cold to stand on deck."

"Thank heavens," she murmured.

He sent her a mock frown. "And although you had no ill effects upon your second outing, I really do think we're challenging fate to take a chance with the rather precarious state of your stomach."

"A gentleman would not mention such an intimate thing to a lady. And besides, I feel wonderful." Her frown did not seem at all mocking.

"I am not any gentleman. I am your husband."

Her flush should have clued him into her thoughts. Instead he found himself bemused by her appearance. She was not strictly beautiful, and yet there were times in which she was, when she turned her head a certain way and smiled. In that instant she made his breath stop. Her teeth were white, and she flashed them often, even her most commonplace expressions ended in a half-smile as if she mocked herself. Her hair was a deep chestnut shade that curled thickly around her shoulders, framing the symmetry of her face. He reached out and touched a strand, threaded his fingers through the hair at her temple. He thought of silk and fire in one errant thought.

"Jered?"

He shook himself free of tangled thoughts, lowered his hand.

"Why do you not ever talk about your family?"

"What is there to say? My parents are dead, my sister and I estranged."

"I think I would speak of my family even if they were no longer here, Jered. Someone only truly dies when they are no longer remembered."

He reached out and tapped her nose with his finger.

"That sounds very sweet, Tessa, but it's not exactly true. Sometimes recollection makes a loss more painful." Knowledge he'd discovered only recently.

She studied him, seemed to measure how closely guarded his borders.

"Was your mother quiet and modest and unassuming?"

He raised one eyebrow. "My mother rode like a demon over the hills around Kittridge, took us fishing, and taught me to sail."

"Then, where did you get your ridiculous notions about wives, Jered? From the ton? That does not sound like you, to espouse an idea from a group you claim to hold in contempt."

He wondered what she would say to the truth? Would she simply accept it or delve further? "Perhaps I did not wish, Tessa, to experience what my father did when my mother died."

"Did he grieve?" She would always question.

"Can someone die of sorrow?" His eyes were fixed on the far wall. How much easier there than directed to her face. "It was as if he'd died in that moment, too. He hardly spoke, barely left his room. When he did go outside, it was to the place she'd died. He would stand there in all kinds of weather, tears falling down his face. Once I found him kneeling there, rocking back and forth upon the ground, his arms clutched around air, as if he held her still."

He looked over at her. "Do not weep, Tessa. It is long since passed. Years and years."

"Has it? Or do you hold it inside still? He must have loved her very much, else he would not have grieved so."

"I really do not wish to discuss my parents, Tessa." He turned away, walked to the windows that overlooked the stern of the ship.

"Don't do this, Jered. Don't send me away."

"There are not many places you can go, Tessa."

"Anywhere but in your thoughts, Jered? I do not wish to pry, Jered."

"No," he said, "only to understand me."

"Is there anything wrong with that?"

"I'm not sure I want to be understood."

She was not content to have him turn away. She reached out, touched his arm. He looked down where her hand rested on his sleeve. So tenacious in her affection. She was difficult to resist.

"Very well, what questions do you wish me to answer?" He went back to the table, looked down at his breakfast cooling on the tray.

"Why, Jered?"

"Why what?"

"You know very well what. Why haven't you touched me? You've been as charming as a courtier, as fond as a brother, but each night, you've simply turned on your side of the bed and left me alone."

Her cheeks were red, and for all her forcefulness, she did not meet his eyes. His intractable wife, embarrassed? It was such a novel thought that he tested it, tipping up her chin with his fingers. She eased away from his touch.

"It's because of the scar, isn't it?"

"What?"

She glanced over at him, then looked away. "I'm hideous to you, aren't I?"

"Indeed you are. So much so that I've spent the last five minutes rhapsodizing how gloriously beautiful you are. I'm surprised I've allowed you to occupy my cabin, you're such a hag."

She blinked at him. Then frowned.

"Of all the inanities you've occasionally pronounced, that has to be the most idiotic. I can cope with your quoting Mother Goose in the middle of the night. Even tolerate your shouting intimacies in crowded theaters. I may as well go so far as to admit that I can quite possibly even endure your presence as a shadow for the rest of my life. But I really cannot abide stupid women, Tessa."

She threw something at him. It was his toast. It didn't hit him, but it was a waste of perfectly good food, especially since it was *his* breakfast. She had taken to eating later in the day, saying that it really did seem to make her feel better to delay a meal.

He picked up the silver condiment set that contained several porringers, one of which contained apple butter. He opened the silver top and flicked his finger into it. A glob landed on Tessa's cheek. Her smile burst forth first, then her laughter.

"Oh, do stop, Jered."

She wiped her cheek, then stepped closer. "Thank you," she said as she lifted both his hands to her lips, cupping the backs of them within her palms as if in offering. Then, she bent her head and kissed the center of each palm, a kiss so soft and sweet that it seemed to spear his heart. It was not an act of passion as much as one of benediction. "That was wonderfully done. But if it isn't my scar, then why?"

He sighed. *Nothing but the truth would serve her, would it?* Yet how could he voice it? Words slid around the roof of his mouth, were captured by his teeth. She had not fared well in this marriage. And yet she'd never ceased to give—of herself, of her humor, of all the qualities that made her unique. He'd been enchanted by her sensuality from the beginning, effortlessly enslaved by passion. That she felt the same he did not doubt; he had eons more experience than she. And yet it seemed a tawdry thing to do to her, to use it to bind her even more closely to him. Honor? A strange word to use in this circumstance, but it most closely resembled it.

He reached out for her, held her close, would not let her turn, or retreat, or escape. "Tessa," he murmured, into her hair. "Please." For what did he ask absolution? He wasn't certain he knew. Only that he needed it. And her.

He went to the door, locked it securely, wondering if he should tell her that he'd never before felt the way he did at this moment. He doubted if she would believe him. He'd given her no reason to ever think him sincere. He drew closed the curtains that shielded the room from the weak sun, encapsulating the room in a womb of darkness, then realized it was the wrong thing to do. He pulled them open again, until the silvery light illuminated the room.

He did not speak as he approached her, realizing with perfect clarity that there were moments that should not be explained or anointed with words. Only actions counted, the movements of his hands upon the fastenings of her dress supported that notion. Her indrawn breath seemed as sharp as a dagger, capable of piecing his heart.

He kissed the shoulder he bared, marveling at the curve of her skin, the bone nestled within. He'd touched a hundred women. Perhaps more. But their skin had never been as smooth, their flesh had not been as supple, their fragrance not as alluring. He kissed the spot where neck curved to shoulder, tongued the collarbone, danced across her throat with teasing kisses. When he dipped and picked her up, she only hid her face in his chest. *Shy?* Or experiencing the same feelings he was having at this moment? A curious sense of being overwhelmed by something he'd initiated but that now carried him farther than he'd dared. He placed her gently on the bed.

His shirt lost two buttons, his fly defeated his fingers' clumsy attempts to open it now. He thought he threw his boots across the cabin; he wasn't sure how he managed to remove the rest of his clothing.

He lay beside her, propped his head on one hand, an indolent position that belied the racing of his heart, the perfect position if he were satiated and comfortable with it, not feeling this raging need. He placed one hand on Tessa's stomach, above the neat triangle of hair sheltering her femaleness. She flinched at his touch, but not away from it. If anything, she curved into him, her hands stroking his chest in an exploratory pattern that was making him quite mad. Her breasts were doing similar things to his intentions, pouting and summoning his lips as if he had no free will. He licked her left breast, sucked the nipple into his mouth, feasting on her with a hunger he'd never felt before.

She tasted like a woman, of soft skin and softer moans. Her nipple was hot, her skin even hotter, a blazing heat he felt replicated inside himself and which he wished more than anything else at this moment to share with her. He wanted to bathe her internally with his heat, warm her from the inside out.

The light gave her shadows and depth, the watery sun lit her skin to the color of cream. Her hair fell down below her shoulders, creating a work of art, a Botticelli if he posed her just so. She was trembling. He reached down and pulled up the blanket, shielding her from the cold.

He placed his hand on her right breast, cupping the mound of it within his palm. Then bent, kissed the scar that marked her perfect skin. His fingers gently traced it, and the small incision below her breast. A shiver of awe sighed through his body, a tremor of fear bled through him as he lay beside her, touching her with sensate and tender fingers. A moment of horror, of incredible pain. It was a miracle she had not been lost to him.

He could see her veins shining blue beneath the perfection of her skin, heard her faint breath, smelled the scent of her. His nose brushed against her temple, the tender, sensitive flesh upon her neck.

In a second gladdened by her smile, he kissed her. Warm and welcoming, her mouth opened to his as if he'd demanded subservience, deserved it. He sank into the kiss, savoring the taste of her, the utter beauty of her response. There was nothing he could do to fight it, nothing he wanted to do. Sparks appeared in the back of his eyelids; he felt as if he were being pulled down into a deep black hole, toward oblivion.

His hands shook, his fingers ached to delve into moist crevasses and plump hillocks so much so that he trembled with the need. He was harder than he'd ever been, the thought of steel running through his mind briefly and humorously. He was sincerely worried about his capacity to finish the act, so immersed was he in the need for it. He felt like a child again, with a child's rapacious appetite for everything delicious.

Passion was a word he thought he knew before today. He'd certainly felt it before, felt the surge of himself climaxing in a warm and welcoming woman. He'd felt lust before, felt himself harden when looking at a particularly attractive female, touched a breast with fullness and plump evocation. Until this moment, with the sound of the sea a backdrop to their breathing, with the gray sky filtering a winter sun, Jered realized he hadn't truly understood passion at all.

Tessa placed her hand on his chest, densely thicketed by hair, then cupped his shoulder, feeling the smoothly curved flesh, the definition of muscles. He made no sound, but it was as if he sighed, an opening up of him, like a door swinging wide. She placed her other hand on the back of his neck and raised her eyes to his.

She allowed herself the freedom of his stillness, all ten fingers sensate, wandering the ridges and hollows of a face she'd known for years and years. *Forever?* His brow was wide and deep, a curl of hair obscured her fingers, she brushed it back into place, gently. His lashes were ridiculously long, his eyebrows thick, the planes of his cheeks carved hollows near his mouth. His nose was aquiline, but not too sharp, his chin definite but not too pointed. It was to his mouth her fingers returned time and again, tracing the full borders of his bottom lip, the smiling contours of his upper, delicately exploring the seam of them, then darting away as if too brazen.

She didn't allow her exploration to cease then, but ran her fingers over the broad column of his neck. His shoulders were warm beneath her palms. Her fingers trailed down his arms, measured the curve of elbow, the strength of his wrists, the broad hands that lay quiescent beneath her exploration.

Placing her hands on Jered was as deeply moving as it would have been to explore the features of her first child, a loving expedition of tender and trembling fingers.

She wanted to feel all of him, trace the angle of his ribs, dart beneath his shirt and feel his flesh, palm the strength of his ankles, the ligature of his calves, cradle the heat of him.

He kissed her ear and she heard his breath, rapid and heavy. The sound of it seemed to melt her heart. She brought her hand up to palm the side of his face. It was a gesture of tenderness in a moment to be remembered forever.

Her breasts felt heavy, their nipples like tiny swords. In a hundred different places, her pulse beat too strongly, sending echoes of feeling thrumming through her blood. If she touched her own skin right now, it would skitter in reaction, so sensitized was she.

She was adrift in sensation and he'd done nothing but hold her, touching her with gentleness and the shivery stroke of a fingertip on her arm, hesitating in the juncture of her elbow, testing there as if pleading permission to go further. Every once in awhile, he would give an odd exhalation, as if he was too filled with emotions to speak and must let some of it escape. She placed her cheek against his chest, feeling that this seduction of the senses had begun when she'd first met him as a child.

She nuzzled still closer to his skin, reveling in the texture of it, the softness of a man's face newly shaven, whiskers tamed, yet hidden for only hours. Her fingers reached up and stirred the hair at his nape, where it curled like that of a newborn lamb. How it must infuriate him, that hint of delicacy.

She'd never before felt this exaltation, this sense of being lifted above and out of herself. It was strangely new and yet frightening. She knew, with a wisdom channeled from her bones and all that she'd ever learned or suspected of life, that what she felt for Jered Mandeville was unlike any other emotion. It always had been. *Love? Or something stronger?* Something that didn't require intellect or wisdom. Something elemental and earthy. All she knew was that she needed him. Now and quite possibly forever.

His lips were infinitely skilled, tasted of mint, a hint of cinnamon, warm to the touch, full. There was nothing to do but match him kiss for kiss, a simple battle joined for the sport of it. She smiled just for a second until he held her tighter, angled his head for more thorough invasion, sent his tongue darting into the recesses of her mouth, tasting her warmth and her receptivity.

Wasn't it strange that a mouth could feel so much? That lips could tingle and pulse heavily? Her skin was as tactile, sending messages of excitement throughout her body. She pressed her lips to his neck, feeling the pulse beneath her lips beat as strongly and as rapidly as her own. Her tongue darted out, tasted the salt of his skin, felt him shudder in response.

His gentleness was somehow too slow, too careful of her. She wanted to urge him to hurry, but she did not, trapped within the web of sensation as tightly as if she were prey and not co-conspirator in this game of passion.

His warm palm flattened on her nipple, a gentle touch despite the insistence of it. She arched against him, feeling the hot tingle of her flesh as her nipple lengthened, silently imploring a deeper contact.

His breath on her neck was warm, stirring emotions and sensations alike. His hands linked at the small of her back, gripping tightly, his head buried in that place between neck and shoulder, it was as if he wordlessly begged for that which he could not name, but which she too easily identified. Jered wanted comfort in the way a child craved recognition and compassion, the instinctive way an infant roots for nourishment and nurturing in one touch.

He moved away and the air eddied between them, sending cold and momentary panic. It could only have been a flash of seconds, time being elongated by sensation and bodily need.

He was draping her in ribbons, skeins of sensation that started at her feet and inch by inch rose higher. Where his fingers lay, a ribbon was born, bright crimson, sunny yellow, a blue to rival that of a perfect sky. They twisted around her, enfolding her in color, binding her to him. She sighed, but the sound emerged as a moan instead, something plaintive and yet demanding, an invocation he soothed with a touch of his tongue.

Her body was beginning to hum, as if a bee were trapped inside, fighting for freedom. It was like nothing she'd ever felt, like no experience she'd ever had. Tessa wanted to move, her undulations instinctive, necessary, as ancient as the act they would soon share. She remained still instead, holding all these trapped feelings together to experience them more fully.

Both of her hands reached up, pulled his head down for a kiss. Into that joining of lips and tongues, Tessa infused all her current longing and hunger, all of the past hurt, and pain, and fear. Then she welcomed him as all women have welcomed their mate, with submission and secret conquering, with love and affection and sublime understanding.

He smiled and sank within her.

It was like torture but without pain, this steadfast invasion. She felt the waiting, a pulse beat deep inside her, measuring the limits of her capacity for endurance. She wanted movement, an easing of the building tension, but Jered did not move except to brush his lips across hers, softly crooning words of comfort. She wanted the brightness, the blaze of explosion, but he only bent to capture a hard nipple in his mouth, grazing it with tender teeth, sucking at it.

This moment made poignant by memory and unvoiced regret was somehow transformed. Subtly lit by a reluctant sun, the room was almost magical, a place of lacy mist, a knoll of sweet earth, a starlit summer sky. Into this silent place came a soft moan, an entreaty, a gasp. She was making sounds, Tessa knew, little sounds that betrayed her body's surprise and exultation as he moved within her, softly, tenderly. Then the sun exploded, showering her with a million facets of light.

Silence again, as hearts beat too quickly and pulses began to slow. Two lovers looked into each other's eyes and each witnessed a naked soul.

No words were necessary.

Chapter 33

A soft tap on the door roused him. He sat on the edge of the bed, gently covered Tessa with the blanket, donned his dressing gown and walked to the door.

"Begging your pardon, sir," Captain Williams said. What portion of his face wasn't covered with whiskers was lined, his skin the color of tanned leather. Most men who'd given up their lives to the sea looked the same, their faces revealed the toll of endless years of scanning the horizon.

"Yes, Captain?"

"I've a bit of concern, sir, about the weather. The barometer's falling rapidly. We've got a good storm coming if I don't miss my guess." Williams would captain the *Isolde* after her refitting, taking her first to the West Indies and then perhaps China. If she could win a few speed trials, orders would rush in for vehicles of her like. Captain Williams's share would be considerable, therefore; he had a vested interest in her safety. The captain had been present from the moment her hull had been crafted, and no doubt felt a parent's kinship for this child of wood and varnish.

"The *Isolde* is seaworthy, Captain. Is your concern because we're only five days out?"

"No, sir. It's just that the ocean currents are normally warmer in this locale, sir. Winter storms are rare. When they do come, they're filled with ice and damn dangerous. Begging your pardon, sir."

Jered nodded absently. "If we headed back to harbor, could we outrace it?"

"I doubt it, sir, but we might be able to put in at another port, sit it out."

"I'd rather we keep on our present course, Captain. If we find the seas too rough, she's fast enough to find a safe port."

There was a moment in which he thought Captain Williams might refuse. He opened his mouth, inhaled a breath. Preparatory to marshaling an argument? Jered didn't know. The man turned smartly on his heel and left.

A scant two hours later, Jered was certain he'd made one of the worst mistakes of his life. An arrogant answer that might well cost him the presence of the one person in the world who was becoming necessary to his very existence.

Tessa lay flat on her back in the bed, both arms spread out, gripping fistfuls of coverlet. The bed was pitching in the air, then rolling back. No, the whole cabin was performing that bizarre ritual, as if engaged in the primary intent of making her lose her dinner. She was not feeling at all well. Chalmers had checked upon her a few minutes ago, and the poor man looked as green as she'd felt. She'd known better than to mention food to him, just told him in a tiny little voice she hardly recognized as her own that she really didn't need anything. He grasped the hidden meaning quick enough, slipping from the cabin with a sigh that could only be construed as relief.

Tessa reached over and grabbed a pillow, drew it over her face. She repeated the curse her brother Stephen had taught her before he decided to join the church.

She gripped the rope Jered had given her. He'd wound it under the bolted bed, instructed her to tie herself in if the sea became too rough. "I don't want you thrown around this cabin like a ball, Tessa," he'd said. "Everything but you is fastened down securely." Then, with a swift kiss on her forehead, he'd left her.

That had been at least two hours ago, before the storm had become so bad she'd begun to pray. Earnest solicitations to the Almighty had been wisely bereft of those bargains made by sorrowful sinners. She did not promise one thing in return for being saved, only murmured the same small prayer over and over, in a chant that grew even louder as time passed and the storm grew louder. "Let it be all right. Please God. Let him be all right. Please God. Let it be all right."

The sky had first been colored pigeon gray, then had shifted to the shade of soot. The wind screamed around the ship as if some great angry beast howled its anger. The *Isolde* bobbed on the ocean as if it were no more than an apple to be plucked from a bucket of water. But this was no child's game, a fact that was made clear each time the ship pitched, seemed to shudder, then shake itself free of the grip of a wave, right itself. Only for it to begin again the next moment.

She felt like a child, terrified and frightened and racing to her mother. Instead, of course, that she wanted her husband. *Don't be a coward, Tessa.* But was it cowardice in the face of this ferocious storm?

Where *was* Jered?

Jered had never seen a tidal wave before, but he doubted anything could be higher than the wave that had neatly sheered off *Isolde*'s main mast. One moment the wave was there, curving toward them like a giant claw. The next it was over them, swamping the decks, pushing the slender ship down toward the bottom of the sea.

Like the other men on deck, he was tied by a rope to the side, a safety harness that could only be trusted so far, considering that twice now waves had washed overboard men similarly fastened. He sluiced the water off his face, breathed deeply in preparation for the next wave's appearance. It came too soon, crashing into them. The storm seemed to accelerate in fury, the roar of hundreds and thousands of gallons of water sounding almost like a growl.

He could barely view the bow of the ship, but what he did see was ominous. The bowsprit looked as if it had been cracked in two and was hanging into the water. The broken mast acted as a drag on the hull, and she needed every inch of buoyancy to fight this storm. Worse, the main mast's height had been offset by the length of the bowsprit; and with the bowsprit gone, it meant the *Isolde* was dangerously top heavy.

He could no longer feel the skin of his face, and his leather gloves had long since been saturated by sea water. His feet were sodden, his boots having paid lie to the claim from his shoemaker that they were impervious to water. Still, freezing was better than drowning.

The weather worsened as the moments passed. It was growing colder. Cold enough to slicken the ropes, to ice the deck. One sailor had simply slipped off the ship, his feet sliding beneath him as if he'd been skating on a pond.

It would be a miracle if they were still on course. He doubted if the rudder was still intact. The force of the waves had the power to crush timbers into tinder.

He looked up at the main mast again. The sea and the sky were the same color now; it was difficult to see the dark mast against the encroaching wave.

If they capsized, they would die. A simple fact. The temperature of the water would shock them first, them lure them all to a quick death. All of them. Even Tessa. And Chalmers, who had fought tooth and nail to be left behind. He should have left them both at Kittridge.

If they died, it would be his fault. His arrogance. His stupidity. *Mine.* A child's refrain. Irritating, but not gratingly so. Patently idiotic voiced by a man full grown. And criminal, if nothing else.

He closed his eyes against the next wave, reaching out and holding on to the door that led to the companionway. The water threw him against the bulkhead, but he was so cold he didn't feel the bruising blow. Tessa would feel nothing after the first five minutes. He would hold her in his arms and curse himself until hell reached out to claim him. *A kind death, Jered. How gentlemanly of you.*

Would she smile as she died, looking at him with that grave acceptance on her face? Or would her eyes sparkle as if death were some great jest whose secret she would soon learn? Would she question him until her lips could not speak anymore? Until she sank beneath the surface of the sea?

No. A thought voiced in his soul, not through his lips. A sickening feeling, not unlike disgust, filled him. He could not let it happen, would not let it happen. *Arrogance again, Jered?*

Yes. Damn it. Yes.

Tessa struggled to unknot the rope, a horrible clammy feeling not unlike that of sickness causing her fingers to shake. The *Isolde* was going to sink, she was sure of it. And she would be afloat in this cabin when it filled with water, forever tethered to the bed.

She would die standing up, if you please.

She slipped on a dress, and over that another. Two pairs of stockings, a comfortable pair of boots, her cloak and a shawl. She wrapped the shawl around her head, let the ends trail to the back, pulled on new driving gloves worn now because they were leather and might protect against the cold.

Tessa stumbled up the stairs to the main deck, looked for Jered, spent only a second framing an excuse for venturing above. Instead her words were trapped by horror, forgotten in the moment she glanced up. In that instant all thoughts flew from her head. She was frozen by the sight of the gray and black monster that bore down on them. Its jaws were white, its neck curved; the wave was taller than St. Paul's. It acted as a bulwark against the wind, stilling sound. That eerily quiet moment seemed like a curious ballet, a delicate and precise execution of strength and beauty, etched in uncertainty and limned in terror.

They were going to die.

Jered turned and saw her. He yelled something, but she couldn't hear the words. The sound had come back, the ship groaned beneath her feet. A long, low, growl announced the arrival of the wave. Jered slammed into her just as it crashed against the ship. He held her against the bulkhead by the sheer weight of his body. She had remained on the top step, and the force of the water threw them both back into the companionway, then tried to pull Jered from her. Tessa grabbed his waist and clung, holding her breath, pressing her face into his chest, chilled by ice and storm and the sudden certainty of death. Water surrounded them, filled the companionway, crashed down into the hold, added weight to a ship already floundering.

A gasp of air. It did not come easily; it was as if she had to take great gasps in order to breathe at all. She shuddered, reminded of another time. She'd survived that, she would conquer this.

Jered held her close, she burrowed closer, needing to be next to him now. Especially now. Her fingers gripped his coat as if they were talons. She would not have been surprised to feel them threading themselves into the wool fabric like large needles. She shivered and clung, gasping, sickened by the taste of brine on her lips. Another quick breath, and she pulled back to look into his face.

"Is it true most sailors cannot swim, Jered?"

She felt his laughter rather than heard it. He raised his head and looked at her. His eyes, reddened by the saltwater, seemed absurdly kind. *Tender, perhaps?*

One prayer answered then, while another still remained in doubt.

"Kittridge!"

He turned, still holding Tessa. The Captain was calling from the weather deck. It, like the rest of the ship, had taken a beating.

"Kittridge!"

The Captain waved to catch his attention, then

pointed skyward. He pushed Tessa back into the companionway so that she was protected, took a few steps out the door, and looked upward.

The ship was no longer top heavy. The main mast had been cracked in two, and the top hundred feet of it carried off by the last wave. The part that remained was dangling offside, connected by ropes that had once held its sails. Now the mast acted as a spar for an outrigger. But instead of keeping the ship from capsizing, the same function such a beam would offer to a smaller ship or boat, the mast added weight to one side. Another good-sized wave, and the *Isolde*'s fate would no longer be in question. Even now, she tilted to port.

Their only chance was to jettison the mast, but to do that, someone must crawl over the deck and sever the ropes that held her to the side. He answered Tessa's question in his mind. *Yes.* Most sailors could not swim. And even if they could, he doubted any of the men aboard this ship had as compelling a reason to save themselves as he.

He looked back at Tessa. She was shivering. Water streamed from her clothes. She pushed back her hair with one hand, remained still as she caught his gaze.

What passed between them in those moments? So damn many things. Too many things. Memory and regret. Wishes and hopes. Remorse and longing. What had his uncle said? *"She has loved you for a very long time."* He could feel it in that moment, a ribbon curling around his heart, shielding his soul. If he went to heaven, dear God, it would be because Tessa loved him. He could not be that evil if he was loved in such a fashion, could he?

Forgive me, Tessa, for shunning you, for being frightened of what you brought to me. You were like the sun, and I like some underground creature, fearful of your radiance and suspicious of your very nature. Forgive me most of all, Tessa, for hurting you.

He wished he could speak to his uncle once more, to quote him something he just now recalled from his schooldays. It was Cicero who said that honorable actions are ascribed by us to virtue, and dishonorable actions to vice. He'd spent his life endeavoring to attain the one. What would it be like to die with the other? He may very well learn.

He turned and walked out on deck.

Chapter 34

~~~~~~~

"**N**o!" The sound of the scream scraped her throat raw.

Whatever Jered was about to do brought peril with it. She'd known it immediately. He had looked at her as if he were saying good-bye. In that second it had looked as if he'd loved her. The man whose existence had only been hinted at, the one who'd laughed on their wedding night, who'd accidentally and effortlessly charmed her, who'd held her so tenderly not an hour before, stared out at her from bleak eyes.

Her scream was tossed into the air, buried beneath the roar of wave and ocean. Jered did not hesitate. She dropped to her knees, both hands clamped across her mouth, eyes stinging with saltwater but fixed on her husband's back. He had reached the weather deck, was bending close to the Captain, shouting something in his ear. The Captain pointed, the cabinet door in front of the wheel was opened and an ax extracted.

The deck was icy and wet, twice he stumbled. Once he lost the ax, and as the ship pitched, Tessa thought it gone forever. But it had become tangled in the rigging strewn across the deck. He retrieved it, bent over by the force of the icy winds. As he moved closer to the edge,

Tessa wondered if he was going to attempt to cut down the mast. It was coated with tar and at least three feet in diameter. It would take hours, and it was clear from the listing of the ship that they didn't have hours.

The rope that ensured his safety was not long enough to reach where the mast lay tangled. In absolute horror Tessa watched as Jered hacked it off, and then stepped close to the edge without any protection at all. He knelt, began chopping at the thick hemp with broad strokes. One rope fell free, and the mast shimmied in position, turning a little but not sliding from the deck. He worked on another, then another, seemingly oblivious to the biting cold and the danger and the swelling waves.

Something caught her eye, and she reluctantly glanced to her right, only to see a wave bigger than the one before approaching the ship. Her breath stilled, time itself slowed.

She screamed his name, but Jered did not turn, did not move. He continued to kneel on the deck, continued to chop away at the rigging. She screamed again, and again. And then watched in horror as the wave swept over the ship, taking her husband with it.

He heard the screams, then realized it was the howling of the wind. He could almost see the shape of the monster in the waves, feel its teeth gripping his neck, shaking. Hot blood poured over his skin, warming him.

The screams came again, fury in the water. A female monster then. A feral creature with sharpened fangs and plundering hunger, frantic to feed her young. She shrieked in fury. He unclasped one hand, realized it held nothing, let it float free. The other now; the other hand held a lightning bolt. Zeus. He was not Poseidon but his brother. Come to claim his dominion. Halt. Too weak a demand, that. Cease. His head lolled to one side, a frigid wave coated with ice chilled the blood pouring down his arm.

The screams were coming from heaven. He looked above him. *Did God cry? Did He weep?* His cheek rested against something hard. Cold. *Dear God, You who are weeping, why is it so cold? Do your tears make ice, then?*

Another scream, a sound. Something pulled at him, then released him. His face slammed into the wall again. He thought it had happened once before, believed himself blacked out for a moment. An exhalation of agony warmed the surface he'd struck. A tongue reached out to taste it. Salt. Wood. Paint. He sighed again, tasted his own blood and spittle. Was he dying? Undoubtedly. But Death would not win easily. It could pluck his flesh from his body, but he would not willingly feed it. He had reparations to make.

God screamed again, and something gripped him, pulled at his flesh. A scream of agony. This time his. *Careful. I hold a thunderbolt within my grasp. Behold, I am Zeus, in kingship to God Himself.*

He found himself being lifted up toward the heavens. Angels, then? *Oh, thank you God.* Not hell, for all his sins. *Oh, God, I do not want to die.*

They had nearly reached him twice, swept back by the waves that crashed against the *Isolde*. Jered hung from the side of the ship. The rope he'd gripped had been wound around his wrist and he dangled there only by that tenuous hold.

Tessa knelt at the edge, a rope tied to her waist. One seaman was below her, another to her side and slightly lower. She would not let them quit, had threatened to cut the lines that held them to the side of the ship if they dared. She'd screamed continuously at both of them when it looked as if they were going to quit before Jered was rescued. Her throat was sore, her eyes no doubt fevered, but her husband was going to be saved. Either that, or she was going to ensure they all died trying.

The third swing across the hull was successful. The mass of rigging was laboriously pulled up to the deck. Tessa turned and signaled, and a chain of men began hauling on the rope. She wasn't certain which one Jered was tied to, therefore, the only thing to do was to bring the whole mess of rigging back on board. Slowly, so slowly that the time seemed measured in months rather than minutes, his fingers emerged, so bluish they were nearly black. Then his arm. She reached down and brushed off the hands that would have assisted her, put her hand under Jered's arms and pulled him to her.

"Please, Your Grace, let me help."

She looked up at Chalmers who knelt by her side.

"I will not let him die." Her face was warmed with her tears.

"No, Your Grace." She looked down. Other hands were bringing Jered's body up on deck. Tessa wiped the tears from her face. They had hardened. Ice?

"Please, Chalmers." She hated it that her voice was shaking. "Please help me." Her eyes stung, tears pooled, then fell over the edges of her eyes. "I don't want him to die." She rocked back and forth, her sobs strangely silent. Or was it simply that they were muted by the storm? It seemed to be lessening, but then her attention had been only on Jered.

"Yes, Your Grace," he said, and bent down to help

her rise. She held on to Jered's sleeve all the way to the cabin, releasing him only when the companionway was not wide enough to allow her to travel by his side. The seamen bore him to the bed, and without stripping his stiff clothes from him, piled the blankets on top of him.

"He'll need as much heat as possible, Your Grace. But I doubt the galley's got a fire lit with this storm."

"Yes," she said, her eyes focused on her husband. She blinked, called herself back to what needed to be done. "What?"

"The galley, Your Grace? Should I see if there is a fire?"

"Yes, of course. Please."

It was frigid in the cabin, but at least the wind did not howl as much. She sat on the edge of the bed, tucking the covers around Jered. He looked too pale, his lips almost bluish. What was best to do? She was very much afraid she did not know. *Think, Tessa.*

The ship listed even more to the side. Had she brought him to the cabin only moments before their death? She tucked the covers around his neck, bent forward, warmed his cold cheek with hers. She was not much warmer, but at least she was conscious.

"Your Grace?" She looked up to find Chalmers at the door. An expression of terror was etched upon his face.

"Yes?"

"I am very much afraid, Your Grace, that we're about to go aground!"

The *Isolde* had fought a valiant fight. Her rigging destroyed, her masts shattered, her rudder lost, and her decks awash, she shuddered with a delicate and almost noble revulsion. Then, as the rocks that lined the coast seemed to beckon, she turned her bow to the west, and with a scrape of hull and shiver of keel, she sighed.

And surrendered.

Chapter 35

"**I** consider it a miracle, Your Grace."

Tessa slanted a look at him.

"Well, if one has to be shipwrecked, what fortuitous circumstance that it should be so near to civilization."

"You do not, then, consider yourself a modern Robinson Crusoe, Chalmers?"

His look of horror seemed genuine. But then, she could not imagine a more gruesome fate than being alone on a tropical island with Chalmers. He would spend most of the time impugning the island, the food, his accommodations and the weather, no doubt.

As it was, he had occupied too many of hours doing just that. Ever since they'd been rescued at Middleston. The *Isolde* had slammed against the rocks in the manner of a child throwing himself onto a feather bed. The shock of the impact was enough to throw her to the floor, no matter the warning. Jered had remained abed only because she'd tied the rope around him, then crept up from the floor and thrown herself atop him, holding on to the headboard bolted to the bulkhead.

The sound of the keel scraping against the jagged rocks had been too much like a scream. Tessa had closed her eyes and held on until the shuddering eased.

For a long time, they didn't know if the ship would sink upon impact, but it seemed that the water was too shallow to bury the *Isolde*. When the first boats had arrived, she had suspected that their inhabitants had been less interested in any survivors as they had been in establishing the salvage rights to the dying ship.

She had felt shamed at her initial thought, especially since the three of them had been escorted to the mayor's house, Jered ensconced in the mayor's bed with effortless hospitality and generosity. Warming bricks and two comforters made the bed a cozy oasis of warmth, but he had still not awakened. He must have suffered a blow, the mayor's wife had commented, evidenced by the swelling on the side of his head.

She'd missed that sign, more concerned that he had not warmed, that his flesh felt rigidly cold. If she did not see the rise and fall of his chest, she could easily think him dead. His right hand was swollen to nearly three times its size, the flesh mottled black and blue. It did not resemble a hand at all, merely an appendage of dubious use. His face was bruised almost as badly. It was quite possible his nose was broken. She and the mayor's wife had stripped his clothing from him, and he lay now in one of the mayor's nightshirts. Her own clothing had been discarded for a flannel nightgown and wrapper made of the same material. Above it, she wore a shawl that covered her nearly to her toes.

Chalmer's presence discommoded her not one whit. She didn't care if her attire was proper or not. All that she cared about was Jered, the arrival of the physician, and her husband's ultimate health.

"Shall I fetch another pot of tea while we're waiting, Your Grace?"

"If you wish, Chalmers."

"Very well, Your Grace."

After he left, she pulled back the covers and settled herself beside Jered. His body felt like a brick of ice; hers was not much warmer. Despite the fire blazing brightly, and the warmth of the room, she felt chilled from the inside. She moved to his side, slid one arm over his chest.

"Do you remember the first time I saw you, Jered? I was sixteen and thought myself so grown. But my mother would not let me attend the dinner in your honor. No doubt she'd heard of your reputation. You kissed me, do you remember? I thought my heart was going to burst. I never told anyone about that kiss. It was a shockingly wicked thing to do, of course. Not as much for you as for me."

She was beginning to shiver, the sensation of waves undulating over her body, causing her to move closer to Jered. She rested her head on his shoulder. "I used to spend hours in front of your painting. I told you things I've never told anyone. That my hair would never do, that I despaired of it ever curling. That my bosoms were getting too large, and surely men who were proper would not care for such luxury of excess as was manifesting upon my body. How I wanted to be a wife. How I wanted my husband to love me as much as my father did my mother. You were the only one who knew how much I hated having six brothers sometimes, and all the really awful things they did to me. I wanted to know what made you laugh. Were you amused by droll humor, by the antics of acrobats or clowns? Which authors did you read, which philosophers did you study? All sorts of questions, Jered." *And you were the only one who knew how much I wanted you to fall in love with me.*

She extended one leg over his. "Do you think wishes ever come true?" She smiled. "Another question. I cannot help it, you know. I was taught to question, Jered. To read and to think and to understand the world in which I live, not remake it in my own image. I was expected to be kind to servants, to care about my fellow man. And if I was not expected to bring honor to my family, it was at least supposed that I would not summon dishonor to our door."

She rubbed her hand against his chest, then pulled the covers up higher, creating a cocoon of warmth. She was shivering in earnest now. Maybe her body was finally becoming warm. And if she was, perhaps Jered could. She pulled her leg up, rubbed her foot down his leg, creating a gentle friction against him. "I shall be very angry if you die on me, especially since I've come to like you. I very nearly didn't, you know. There was a great many times when I found myself struggling with the fact that while I might love you, you weren't a very likable person."

She sighed, rubbed his chest a little harder, extended her range of motion to his shoulders, down to his stomach. His body should have felt lax beneath her hand, pliable, but it felt strong and firm. For all his rank, he was not indolent. He played as hard as most men worked, and controlling a perch phaeton was not an easy task, at least that's what one of her brothers had told her.

"You are a hero, you know," she said, stroking her leg and her arm up his body. "Without you cutting the mast free, it's quite possible we all might have died." *Stroke, rub.* "Captain Williams had high praise for you, said it was a pleasure to be employed by such a man as yourself." *Another stroke.* "You won't let it go to your head, will you? Jered, I say this in the most loyal and wifely of ways, but you can become almost insufferably arrogant at times.''

He was not moving. He felt measurably warmer but not enough to suit her. *Could someone die of this? What had one of the sailors called it? Ice sickness. "Heard tell t'weren't a bad way to die.''* She pulled the covers up closer, tucked them around his chin.

"You were right, you know. I've had too many weeks to think about it. I was trying to change you. I imagined you before I knew you. But one person ought not to try to alter another. I know that now, just as I know that I truly do not want you different." She leaned her forehead into his side, burrowed close. "Except of course, that I want you warm and well and smiling at me.

"Please, Jered." He may die, despite her efforts, despite her chattering to him like a magpie, or the heat she'd willingly shared from her own body. "Please, Jered," she said again. Another prayer.

"What is wrong with her voice?"

He lay with his eyes shut. Tessa had left. He'd heard her close the door softly behind her. Why, damn it, did he feel her absence so acutely? The sounds of a washbasin, a pitcher solidly meeting the top of a commode distracted him from such unwelcome thoughts. Chalmers, forever caring for him.

"Well?" Another sound, a brush of something against leather, perhaps? Of course, he was about to be shaved. *Above all, do not let us get slovenly in appearance. It would never do.*

"I suppose it was due to her screams, sir."

His eyes popped open. "Screams?"

Chalmers stropped the razor with perhaps a bit more force than necessary. "Yes, your grace. She refused to let them abandon you. Threatened to shoot them, I believe, if they did not pull you from the side of the ship."

He closed his eyes again. Something squeezed his chest. So much for intent, then. *Face it, Kittridge, as a hero, you're a dismal failure. Your wife must save you from yourself. You wallow in depravity with much more grace.*

"Where the hell are we?"

"A town called Middleston, I believe, on the coast."

"We never made it to Scotland, then?"

"No sir."

"And the *Isolde*?"

"She went aground, sir. I expect she's fodder for the wreckers now."

The thought of the *Isolde* being picked clean was not one he wished to contemplate. She was a beauty, and he had sent her to her doom. *Very well done, Kittridge.*

His uncle would not be pleased. The knowledge attained had been too highly purchased. Yet at least they knew that her mast had been too tall for her length, that she was dangerously overbalanced in rough seas. She needed to be longer, with sleeker lines, with three masts instead of four. A ship like that could scud the oceans, clip the waves themselves.

"And the men?"

"Three lost, three injured, one bad. Her Grace insisted the physician see to them, too."

The physician had made an inventory of him earlier, and Jered had been half-amazed, half-amused to find himself relatively intact. His wrist was broken, his hand throbbed like blazes, and he was certain he would never again be completely warm. His head ached and his nose was broken. A litany of injuries. Or of failure.

A damned doomed voyage. Except perhaps for memory, and that he forced away. He did not want to think of Tessa at this moment.

He turned his head away, surveyed the window to his left. It was snowing. Great flakes of it. No doubt covering the ground and making travel dangerous. He didn't feel a surge of excitement at the thought, only an odd weariness, as if he'd not slept for days.

"Can you hire a chaise, Chalmers?"

"If you wish it, Your Grace."

"I wish it," he softly said. "I want to go home."

"Are you certain that it is the wisest choice, sir?"

He glanced at his valet. His face looked pinched. From withholding all those condemnatory thoughts? "Thank you for your concern, Chalmers, but I will be fine."

"I was not thinking of you, Your Grace, as much as I was the duchess. She's had no sleep in the past two days. I doubt travel will aid her in any great degree."

"Then, she can choose to remain here, can she not?" He turned away from that disapproving look. "And send word to my interfering relations that I want them gone from Kittridge before I arrive."

"Kittridge, sir?"

"Yes, Chalmers. Kittridge. I find that the thought of London is particularly unappealing at this moment."

It was evident from the beginning of the journey that a hired post-chaise was not up to Kittridge standards. The springs were quite loose, the upholstery sagging, the benches hard as iron. There was a smell about it that hinted at tobacco, and too much perfume, something stale and sickening sweet.

The horses, too, were sorry nags. Not matched, and one even looked so sway-backed, Jered almost shot it to put it out of its misery. The trip home seemed as doomed as the voyage to Scotland had been. Except, of course, that the days were spent in what passed for silence among the three of them.

The first day, Tessa slept for most of the day, wedged into the seat while he and Chalmers occupied the opposite bench. The second, she dozed, more often than not coming awake at the lurch of the coach or the sound of an approaching town. She did not look well, her eyes appeared haunted, at least that's what he thought on those rare occasions in which they actually looked at each other. He would have thought her stomach bothering her again, but made no mention of it. To do so would have hinted at a caring nature, and everyone knew he was not possessed of one. Strange, though, how her malady seemed to afflict her once and then was gone, as if she'd only to experience once to learn it and having done so, it was not necessary to repeat it. Not unlike virginity, he mused, and then smiled at the utter nonsense of such a thought.

For all his wife's evident fatigue, she looked better than he did. A child's monster could not have looked more hideous. Beneath his eyes were pockets of yellow and brown bruises, his nose was plugged full of linen, his hand bandaged and wrapped. He looked slightly worse for his adventures.

"Are you married, Chalmers?" There, a question to slice through his thoughts. How odd that he didn't know.

"I am a widower, sir."

"Is it possible, Chalmers, or have you grown even more stiff in the past week?"

"I do not know what you mean, Your Grace."

"Any children?" Very well, he could play this game, too.

"One, sir. A girl, lives in Hampstead."

"Do not tell me you are a grandfather yet?"

"Twice over, Your Grace."

"Do you ever see them?"

"Not as often as I wish to. There never seems to be enough time."

" 'But at my back I always hear, time's wingèd chariot hurrying near.' Marvel had it right, don't you think? Wish to God we possessed a winged chariot at this moment."

He glanced at his wife. She was staring out the window. An occupation that would do little to alleviate the boredom. At his look, she turned her head.

"Are you feeling all right?"

He smiled. "I would ask the same of you, but then I've been forbidden to. A surfeit of usage, I believe. You could do with some pampering, Tessa. I would recommend a long ocean voyage had it not been for our recent experience. Perhaps the waters at Bath. But then, I doubt you would be able to tolerate the pretensions of their society. They are not a laudable lot. They bow too heartily at the presence of a sir or lady. Their gossip is not of the latest vintage. Their manners deplorably pedestrian. Yet they have the most cunning way of slicing a woman's reputation and enhancing a rake's. I do believe I attained my greatest stature at Bath. When I was but a youth."

He leaned his head back against the seat, closed his eyes. Did she stare at him still? Was she with child yet? Let her be with child, and let it be an heir, so that he might leave her at Kittridge and count himself one of the fortunate ones. She jarred him, disturbed him in some elemental way, caused him to recall things best left forgotten. Opened a door into his soul that should be left closed and banded with iron. With her curiosity, with her tenacity, she'd soon find out he was not whole at all, not with a soul charred and shrunken.

He'd thought himself capable of offering her friendship, but instead, he nearly killed her because of his character. An undying arrogance. He could, possibly, be excused for it. But not for cruelty. Could he do nothing right? He found it easier to slip into the role he created for himself sixteen years ago. A man devoid of feelings instead of a child cut raw by them. Not loss, not despair, simply no emotions at all.

"I owe you thanks, I believe. A great deal of it, if all the stories I've heard of you are true. You are quite a behemoth in your own right, you know. Sailors will speak of you with hushed reverence, figureheads will be carved in your image."

She said nothing. Silence was perhaps not the wisest course for her to take at this moment. It irritated him. If he must experience a sentiment, let it be irritation. That could easily be coaxed from his lexicon of previously used emotions. He'd often felt irritation.

Yes. Irritation was better. He'd heard almost every word she'd said to him while he lay in that rigid cocoon of ice. He'd felt pickled by the cold, preserved for death. Instead into this white wasteland she'd come, her voice a beacon for him to reach for, her body warming him by slow degrees.

"Please, Jered." He'd heard that, too. A woman not born to beg, but doing so with eagerness. Her voice was husky now, the legacy of a thousand screams on his behalf. To God, to the wind, to the angry sea. It was

almost more than he could bear. Certainly more than he deserved.

How could he tell her that every time he wished to do something correct in regard to her, he ruined it? He'd nearly killed her.

"You are doing it again." He looked over at her. "Shutting me out. Becoming perfectly odious. It's taken me a long while, but I've finally figured it out, Kittridge."

"You seem excessively angry, Tessa."

"The word is enraged."

"You are no doubt tired. Fatigue can add to the potency of emotion."

"I'm bloody enraged, Kittridge."

Chalmers was becoming flushed. At his valet's stricken look, Jered shook his head. "We are embarrassing Chalmers, my dear."

"Chalmers may well have a great deal more to be embarrassed about in the course of our marriage."

"Indeed?"

"Don't use that tone on me, Kittridge. I am not one of your doxies."

"Your Grace, it would be no hardship for me to sit with the driver—"

"Do be quiet, Chalmers," Tessa shot back.

"As a matter of fact since our marriage, I've had no doxies."

A moment of silence while she digested this. "Is that the truth?"

"Yes." A glance at Chalmers. He seemed entranced at the view of snow-covered landscape. "When did I have time, my dear? If not physical stamina?"

Chalmers made a sound like a moan.

"You aren't going to ask what I'm talking about, are you?"

"There are a great many times in the course of our marriage, Tessa, in which I have been superfluous to the conversation. You simply continue on."

"Another technique of yours, Jered. Quite a good one, actually. Anger the opponent sufficiently and they become distracted."

"Are we opponents now?"

"Another distraction."

He smiled. He actually enjoyed sparring with her.

"Very well. What monumental discovery have you made about my character?"

"Your Grace—"

"Not now, Chalmers," he said.

"You prefer being contemptible, you know. Being happy absolutely terrifies you."

"Is that correct?"

"Yes, it is. So much so that you immediately revert to being a pompous, insufferable, arrogant ass the moment you discover you aren't miserable."

"Your Grace, really—"

"Shut up, Chalmers!" they each said in unison.

Chalmers curled into the corner. Tessa retreated to a glaring silence, and Jered concentrated on the view.

Chapter 36

"I cannot go home until I've shot you," the Earl of Wellbourne said. He stood in the doorway to Jered's library, a short, squat man, with a rather rotund stomach, which seemed to have increased in girth each time Jered saw him.

In direct counterpart to his words, however, there was a smile upon his face. The earl didn't look like he wanted to kill him.

Jered put down his quill, leaned back in the chair, and surveyed his visitor. His father-in-law had long since, no doubt, been given the run of his home, which was why he had not been announced. "A duel? Or am I supposed to just sit here and let you shoot me?"

"I believe," Gregory said, "that I would just as soon you remain where you are. I could possibly manage the feat quite nicely. I confess that I am not the best of shots, you see."

"Is it necessary that you shoot me, or would some other weapon be preferable?"

"I am not, regrettably, much of a sportsman at all. I do like fishing, but I don't suppose I could do you in that way, could I?"

"Does Tessa get her habit of questioning from you, or her mother?"

Gregory smiled. "I'm afraid it's all Tessa. When she was a little girl, she used to ask the strangest things. Not why is the grass green or the sky blue. She wanted to know if clouds were God's way of talking to people. Or if flowers knew what color they were going to be when they were only seeds."

"You had your hands full."

Gregory nodded, still smiling.

"Am I allowed to inquire why I am to be killed, or is reading the condemned man a list of his sins not allowed?"

"At least you admit it might be a list rather than just one. That shows improvement, you know." He approached a chair facing the desk and, at Jered's nod, occupied it.

"Oh, I shall be the first to admit that I'm flawed. I assume, by virtue of your mission, that you are without faults?"

"Saint Gregory, you mean? It sounds wonderful. I'm afraid, however, that I cannot claim the title. If nothing else, my progeny would hoot with laughter. They are, you see, an added reason for my presence."

"So, you shoot me on Tessa's behalf?"

"Oh, not on hers. On the boys', of course. It's either myself as their representative, or all six of them doing it on their own."

Jered fingered the quill, dropped it back on the blotter. "A veritable plethora of sons."

Gregory raised one eyebrow. "You know my wife. Therefore, you understand the attraction."

Indeed he did. Helena Astley was a thorn in his side,

a tigress determined to protect her young. All the same, she was an exquisitely lovely woman.

"My sons do not believe you have treated their sister at all well."

"And you no doubt share in that viewpoint."

"I must confess I do."

"As do I." He smiled at the look of surprise on his father-in-law's face. "How can I not? She's been shot, nearly frozen to death, and shipwrecked."

"Do not forget kidnapped."

"I hardly think that's a punishable offense, since I am her husband."

"I still think it should be listed."

"Very well." Jered leaned back in the chair again.

"I do not suppose I would escape unscathed if I murdered a duke," Gregory said.

"There is that to consider."

"What are you going to do about this, Kittridge?" There was solemn anger in the man's eyes, all irony whisked away in a blink.

"I don't have the slightest idea," Jered confessed. And he didn't. His supreme gesture of sacrifice had been nullified by its idiocy. His wife had had to save him from himself. He'd wanted to prove himself worthy of her, and all he'd done was illuminate some additional faults heretofore kept hidden. He'd screamed, damn it, when his wrist had been set, found himself moaning and petulant like a child with a fever. *Not exactly the stuff of legends, eh, Jered? No knight with white horse.* Hell, he'd probably spear himself with his lance if he tried that trick. And there was a perfectly good set of armor in the north hall, too.

"She's not at all happy."

Since Jered had not seen his wife in three days, that

knowledge had been spared him. Still, he could not claim surprise, could he?

"My wife says she's been crying, and I truly do not like Tessa to be unhappy, Kittridge. Aside from that, when my wife is upset, Dorset House is not a pleasant place to be. And I cherish domestic tranquillity."

Jered didn't see how Dorset House could be that tranquil with all those children milling about the place, but he wisely refrained from commenting. "I understand you've been working with Wilberforce."

The change of topic evidently startled his father-in-law. Jered profoundly hoped so, he had no intention of discussing his marriage with anyone. Father or no father, there were times when parents were simply meddlesome. He wondered if Helena Astley had ever been versed on such an idea.

"Yes, I am. Why?"

"Will he reintroduce the motion?" The House of Commons had recently voted to prevent further importation of slaves into the West Indies. The motion failed by a close margin.

"How else to get it into Lords?" Gregory questioned.

"Do you need some assistance?"

Another surprise, evidently. His father-in-law looked decidedly unimpressed.

"Why would you offer?"

"It's a damned sight better alternative to being shot, don't you agree?"

It occurred to Jered that it was the first time he'd ever heard his father-in-law's laugh.

He might as well be in London. He had effectively shut her out of his life. People came to Kittridge at all hours of the day and night, and he welcomed them, his library door closed behind his visitors. Sometimes she heard laughter; sometimes only the drone of conversation.

The days aboard ship might not have ever happened. The camaraderie, the sweet, heady pleasure of that afternoon when she'd felt tenderness and love from him. Maybe it had only been her imagination, a wish she'd had that had come true inside her mind. Perhaps they had not sat and laughed and told each other stories and played cricket and cards.

There was nothing left of the man she'd come to know, the one who'd held her close and whispered her name as if it had been some precious and secret word. Inherent in this man's speech was arrogance and ducal authority. He held himself aloof, above everyone else, apart. Even from her. Especially from her. He'd always done that. But once she'd not allowed him the distance. She'd followed him and burrowed into his life and demanded a place beside him.

Why did she think such actions would now be futile?

Had she truly imagined that look in the companionway, as he'd stared at her? It had been as if he'd said good-bye, as if his heart had been in his eyes, and all the emotions in the world spread out for her to see. There was nothing there now, only a coldness of which she was chillingly familiar.

What hope she'd felt when he'd first stirred, regaining consciousness after hours of worry. She'd rushed to the bed and called for Chalmers, and only then for the physician. The duke would live. That was it, then. The duke lived, but the man had disappeared.

Arrogant man. His bruises had faded to yellow and brown and he looked quite liverish. His nose no longer wore that hideous bandage, although his wrist was still wrapped. He'd taken to carrying his walking stick in his left hand and holding his right tucked into his pocket. He should have looked ridiculous, but of course he did not.

Only like Jered.

She couldn't stop from crying at odd times, such as when she'd received a letter from Peter Lanterly inquiring as to her health. She'd written back, telling him that she was quite fine, that her scars were fading and that she had no ill effects from the operation. She did not remark that she'd been nearly drowned since, and had recovered quite well from that also. She remembered that enchanted afternoon, when Jered had made love to her, touching her so delicately and with so much reverence it was as if she were precious and fragile. Then dissolved into tears because he'd not touched her since. Had not even glanced at her in the hallway. Except for his bruises, that time might not have happened. And as soon as they were faded, she was certain he would be returning to London.

She would not return with him. That lesson had been weeks in the making, but she'd finally learned it. He did not wish her as his wife, and she could be nothing less.

It was an eerie feeling staring at his own portrait and feeling a sense of resentment toward the man who faced him. Almost as idiotic as swearing at the looking glass, but then, he'd also done that in the last week.

"You immediately revert to being a pompous, insufferable, arrogant ass the moment you discover you aren't miserable."

He was very much afraid she was right. And yet he had memories of laughter and joy in his life. All predating his mother's death. He had denied her loss for so long, the aching pain of it perhaps never felt in its entirety. *Could such a thing be possible?*

"No, Jered, we have to return. Your father expects us, and I've promised to read Susie a story." A hand had pushed back her hair, her bright smile mimicked the afternoon sun. "No, do not look like that. You managed to soften my heart when you were four with that look, but a pout will do you no good now." With a laugh, she was off, heading back to Kittridge. A few moments later, he had heard the horse's screams, found her lying there.

Was that the instant he had changed? Or had it been when his father had died? He'd learned a lesson then, one almost rendered perfect by his repetition of it. It was easier not feeling anything.

Being numb was easier than feeling pain. Being numb rendered you almost invincible. He had kept his friendships superficial and shallow, avoided his relatives because they pulled him from behind his solemnly erected walls.

He had retreated from Tessa with single-minded terror only because what she promised him with her acceptance and her love was something he could not bear to feel. Alive.

And the depravity, Jered? The only way to penetrate the numbness. The only way to feel anything, and occasionally he wished to prove himself among the living. Not yet entombed. Excitement, danger, defying law and custom and rule. He'd grown to need all of them, simply to feel alive.

A paralyzed limb cannot feel a pinprick. But a numbed soul? A woman's gentle laughter. A bushel of questions. A shattered vase.

The young man in the painting was a specious gentleman, one filled with contradictions that were obvious to him as he stood there. So desperately needy and so painfully lonely, yet refusing to acknowledge the hollowness of his heart and his soul. The cavern of his soul resounded with denial.

His uncle was wrong. True evil was not intent. It was habit. It was the absence of love simply repeated over and over, until even its absence no longer had the power to wound.

Why did this painting disturb him? It portrayed him very well, a few less lines around the eyes, perhaps, a less sardonic smile. The eyes were the same, his hair appeared similar, even though the style had changed. Nothing about it was glaringly wrong, except that he could not see himself in this young man. An effortless gift of knowledge from his wife.

A little lowering to admit that his understanding of himself had been prompted only by marriage. If not for that momentous occasion, it was quite possible he might have remained as he had been. Not a happy man. One immersed in activity because it was easier to live in a cacophony than it was to live with himself. He could not remember a time, except for this past week, that he had ever remained alone and quiet, absorbed not in what occurred around him but in his thoughts.

He had been, for all his questioning of himself, for all the inadequacies that measured him, all the insecurities that pummeled him this week, almost vibrantly happy. It had astounded him that it could be so.

"I fell in love with him, you know," Tessa said, as if he'd conjured her here. But then, it was her sitting room, a natural place for her to come. He glanced back at the painting.

"He is an idiotic young man," he said. She was smiling. *Was it a sad smile?* Now was the time to confess all of his soul. *Coward, Jered? God, yes.*

"He listened quite well to me. Was very patient. Did not seem to mind all my questions."

He smiled. *"A captive audience, then. Poor practice for the reality."*

"Oh, I don't think so. I thought the reality quite spectacular."

He watched her walk away, clenched his left fist tight, and then, empowered by more than simple irritation, by something bordering on confusion and rage, he threw his walking stick at that damn idiotic portrait.

The fool just continued to smile at him.

Chapter 37

He found her in the gazebo. It was not a difficult feat; she disappeared there most afternoons with a book. For the past week, he'd watched her as she stared off into space. What was she thinking? It wasn't about him, that was for certain. She seemed to have adequately banished him from her mind.

She didn't move as he approached, only turned her head and watched him. He placed his good hand on one of the pillars supporting the structure, his booted foot upon the first step. The man he'd become in the last week was hesitant, uncertain. They were not easy emotions. They irritated him. No, they frightened him.

She tilted her head, her soft smile neither welcome nor dismissal. Dear God, she was lovely. Something in his chest turned over, lay flat upon the ground, tail wagging, begging.

''I'm selling the house in London,'' he said as preamble.

''Really?'' Damn it, didn't she know what a sacrifice that was?

''And I've given up my memberships in my gaming clubs.''

She smiled, a polite and utterly apathetic gesture. "Why on earth would you do that?"

Silence, while he worked up his courage.

"Because I'm willing to begin again," he said, "to change my life."

She blinked at him. She did that when he'd startled her. When, for once, words failed her. It had not happened often, but enough that he was charmed when it occurred.

"I've hired a secretary who will come to live here in a week. A recommendation from your father. No doubt he's a spy."

There, that coaxed a real smile free.

"My one attempt to be honorable failed miserably, but it doesn't mean that I could not learn. It is, you see, so much easier to be a reprobate. Sliding down into hell without an effort lifted to improve. 'For where we are is Hell, and where Hell is, there must we ever be.' "

"You were always honorable, Jered. You didn't like being so, but you were. If you hadn't been, you wouldn't have arranged for your own gold to be stolen. You would have joined those who took their fill of the prostitutes at the tavern. You would have found time and stamina for a mistress. You wouldn't have loaned your box to the Crawford sisters. Your problem was that you simply didn't expect to be happy, so you went about ensuring you weren't. I'm very pleased you're feeling good about yourself."

Why did he think she was slipping away from him, into a world of polite indifference?

"I've been an idiot, Tessa. I've been wrong." There, that confession should crack that polite facade. Except that it did not.

"We've both been wrong."

Did she mean about loving him?

"I've made mistakes." He lifted his hand, a gesture to silence her response. "Do not tell me that both of us have made mistakes. Mine were worse."

"Very well," she said, and a small smile played around her mouth.

"I love you, damn it." Not exactly a romantic declaration, but one from the heart.

She blinked at him again.

"And if you cannot forgive me for all the anguish and pain and grief I've put you through, then I'm not the one riddled with arrogance in this family. Isn't it enough that I've rearranged my life? I've made lists, damn it, of all those people I know who might possibly be worthy enough to associate with you. I've donated a sizable amount to the church steeple fund, endowed a home for grizzled war veterans, and promised to support three orphanages. I have even invited your entire family for dinner!"

When she said nothing, he admitted the final capitulation. "I sent your mother a note, asking her to tea."

"You love me?"

"Didn't I say so? I am only too aware of my many faults, Tessa, but I am trying to mend them. The least you could do is applaud my attempts."

"I applaud them," she softly said.

"Well, think about the rest," he said, suddenly more irritated than he could ever remember being at her. "Most women would throw themselves into my arms, Tessa. A great many of them would be squealing for joy right about now. I've never said those words to another living soul, and you just sit there staring at me."

Nor did that announcement seem to compel her to

move. She just looked at him as if he were some sort of gorgonlike monster she'd imagined in a particularly hideous dream.

"I know you love me. I'm not perfect like some damn portrait, but I know you do."

Was she frozen into place? And what did that look in her eyes mean? As if they were tender and pitying. It looked as if she was beginning to cry. Damn it. A declaration of love shouldn't inspire tears.

He had only one resort, to grab his tattered dignity around him and leave before he humiliated himself even further.

By getting down on his knees and begging.

"I am not so sure that what you're doing is wise, Tessa."

Tessa looked up at her mother, fastened the last button upon her cape. "Mother, I love you. I admire you and respect you. And I hope that you understand what I'm about to say."

"But you want me to go away?" Helena smiled at her only daughter.

"Not go away exactly," Tessa said.

"But leave you and Jered alone. To work out your own problems."

Tessa smiled. "Yes."

"I remember saying the same to my mother-in-law," Helena sighed.

"Did she?"

"As your father reminded me recently, she did not."

Tessa stepped up on one tread, kissed her mother's cheek. "You mean well, Mother, but I wish you would concentrate more on Harry. There are signs he will be even more a rake than Jered."

"Do you really think so?"

"Not only that, but it's not long before a few of the boys should be married. If not affianced."

"You simply want me to bother someone else for a while."

"Just a bit," Tessa said with a smile.

"I hope he's worth it."

"He is." Tessa pulled her gloves on, smiled at her mother once more.

"Are you very sure?"

"How sure are you that you love Father?"

"That much?"

"I'm afraid so."

"You know, of course, that it means I shall have to come to like him," Helena said in disgust. "He invited me to tea, you know. I haven't answered him."

"He's very likable," Tessa said as she motioned to the major domo to open the door. "He just has to realize it."

She'd taken Chalmers!

Not only had she left for London, but she'd taken his valet! Not that he'd never undressed himself before, but damn it to hell, his wrist wouldn't move, and the bandage wasn't easily coaxed either in or out of any of his sleeves.

The fact that his best coach was gone only stretched his temper further. The vehicle that remained was one sorry piece of equipage, designed to haul produce from the market. It had only one seat, and it sagged, making him feel as if he was still aboard the *Isolde* in the midst of a raging sea.

He was almost certain he did not like his wife. No, there was no uncertainty about it. He was decided. He did *not* like his wife. She'd made a mockery of his life. Following him, badgering him to change, then refusing to appreciate his embracing an honorable existence. She'd castigated him, shamed him, infuriated him. Not to mention her ominous silence the one and only time he'd ever expressed love for a woman. Weakened him.

But he'd never been bored.

A slow smile wreathed his lips. He didn't even know he was smiling until the cold nearly froze his teeth solid. He felt the way he had when robbing a coach or doing something forbidden. Excited. Alive. Traipsing after her in the dead of night. Idiot woman had stolen his valet.

Those inhabitants in the cottages lining the road heard the sound, rolled over and pulled their covers closer to their ears. It was the wind, of course, and not laughter they heard.

"What do you mean, she's gone?"

Chalmers handed him a note. His valet looked the worse for wear. But at least he didn't smell of onions. Jered opened the note he'd been handed the moment he'd entered the door of his London town house. He read the five words, his stomach answering with a gleeful dip as if it were in imminent danger of catapulting into the air. "She said it was either that or robbing a coach, Your Grace." A trilling little laugh escaped the valet. "She said she didn't like horses much."

"Are you hysterical, Chalmers?"

"I do believe I am, sir."

He stared at his valet. "You just let her go off like that?"

"There was not much I could do, Your Grace. Her

Grace can be quite overwhelming when she chooses to be.''

Since he'd felt that way more than once, Jered could only silently agree.

"Besides, sir, she borrowed her brothers. Do you know she has six of them?''

"They're all here?''

"Indeed yes, sir. And may I venture to add, Your Grace, that they don't seem well-disposed in your favor? I spent a great deal of time in their presence, and I must say I've never seen a more violent group of young men. The youngest, sir, seems to be quite willing to use your bones in a soup, I believe he said.''

"Are her parents here?''

Chalmers shook his head.

"Why the bloody hell did she kidnap you?''

"She said, sir, that you might not know she was gone, but that my presence would be sorely missed.''

"I should beat her.''

"Quite, sir.''

"But we both know I won't, don't we?''

Chalmers only giggled again.

The Pleasure Palace was as it usually was, tastefully, silently discreet.

Instead of taking the stairs, he swung around to the back, tapped quietly on a door. It was answered by a woman of middle years who provided the information he sought. He found himself being lectured on the inadvisability of importing talent in view of the anonymity offered to the patrons of the establishment. He smiled tightly, wished both his hands worked. The better to strangle her. The particular morsel in question was waiting his pleasure on the second floor. He declined any further information. In this case, ignorance was much desired.

He used the key given him, opened the door to find a room lit only by the light of one taper. Shadows filled the room, but the one candle illuminated his wife. Draped in silk, naked, and lying on the bed.

She said nothing, simply smiled at him, an odalisque promised for his pleasure. There were rooms of such women in this place, but he did not tell her that. Why? None of them had eyes that could drown him in warmth, or a smile meant to heat his soul.

She terrified him. The truth of the last moments, in stark and unrelieved simplicity, disturbed him more deeply than he would have imagined. It was a feeling not unlike a lion who paced a cage restlessly for years, who, once given liberty, remains in that same pattern of restlessness, uneasy with the broader scope of freedom. He pushed it aside. The lion died lonely. He had no intention of doing so.

"You stole my valet." A patently idiotic remark, of course.

She seemed to recognize it as such. Her smile broadened.

He went to one side, slid tight and latched the viewing window, then repeated the action on the far wall. No one was going to witness this next denouement. He moved closer, realized he couldn't pull off his own damn coat. He extended his arm to her.

"Tessa," he said.

"What, Jered?"

"Tessa." The words stuck in his mouth. How very odd that he'd never asked before. Not once. Never in his life. "Help me," he whispered. "Please."

She sat up and pulled the cuff out gently, away from his bandage, then slipped the coat free.

"I really do love you, you know."

"You might sound a little pleased about it."

"I am terrified. *You* terrify me. All my happiness seems caught up in one of your smiles."

"Oh, Jered, that was lovely."

"I am descending into poetic madness. Do you know I laughed like a wild man all the way from Kittridge?"

"Truly?"

"I smell of onions. You stole my coach." He moved closer to the end of the bed.

"I quite like onions, and I'm sure it didn't hurt you that much to ride in a wagon."

He surveyed her position. She'd sprawled out on the bed again, only barely covered by the square of silk. "Do you love me, Tessa?"

She smiled. "With my whole heart, Jered."

"It's about time you said it."

"I doubt you would have wished to hear sooner." He nodded, accepting the truth of that remark.

"I've only one good hand for the moment," he teased, "else I'd join you."

"Are there no other positions?" Her grin was delightfully wicked. He closed his eyes, said a quick prayer, blessing the day he discovered a young girl sitting beneath a tree. No, not just for that, but for also keeping her safe. And for granting him a bit of sense. Enough to see love when it stared at him with large and warm brown eyes.

"There is one, but it requires a rocking movement, a love of riding and some height. Do you think you'll become ill?"

"I'm quite willing to risk it," she said, smiling.

"Very well," he said, and leaped onto the bed.

A few moments later, the madam of the house frowned, looked up at the staircase. Really, there was no need for all that laughter.

Was there?

Epilogue

"**G**ood day, Chalmers," Tessa said as the valet entered cautiously.

"Good day, Your Grace."

"Are you quite ready for your holiday?"

"I am, and thank you again, Your Grace."

"It was not I, Chalmers, but Jered." She sat up, grabbing the sheet around her and whispered, "He's developing quite a sense of family, you see, since his sister and her family is arriving tomorrow. And you really must see your grandchildren more often."

Chalmers smiled. "Quite so, your grace."

"I don't know what she's telling you, Chalmers," Jered said, his head buried beneath the pillow. "But whatever it is, it's wrong, I'm certain of it."

Tessa swatted him on the back.

"Don't let him browbeat you, Chalmers. He's an autocrat and a despot."

"As you say, Your Grace."

"Good God, Tessa, now you have him agreeing with you." Jered's head popped up from beneath the pillow. "It's insurrection, is it, Chalmers?"

"On no account, sir."

"We are all totally terrified of your consequence,

Jered. Why I tremble at the very thought of your irritation.'' She smiled brightly.

''I'll dress later, Chalmers,'' Jered said slowly, eyeing his wife.

Without calling attention to himself, Chalmers backed out of the doorway, closing it securely behind him.

''You're playing hell with my schedule, you know. I'm to meet with your father and some of his cronies. We're embarking on a campaign for Lords next year, storm them with brilliant rhetoric.''

She only smiled at him.

''Chalmers doesn't quite know what to do with a duchess in attendance so often.''

''My parents sleep together, Jered. It's something I could become used to without much trouble.'' The smile broadened.

''You're delightfully lovely this morning.''

''You say that every morning,'' she said, falling back onto the pillow.

He raised himself up on one elbow and watched her. She was almost luminous, as if the sun dwelled within her skin.

''It is true every morning.''

''You say that, too.''

''Am I becoming redundant, then?'' His fingers traced down her arm, from elbow to wrist.

''Excessively so.'' She sighed, then rolled so that she was facing him.

''Are you going to become ill again this morning?''

''I do believe that is past.'' Her voice was soft, matching his mood, the utter peace of the early morning. He'd found he liked rising with the sun. It made him feel positively Spartan.

"Good. It was a deplorable way to begin a morning."

"I am so sorry it disturbed you," she said, her smile changing tone to become gently teasing. Her hand reached up to touch his face, fingers gently tracing the line of his bottom lip.

"You realize of course," Tessa said, "that this changes everything."

"Oh?"

"While I know it was your initial idea to keep me here at Kittridge once I was with child while you returned to London, it simply will not do."

"It won't?"

"No. You're going to be a father now. And fathers must supply all manner of things to their children." She lay back against the pillow, smiling.

"Such as?"

"Knowledge and love and hugs."

"And brothers and sisters, too."

"Of course."

"But not six of them, surely."

Her smile was excessively mischievous.

"Is our marriage to be dictated by your parent's example, Tessa?"

"Well, it is an extremely happy union."

He recalled his mother's smile, his father's very real grief. Another happy union. Would he have not felt the same as his father if Tessa had been taken from him? He was all too aware he would have. And perhaps, if his son stood in front of him, strong and able and alive, there might be a time in which he cried out in accusation and pain. *A moment of forgiveness, Jered?* Perhaps one long overdue.

Jered leaned back among the pillows and studied his wife. A thin beam of sunlight struck her upturned face.

Her lips were solemn, her eyes closed. She was encapsulated by radiance, an oddly garbed angel. In that instant, he felt blessed. Not by the nature of his position or by the possessions that were his to steward but by silence and peace in a room far away from London and his past. His hand reached out in reverence and rested against her cheek. She accepted his touch with a soft murmur, placed her own hand over his cooler one as if to warm it.

It was, he thought, a patently ludicrous notion. One was not supposed to adore a wife. It simply was not done. In fact, it was practically forbidden.

He grinned and reached for Tessa.

The branches of the trees were covered with curling leaf fronds. Slowly, joyfully, they unfolded their eager faces to the sun. Somewhere a bird warbled a spring greeting. The song was taken up and multiplied a thousand times until the air trembled with the sound. Forest creatures, rabbit and fox and squirrel, peeked out of their burrows to greet the spring.

A gentle breeze tumbled through the buds of newly opened flowers, caressing daffodil and rose, whispering a refrain as it passed. Barely heard, it tempted the listener to linger awhile, decipher its faint music. Those who did so were inclined to smile, and then press on, certain they had been mistaken after all. Surely it had been a trick of the wind. But if they had stopped once more, they would have been convinced of what they'd heard.

And they lived happily ever after.

Next month, don't miss these exciting new love stories only from Avon Books

In Scandal They Wed by Sophie Jordan
Chased by scandal, Evelyn Cross long ago sacrificed everything for a chance at love. Bound by honor, Spencer Lockhart returns from war to claim his title and marry the woman his cousin once wronged. But as desire flares between them, honor is the last thing on his mind…

The True Love Quilting Club by Lori Wilde
After twelve years of shattered dreams, Trixie Lynn Parks returns home to the ladies of the True Love Quilting Club… and the man she left behind. Sam Cheek is no longer a carefree boy, but as chemistry sizzles, could he be the one to mend her patchwork heart?

A Most Sinful Proposal by Sara Bennett
When the proper Marissa Rotherhild makes him a most improper proposal—to instruct her in the ways of desire—Lord Valentine Kent has never been so tempted. Though he's every bit the gentleman, he knows even the best of intentions is no match for a passion as desperate as theirs.

His Darkest Hunger by Juliana Stone
Jaxon Castille has long hungered for the chance to make his former lover, Libby Jamieson, pay for her deadly betrayal. At last the hunt is over…but the Libby he finds is not who he expected, and the truth is far more shattering than anyone imagined…

Unforgettable, enthralling love stories,
sparkling with passion and adventure
from Romance's bestselling authors

At Avon Books, we know your passion for romance—once you finish one of our novels, you find yourself wanting more.

May we tempt you with . . .

- **Excerpts** from our upcoming releases.

- Entertaining **extras**, including authors' personal photo albums and book lists.

- Behind-the-scenes **scoop** on your favorite characters and series.

- **Sweepstakes** for the chance to win free books, romantic getaways, and other fun prizes.

- Writing **tips** from our authors and editors.

- **Blog** with our authors and find out why they love to write romance.

- **Exclusive content** that's not contained within the pages of our novels.

Join us at
www.avonbooks.com

AVON *An Imprint of* HarperCollins*Publishers*
www.avonromance.com